Shadows

of an

Angry God

Shadows

of an

Angry God

Marianna Palmer

Any references to historical events, real people, or real places are used fictitiously. Names, characters, and places are products of the author's imagination.

ISBN 9798396254275

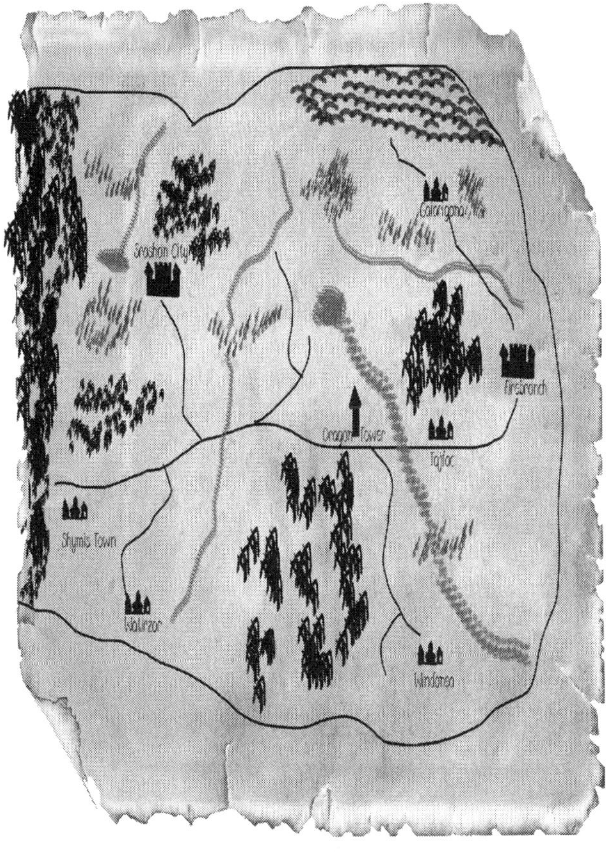
Srashan City
Firebranch
Dragon Tower
Tajfor
Shymis Town
Windonea

Map of Telda

Chapter One

"Dertujia! It's moving to your left," Xorna yelled. Dertujia nodded and jumped aside as the giant hoof landed where he had been. The centaur whinnied in annoyance. Wild hair fell down its back. Giant muscles rippled as it tried to trample Dertujia. The glowing eyes had no sense, nothing more than rage.

"Thanks for the warning, Xorna," Dertujia said wryly. He rolled to the side as the centaur reared. "It really wants to cause more destruction, doesn't it?" Dertujia added.

His impulsive friend waited for nothing. Without even responding, she launched herself onto the back of the centaur.

"Don't be a fool, Xorna!" Dertujia yelled. He knew that was the worst way to stop a rampaging centaur. And, sure enough, the beast took off with Xorna. Ripping the grass with its heavy hooves and ignoring all of Xorna's attempts to soothe it.

Centaurs! Blind and stupid animals. And more than deadly.

Dertujia groaned and ran after them, drawing his sword from his hip as he did. His red armor glinted in the sun as he rushed toward the running figure. He could hear Xorna's shrieks as the figure grew dim. He stopped and panted. *I can't outrun a centaur,* he mused. He looked toward a tree towering over him and got an idea.

He climbed it quickly, using his sword as a handle. He went out on the edge of a sturdy branch and jumped. *I hope I can make it.* His body flew through the air and landed on the branch of another tree that was perpendicular to the one he had climbed. *I really didn't think that would work,* he thought with happy surprise.

He didn't waste any time thinking more about it. He ran from tree to tree quickly gaining on the centaur. Soon enough the two came into sight. Dertujia reached the last tree and realized he was directly over the centaur now. He smiled and jumped.

He landed right behind Xorna who was looking at him with a gaping mouth.

"I can't believe you jumped," she said with a shake of her silver hair.

"It seemed like the thing to do," he grinned recklessly. The centaur, now really annoyed, started galloping faster. Given that the trees were sparse, it could go into an all-out run.

"Now what?" Xorna asked with amusement. If either of them jumped at this speed, it could prove fatal. A good landing meant nothing. The centaur sped up even more, nothing halting its run.

"I get nasty," Dertujia said with a glare. He shoved his sword downward and into the centaur's back. A shriek of pain and rage echoed from the beast as blood poured from the wound. It suddenly stopped, skidding in the dirt, and belched dust into the air. As if it just noticed it had riders, it reared and bucked wildly. Losing their balance, both Xorna and Dertujia fell onto the ground.

He stood up with a hiss only to see Xorna glowering at him even as the centaur turned.

"What?" he asked, holding his sword out as a warning.

She held hers as well, a warrior through and through. Yet she still said the same thing she usually did. "Stabbing it was a bit unnecessary, wasn't it, Dertujia?" She wriggled her shield, as if it could stop the beast, had it a mind to attack.

They both walked closer to the breathing and huffing animal. But Dertujia answered. "It got us off the back, didn't it?" Dertujia scowled. He looked at the wounded centaur who was eyeing him back. "I didn't even hurt it badly, see?" He pointed at the wound, which was rapidly sealing. Centaurs had double healing of humans and horses combined. The only clue of Dertujia's attack was the drying blood. Too bad the intelligence wasn't even near a horse's.

In addition to the sweat on the flanks, there was fresh blood. It had trampled a child this time. The poor boy hadn't seen it coming,

"Still," she murmured. "It could have ended peacefully, not violent."

"We'll argue later," Dertujia said as the centaur decided to charge. It obviously didn't like him.

Its burly furry arms rammed his sword, taking the brunt and not even flinching. His sword was knocked from his hand. A mighty kick flew towards his head, but Xorna swiped at it before it could connect.

Dertujia gave her a nod. "Thanks. Now let me finish this."

Dertujia jumped and kicked the centaur in the chest as it passed again. He pulled a coil of rope off his belt and twirled it in the air. Letting it fly, he lassoed the beast around its humanoid neck. He tied it tight and pulled another rope. This one was sent around the legs. Soon, the beast was completely subdued, except for the occasional kick.

"I still think we could have reasoned with it," Xorna said, taking in the tied, thrashing form.

"Centaurs look like us, Xorna, but they're not human," Dertujia said, his already deep voice getting even deeper with emotion.

"But we have no clue on that. My years as a hero have told me to look past the obvious," Xorna said with a shrug of her armor.

"We've had this argument before. They have only the minds of beasts. Look at it," he said and gestured to the wild eyes of the centaur. "It has trampled people, destroyed crops, and even killed animals. Today it killed a young boy. And why?" He paused and looked at Xorna who remained silent. "Because," he answered his own question, "it was in an animalistic rage. It didn't kill for food. Or even territory."

"I don't know," Xorna said. She grunted as she untied the legs, pushing the beast to its feet. It had given up, docile now. For the time being. Like a dog on a leash, Xorna walked it down the road and towards the village of Shymis, a little village at the bottom of endless peaks.

Dertujia's home. Though he saw it rarely. Being a hero from a young age, his real home was whatever path led to villainy.

The road was newly paved with morningstones. Fresh and bright like a dawn sky. On the sides, purple flowers peeked out from the soft grass that led to meadows. Farmland built up around the village, but all stopped at the sharp mountain line.

Xorna was steaming as they entered between the two wooden pillars that welcomed them to Shymis Town with a handmade wooden sign swinging up in between.

The sound of burgbugs sounded. Little chirps. They were active. They knew death was here. They always sung when someone died.

"You should have tried. One word, one comment. Maybe we could understand them."

Dertujia gripped his hands into fists. "Never. There is no understanding evil."

Xorna spit on the ground. The shade from the familiar round Veil Tree hit her beautiful face, reflecting her freckles and her scowl. "It's that kind of attitude that caused the war to start between us and Watirzor." Dertujia stopped and fixed a stern gaze at her.

"They attacked us first," he said with an edge to his voice. "And it's your kind of attitude that made it last so long. The king should have been harsher. Maybe we wouldn't have lost so many."

Xorna had no retort. She was becoming a peacemaker. A lifetime at war had softened her, not hardened.

"Fine, if you can't see reason, let me tell you this. The centaur trampled Vonon. He was just seven. He'll never celebrate his eighth birthday. Never go into the forest at twelve to prove he can find his spirit animal. Never get married or have a family. His family line dies with him as he was an only child. This beast …" Dertujia glowered at the centaur, but its eyes glared back. The rope around its neck kept it from attacking, but only because it was terrified of suffocation. "Killed a boy. Its life should be taken. Or do you not believe in justice?"

Xorna stopped looking at him.

"Let's just get the centaur to the prison," she muttered and started walking faster. Dertujia sighed. This wasn't the first time they had had this argument. Dertujia believed in victory at any cost; Xorna only wanted peace no matter what. *I think someday she will have to see reason.* He shook his head and pulled the centaur toward the prison at the end of the village. It wasn't large, but it was the only stone building in the area. The king had commissioned it to hold any lawbreaker until they could be taken to the main prison in Srashan City, the leader of Shymis.

The assistant saw the centaur, gaped, but wasted no time in squeaking the heavy gate open inside. The centaur walked in and roared as soon as the rope was taken from its neck. As the assistant slammed the door in its face, Dertujia could hear it slamming against the walls. Hopefully, the evil thing would knock itself out.

"Someone will come pick it up," Dertujia said, as the two left the nervous looking assistant behind. The sun hit his eyes, and he shielded them as he took in the sad face of Xorna. She was no longer judging. She felt the evil of the world too hard. Sometimes she just couldn't see where it came from.

"Yes, it will be executed." Xorna sighed and looked back at the prison.

"It also could be set free," Dertujia pointed out, but he didn't know what would become of the beast. Nor did he care. He had done his job. He had saved the lives of everyone in this village. Xorna had too, though she was more reluctant than he was about the end of the beast.

"I am going home. Come get me if you need anything," Xorna said.

"Tell your sister hi, for me."

Xorna nodded and shuffled down the path that led to her house.

***

Dertujia walked down the dirt road between the scattered houses. The road wasn't traveled much. The village was way too small to get many visitors. It was mainly farms and the like. The major trade happened more to the north.

"Hello, Dertujia," a woman's voice yelled out. Dertujia tried not to groan. He recognized the voice. It belonged to Leahnina, a young woman who was his biggest fan. After plastering a fake smile on his face, he turned to see her running up. She always watched for him from her home, staring out the box window until he showed up. She was a relatively pretty young lady with hair as black as night with patches of blonde interwoven in. Her cheeks were rosy red, and she had a nice figure. A lot to look at on top and wonderful hips that could get into his dreams. There was just one thing that made Dertujia not like her.

"Good going with that centaur! I heard all about it," she said quickly. "Of course, *I* already knew it was going to happen. The future is an open book to me."

He didn't know whether her blathering on about how much she knew the future was an endearing trait or if it made him want to throw her into the nearest pond. None of her prophecies came true.

On second thought, some had, but they were only that a freeze would come when one could feel the sharp chill to the air, or that a woman would have a son when she had had three already. Useless.

Now she was intent on telling him his future. As if he would trust her. "That's nice, Leahnina,"

Dertujia said politely. "Can you see how this conversation will end?"

"Um," she said uncertainly, but then arrogance covered her face again. "I don't need to be an oracle to do that. You will invite me for dinner at your house."

"Will I?" Dertujia muttered. She looked at him, hope burning in her eyes. "All right, fine, come. You can draw the attention from my parents off me." He motioned his head, and she eagerly followed. *Like a puppy,* Dertujia thought with disgust. He tried to stop thinking that way. Leahnina was a perfectly nice woman. The walk became silent, but Dertujia didn't try to talk. There were just too many things he didn't know about the woman beside him.

She had no parents and lived on her own. She wasn't a native of the village. She had lived in the city up to almost womanhood, but she had moved to Shymis a few years ago. Now she did odd jobs around town. No one quite trusted her, but she was so helpful, all they could do was accept her.

Dertujia preferred not to look at her. Her eyes had such … expectation. He was pretty sure she worshipped him like he had seen some worship the long dead gods.

The dirt road soon ended, and he reached his house. It was one of the bigger houses in the village, a gift from the Srashan king when Dertujia had saved his life a long time ago. It was tall with white walls and a red roof. His mother had placed many flowerboxes at the base of each window. It made the white much more appealing. Turrets struck the sky with rounded roofs and narrow windows.

He pushed open the door, gratified to hear its familiar wooden groan. He was home. He hadn't had to leave longer than a day to capture the centaur. None had called for him. Maybe he could be here for a while. To revel in home.

"Dertujia!" a woman, named Brani, yelled when she saw him. She had been sitting in the wide living room on the Koorsgald down chair. An expensive item.

Her red hair was swept up into a jeweled comb. Dertujia had gotten the color from his mother but the height of his father. "You're safe! Are you hurt? Did you break anything?" she said as she grabbed a hold of him in a ferocious hug.

"Mother, I'm fine," Dertujia said as he untangled himself from her. "Look, Leahnina has come to dinner."

"Oh, hello, dear," his mother said politely, but then turned her attention back to Dertujia. "Come inside. We want to hear about all of the centaur's tricks. And I want to make sure you're not hurt." She ushered him towards the table.

***

Hours later, his parents still hadn't heard enough about the raging centaur and how he defeated it. Dertujia was getting a bit tired, but his parents didn't seem to care. Leahnina was still talking animatedly about how she had foreseen the whole thing.

"I knew he would win—"

"All right," Dertujia finally interrupted. "I'm sick of talking about it. The time we've spent just speaking about the event has taken longer than the actual defeat."

"But Dertujia," his father, Kaytal, spoke up. He was sitting at the head of a rather large table. Kaytal brushed his dark blue hair away from his eyes and reached for a glass of strawberry wine. The food had been good, but Dertujia had picked at it. Something was off. He couldn't place what it was. "Despite what you think, your adventures are actually very entertaining for us. So, let's keep talking about it."

"Go ahead," Dertujia said, "but I'm leaving." He stalked out, not really caring if they followed him or not. All they wanted to talk about was how he had defeated the centaur, not about how he felt about it or anything else.

He felt empty. Hollow. Xorna might have been right. He looked towards the sword as an answer. But he couldn't second guess himself. When evil showed, he killed. That was the way it had always been.

Sometimes he just got tired. Exhausted really. What was the point to it all? Every time he left, he came home exhausted. His parents had another new piece of furniture or jewelry. But he had nothing.

Outside, he took a deep sigh and just breathed in the night air. He loved this village. It was quiet, peaceful, and his home, but he didn't belong. He wished he knew where he did. The villagers called him a hero, looked for him and

Xorna, praised them until the songs hurt his ears. But they didn't feed him inside. Nothing did. He grew hungrier every day.

Maybe this was what getting old did. No, he had no signs of wrinkles, no gray hair. He had only reached a third of his life marker. Still young, but time to settle down? Impossible. His parents wouldn't let him. He had to be a hero, maybe to the point of death.

He had removed his armor and let it rest in his room. His parents kept it like a museum. A monument to lack of change. He still felt like the sixteen-year-old he'd been when he left for the first time to seek out evil. To fight like his parents always wanted.

But his muscles belied that. His arms were bigger than any man's he'd seen in Shymis. His shoulders could hold the weight of the world. Scars ran down his sun bronzed skin. His hair had grown too long. Red hitting his large back.

He was no child. But he didn't feel ready to be grown.

"Who am I?" he asked the night sky. Silence answered. Everyone was inside at dinner. Tomorrow would be the start of the fall harvest. It'd be winter soon, and plans had to be made to sustain the village through winter.

A life that Dertujia was separate from. When winter came, he had to travel. He couldn't stay home and enjoy the comfort of the fire. No. Winter was the busiest time for war runners. They didn't do the work of storage over the summer or fall. They'd steal from others for their survival. He'd have to stop them.

"Why?" he asked. "Why does it have to be me? Why must I always fight?"

Suddenly, his ears perked up at an unfamiliar sound, the sound of a bird cheeping its head off. It was the wrong time of year for the migratory birds to be here. And he had never heard that kind of chirp before. Then a soft voice said, "It's okay, little one, come out." Dertujia wrinkled his forehead and started walking towards the sound. The cheeping continued, but then an unmistakable sound of a baby's cry filled the air. It was coming from a lighter part of the forest.

Dertujia slowly wandered through the overgrown plants. Some hit his waist, leaving a mark of wetness from the recent rain. He kept going, always towards the sound of the bird. The trees were silent, but they ignored him, almost as if they were watching something else. Dertujia saw a pleasant glow lighting up the corner of the woods. He went towards it. A clearing showed, a glow lighting up everything. A beautiful woman with pale blue hair. She was the source of the glow. She knelt down and held her hands out. An inner glow spread through her skin. Then Dertujia noticed she was holding a baby with large white bird wings. As if a giant dove had attached itself to the baby.

Confusion took his brain, but he knew one thing. How to be a hero. "Is there a problem?" he asked, but he startled her, and she jumped a few feet. "I'm sorry," he said.

"I didn't hear you," she said, still trying to calm down. "Why didn't I hear you?" she asked. She didn't direct the question at Dertujia but at herself.

He couldn't answer her. He thought he was making enough noise. He hated the dark and hadn't wanted to surprise her. A feeling from his own mind. No one should sneak up on someone unless there was plenty of light. "You and your child shouldn't be in the middle of the forest," Dertujia said kindly.

"It's not really my child," she said and gestured at the child with wings. She put him on the ground. The light bent around him, and he bumped and groaned. His skin stretched; his face widened. He grew. In seconds, he was a full-grown naked adult male looking around like he had never seen trees before. The surprising thing was, the being was less than half Dertujia's height, and his bones were easily viewable.

Dertujia jumped back. He had never seen anything like this before. "I just created him out of starlight and moon-tears," the lady smiled. "He's the start of a new lifeform." She looked him over and started musing out loud. "What should I call it? It will like to fly. The sky will be its home."

"How about Flitelike?" Dertujia proposed with a smile. He was almost positive he had fallen asleep at dinner and was now dreaming.

"I like that. Well, young one, I dub thee a Flitelike. You will love peace and happiness. You won't want to fight ever."

"That's not entirely true, Sister," a thick voice said with venom dripping from his tones. The woman gasped and looked up, and Dertujia did the same.

A man that seemed taller than the trees stood before her. He had eyes that were so thin they were barely slits, and a face that was so sharp it matched his eyes. Black hair roared out around his face like a lion's mane. There wasn't an ounce of fat on him. He was narrow and lean. He wore what looked like a suit of skin. It clung to all his perfect muscles.

"Eropus," she said with confidence. "Having a bad day?" she added mildly.

"I'm having more of a bad existence, with you constantly in it, Sister."

She shrugged and turned away as if she wasn't impressed, but Dertujia saw the hidden fear in her eyes. Dertujia decided to step in.

"I don't know who you are, but I would suggest you leave this place." He didn't know why. Dertujia had no armor, no weapons. If this man was a threat, there was little he could do. The man looked at Dertujia.

"Who is this?" he asked, his thin lips twisting into a smile. "Your protector?" He shot that to his sister.

The woman glanced at Dertujia. "No, just a brave man, who shouldn't be here." She looked more nervous than before. "Leave this place."

"He doesn't have to worry," Eropus said. "Besides, I would like a witness to this spectacle.

Your new creation," he added with a sneer. "Peaceful, happy, right, Sister?"

"Look, if this is about the Arachnialons—"

"You destroyed them!" Eropus yelled. "They were going to be a dangerous, deadly weapon! And you turned them into happy-go-lucky fools."

Dertujia couldn't move. Couldn't blink. Something was very wrong here. The names they threw about. Unfamiliar, strange. Dertujia had traveled the land of Telda. He had seen a lot, heard myths and legends. Those names weren't like any language he had ever heard.

And these two? Were they human? No. Something more. Gods. No, they couldn't be.

"I didn't want to think of those creatures having to listen to you. And the damage they could have caused the humans ..." The woman, the goddess, had a tear in her eye. She held her stomach as if just speaking about the creatures hurt her.

"It would have been beautiful," Eropus said. He too held his stomach, but it was not in pain. It was in anger. "But I will have my revenge. And you haven't stopped my plans, Little Sister. You've just delayed them. And in the meantime ..." Eropus glared at the Flitelike, and gold balls flashed out of his eyes towards the innocent being. They swelled around him until they started changing him. His face grew angry, and his posture tight. A sword appeared in his hand, and he started screaming in anger.

"There, pleasant new creation, isn't he?" Eropus mocked. "He will only want war. Hc will murder even his own. He will fight. And he will die, like all of them will. I'll see you later, Sister." Eropus flashed a few times and then disappeared, followed by the Flitelike as he angrily flew into the sky. The woman looked devastated.

"Excuse me," Dertujia spoke up, now convinced he wasn't dreaming, "but can you explain to me who that was, and what's going on."

Chapter Two

Dertujia waited for an answer from the woman as his thoughts tried to sort out what he had seen. *She created that creature, and that man ruined it.*

"I am the goddess of life," she said eloquently. "That was Eropus, my brother. He wants to control this world, and everything in it. I just want peace."

"Yeah, so do I." Dertujia paused. "I want to stop this from ever happening again."

"This?"

"Well, I am just a casual observer, and I certainly don't understand the whole of what just happened. But it seems an awful lot like you two create … beings."

"We are gods." She nodded and looked towards the sky. "We were born of star dew and moonbeams. A long time ago when mankind didn't exist, we came into being. But now we try to stay out of view."

"I didn't need a history lesson. I just heard your struggle. You both create and then ruin each other's creations. It's barbaric."

The goddess drew herself up tall. Offense breathed out of her regal form. "I only prevent the creatures made by my brother from suffering. He destroys mine."

"That doesn't seem to be a very stable relationship for us mortals or either of your creations. Can't you make peace?"

She shook her head. "Eropus has been wounded. The gods are dead, most of them. Surely, you know that."

Dertujia nodded, feeling the cool air lick his arms, making goosebumps. Somewhere inside he still heard that wild shriek of the flying, newly made creature. "Did they die of starvation when the Immortal Tree withered?"

The goddess slid down to a rock to sit and gestured for him to sit next to her. He knelt down, watching her face. She was a god. Yet she was his equal. No pretense or arrogance. Not like Eropus.

"The Immortal Tree was burned," she corrected. "By a human's hand. The human found out that if we don't eat, we die. One by one, my family succumbed."

Dertujia blanched at the pain in her voice. He had never gotten used to suffering. He usually allowed Xorna to comfort grieving villagers while he ran. But tonight, in this clearing with a goddess, he was the only one here.

He held her hand to his chest.

She gave a small smile. "It is nature for all to end. Gods and mortals. They keep the cycle alive. It was probably wrong we live so long anyway."

"And? Eropus and you? How did you survive?"

She gazed up into the trees, seeing far off. "I am life. It feeds me. New birth. Humans living and laughing. Love and friendship. There is no lack of food for me. But Eropus? He was the god of love."

Dertujia blinked, seeing that evil wrathful god in his mind. Love? Really?

"The trouble is," the goddess said. There was amusement in her voice. "Humans don't need help in that department. If they fall in love on their own, he gets nothing. Maybe he could try harder, but he despises humans now. They killed our family."

Dertujia gazed at her. Something in his soul stirred. Somehow, she was a reason to continue. A path. He didn't know why. She was just a wonderful being who could be killed by starvation. "What are the Arachnialons?"

She tilted his chin up, gazing at his face. Her scent surrounded him, taking him on a journey without him going anywhere. Past the stars towards the moon.

"Eropus made them out of spite. Spiders mixed with humans. They were meant to be a plague on mortals. Taking their territories, stealing lives. Trapping and poisoning any who opposed them. I gave them love.

"Now they are vegetarian."

Dertujia tried his best not to laugh.

"And Eropus hates you for it."

She nodded. "He's always hated my interference in his masterpieces, his words."

"So, he destroys yours. That Flitelike is now dangerous."

She nodded, a crystal tear falling down to his hand. "I'm afraid more will suffer. Eropus isn't finished with destruction."

Dertujia shook his head. "It might have escaped your notice, but I am a hero. Raised to be one since I was seven years of age. I used a sword when most kids played with toys. I have defeated war runners and evil all my life. I can stop him."

She gave him a soft gaze and then gestured. A table set with food appeared. "Sit and eat, it is obvious you wish to talk more."

Dertujia sat but then said, "Not talk. Fight. How can I stop him If he wishes destruction? What can I do?"

The goddess just smiled. "Not much I'm afraid. He even now drains the world to fuel his evil creatures."

Dertujia's jaw dropped. "Wait, back up. You are saying he is draining the world?" This was unfathomable to him. How could anyone, even a god, drain their world of Telda?

"It's a long story. But I'll tell it to you if you'd like."

Dertujia nodded.

She reached out for a pitcher of red juice, but to his surprise she poured him a glass and didn't drink herself. As if she didn't mind serving him. Him! A lowly human served by a goddess.

"As I said, Eropus can't eat love without being directly responsible. As much as he despises humans, the last thing he wants is for them to couple and feel joy. Happiness. He chose a new sustenance. The world around us has energy beyond measure. He has burrowed into the world and taken its core. Now it is inside him, he wears it like a heart."

Amazing. "That destroys our world?"

"It will wear out. With that, new disasters will become prominent. Earth tremors, winds that move trees. The death of the very sky above our heads."

The idea warmed Dertujia. This was it. His purpose. The reason he had to fight. The path he had gone on since he was young. "Tell me where his home is. I will go and destroy him. Oh, I can destroy a god, right?"

She shrugged. "I honestly don't know. Can you strike a death blow? Yes. Will he allow you? Not so clear. But his home is far away, past many villages and dangerous lands, further, I'm betting, than any land you've ever traveled. I will give you one blessing."

She blew a kiss at him which formed a green star in the night air. It hit his forehead and slipped in. He felt it inside his brain. Suddenly, he knew exactly where Eropus' home was. That'd make this journey easier.

"I'll set out tomorrow. By the way, what is your name goddess?"

"Bynneeshia. But mortals like shortening things. You can call me Neesh."

"Neesh." He nodded. He was starting to grow a fondness for her. He wondered if it was all by his choice. This goddess could be manipulating his emotions. Still, he trusted what she said as truth. Dertujia had seen the look in that maniacal god's eyes.

***

True to his word, Dertujia spent the evening preparing for the trip. His return to the house had thrown everyone into a tizzy. His mother was most vocal, but to his surprise, Leahnina was the quietest. After he had made his announcement, they were surprised. But nothing lasted long. How many times had Dertujia left to save another village? Granted this trip was a lot longer, but it was nothing out of the ordinary. His father praised him. His mother worried.

Leahnina did nothing. He grew increasingly worried about her more than anything else. And he wasn't at all surprised to find her face next to his window as he put the last change of pants into his bag.

He pushed open the wooden beam attached to the old glass and looked at Leahnina. "Yes?" he said simply.

"I have to come with you."

Dertujia laughed. "You know Xorna is the one who usually accompanies me. She is already packing at her place now. We'll leave on her wagon in the morning."

Leahnina nodded, fingering her hair. Funny, it always had light patches of blonde in it, but it was the first time, under the silvery moon, that he saw that they were more than ever. "Then you can easily fit me."

Dertujia let his tongue hit between his teeth and his lips. Taking her with them was beyond complicated. Leahnina was a soft villager woman. She had been pampered by city life and by her parents until they both died from fever. And even after coming here the people of the village felt sorry for her and gave her everything she could ever need.

And the goddess had said that they would have to go far to find Eropus's dwelling place. That was all the guidance she gave verbally, but ever since they separated company, Dertujia had felt the calling in his heart. He knew where he had to go. The journey would be hard. Most villages ended far before the Wild Areas. The ones where monsters bigger than a house roamed. And other villages popped up. But as Eropus' lands became more, villages were sure to be lost. No way would a god as evil as Eropus stomach his worst enemy to live near his home. There would be little food, water, or comfort. And Leahnina wanted to go!

"If you don't let me come, I'll follow you," she said stiffly. "And you'll see how fast I die without a hero to protect me. Then you'll see how heroic you are."

Dertujia groaned. Leahnina always manipulated everything. "Then come!" he barked. "We will leave at dawn, and then Xorna's wagon will go as far as the roads do. Then we'll have to walk."

Leahnina didn't look daunted. She just grinned and turned to run away into the moonlit night. "Why?" he asked before she could.

"I see your future," she said simply. "I know you'll need me." Then she was gone.

Dertujia sighed. Sometimes he thought that Leahnina was a good friend. Sometimes she drove him to his last nerve. But tonight, she seemed to genuinely care about him. More than he did her. That wasn't good at all. But sometimes … when her hair shined under the moon, there was something he felt. In the vicinity of his heart …

But he had given up on love a long time ago. It was dangerous in a hero's world. Especially to one who couldn't fight at all. Truth was, Xorna was way more a match for him. If they were to settle down, it would be Xorna he'd marry. She once said they were compatible enough, and if old enemies came looking for them, they could easily fight them off.

And that was logical. Except …

Xorna didn't look nearly as pretty under the shining moon.

Dertujia shook his head and settled into sleep. The moon winked and went out, and the hazy gray sky of dawn filled his empty room. Dertujia was already outside securing his stuff on the wagon. Xorna and her sister, Gampralle, were in the front. Dertujia looked around and smiled. It looked like Leahnina was oversleeping—then Leahnina came shuffling her feet. Dertujia had almost hoped she would stay behind. Slept in. But she was here. She had even braided her hair for the journey and brought her own pack. No one had told her what she needed, but she was smart. She had brought an assortment of things. Dertujia cursed inwardly but helped her up onto the wagon.

Gampralle greeted Leahnina and urged the horses forward.

The wagon trundled over the lonely morning road, as the sun kept rising, making the area glow. Mornings always made Dertujia feel alive and whole. Finally, they reached the end of the road and Xorna sent her sister back, with a hug and a promise that she'd be careful. Not that Gampralle worried too much. She knew Xorna was a great warrior. The trio sat down on the side of the road to enjoy a light breakfast.

The first part of the journey commenced. It didn't take long before Leahnina started complaining. She wasn't used to eating outside, so sand got in her teeth. She had never walked long, so her feet hurt. She got bored of the long roads. Dertujia and Xorna were already making plans in their heads to fill the hours. But Leahnina did nothing but mutter. Then she started singing.

Irritated, Xorna broke into a new topic, just to shut Leahnina up. "News came from Srashan

City. The centaur is set to be executed tomorrow."

Dertujia sighed. He expected that end for the beast. It didn't sit well on his shoulders, but he understood. If they just let it go again, it'd kill more.

"Really?" Leahnina asked.

Xorna shot her a look. Dertujia could have told her Leahnina was just curious. "Yes. Don't tell me you're for that."

Leahnina showed that she was thinking about it. "Yes, and no."

The hills pushed the road upwards. All around, brush started striking out making for hard walking.

"How can you think anything other than the fact that it's inhuman?" she demanded.

Dertujia groaned. "Xorna, it's not inhuman to save lives."

Xorna grabbed a long stick off the side of the road and pulled extra leaves off of it. She was fashioning a walking stick. She always did that at this time of any journey. "You didn't save the centaur's life. You condemned it."

Dertujia glowered. "You helped. And I'd do it again."

"What do you think?" Xorna said and pointed the wooden staff at Leahnina. She wanted her on her side. If Leahnina played it right, she'd have an ally. If not, Xorna would work her hardest to ignore her.

Leahnina considered it. Dertujia felt surprise fill his belly. She wasn't judging quickly like most of the villagers did. She waited and thought. If she agreed with Dertujia, what would he think?

She finally stumbled over a rock and answered. "I think it was a no-win situation. That centaur killed a child. It was out of control. The problem with a human body and a bestial mind is never knowing what side of the coin the creature will fall on."

Xorna stamped her feet as they walked. "You are impossible! An innocent being is dying at noon tomorrow. And you two think it's right."

Leahnina looked angry herself. "You have a strange definition of innocence. Just because something doesn't have control over what is done, doesn't give it that particular quality. What would you have them do?" she demanded. "Set it free and risk it killing again? Or imprison it forever?"

"Kinder than killing."

Leahnina's face fell forward. Two burning eyes peered at Xorna. "Kindness is a strange thing. Let me tell you a story."

Dertujia's ears perked up. Leahnina told wonderful stories. "There were two bandits once. They grew up together. They were starved their entire childhood, and, because both sets of parents didn't want children, they were cruelly beaten. They grew mean."

Xorna's footsteps slowed—she was listening. "Okay, so?"

"One night, when the stars were out but no moon showed, they broke into a woman's house and were about to rob her. She caught them in the act. One knocked her on the back of the head, but her screams drew her neighbor in. He stopped them both, but in his kindness, because he knew what made the thieves steal, he didn't kill them. He called the magistrate. He too felt pity on them."

"Is there a point to this?" Xorna complained.

Dertujia hushed her. He wanted to know the end to the story.

"The thieves were allowed to go free. They were given a house, jobs. There were even matches made for both thieves. But it wasn't enough for them. They wanted to be paid back for their lives of abuse and starvation, so they continued to steal."

Xorna rolled her eyes and shot a look at Dertujia. She clearly though Leahnina was like him. Truth was, Dertujia didn't know where this was going to end up. And he had no idea what it had to do with the centaur.

"One night, when the stars were spattering the black velvet sky, and there was no moon, they broke into the same house again. They murdered the woman and the next-door neighbor and ran off with all their treasures."

"Good grief! That's ridiculous," she spat. "Why would you make up something like that?"

"I didn't make that up." Leahnina stared at the ground, watching her feet, whimpering from time to time. "My feet hurt," she declared.

"Um, Leahnina," Dertujia said kindly, trying to stop her from going off on her complaints again. “What was that? The point? And where did you hear it?”

“That was my grandmother who died. She was well off. I lost her. The point is once a man has thrown off his desire to be human and shows the beast, then there is no saving him. Those thieves, when they entered my grandmother’s house, didn’t have to attack her. They could have just run into the night. The fact that they’d attack once, without cause, just for money showed that they turned off their ability to be men. They should have been at the very least imprisoned. But no one should have let them go free. The neighbor died for his kindness, and the magistrate has blood on his hands. I miss my grandmother to this day because of kindness.

“Justice … that’s the true end. It doesn’t have a preference. It doesn’t have mercy. It judges.”

Xorna didn’t know what to say. “But … the centaur isn’t like that. It’s just a beast.”

“So were those men. But they can still kill. I know. You dismiss the life of the boy who never lived by ignoring the centaur’s crimes. I won’t. Never. I will judge. And I don’t care if it’s harsh.” Leahnina’s face crumpled. “My feet really hurt. Can’t we stop?”

“For the love of the mountains, woman,” Xorna exploded. “We have only been walking for a couple hours.”

Tears came to Leahnina’s eyes.

“Let me see,” Dertujia said with a look at Xorna. They stopped, and Leahnina took a seat on a huge black boulder that was stuck into the shrub by the side of the road. The sun was already shooting overhead. Trees caught its burn, but they were too far off to do much good.

He slipped off Leahnina's slippers and groaned as he did. They were just fabric. No protection from the rocks of the road. It wasn't at all surprising to see that her feet were covered in wounds.

"You're bleeding!" Xorna said surprised. "Don't you know how to wear travelling shoes?"

"I've never gone far. Ever since I left the city I've been in the village. I didn't know."

She still sounded like she was about to cry.

"Xorna, go and get us some lunch, would ya?" Dertujia asked, and she gave him a look.

"With pleasure." Then she was off. Dertujia could swear he heard her muttering under her breath, "The two of them are perfect for each other. Hearts of stone."

"Did that story you told really happen?" he asked. He poured some water over her feet and then rolled up the cloth of her slippers to make padding for some shoes he would fashion. He stripped some bark and started sewing up a pair of shoes that might take the brunt of the walk. Not much. The damage was done.

Leahnina nodded. "I visited my grandmother whenever I could. She told me of the first attack, and she was scared. She knew they'd be back, but nobody listened to her. I want those men dead."

Dertujia wrinkled his nose. "Where are they now?"

Leahnina shrugged her tiny shoulders. She seemed so small—so vulnerable. "I guess they're on the run. Word was, they retreated to Bandit Road, but I'm not sure. They're alive, and Grandma's dead. I don't know …"

"Xorna is livid at us. I, too, think the guilty should be punished. But I think you made her think."

Leahnina watched as Dertujia's skilled hands pushed and prodded a piece of bark to go over her feet. "How can she not want perfect justice when she's seen so much?"

Dertujia sat back on his heels. The new shoes were on Leahnina's feet. "*Because* she's seen so much. Some people do reform. Some do turn over a new leaf and make the world a better place.

"See, a few years back, Xorna saved the life of one war runner. She gave him a second chance because he told her the sad tale of his life. But he wasn't like the thieves who killed your grandma. He's now a great man and a great leader.

"That changed everything for Xorna. It made her think of how many she had killed that might have been good men."

Leahnina laughed, but it was bitter. "I don't believe that. People don't change. They might switch sides, but they stay true to who they are. Murderers in peacetime still murder. Peacemakers in wartime still bring peace. You can paint a butterfly yellow, but it will still fly the same."

Dertujia smiled and cuffed her shoulder gently. "Why, Leahnina, I didn't know you were a poet."

She stared at him. "There are a lot of things you don't know about me."

That made the air uncomfortable, but Xorna came back with two or three flying rabbits (it was hard to tell the amount with all the feathers), and then made lunch. Nothing more was said.

The rested warriors … The somewhat rested two warriors and one completely unrested Leahnina, left again after eating their fill. Leahnina hung back until Dertujia had to urge her faster. They made good time and spotted the hills of Argona Canyons. The Argona Canyons were supposed to be, according to the map that Neesh put in his head, the marker that was the first step of this journey.

Dertujia felt that the evil god lived far beyond them. Thankfully, the journey remained uneventful. Lots of walking, lots of sun-ups and sun-downs. Catching food, finding places to sleep, and listening to Leahnina complain on and on every single minute of the day. She only quieted when they passed the dry brush fields and finally the landscape turned tall.

Chapter Three

The Argona Canyons were vast long mountain ranges, snaking north with rock so red you'd swear it bled. Many times, the parallel mountains reached together to form almost a cave.

It was one of those enclosures that Dertujia and Xorna chose to throw their packs on the ground.

Leahnina moaned as she collapsed against the wall. "Why did I want to go on this journey? It's hard."

Dertujia gave Xorna a wry glance. "Leahnina, we have only walked."

"For a very long time," she complained.

"Well, gods grant you we actually stay away from all bandits," Xorna said. "What kind of softness are you used to?"

"I do all my own work!" Leahnina defended. "Besides, bring on the bandits! I'd rather have bleeding than blisters!"

Both Xorna and Dertujia laughed at that. "Well, I don't want to bleed this night," Dertujia

said. "I'll climb the mountain and scout out any enemies that might be following us."

"I thought I'd do that," Xorna said quickly with a glance at Dertujia which clearly yelled, "Don't leave me alone with Leahnina!"

"Alright!" Dertujia said. "I'll start some dinner."

"Ooh! Great! I am so hungry!" Leahnina said. Xorna snorted and walked outside. He could see her testing the walls for a firm grip and then pulling out her ropes and harnesses. Normally he'd be with her to make sure she didn't fall, but he could tell Xorna wanted a break from Leahnina, and he didn't want to leave the new traveler on her own. Xorna could climb the mountain by herself, but Dertujia didn't think Leahnina would like to be abandoned by the two of them.

"Leahnina … are you going to be offended if I tell you something plain?"

Her eyes flashed as her head snapped up. "No," she said evenly, but there was venom in her voice.

"Oh, good, because it seems very much like you'd get mad."

She set her mouth. "I'm not going back."

Dertujia sighed. He grabbed some fire-starting stuff out of his bag and put the fire where the smoke would use the wind to go out of the cave. "You don't belong here. There are all sorts of merchants and waggoneers around here. I'm sure we could find someone nice to give you a

ride—well, even if we have to pay him or her—no more blisters."

Leahnina brought her knees to her chest. "You think I'm a burden, don't you?"

"Right now … yes." He owed it to his friend to be honest, and he owed it to the goddess for it to be brutal. Leahnina had no business out here. "You can't fight, cook, climb, or walk. You've done nothing but complain. Xorna's fed up with you."

Leahnina stared him in his eyes. "But not you?"

He cursed inwardly at his word choice, but he couldn't lie. "No. I was like this on my first long journey, and I'm sure Xorna was at one time—some time. Maybe when she was small."

"I can't imagine Xorna ever being like I was on this journey. She's so strong."

"She had to learn that," he insisted. "So did I. So do you, but this journey will only get harder."

"And so will I. I will match the journey. It will make me tough. Please give me the chance to show you how useful I can be."

"How?" Dertujia demanded. He had hoped she would take the bait and leave.

"You both have brawn, and I'm sure you have brain, but I'd bet I could beat both of you at chess."

Dertujia grimaced. "That dumb game where it looks like you are trying to rule the world?"

"Yes!" Leahnina crowed. "It takes tactics and strategy. I'll bet that that evil god won't just

let you walk in and stop him—in fact, I'd bet he could wiggle his finger and kill you."

Dertujia gestured to her feet, and she yanked off her newly made shoes. Dertujia grimaced at the bleeding wounds and did his best to wash them, spilling water from his waterbag in a trickle down her lovely skin. He paused for breath, not sure where he was getting these thoughts. They seemed invasive, not his, but they were. And they were wonderful. And distracting. "You think so little of my skills?" Dertujia gave her a wry grin. Finished with her feet, he leaned away from her and his thoughts.

"No, of course not. But I do know … well, let me ask you this. Did you catch that centaur by matching his speed?" She challenged him with face and form. An equal.

"No. I couldn't."

"Exactly. You used the trees to gain advantage. I may have looked like I've only complained, this journey, but I was also thinking. You can't possibly hope to win by walking into a god's home and killing him—one who not only changed creatures' essences at will but also is draining our world. I don't think you'll win—in fact, I'm sure of it."

Low flames caught the roughage as the fire started. It flickered across the cave, lighting up Leahnina's face while the overhang cloaked her forehead in shadow, as if she was wearing a hood. He suddenly got a chill. She wasn't just saying this—she knew.

Laughing it off, he pulled the mounds of meat covered in salt onto a spit over the fire.

"So, what would you have us do?"

"I say you do two things. Get more allies and get more power." There was a strange hollowness to her voice when she said that.

"Leahnina … you're scaring me."

She laughed, and he joined in. "Don't be scared. I've told you. I'm an oracle. Will you do as I say?"

"Tell me my future," he joked and listened. It wasn't a bad plan. Conveniently enough, Leahnina's plan had two stops before they even reached the road to Eropus' kingdom. One was to a town where mercenaries could be bought, and the second was (not in this order of course) to go to a place called Dragon's Tower. Travelling there could draw out any latent power. If any who entered owned anything, they'd be told, and, if Dertujia or Xorna had anything, it'd be that much more they would have to defeat Eropus.

It was logical, and even Dertujia knew it was best to have safeguards for any encounter with a villain—especially a god. Still … there was an inkling of worry about *how* Leahnina knew these things. At the beginning of this journey, she had no clue what the best way to attack was. Now, like a flash, it had come to her.

It unnerved him. Okay, yes, she had predicted that one storm a few weeks back, but nothing else, and all these extra powers were new to Dertujia. It was too much like those gods.

Even so, he plastered a grin on his face, and the plan was set.

The pathway to the tower was a bit more treacherous which was why Xorna didn't much like the idea, though she had approved of Leahnina's idea. Dertujia could see her estimation move up at the thought process Leahnina used. There was an active volcano pouring lava underneath already hardened stuff. A path was there, but it moved over flowing lava.

"It's a bit shameful really that we didn't think of it, you know," she pointed out as she set one of her feet gently on the slightly writhing volcanic ground. Each step was careful. One wrong move, and they could go right through to the hot lava just inches below the surface. So, no running or speed. Since it was slow going, conversation was the only thing interesting going on.

"To think, Dertujia, we were going to just walk into an evil god's home," Xorna whispered as Leahnina took a step further behind them.

"It's what we do. Give the enemy a chance to explain their side—though before we always had our abilities to back us up. But a god is different."

"We were so … used to all this. People call for our help—we go. We've become jaded, I believe. Everything crazy is normal." She paused and stopped, taking a deep breath. She tested the rocky dirt. "Thin ground here … tread quietly."

And they stepped even lighter. Conversation halted as well.

Leahnina surprised both and didn't … well, complain. She seemed to be slipping into the rhythm of adventuring. Dertujia felt a smile cross his face. Leahnina was growing.

Xorna smiled as well. Though, he could feel the edge to his old friend. She knew that this lava road was the first place where she could truly lose her life. Before her skill kept her mortality at bay, but now a missed step could be the only thing between this life and the afterworld.

Conversation stayed away as they walked the black ground, and hours passed before any of them breathed easier.

"I see the tower." The lava had become much more stable here. It had settled down to a few feet of rock between them and the flowing heat. Leahnina pointed and clapped. "I was right!"

"Of course you were. You had heard about it—read about it. The travelling bards …" Dertujia said warily.

Leahnina's smile faded. "Maybe you're right. No matter. I only saw it for real—I mean in person now. It's … ugly, isn't it?"

The tower she spoke of was still at least three days travel, but it struck from the horizon like an ugly and tall brown mole with a rounded top, and a huge, sculpted, black-as-coal dragon wrapped around it—base to top.

"Well, you were right about the tower's location. I hope you're right about the powers as well," Xorna spoke. "Let's make camp. I don't want to be travelling over more ground that's treacherous tonight."

Leahnina and Dertujia agreed, and they found some flat ground on which to throw their stuff down.

Much like the previous nights, Leahnina took off her shoes and rubbed her feet. They were bleeding, but Xorna surprised them both and quickly tore pieces of fabric off her first aid kit and bound Leahnina's feet.

"The more they tear, the more they'll protect. Soon you could walk barefoot over that hot ground and not care."

"Hey! I could feel that heat even through this thick bark on my feet. I think they even smoked a bit."

"Just a joke," Xorna said, but she smiled.

It seemed delaying the actual interaction between herself and a god had put her in a considerably better mood.

"Leahnina, I've given what you've said some thought. About kindness. Dertujia and I have had a lot of disagreements about it, but he couldn't put such a face to the suffering you endured. I shudder to think of your … the crimes against you. I don't think murder is ever an answer … but I don't know if I know the answers to every situation anymore."

Dertujia gave a mock gasp. "Surely not! You know everything, Xor."

She cuffed his arm. "I'm still right about the centaurs."

All shared a laugh.

"So, what powers do you think we'll get?" Leahnina asked. "I will … well, I don't know."

"I want lasers coming from my eyes!" Dertujia stated.

"I want the power to make anyone fall in love with me," Xorna joked.

"Come on!" Leahnina groaned. "Seriously! What do you feel?"

Dertujia shrugged. "I honestly don't know. I've always been fast, strong. What is that?"

"You always had trouble falling asleep at night," Xorna teased, not taking Leahnina's plea for seriousness seriously. "Maybe your gift will be insomnia!"

"If that's true, I'll return it!" Dertujia joked back, kicking Xorna's foot.

"I am surrounded by clowns!" Leahnina complained.

Dertujia gave her an apologetic shrug, but the truth was he had never really felt anything. Yes, the night always bugged him. He felt more comfortable in the day. As if … his friends were all around. At night, nothing at all. As if he were dead or blind. He didn't know why that was, but it was. He slept during the night to match the others in the village, but he'd have a more peaceful sleep during the day.

The days towards Dragon's Tower were mild, and soon they left the volcano far behind. Every day, the brown and black tower rose taller in front of them until it reached far above their heads, and the dragon's shadow captured them.

Finally, they reached the base. A gigantic shiny metal door greeted them. Black dragons were carved across it. It was the only way inside.

"That doesn't look like a light door," Xorna said mildly.

Dertujia nodded and gestured for Xorna to help him.

But to their surprise the door swung open easily—much easier than it should have, given the size and breadth. Dertujia shared a look with Xorna but walked forward. They all took a collective breath as they entered.

The first floor had one big round marble floor with spiraling staircases that led up to the left and right. The concaved walls were lightly decorated with swirling, silver magic symbols and equally silver wall sconces that kept the area light with little flickering torches.

"Well! We're here, Leahnina," Dertujia said. "Now what? Climb those stairs and hope for the best? Isn't there anyone to greet us?" His voice echoed until it was swallowed by the upwards air.

"I am far from the expert here," Leahnina answered, moving her head back and forth.

"Do not query." A voice filled the area. "It will be answered without the question. Your will will form your why."

"Well, that makes sense," Xorna said wryly. All three had jumped when the voice flew through the room like a restless bird, and they were now back-to-back. Xorna and Dertujia weapons ready and Leahnina with nothing but her fists up.

"One by one, you may come, choosing the stair that your will desires. Down path will be formed. Outside lies no power. Within is the only way."

"What does that mean?" Dertujia asked.

"I think that if the staircase leads you outside you have no inner power," Leahnina mused.

"How could it lead outside?" Xorna demanded.

"A teleport spell. Haven't you heard of them?" Leahnina asked with an arch to her eyebrow.

"No," Dertujia said, "but I've seen disappearances before."

All quieted. War or peace, Dertujia and Xorna weren't used to magic.

"I'll go first," Leahnina declared and trotted off before Dertujia could stop her. He would have chosen to go first had she allowed him.

Leahnina didn't deliberate before choosing the left staircase, and then she was … gone!

One moment her shoes hit the stairs in rhythm, and then all was quiet.

"Leahnina!" Dertujia yelled out. But there was no sound in Dragon Tower except for Dertujia's and Xorna's yells.

"Quiet yourselves," the voice spoke. "Leahnina, daughter of destiny, child of no one, has been judged. You will see her, either now, if you wish to leave, or when you complete your trial. Choose!"

Dertujia looked towards Xorna, but she just shook her head. She wasn't about to let him go next.

And she too vanished much like Leahnina.

Finally, after what seemed like eternity, the voice spoke again. "Now you … unless you choose to leave …"

"No, I don't. I wish to know what abilities I have. But who are you? Where are you?"

"I am the light when the sun goes down. I am the fear of the brave. I am nothing and nobody."

"And that means what to me?" To the silence, Dertujia huffed. "Alright, fine … Then where are you?"

"Between the edges of the world."

"Do you have a form I can look at?"

"If you desire … but know this. You will expect me different—you will be afraid."

"Ha!" Dertujia declared. "I fear nothing! I have been fighting since I could hold a sword. Nothing exists in my emotion anymore of fear!"

"Silly." Then the voice, instead of reverberating off the walls, coming from the walls themselves, came from above.

With a screech, a massive black dragon filled the tower, landing in front of Dertujia. His jaws stuck out into an awful snout filled with sharp teeth. Massive wings curled around his back. Scales like fallen leaves in a pile adorned an overgrown body.

"Yes, you think me to be a monster."

"A dragon," Dertujia said, holding his sword out. He couldn't help it. This was what Xorna once spent a whole year on before she met him. She had filled his ears with horror.

He looked for the weak spot …

"Do not bother!" the monstrosity glared. "I am the tower. I judge souls. I bring out talent. Choose your staircase or leave."

Dertujia felt his heart slap into his throat, filling his soul with the sound. His instinct—his training was to kill.

But wasn't this what Xorna always talked about? The dragon was doing nothing except offering to help draw out Dertujia's power.

And he had his sword ready!

"I choose …" he said with difficulty. "I choose," he tried again, "the left staircase." And he walked towards it, turning his back on the dragon.

He felt exposed as if he was naked—no, as if he were a newborn.

That dragon could rip him to shreds, and he had his back to him as he climbed the stairs.

Suddenly … he couldn't see. Memories assaulted him, ones he had forgotten, lost. He was five and had almost fallen in the well—the shadows … the shadows? They had warned him.

The daytime was pleasant, because there were so many shadows—the sun crept over everything bringing them to life. When it left, darkness smothered most shadows. Light brings shadows. Darkness brings nothing.

A quiet whisper in his ears begging to be noticed.

He … was shadows—knew shadows, mastered shadows. Dertujia was the master of shadows.

That was his hidden ability.

Darkness filled his brain, but seconds later, he was outside the tower, next to Xorna and Leahnina.

The trio was silent as they traveled now, onward to getting the next stage of Leahnina's plans. None of them wanted to compare notes—to talk about the powers that had been awakened in them.

The roads became more traveled, telling that a town was nearby. The very town Leahnina had predicted. Dertujia wasn't asking anymore of how. He felt every shadow even from far off. With time, and training, he would be able to talk to shadows across the world.

The sheer power of his abilities had taken a toll on him.

Xorna was too quiet, which made him nervous. She always had an opinion, but the days and nights that passed, the only real conversation was where to get food, to sleep, and how many miles to where they were going. Even their final destination was ignored.

Chapter Four

Finally, about two days' travel before they reached Tajfac, a walled city, Leahnina was the one who broke the silence.

"Okay, so, maybe," Leahnina said. They were all sitting next to a fire. The sun to the point of almost setting. "Instead of going to find that evil god, we should go and find that religious order who has devoted their lives to the unspoken. I'm sure they'd enjoy our silence."

That caught Xorna off guard, and she laughed out loud. It was nice to see. Her eyes had been so shaded. And now as she sat against a tree with the firelight making her face glow, she almost reminded him of the old days. Everything had changed after that tower.

"I guess so," Dertujia said. He didn't find it so funny. When he talked, he almost heard an echo. Not an echo of his voice really, a standing to attention as if all shadows in the world waited for his orders.

"So, I'll go first!" Leahnina said and stood up, nodding to both. She straightened her traveling cloak and rotated her shoulders to get the kinks out. "I have the ability of future telling. I can tell we'll find six mercenaries who will all die in our battle."

Xorna blanched. "Truly? You can see that?"

Leahnina nodded. There was no smugness to her tone. Just a quiet majesty. Dertujia's breath caught just as bit. He had never felt this way for Leahnina before. She had matured. What had she seen? What *did* she see?

"How can you tell?" he asked. "I mean, can you see the events? Is there a way of avoiding them?"

Leahnina sat back down and gave him a small grin. "The future is malleable. I don't know how you'd save the mercenaries. But I'd pass if I were you. These mercenaries, the only ones who would dare come with us, will be murderers and brutes. The world will be nicer once they're gone."

She shook her head. Her hair flickered and fell like it was liquid, cascading down her shoulders. Had she truly been this beautiful before? Or was his mastery over shadows making him see everything more?

"Your turn!" she announced. "I can't see what you've gotten. I mean …" She looked at Dertujia and then blushed at the obvious awe in his face. "There's a whole lot of darkness around. I don't know why."

He took a deep breath and nodded. "Maybe I should show you why." He felt for his newly discovered friends. The town had horses. Their shadows were wild, trapped by the casings of mankind. But he could free their shadows.

He called. To show off just a little—he wanted Leahnina's awe—he stood up and reached his hands out. "Shadows, come to your master. Make yourself flesh."

Dertujia felt a sickening sensation in his chest as suddenly they just rushed forward, extra black against the darkness, flickering in the flames' light. It hadn't even been difficult. He had spent years training with a sword. He had dropped it more than he could count. He had to develop a sword hand that allowed his grip to remain strong, and *that* had taken years.

But one beckon, and shadows were here. He could have summoned one of those giant lizard-like beasts from the land of the Reapers. He could summon that centaur's shadow.

He could use his friends' shadows. The power was limitless.

Untapped. Terrifying.

"Wow!" Leahnina exclaimed. "Can I pet them?"

Dertujia wasn't sure. But he nodded. Somehow, he wasn't surprised when Leahnina could. She even hopped up on its back and rode. It didn't throw her. Because Dertujia didn't want it to. Otherwise, it would have. He had complete command.

"That is incredible!" Xorna said and hugged him. She, too, was amazed. "Dertujia, if I was honest …" Xorna only said this because Leahnina was far enough away. Leahnina was enjoying riding around, the fading sunlight on her hair. Dertujia enjoyed it as well.

"I was scared." It sounded like she was admitting to murder.

He turned to her with surprise, ripping his wandering gaze off Leahnina. This hadn't happened before. It was her power, he decided. Leahnina was more attractive now because of it. That was all.

"You, Xorna? You were scared?"

She threw her hands up in the air and dropped to the ground. As she tended to whenever she emoted, she grabbed her sword and started taking care of it to make sure the blade was as sharp as it could be. "We were going up against an evil god. You may have met up with this goddess, but I didn't." She paused to pat her chest, the sharpening stone in her hand making a dull thunk against her armor. She wore it even in the night, no matter how uncomfortable she was. That had never happened before. Now, her silver pounded metal shaped of twisted vines was her best friend, her nightly companion. Finally, Dertujia saw what he should have from the beginning.

As much as it shamed her to admit it, Xorna was terrified of everything that was happening.

"And he's draining the world!" Xorna continued. "He needs to be stopped. But when it's a war runner or a corrupt king … A person mad with power or even the centaur that I had my qualms about bringing in, I always knew what to expect. But magic? Powers? That stupid tower which gave you abilities? It's so beyond me. I signed up to fight evil in men, not gods. I can't …" She shook her head and gave an extra harsh swipe to her blade.

"And ever since we started, I've had the worst feeling. Like … this can't end well."

Dertujia nodded. He should have seen this sooner. The trouble was Leahnina had been a distraction from the beginning even before her powers. He didn't know how or why, but Leahnina had taken possession of his heart. He had fought it. His life was wars, not family. But he couldn't help it now.

Leahnina was too important to him.

"If you want to know for sure, ask Leahnina," Dertujia said, his eyes wandering again. The shadow horse was faltering.

Suddenly, it disappeared, and Leahnina fell to the ground.

"Leahnina!" he yelled and rushed to her side.

But to his relief, she was giggling. "That was fun! Why'd you try to kill me?" she asked Dertujia.

He tried to chuckle. But all he could do was kick himself. The torchlight around the stable he had borrowed the horses from had gone out. No light. No shadow. No wonder he felt so alone at night. Only by the light's power did his shadows exist, and in the day … light was everywhere. So, his powers did have limits after all.

It cheered him up. He was no god.

Leahnina was getting tougher. She only rubbed her hind end and sat down again. "Okay, so shadows and future against a god. Xorna? Please tell me you have like fire control or some kind of earthquake?"

Xorna shook her head. She quietly laid her sword down. "I went outside. The tower gave me nothing."

Dertujia and Leahnina stared at her. She met their gazes with a snarl. "So what? That just tells you I don't need any razzle dazzle. Sword and shield. Armor. I fight with my fists and weapons or not at all."

Dertujia wasn't as distracted now. He could see the pain hidden away. She was left out.

Was she going to make it? Did the talents she have at warfare give her enough to survive this?

"Leahnina, tell us what happens." He reached out and took her hand. Her shadow flickered in his mind. As if … he could tell she was breathing harder because he was holding her hand. Just as an experiment, he rubbed the back of her knuckle.

Yep, definitely a connection. He grinned but tried to get back to what he needed to do. "Can we beat Eropus?"

Her eyes shaded. She looked across the world, across time. But this time it wasn't her shadow that flickered. Her entire face went in and out for a split second.

"Leahnina," Dertujia swore.

She didn't listen. She opened her eyes and answered. "I can't see everything. But I know this. You will defeat Eropus. He will die by your blade."

Dertujia laughed. Even Xorna smiled. "That's wonderful." He released her hand. Ignoring his own disappointment, and the shadow's …

Xorna opened up a map and peered over the squiggly lines. "So, what can we do about the mercenaries? Should we even involve them if it means their death?"

Leahnina and Dertujia shared a look. Moral dilemmas were presenting themselves before them. What choice did they have?

If Dertujia went and got those six men, he'd have aid, and they'd be out of commission. But he would be sending them to their death and not in combat.

"They will help." She bit her lip. Her eyes went clear. They came back, albeit slowly. "If we don't use them, Xorna will lose a finger. I will be …" She gasped. She swallowed. "I will be killed."

That was the end of moral dilemmas. No, he would not risk Leahnina. "Can we get to town tomorrow?"

Xorna poked her finger across the map. He could tell these events troubled her. But she was getting it. Trade off a bunch of evil men's lives for a good woman who was their ally. Even Xorna wouldn't resist that.

"We can be there by noon's sun tomorrow." She folded up the map and started removing her armor. Having a fortune teller who knew the future by her side had calmed her. "I do wonder," she started as she pulled her traveler pillow up under her head and flipped the blanket down on top of her. She placed the armor by her bedroll and fell against the ground in her undertunic. "Making decisions like these, does it elevate us? Only the gods usually do that. Knowing what's to come, choosing who lives and who dies?"

Dertujia pondered that as he fell asleep. Surely one or two decisions to save a good woman and kill evil men didn't make him a god. It was just this one time. Nothing would come of it.

Dertujia was no god. He'd only make these decisions to defeat an evil being. Then he'd go home.

Once again, he reached his hand out for Leahnina, who was waiting. She squeezed back. Under Xorna's heavy breaths of sleep, he asked her, "Do we stay together, Leahnina?"

Her answer was comforting and yet somehow as terrifying as his control over the shadows. "For centuries, my beloved."

A smile hit his face as she traced his wrist with her fingers. He reached up to her forearm and held on.

Leahnina was now his comfort. She knew what would happen. He would always have her. They fell asleep, arms connected.

The shadows died as the clouds obscured the light and the fire burnt out. They were reborn again as morning hit.

Dertujia awoke, still smiling, his arm around Leahnina's.

The conversation was much livelier the next day. The secrets had died, and they could show what they wanted. Xorna kept her fears away from the conversation—she didn't want to seem lesser in the eyes of Leahnina—but everything else was on the table.

"Are we getting a room?" she asked. "Or camping outside, going in, in the day, and finding these doomed mercenaries?"

Leahnina rolled her eyes. Xorna still didn't like it, and she let the two of them know it every time she mentioned them.

"A room," Dertujia said firmly. "I don't like a town being at my back as well you know, Xorna."

She gave a heavy sigh as if he was being impossible, but she nodded. Leahnina blushed a bright red, and Dertujia wondered if she was seeing a future or if she was just imagining being alone with Dertujia in a soft bed.

His own mind wandered. This was so new! He had feelings before. He would have had to be dead if not, but his parents had instilled a high sense of honor in him. Going to bed with maidens meant lack of control. Whether from what could come of it or being trapped in a relationship he had no time for. But Leahnina … the idea had merit.

Neither trappings seemed so bad to him now.

Xorna, reading both their faces as if they were scrolls, snapped her fingers in front of their eyes. "It will be *one* room for the three of us. No extra stuff."

Leahnina actually groaned out loud but covered it by coughing. Dertujia managed to hide his disappointment. He had forgotten the third person here. So easy to do when he stared in Leahnina's eyes. That tower had changed their relationship—had changed everything. He couldn't deny any feelings.

But tonight, he'd have to deny his body longer. It wouldn't be fair to Xorna for her to be around two lovers.

They let her go ahead, and he gave Leahnina a glance. "I have feelings for you," he said stiffly. "I just wanted you to know." Okay, so this was harder than wrestling that bearman! What if Leahnina didn't feel the same?

"I know." A knowing look passed her features.

Of course, she did!

"And?" he asked. "If the feeling is not …"

She stopped and stared at him. With that one look, he knew. But still …

"I called you my beloved!" she said.

He pursed his lips.

"I said we'd be together for centuries." Now she was miffed. "You need more?"

"Kind of, yeah. I know you were just using hyperbole with the word centuries."

She didn't answer. A chill hit him, but he rallied forward. "Look, Leahnina, we were just friends before this. You were an annoying fan, not a … partner."

She blushed again. Dertujia *really* wished he could see what she did, and the images that were going through her mind. “Dertujia, we were meant for each other. I always knew that.” Her face twisted a bit as if she would cry. “I may have been an ‘annoying fan’ to you, but for me you were always the one. My master. My slave.”

Dertujia shook his head and drew her closer. “Neither. Partners. I don’t want a servant or to be a slave. I want equality. Give and take. Can we promise each other this?”

Leahnina reached up and kissed him, pushing with more force than she should have had. “I promise you I’ll never leave you.”

“I’m growing *very* old!” Xorna said with a scowl at the two of them. And yet did Dertujia see a smirk?

His old friend was happy for him.

They continued their journey. The road started having stones. At first, they looked random and then a definite pattern started breaking out. Soon the stones were so pressed together no one could mistake it for anything other than what it was: a road.

Signs started appearing, telling how far Tajfac was.

“How unnecessary,” Dertujia said. “We should just walk until we get there. Who cares how long or how short it is away? Knowing won’t change the distance.”

Xorna snorted. “Look, Dertujia, *some* of us like knowing what comes ahead so we can plan. Like, look, that sign says we’re about three thousand steps away. Now, I don’t know if I have the energy for three thousand steps, so we’ll stop under that tree have a drink and something to eat, bind wounds, and then go on."

Leahnina bit her lip. She knew Xorna meant her. "No need!" she said quickly. She pulled off her Dertujia-made shoes and wiggled her feet in the air. "I don't have injuries anymore."

Xorna threw her hands up in the air. "Great! Was there anything that tower didn't give you?" She walked over to the tree and sat down with a huff. "No good tower. Didn't give *me* anything. No powers, no healing ability. Misbegotten building of stone and dirt!"

Dertujia shared a smile with Leahnina, but they followed Xorna's lead and sat.

"One problem, Xorna, my friend, if you can stop muttering long enough to listen. We have no supplies. We were going to get our bags filled in town. But right here and now, we have little water and no food."

Xorna surprised him and didn't groan. She rolled her eyes as if he was being utterly impossible. "You controlled that horse to come last night when very little shadows existed! What, can't your new *powers* bring us food and drink? I want a vegetable burger and grapemint wine. Thank you very much."

Dertujia's jaw dropped. But to his surprise, Leahnina piped in. "Cheese and rain-chicken ravioli, please! Oh, and that bubbling water."

Dertujia groaned. "What do you think I am? A waiter?"

It was Xorna's and Leahnina's turn to share a grin. "Yep, sounds about right." Xorna sat back and wiggled her eyebrows.

Leahnina giggled. "Absolutely. But, Dertujia, you can bring us the shadows. Can't you make them bring us something too? That horse was form until the shadow died."

Dertujia hadn't really thought about the possibilities of his new power. He hadn't wanted to. But he was hungry. And thirsty. And suddenly the vase-roast his mother had made before this journey popped into his mind. But that wasn't all. That drink he had once. From the Immortal Mountains. It had been an offering from the deepest parts, only meant for the gods to drink. Dertujia had snuck a sip and had been overcome with pleasure. It was a good thing the gods hadn't minded. Not that any of them watched over that place anymore.

"Okay, then, your demands are met," he said and reached his hand out. As an afterthought, he suddenly realized eating vase-roast on the ground wasn't exactly his style. A table … the shadow reaching up tall, from a right angle as the sun streamed in through a window. It popped up, a little tilted but more than enough to sit at. Chairs followed.

Then he sent a summons across the land. Wherever food existed, the shadows around listened. In only minutes, the requested meals sped across the landscape, carried by shadows. Leahnina wasn't surprised, but Xorna's jaw dropped as the aroma entered her nose.

"You did it! So, I won't lecture you on eating meat." She grinned, but Dertujia knew she would have. He took the bait. He shouldn't have. It was an old argument.

"You can't stop eating meat just because one out of a hundred thousand Teldians are turning into animals, Xorna. You just can't. That's illogical." He flicked his fingers and shadowy silverware appeared. Funny, he could have brought real things forth, but he preferred the black shadowy look. Not there, but there. Only the food was real, and, he supposed, even the shadowy version could have given him sustenance. Not that he wanted it. The bite he brought to his mouth sent him back home. Under his parents' roof, before all this had begun.

"But you could be eating a human, you know," she pointed out.

Leahnina was already digging in herself, draining the bubbly water in one go, and Dertujia brought more. "I'm new here. What are you talking about?"

"God of animals." Xorna was short and to the point. "He died. Threw his own power into the world. Anyone it touches transforms. Some turn into animals completely. Others get the ability to change at will back and forth. That's why I eat vegetables and that's all. I am no cannibal."

Leahnina smirked. "But what if the god of vegetables dies?"

Xorna pointed her burger at her as if she was stabbing her. "There is no god of vegetables, fruitcake."

Leahnina giggled. "I actually agree with Dertujia," she said slowly. "Meat is a vital part of our diets. If we stopped completely, then we'd suffer nutrition loss. It can't be stopped completely just because of a chance of eating …" She trailed off. For a minute, Dertujia thought she was crying, but then he saw that the shaking she was doing was because she found this whole thing funny.

"A human turned into an animal!" She chortled. "So funny. What a fate!"

Dertujia hid a smile. Xorna glowered. It was hard for his old friend to have two people against her and her beliefs. But it was wonderful for Dertujia. Who knew Leahnina had shared so much of what he thought? It was a shame he hadn't realized before.

"It's okay, Xorna. I'll just bring forth only animals who don't speak. Does that please you?"

"I'll never eat meat again," she declared. "Even if it doesn't speak, it could be … I mean, he or she could be a child of a human. It's horrible. If you think about it."

Dertujia wiped his mouth with a shadow napkin. "Most things are, if you think about it. Let's not think. Let's eat and enjoy." He looked at his two friends and smiled. This was the best part of the journey so far. Eating and drinking with friends, even with arguments—having camaraderie. He never wanted to forget this.

The meal ended, and he sent the shadows back.

"Where did it come from?" Xorna asked as they started traveling again. "The food?"

That stopped Dertujia. He had only felt out for the shadows and the belonging items. He hadn't thought about the source. Had he just become a thief then?

He should have felt worse. He didn't know where he had taken it from. But … they were hungry. And going to save the world! Surely a few people could spare food to feed them.

Leahnina shared a look with him and quickly said, "I see that it came from a place with abundance. They neither miss nor care about the food being gone. No worries, Xorna."

That relieved Xorna. She didn't say much more. It ended what would have been a lengthy lecture.

"Is that true?" Dertujia asked under his breath.

Leahnina shook her head. "I don't know where the food came from. But I'm fed and happy. I don't need indigestion thanks to a guilt trip." She glanced at Xorna. "It's amazing."

They both stared at Xorna's back as she walked ahead of them, bending down to sniff a flower and inhale its scent.

"She seems so innocent sometimes," Leahnina continued. "She doesn't get the fact that sometimes the ones in need have to take without guilt. I'd love her to tell a starving man not to eat an animal that used to be human. Ethics have to change. Morals are subjective when you're desperate."

Dertujia stared at Leahnina. He never knew she felt like that. But he recalled the bandit story she had told about her grandmother. Leahnina had a different idea on what justice was, and what was wrong and what was right.

He reached out to squeeze her hand. "I should have had you on all my journeys. I didn't even realize I was missing you."

They swung their hands in unison as they made the last three thousand steps into Tajfac. Just as Xorna said, they walked under the archway into the city just as noon's sun spread out overhead.

Chapter Five

Tajfac wasn't a city Dertujia was familiar with. There had been little to no cause to come this far east in his travels. The difference here was incredible. Dertujia was used to buildings, sure, and some of the cities he had been in had them thrusting into the sky as if they were trying to fly off the ground. But all of them had been built with wood and earth or stone, something natural.

But what made up Tajfac was a shiny substance, like a sword's blade or a shield's surface. Every single building was square with square windows and square pathways leading through the city. If the signs leading to the city were needless, the ones in the town were downright gratuitous. Each one, cut out of the same metal, and just as square as the buildings, told you where any location in town was and how far.

Bordering the very unnatural paths were flowers and minimum grass, but both were wan and ugly, barely surviving. The grass was brown and hanging on.

"Horrible place," Dertujia said.

"The future," Leahnina said mysteriously. "It's convenient. Each person has a house, and the new improvements make farming unnecessary. I see their future. It is mechanical. Large vehicles, round and fast."

That sounded even more horrible. It was no wonder they would pick up the mercenaries here.

Luckily, the signs told them where the local mercenary guild was. As one might expect, it was square and metallic. But this building had swords crisscrossed over the entrance.

Dertujia looked at Leahnina and pursed his lips. "Perhaps you should stay outside. Mercenary guilds are rough places. They don't care about who you are. If you have money, you might hire them. Or you might turn their eyes on you. Especially with the men you've seen, it could prove to be dangerous."

Xorna nodded. "You are the wrong type to go in. They will size you up and find someone lacking."

Leahnina glowered, but she was outnumbered. She walked across the street to what looked to be a pathetic garden full of barely surviving grass and trees and sat down next to a group of people who were all stretching their bodies, paying no attention to Leahnina.

"Good," Dertujia said. He gave Xorna a grin. "Thanks for backing me up. This place might be rough. If I'm right, they'll size us up too and find competition."

"Story of our lives," Xorna agreed. "What are they doing?" She pointed to the people near Leahnina.

Dertujia looked to the group who were now kneeling and bowing as if praying, reaching their hands far overhead. "It looks to be the same exercises we do to loosen our bodies, and yet it's stranger than I'd expect."

"It's strange that villagers are doing it," Xorna agreed. "I thought it to be unique to warriors."

"Another new invention." Dertujia was quiet. He didn't much approve of change. The world was changing around him. What would happen if every village was like Tajfac, all metallic and shiny when before it was in communion with nature? Dertujia wouldn't be able to take it.

"Shall we?" Xorna asked, and they opened the heavy front door. Inside was as ugly as they'd expect. There was one counter far across the way, but the main room was the only one, scattered here and there with tables. Far in the corner a solitary staircase headed upwards. The smell of old ale and body odor assaulted Dertujia's nostrils.

The people here were about what Dertujia would expect. Not for who would work with him but for who he'd fight against! In fact, he thought he recognized a few.

Keeping one hand on his sword, he sent his summons through the room. The light from outside spread in, making for nice and thick shadows.

The people here didn't know why they couldn't move at all as Dertujia and Xorna headed over to the counter.

The person behind it was one of those skinny guys who never saw any action but acted as if he did. Going home at night and telling stories about all the mercenaries while he stayed safe inside his home. Gray hair with a pale face and watery eyes that looked at the two, wondering why no one was walking up to them.

"Um, welcome to the mercenary guild," he said. "Are you looking or finding?"

Xorna leaned forward. "What's the difference?"

He gave a nervous giggle, trying very hard not to gaze too long at Xorna. "Looking is work and finding is wanting someone to work for you."

"Clear and succinct," Dertujia said rolling his eyes. He decided to address the room. "We're going after the evil god Eropus."

Mutters attacked the room. Even as frozen by shadow as they were, they could still emote. No one there could forget the name of evil.

"We need some people to help us," Xorna said in a loud voice.

No one dared look at Dertujia. As fearsome and bloodthirsty as they were when he entered, none of them wanted anything to do with this quest. Minus, of course, six. Only six mercenaries would raise a voice. Dertujia wasn't surprised.

"What's the pay?" a man in a table near the door spoke up. Dertujia allowed the shadows to leave him. But a quick glance made Dertujia know he would never have chosen him if he had a choice. The man moved almost as if he would attack every five seconds. Many different vials were on his belt. Even from here Dertujia could guess they were poison, a most dishonorable way of attacking. His hair was greasy and unwashed, and so long, one could tell he had never gotten it cut.

Dertujia groaned inwardly. What could he say to get more mercenaries?

"How much will I get if I go against the great God Eropus?" a squeaky voice called from a square table.

Dertujia and Xorna exchanged glances. The morals were clear on her face. Offer a huge amount of money and never really be able to pay up or just tell the truth. To his surprise, she just nodded. As if she was fine with it all. Was his friend changing? Or did she just see the greater need here?

"I will pay one hundred thousand Gilars to any person who joins us. We are going after a dangerous foe, and we pay well."

Another person was allowed to stand up, but this guy Dertujia knew. Short hair that only grew long over his ears. Green and black tunic over soldier's boots that weren't his by right. A long thin blade that was slung over his back. He marked every part of his body with ink depicting bloody battles.

"Ah, it's strange seeing you when we aren't separated by prison bars. If I agree to this bargain, will you come after me? Or would you pay me and leave me to spend it?" He gave a grin and wave to Xorna who smiled back, whipping out a knife as if she'd like to throw it at him.

"No, Dolawa, I'd let you go free."

Dertujia didn't look at Xorna to see how she was taking this lie, but he could tell that she actually didn't mind for this guy. Dolawa was a piece of work. Definitely worth what his future was.

"Good to know."

Once again Dertujia let his shadows go. Another familiar face. She was a thick woman, maybe a giantess, and even a Reaper might not want to eat her. She wore some woven armor and a large ax. She had murdered an entire family before Dertujia had stopped her.

"What is this, Icamea?" he asked. "A mass jailbreak?"

"We teamed up," she said. "We needed money. We didn't think you'd come to Tajfac."

Usually, she'd be right. If it weren't for Leahnina, they wouldn't have. "Business. Well, will you help?"

She laughed and gestured to three other people. Exactly six. Two Dertujia knew, but he had seen the others on the way out of the Gaiarigonian prison. Murder was just the smallest crime these people were guilty of. Patricide, terrorist attacks, assassination plots, and worse. Dertujia was going to bring them all along.

He shared a look with Xorna. There was no guilt in her eyes, except for the stuff that told her she was being a judge, jury, and executioner for these people. But she had to do it. She wouldn't let these monsters live when Leahnina would die.

"For one hundred thousand Gilars, I'd go up against the god of evil. Payment in advance of course," Icamea demanded.

Dertujia laughed and crossed his arms. "Payment before we go into the lair of Eropus."

The group was so transparent. Dertujia could see that they planned to take their money and run. In the meantime, they'd pretend to go along.

"Meet us outside the city with mounts tomorrow morning. We'll be going far." Dertujia nodded and walked out.

Xorna followed. The door closed and they could hear the room erupt inside. Dertujia knew they were exploding about their lack of movement. Silly sheep. Take away their freedom for one second and they go crazy, but they gave it up willingly every single day whenever they drank too much or ate too much or smoked too much of their favorite weed.

"I don't like this," Xorna puffed.

"Neither do I. But Leahnina knows what she's talking about."

"Yes, exactly." She was so angry, neither noticed that there was a much larger crowd than when they entered, all heading toward one person sitting in the park. People would leave either sobbing or laughing, but Dertujia didn't pay much attention to them. He was intent on his old friend.

"Because they're going to die?"

Xorna gave him a wry look. "Dertujia, I know I give you a hard time, but I'm no idiot. Those people should be shoved back into the deepest pit they escaped from. I'd like to know how the prison was overcome. I look forward to when they won't stain the air with their breaths anymore. I would kill them if given half a chance. But! They'll be traveling with us. With Leahnina. She's no warrior. She only has the future. We'll be sharing close proximity." She shuddered. "I can't be the one to kill all of them on this journey."

Dertujia laughed. "My shadows will keep watch. One wrong move, and their own shadow will strangle them. Not to worry. No one will hurt Leahnina."

Xorna nodded. "Dertujia, what is it with her? You have changed. You treat her like she's a precious gem. To be worshipped. But I know you. You didn't want to be trapped." She shot an irritated look over her shoulder. "Gods, can these people stop being so loud?"

The people were almost buzzing with energy. Dertujia ignored them and focused on what she said. "Xorna, I've lost my heart. Leahnina has taken it. I don't want it back. I can't truly describe it. I'm no poet. But it's like we are meant to be together for a very long time. It's as if my shadows were blocking my feelings for her.

But now that I can control them, they let me see the truth. She knows …" He put his fingers to his chin. "She knows what it's like to have so much power. She knows where I'll go and how everything will turn out. I can't help but …"

Xorna held up a finger. "I can understand. I just don't know how you will settle down after this. Will you? Have I lost my partner?"

Dertujia laughed. "Xorna, you are assuming we survive this."

Xorna made a face, but the crowd around gave them no more peace. People were pushing in from every street, bumping into Dertujia and Xorna.

"Disperse," he said irritably. One by one their shadowy feet pulled them away to reveal …

"Leahnina?" Dertujia said. She was the one sitting in the park. The one everyone was trying to get to.

She was gesturing wildly to a man sitting at her knee, listening in rapt attention. Telling the future.

"You will marry and have a long family line. You will create the vehicle everyone will use."

"And, what about tomorrow. Will it rain?"

"Buckets. Keep your windows closed. And remember look for the woman with the rose in her hair. She will be your wife."

He kissed Leahnina's hands and ran off, happier than any person Dertujia had ever seen. Dertujia and Xorna strode up to Leahnina.

"Is it too much to ask that you'd keep a low profile here?" Xorna asked.

Leahnina looked up with guilty eyes. "One person wondered if they'd be able to make it home in time to meet their son. So, I …"

Dertujia laughed. "Just told everyone their future. Wonderful. But no more. None!" he boomed to another person taking Leahnina's hand. When he didn't let go, Dertujia crunched his hand into a fist and pulled the man up into a tree. "They don't listen really well."

"I am important." Leahnina's eyes shined, and Dertujia's heart gave a sympathetic bump. How many times had Leahnina been unimportant before?

"Always," he said with meaning, and she gave a happy smile. "Now, let us go to an inn. Soon, we'll leave this nature-less city. We will meet up with our … allies outside the wall in the morning."

And they walked. Dertujia had to use his shadows to keep many future seekers away. But he found out something. His powers were not omnipotent. Too many wore him out. Too many people clustered together had too little individuality to control. When they came together, their one shadow was chaos. But many settling apart made it easy. Like being heard in a large area versus a small room.

He had to keep that in mind.

***

There were a few inns in Tajfac, but most of them were modern. Flashing lights showed them from a mile away. Xorna led the two, while Dertujia stayed back with Leahnina. She had gotten a following. People were asking for their futures, trailing her from the park to the inn. As it got darker, their shadows grew more and more hard to control until Dertujia genuinely grew worried about his ability to lose them.

"Stop," he begged as Leahnina told a couple when their child would be born. "You are making a name for yourself."

Another inn, Cotton Rove Inn, was bypassed. The sign itself wouldn't allow sleep inside: it was so bright.

Xorna didn't even turn her nose up at it as she kept going, looking for a place to rest their head that wouldn't blind them.

"And what is wrong with me having a name for myself. I am an oracle." Leahnina turned to greet another. A baker by the looks of him. Flour on his apron, a big gut, and a tired face.

"I already know," Leahnina said. "No, you didn't ruin your chances. Put the coin in the bread again. The mayor will find it and will be happy. He will help your political leanings."

The baker beamed. "You are amazing." He rubbed his floured apron, smearing it across his fingers. "King Veriton should know about you. He would pay good gold."

This was becoming tiresome.

Leahnina finally gave it a break though. "No, I am done now. King Veriton will just have to rely on his own soothsayers."

The baker backed away, but his eyes were calculating.

Dertujia put him out of his head. Xorna had finally stopped in front of a cute little inn, no flashing lights. Just a swinging sign that said, Beds.

"Perfect," he muttered.

The inside was even humbler. A wooden floor with only one stretch of wood that made for a counter. A few tables that were part of a breakfast nook. Swatches of quilts on chairs in front of a soft fire. The night was a little chilly.

Xorna threw down coins, and the innkeeper greeted them with friendliness. But no overt interest.

There was only one room available, so the trio moved upwards onto the second level. Their room was on the end.

"I need a bath," Xorna announced. "I'm going to ask the keeper for help. You two can wait."

She handed the key over to Dertujia and turned around on her heels.

Dertujia unlocked the dull metal lock and swung the heavy door open. There was a broad bed with a similar décor as the bottom floor. Quilts across chairs and the bed.

Seconds later, a mouse of a boy rushed in. "Need a fire?" he asked.

Dertujia nodded, and he got busy. Then he was on his way.

"Are you angry with me?" Leahnina asked as she threw her pack down on the floor, then slipping back on the bed, sighing with pleasure.

Dertujia couldn't think straight. Something about Leahnina had touched something in him. Her being on a bed sighing in pleasure, and Xorna taking a long bath, it gave rise to an imagination he hadn't been aware of.

He struggled to remember why she'd ask that. "Your powers," he said. "They aren't things to play with. Those people … what if you had given them a bad future, and they blamed you? Or what if they wouldn't take no for an answer. That baker? He's a power grabber. He wants it."

Leahnina gave him a hard glare. "Dertujia, I want to use my newly discovered powers. Is that so wrong?"

He shook his head. He had used his own. "I don't judge you. It's not my place."

Leahnina swung her legs, touching the blanket under her. "Maybe I want it to be your place. I don't want you to disapprove of me."

Dertujia wanted to answer, but suddenly there was a loud knock on the door.

"Rise and make ready for the king!" a voice proclaimed.

"Okay, yeah, that figures," Dertujia said. It was like he had eaten a bad dinner. "He works fast."

Leahnina gaped. "The baker?"

"You don't know kings, Leahnina. If they hear about something powerful, they try and take it. And anyone who brings it to them has their own power."

Leahnina snorted. "He only wants me to tell him where his lost son is. Enter!"

Dertujia had to chuckle. She was ordering royalty about.

Three people entered the small room. Two guards took the flank by the door, but King Veriton came in after. He was a wiry guy, thinning gray hair and watery eyes.

"I received word that you can tell the future." He addressed Leahnina and ignored Dertujia was there.

She nodded. "Your son has been kidnapped by the Rouge Woman."

King Veriton blanched. "Oh. She, uh, has. I don't understand why."

Leahnina giggled, walked forward and took his hand. Faking a kiss to it, she whispered under her breath, "Yes, you do."

Dertujia's flickering shadows amplified his hearing. His newly found powers were weak, thanks to nightfall, but strong by the fire's shadow.

King Veriton swallowed, glancing around the room. The guards hadn't heard. "Is she … Will the boy be hurt?"

Leahnina shook her head. "No, and you also know why."

King Veriton rubbed his head. "Will she return him?"

"Only if you announce her. I'd do it, King. She knows the truth. You are king. No one will be upset."

King Veriton gave a wry smile. "None?"

Leahnina chuckled. Her face did the flickering thing. Like the fire. "Oh, she doesn't care. Trust me."

King Veriton nodded. "Thank you, seer. I am amazed. If all you say is true, I'll be back."

He turned and left, the guards following. A brush with royalty ended with such ease.

"What was that all about?" Dertujia asked.

Leahnina rummaged in her pack on the floor, slid down to the mattress and started brushing her hair. "King Veriton has an illegitimate heir. When the babe was born, he snuck him into the birth bed of his wife. She hadn't known hers was stillborn. Both babes were born on the same night. But the Rouge Woman, let's just say she is not royal. She wanted her son back."

Dertujia blinked. "Are you telling me he was unfaithful to his wife?"

Leahnina let out a laugh. "I forget as much as hero you are, you're still a simple villager who could never imagine infidelity. Truth is, Dertujia, men wander more than you think. So do women."

Dertujia sat next to her, troubled. It seemed so sordid. So wrong. "I'd never do that. It's dishonorable."

Leahnina hit his shoulder with her brush by mistake, but she dropped it and reached for his armor. "It's heavy. Tonight, you should be free."

He nodded and allowed her slim fingers to undo his belts. His armor dropped to the floor, leaving him in his soft undershirt.

"Dertujia, are you saying you'd never stray? Ever? Even if there were a more beautiful woman. Or a more tempting prospect?"

He turned his head to gaze at her. The fire warmed his cheek. His shadows told him of Leahnina's desire. Her elevated heartbeat.

"Never. If I marry, I will stay married. I'd never leave …" He couldn't finish his statement, but she understood.

"I believe you."

"That's enough," Xorna said walking in, carrying her armor and undershirt in one arm and wearing a fuzzy green bathrobe. "I'm going to sleep. The water is being replaced for you."

"Oh, I am so ready!" Leahnina said and rushed out the door before Dertujia could protest.

"It looks as if I'll get the last bath tonight," he muttered.

Xorna took her own brush out and started going through her hair. "You're both hopeless. I swear, you won't be falling in love on this mission. It's too dangerous."

"I know," Dertujia muttered. But it was becoming too late for that. He had denied Leahnina's place in his heart for years, pretending she was an annoying fan. But it was her face he had looked for every time he returned home.

It was her approval he wanted.

Now that she could see the future, she became a great ally, but something to protect as well. He couldn't be free of her, and he wasn't sure he wanted to be.

"A king visited in your absence," he noted.

"Ah, gods deliver us," Xorna responded and fell backwards on the bed.

After Leahnina finished her bath, Dertujia took his, and the three slept together in relative comfort. Xorna had taken the place between Dertujia and Leahnina, giving both respite from their wandering minds.

As Dertujia fell asleep, he thought, *This journey is getting more complicated.*

***

The morning dawned with no trouble, and the trio snuck out of the inn without anyone catching them for future telling. On the way out of town, Dertujia paid for three mounts. Sad looking Broobits, a tall lizard like animal with a long tongue, thick backs and eyes that were hollow. They were good enough steeds, but Dertujia vowed to set them free as soon as he could and *not* return them to this misbegotten city that mistreated them.

The mercenaries met them as promised. Not a one was even close to trustworthy. Oh, sure they said the right things, smiled large smiles, but there was something in the eyes. Even if he had never met them before, Dertujia wouldn't turn his back on even one of them.

After everyone introduced themselves, they started moving. Quite a few of the mercenaries looked at Leahnina like she was a gem. Only about two actually wanted her future telling, though. It amazed Dertujia to find out he wasn't the only one who thought of her as beautiful.

They made an odd procession. Like an army, with the leader far ahead of the ones behind. Across the dour landscape, which had turned brown and desert like, the company struck out obvious with all the colors they wore.

Not one of the mercenaries supported any kingdom or cause, but they still clung to a false allegiance, a union with the mercenary guild. While Dertujia, Leahnina, and Xorna wore the traditional red traveling cloaks, especially as the air grew chilly, the mercenaries wore the hoods of the guild. Pure silver mixed with gold. They wanted people to know when they were coming.

Dolawa had courage to ride up next to them, acting as if he were part of the group. But the way he simpered towards Leahnina turned Dertujia's stomach.

"My lady Leahnina, you look so beautiful in the sun's ray." Dolawa said on more than one occasion. A strong feeling of jealousy roared up. It burned so fiercely he had to separate their group from the ones following. Otherwise Dertujia would have run Dolawa through. It made Dertujia comfortable that Dolawa couldn't have any more intimate conversations with Leahnina.

When the sun started its nightly trajectory on the first day, Xorna shared a look with Dertujia. He understood. He quickly just made camp for the night. Dertujia's shadows were weaker during the dark hours. There was no moon, and pitch black were the nights here.

During this blindness, Dertujia knew Dolawa would probably make a move towards Leahnina, and if she refused … Dolawa wouldn't acquiesce. Dertujia asked Leahnina to stay with him in his tent. Dolawa didn't seem angry, but Dertujia thought he heard, "She can't always be in your tent."

He slammed his bedroll down inside, and he heard Leahnina giggle.

"What?" he demanded. "This amuses you?"

"Your jealousy does," she admitted. "It's nice to know that after all these years you feel as deeply as I always have."

He stared at her. "Yes, but this goes beyond. That monster in human's skin *wants* you."

"I am not as helpless as you think, Dertujia." She unrolled her bedding. "My powers grow every day. I don't just tell the future … But that ability does tell me one day I'll be mighty. One day I will control time itself."

Dertujia smiled. "Well, until then …"

She snuggled up to him, putting her tiny chin on his shoulder. "You worry too much. You don't have to. Not about me. I watch out for my own wellbeing. Trust me, if I saw a future where Dolawa accomplished anything, I'd do … certain things to prevent it. I am no longer a wilting flower. I am a thunderstorm without end. Spinning and roaring. I am not who started this journey."

Dertujia caressed her chin and fell into her eyes. "Leahnina, I hope that isn't true. I love you now. But I still want that woman who was my friend. Don't change."

Her head slipped down to keep her view away. "But I will change. Both of us will. That's what happens when you face evil. And Eropus *is* evil."

Dertujia frowned. "You've seen this god then?"

Leahnina nodded.

"Then what shall we expect?"

"He can rip the world apart. I fear him … more than anyone else. His power takes away from mine. I see no future after we encounter him. Bits and pieces. But there's no firm outcome. Nothing."

Dertujia lifted her chin and kissed her to offer some comfort. She wrapped her arms around him, and they spent the night just holding each other in their arms.

Chapter Six

The next morning, they traveled into a new land. It had no trees. No brush. No water. Gray and white sand blew across their path. Dunes went on for as far as Dertujia could see. Nothing else could be.

"The desert of death," Dolawa said coming up behind Leahnina and Dertujia, making a few kissing noises at Leahnina. "Nice place. If we're going into that, I'd suggest you use your shadows to save us all. Or would you rather go around?"

Leahnina ignored him and looked only at Dertujia and Xorna. "There is a chance of survival if we go around. Anyone who enters this place dies. It's supposed to be endless."

Dertujia shook his head. How could the gods make something as dangerous as this? "We go around," he decided. They turned from the vast sand in front of them and started skirting the perimeter.

Finally, the heat of the desert disappeared, and green hills took its place. Big mounds, some with grass, some with bright white flowers. Many legends circulated about these hills. One being that lovers came here and were bonded forever.

It was a pretty place, a nice one for a picnic. But something unnerved Dertujia. It was Leahnina. She didn't seem as relaxed as such a tranquil setting would suggest.

She frowned and looked back and forth, seeing something far in the distance.

It turned out it was closer than he thought. Suddenly, they were surrounded on both sides by an army coming up over the hills. A thousand men in one kind of armor marched forward.

They sure looked official.

"You!" a man yelled. He wore a grayish green armor and a matching helmet with a long yellow plume, a soldier in name only because he'd never wear that stupid thing into battle. More than likely he'd let everyone fight, while he ran away when things went badly.

Dertujia drew himself up to full stature. He never liked soldiers with too much power. "Me?" he asked.

"Yes, you. Are you the one in charge?"

The mercenaries were fanning out, drawing daggers, swords, or whips. They were ready for a fight. He wondered how many of them had been inactive in the recent years.

"I am Captain Bartoe. King Veriton has sent me and his men to bring the soothsayer. The fortuneteller. The woman who has knowledge of the future."

Dertujia cast a look at Leahnina who only smiled. Ah. This was what she had been foreseeing. Soon the mercenaries would meet their end. Good. Even now Dolawa looked like he was waiting for a chance to run off with Leahnina. Guys like that normally got what they wanted. Not this time.

"She will not be harmed," Captain Bartoe assured. "She will be a wonderful addition to the king's forces. A person who will tell him how his kingdom will fare. As long as she tells him right, she will live a happy and wonderful life."

"A bird in a gilded cage," Dertujia muttered. He had very little patience with kings. "You can ask her yourself," Dertujia said louder. "Leahnina, do you want to go with them?"

She laughed out loud. "I am already on a mission, thank you for asking. But even if not, I would never work for a king who would imprison me. Tell your master, dog, that I am a free agent. And no one will have me."

She gave Dertujia a hidden look at the end. She might as well have added, "Except you, Dertujia."

He shook his head with a smile. But he got his shadows ready.

"A pity. But my orders remain the same," Bartoe said. "You are to come with us, no need for your permission. Take her."

With a mighty roar, the army attacked. They sped down the hills, uprooting flowers and grass. Their shadows were united, a massive force. Dertujia tried to drag them down, but they were too heavy. He grunted as he took down a few men, keeping Leahnina behind him. Whatever magical powers she'd have some day, for now all she could do was tell how this was going to turn out.

But that small detail gave Dertujia faith. Because if not, he would have been terrified. His love, his one true love who he couldn't lose, was starting to look to be a valuable commodity. Her dignity and beauty were desired by men. Her powers were desired by kings. And combined, she was the most precious prize the world had. Now, to him, he already knew that. It was the rest of the world that frightened him.

He could lose her. Never before had Dertujia had anything to lose but his life. Well, of course, he feared losing Xorna. But losing a partner who knew what she was doing, who accepted that death was one of the consequences of their lives, was one thing. But to lose someone who hadn't really known that consequence, who in a lot of ways was just an innocent child? Though she wore the body of an adult, the pain in her life had created something that had stalled her growth.

He would have been frozen in fear if the outcome wasn't for sure.

All around the battlefield, the mercenaries and the army fought.

"Now, Dertujia, let us go," Leahnina whispered in his ear. "They will battle each other. We will enter the desert."

Dertujia turned towards her, shock on his face. He knew the mercenaries would have to die, but to abandon a fight?

"It's the only way," she murmured.

Dertujia trusted her. He had to. He gave a retreat whistle, one that only Xorna would recognize.

She turned to him with a gaping mouth and elbowed the soldier coming up from behind. But she knew not to mess with the retreat whistle. It meant life or death.

Cloaking them with the shadows of the hills, Dertujia led them away, listening to the screams of war.

It was a slaughter. The mercenaries all died. Dolawa did when he looked for his chance to grab Leahnina and run off, getting a knife in the back. The rest ended more honorably, but they took out a good share of the army that was after Leahnina.

At the end, Captain Bartoe called his men together and desperately looked for any sign of his prize.

"Not here," Bartoe said. He wouldn't return to his king emptyhanded.

"Shall we return? We've lost a third of our men," an underling said. Not important enough to remember his name.

"No. We go on."

"But they've headed …" His underling shook his finger in the direction of the vast desert. Only known as a place that someone went in but never came out. "There. We will all be killed if we go through, Captain. And if we don't, we'll never catch up."

"Damn!" Captain Bartoe cursed.

A slow hiss hit the wind. At first Captain Bartoe didn't think anything of it until a voice whispered in his ear. "Problems, mortal?"

He jumped and fell, scurrying away from the evil voice.

The man … god in front of him was as real as the hills around. As real as His Majesty's anger, as painful as the punishment that would reach Bartoe if he returned to his king without the woman. "Who are you?" he asked.

"You know," he answered. There was a sly grin on his face as he looked around the army. Most were looking anywhere but back at him. A few were even on their knees, their foreheads pressed hard into the ground.

"You want a way around the desert? You want your prize?"

Bartoe nodded. He feared this god, sure, but he feared the king more. "Of course."

"Well, let's just say I know certain tricks." He walked up the hill, his pale robes fluttering in the breeze. He was a perfect specimen of power. Even as thin as he was. His hair roared around his head.

But he was helping Bartoe. That was good enough for him.

"Desert, move." The god's hollow voice sounded like wind in a tunnel. "Move and never settle. Come back only when Bartoe is in place."

He turned as if to leave, even as a roaring sound came. Wind mixed with rock. Dust and mineral settling together.

"Why?" Bartoe barked out.

Eropus turned one slit eye towards him. "Because. These mortals think I won't put up a fight. I'd like them to know I will. Tell them if you see them that Eropus wishes Dertujia the best. And that he has made this a personal fight when he didn't have to. He could have left the goddess alone. But, instead, he helped her. That will be his most regretted mistake. Tell him. If he survives the desert."

Then Eropus was gone. Bartoe returned to his confidence. "Get up, you whining mongrels. We need to get to the other side. We will find a weakened hero with no army."

One of his men looked down at the ground.

"What?" Bartoe demanded.

"That was Dertujia and Xorna. They saved my life a long time ago in Windonea. I don't think …"

"Your king demands the fortuneteller. You will go past heroes and debts."

"No." He turned and walked off. He didn't even feel when the sword slit his neck. He fell, and everyone looked at Bartoe.

"No deserters. Do you understand?"

The army nodded. They left the body-littered ground, some who died in battle, and the last who died because of a battle of conscience.

***

The desert winds howled. The sands skittered, roaring around their faces. Dertujia kept a shadow barrier up around them, so the sand spilled harmlessly around, but it wasn't easy. The shadows from far away weren't coming, not in this death, but even with the cloud around them, there were plenty of shadows to use.

Problem was, they were as tempestuous as their casters. Wild and angry.

"This desert is known to be endless," Xorna said with a glare at the sand.

"Lies," Leahnina argued. "People only say that because they were beaten by it. But I see us on the other side."

"And why didn't you share that fact with the mercenaries?" Xorna asked. "You led us to believe we'd all die. You only set up the path with their own doom." The sand bit at the shadows. Dertujia narrowed his eyes and pushed back. He didn't agree with Xorna. Problem was he didn't disagree with her either. Leahnina seemed to have set a needless death in motion.

Leahnina stopped and turned back. The brown wall of wind behind her made for an impressive backdrop to her wild, two-toned hair. "Xorna, please don't question me ever again."

"Oh, ferocious," Xorna joked. But Leahnina looked it.

"If we had continued in here, the army would have still come after me. But they would have had a lot of the advantage. The shadows of the sand aren't listening as well to Dertujia as they should."

Dertujia blanched and cringed under Xorna's look. "Okay, she's got a point there."

"I would have died!" Leahnina said with a snarl. "I have seen my own death countless times since that dragon tower. It's like I'm … marked for death. I have satisfied luck's bloodlust for the time being. But what would you do? Let murderers live when you yourself died?"

Xorna sighed. "I hate this. I had morals. You, both of you, are wearing them down. I like the fact that Dolawa died. That bastard had no respect for either of us. But who am I to turn into a judge?"

"You are the better person," Dertujia said, his own conviction rising up. What he had always believed in his life since he picked up the sword of the hero. "Heroics give us fame, sure. Trouble and struggle. But it also gives us a responsibility. We do have to choose who lives and who dies. Especially now that we have the knowledge of the future, we can make better choices."

Leahnina reached out for him, squeezing his hand. He drew her close and let the shadows tighten as he kissed her.

Xorna groaned. "Okay, lovebirds. I don't need this. I feel like an extra sword when one has two. So, please knock it off."

Dertujia deepened the shadows so Xorna couldn't see them.

"Oh, yes, that's much better," Xorna sneered. She hit him on the shoulder, and he let the blackness dissolve back to a shield.

"Sorry, old friend, but I just found her after all."

"You're sickening," Xorna said, but her lips turned up. "Can we focus? Leahnina, when will we be free of this abominable desert?"

"I'm not sure," she admitted. "My powers aren't perfect. Until after at least …" Leahnina's face crinkled as Dertujia watched her. He was becoming quite accustomed to that look.

"And what is on the other side?" he asked.

Xorna held her hand up as she swayed around a dune that seemed to rise up in front of them. "No, don't ask her. Let me try. Death. That's what she sees."

Leahnina laughed. "Yes, Xorna. You're right. My visions see … that mainly. We're on a horrible journey."

Dertujia didn't disagree. How could he? "How about we try and make camp? I do not like sand. Every step seems to take three."

They agreed on that and settled down. Dertujia kept the sand at bay as they tried to eat. Night fell and brought cold. All three bundled up together, to keep warm. Icy cold knives of wind dug into their arms, and Dertujia's shadows whispered away to nothing.

The tents wouldn't stay up in the wind. There was no shelter. Nothing to do but miserably cower together and wait until morning. Dertujia was amazed. The gods he had met were so powerful they put even his shadows to shame. But this desert with its wind and death was more powerful than either. It took down time itself.

The next morning dawned, and they had to dig themselves out of a small dune made during the night. It was hotter than the previous day. The water was running out, and they were still no closer to the end of the desert.

The trio spoke little, to save their rasping voices, and the journey continued.

And continued. And continued.

Days passed. The water trickled to nothing, and Dertujia stared at his friends. This was the end. Leahnina had been wrong. This desert continued forever!

"It has an end!" Leahnina rasped. "I don't understand."

Dertujia put a calming hand on her knee. "Let us not fight against the end. Rest in my arms. We'll take on the new journey together."

They had fallen to their knees without noticing.

Xorna laughed, but it was loud and angry,

"What, my old friend? At least we meet our end together."

"I was just thinking." She tiredly pulled her silver braids down into a flying swirl. "A few years ago, we were up against the wall. The gigantic red *thing* was going to eat us. Eight arms. Ten feet tall. It had already sucked in a whole village."

Dertujia held Leahnina's head to his shoulder as she sobbed dry tears. There wasn't much water left. "And?"

"You said, 'I choose when I die, not you.' And you charged that Octogob. Right down the center. You startled the creature so much he missed that you were rolling under him, slicing his … um, I'll be a lady and say parts. The scream he made! But you didn't stop. You sliced that thing to ribbons."

"Point?" Dertujia asked. He wasn't feeling so well.

"You chose when you'd die then. Now you're giving up because of a little bit of dirt and wind. Some hero."

Dertujia gaped at her, but Xorna raised her eyebrows in challenge.

She was right! Dertujia didn't give up. Never had. But this journey … He had assumed it was a death knell from the beginning. He was just giving into it now.

But no. Wasn't he the hero of Windonea? The tamer of the Reapers? The champion of a goddess and the winner of the king's jewels? He had fought giants and diseases with equal ferocity.

No, he wouldn't just give up. Not when he could fight.

He racked his brain, trying to figure out a solution. Getting out of the desert was useless. He didn't know when that'd happen. Calling forth shadows was also useless. He only had the dead land's power. He couldn't go up. The sky was endless.

But down? Deep down. Underneath the sand. Underneath the endless heat. Where water would exist.

He stood up and crunched his fist. He summoned forth the wind's shadow and spun it into a tornado. It dug down, further, further.

"What is that?" Leahnina demanded in a horrified voice.

Dertujia almost laughed. How could she be so scared of his powers when they were going to save them?

"It's fire," Xorna answered. "Coming from the sky. Aiming at us."

Dertujia got the point. His awesome powers weren't scaring Leahnina. It was something else. Another thing. He kept digging, faster and faster.

Then … there was another shadow coming in. Stone. Cold. Not sand. He opened his eyes. Solid stone. That was just great! He was tunneling into solid stone. Yeah, that'd save them!

It looked to be the top of a building, all square and poking its head out of the sand. He had managed only to unearth that much.

"Words, Dertujia. Look down." Xorna was insistent. Dertujia didn't listen. He looked *up* not down. It was in the sky that fire lived. Spinning around, trying to find them.

"I know what they say. They are … my words," Leahnina said confused.

Xorna would have snorted. But there was danger all around. No time for that!

"What do they say?"

"Speak for me. Ask for me. The passage is a way. A tunnel that will guide you."

"Whose name?" Dertujia demanded, too terrified as the heat increased ever more.

"Padonum. The goddess."

Dertujia had no clue what any of this meant. Why it was in Leahnina's words, whatever that meant? Or what any of this meant. All he knew was that one goddess trusted him. This goddess would save them. "Padonum," Dertujia yelled. "Save us!"

The fire hit harmlessly against the stone. The trio was gone.

Chapter Seven

Dertujia felt as vulnerable as a baby. How fast he had begun to rely on his shadows. But this place was dark. No light. No shadows.

"Xorna?" he called out, sounding young. He had always relied on her to save him. "Leahnina?" Someone else he relied on.

"Here," Xorna responded.

"Me, too," Leahnina added.

"Calm down, Dertujia." Xorna sounded like she was smiling. She liked it when he looked to her.

Leahnina rushed to his defense. "He is *not* excited."

Dertujia couldn't help but smile himself. Leahnina didn't know him that well. She still worshipped him. He decided he didn't want to lose that just yet. "Yes, Xorna. I am fine. Do you have something to light this place with?"

"Way ahead of you. I've explored this place with my fingers. There are torches on the walls. I can light them, and I'm next to one now."

The next minute the room was filled with light.

Xorna had a flint and had gotten a spark. "I only lit one," she said plaintively. "All this magic …"

"Padonum has aided us," Dertujia said. "But who is she?"

"Maybe the owner of those items," Leahnina said and rushed across the room. She was way too excited about something that Dertujia hadn't even spotted yet. He took a second to reacquaint himself with the shadows from the flickering torches. Warm and friendly, after so long without living.

A huge room was around them with only one doorway out. He could see it met a long and winding tunnel that presumably would get them out of here. The whole place had the same tiles, silver with etchings of golden letters the same. And …

"Water!" he yelped. He rushed across to a pool and gestured the others over to it. How could Leahnina have missed this to go to some items that were on a dais far across the way?

Xorna ran to his side, and Leahnina followed, reluctantly. Then all drank their fill.

"Let us fill our waterbags," Dertujia suggested.

Leahnina shook her head fast. "No. Don't. This place … I have a feeling. It's so strong."

"Your future telling?"

"And the past." Leahnina didn't explain that. "Look, you take what you need. You don't take more. If you do …" Her eyes shifted around. "Bad things happen. Just don't take more."

Dertujia trusted her. Besides, freedom from the desert couldn't be long now. Their little group's thirst was quenched, and the tunnel would get them out of here so they could get more water at a nearby town. "It's strange," he said now that he could think. "Those fireballs coming just as we found this."

"Someone is watching this journey," Leahnina said. "Someone is against us."

"Hm, give you two guesses," Xorna joked. "I think we're seeing the first signs of our adversary. Eropus is scared of us."

Dertujia wasn't so sure. More likely he was playing with them. "And the items," he finally asked walking over to the little golden dais. Shapes of waterfalls fell down in golden splendor, and the only cloth in the room, ageless, spread out to reach them.

The items that had so infatuated Leahnina were three. A small box engraved with pictures of gods, a glowing green pendant, and a large mirror.

They were normal enough, no embellishments or anything amazing but Leahnina looked at them with love.

"We take them," she decided.

Dertujia was more than confused. Leahnina kept surprising him. She had her futures. Her attitude. Now she wanted these seemingly useless things.

When she caught his look, she immediately defended herself. “They are full of magic; don’t you feel them?”

Dertujia was loath to admit he didn’t. No matter his shadow control, that didn’t tell him what Leahnina’s visions seemed to. He glanced at Xorna who threw up her own hands as she turned her nose up at the items. Trinkets were never her forte.

“What do they do?”

“This is Padonum’s box. The very blood of our planet runs through it.”

“So glad you cleared that up,” Xorna said. “Helpful, how?”

Leahnina just shook her head. “You could control …” Then as if she lost whatever vision that gave her the knowledge, she trailed off and suddenly brought up the mirror. “Padonum’s mirror.”

Now, this did seem to keep Dertujia’s attention. It was so clear, even as he gazed at his dirty reflection, he could almost see everything—the world from a top down view. “I sense it,” he said quietly.

Xorna growled and started polishing her sword, sitting down with a great big sigh. It still irked her that the two of them had so much power while she had none. “You both sense magic, hurrah.”

Dertujia tried not to laugh. “What about the pendant?”

“It controls the sky.”

Dertujia narrowed his eyes. “Wait, earth and sky? And the mirror is shadow, isn’t it?”

Leahnina grinned. “Yes, it is.”

“Three elements of our world. These items connect with them.”

Leahnina nodded. “Now you’re getting it!”

“Who was Padonum?” Dertujia asked. He was already unnerved to know one goddess, but now he owed his life to another. Someone he hadn’t met. And now Leahnina held her items.

“Padonum was a goddess who—”

Xorna jumped up. “No. Stop. We have no clue how far this tunnel goes. We don’t have time for a history lesson. We haven’t gotten very far, and we’re on a mission, remember?”

Dertujia nodded. But he didn’t like it. Leahnina wanted these items, but could they really take them? There was no time to wonder.

Xorna was right. That desert had nearly killed them. As it would any future traveler …

“Just one moment,” Dertujia said, thinking about any others who could be trapped in the desert. If they found this place and took more than their share of water, then the bad things Leahnina saw would come to them.

He started etching out a warning in the wall, telling future travelers to be wary of taking too much water.

“Why did you use the language of the goddess?” Xorna asked curiously, tracing the carved letters in the wall.

“If anyone is here, they know her language. We can’t be sure they’ll know ours. I want to make sure they know not to touch what they should not."

Xorna shrugged. They gathered up their small supplies, took one more lingering drink from the spring, and then they left the small cavern. Leahnina had the items.

This had turned out better than he could have hoped, really. As he took in his friends in the low light, cast by torches that flickered but didn't go out, he saw black patches, singed by the fire that would have burned them.

"I don't understand any of this," he murmured. "You and this goddess. The fire that burned. The endless desert that shouldn't have been. In one breath, I seemed to have fallen into a whirlpool of magic and danger."

"They're gods," Leahnina filled him in. "They have powers above and beyond any of us. What I wanted to say was that the goddess lived here. When the mortal who made a vendetta against the gods came, she hid in her desert. For that, Eropus brought down fire to kill anyone who'd use the desert as a shield. She left water for those loyal to her, an escape."

He brushed against the darker part of the walls. It was dry, no slime, no sharp edges. It seemed the trio was the only thing alive down here.

"But how do you know? You could tell the future. Now you can tell the past?"

Leahnina touched his arm. "I don't know either. I just felt her out. I saw things. These items will help us."

Dertujia grinned, but he wished it wasn't so dark around, that they weren't travelling further and further away from water to an unknown destination in hopes that it'd lead out of this death.

"What is down here?" Xorna asked.

The lights cast shadows. Dertujia couldn't feel anything. "Nothing. Just us."

"But I heard …"

Dertujia heard it too. A wind against leather sound. A light scraping as if someone was coming towards them.

"What is it?" he asked Leahnina.

She shook her head. "I don't know."

She didn't know.

They froze as the sound came closer. It echoed through the tunnel. Still no warnings. Not from Leahnina's future telling, not from his shadows. Xorna's keen ears knew something was coming.

"The wind moving around it, the thing's fast. The sound. I've heard it. Oh, bats."

Dertujia relaxed. "Are you telling me you're worried about a bat?"

Xorna's shoulders tensed, making her armor move. "That's no bat. It just has leather wings."

Now Dertujia could hear it. A whooshing sound, a bird? The torches went out.

Darkness spilled around them. His shadows were gone.

The trio took their right stances. Xorna and Dertujia were used to being back-to-back when an unknown enemy showed. Leahnina followed suit. They pressed against each other, not seeing anything.

"Who has dared enter the Endless Tunnel? Who has a death wish? Who has trespassed in my lady's sacred temple?"

Dertujia held his sword in his hand, but he couldn't see anything. "It is I, Dertujia. My companions are Leahnina and Xorna. Maybe you've heard of us. We're on a mission to defeat Eropus, your lady's enemy."

The strange sound came to a stop. There were the sounds of Xorna's bat wings, but they were large. The torches flickered back on.

Dertujia came face to face …

No, not a face. There was an eye.

"You're an eye," he said calmly, feeling an eruption of terror coming from his heart. But one thing he learned was never to show fear.

The thing was monstrous. Huge. Almost as big as the tunnel. Its wings were far from bat like, spread wide above them. Thick and ribbed with curling ribbons dripping from them. The eye itself had hair lashes that swept down with no lid.

The pupil was a long thin oval, seaweed green but surrounded by a bloated white circle. It couldn't blink. The only thing it did was sweep its lashes over its pupil.

"How observant. I am more than an eye. I am the justice for trespassers. I kill without conscience. You aren't supposed to be here."

Dertujia nodded. He could feel the joined terror they held. An eye wasn't supposed to be speaking to them. It was drilling thoughts directly into their brains.

"Did you hear me? The enemy of your lady will meet his end by my blade."

The eye snorted with no nose. Laughed with no mouth. "I think not. The three of you are scared children, quivering in my presence."

Ah, it was right. But, strange thing, Dertujia was only scared as long as nobody mentioned it. But when the enemy spoke it, the fear disappeared.

He held his sword out. "Leave us be, or we'll see if an eye has blood."

A rumbling sound met his words. Impossibly, the tunnel grew even smaller. The torches went out, and darkness took over.

"Can you feel smaller, humans?" the eye asked. "I control the very land around you. Tremble as you die."

That was enough. Listening for the sounds, the flapping wings … He skirted forward, his feet making small movements as he felt the earth move underneath.

No. This eye had no idea who it was dealing with.

The noise …

The flapping wings, obscured by the shaking earth.

"You want to play?" Dertujia asked. He whipped his sword out through the darkness. He crowed inside as a swishing sound filled his ears. The earth stopped. The tunnel widened.

He swiped again. Blood dripped. A thick sound of falling. The torches spilled light onto the area. His shadows came back, but Dertujia held his sword on the eye, which was on the ground. Its wings flopping on the floor next to it. Unattached.

"No wings, no flight, bloated wonder," Dertujia said. "Now we will leave, and you will tell us how much longer to an exit or I will run my blade through your ugly body."

The eye bounced to movement, jumped into the sky, and fell down, bouncing again.

"You removed the wings," it said. It sounded … happy?

"Yes, I did."

The eye bounced again. Dertujia thought flying was bad, but it was way worse to have this thing making the disgusting squishing noises as it bounced around, sometimes hitting the wings and making for another grotesque sound.

"I was cursed. The wings are my second affliction. Thank you. To answer your question, you will be out in the north part of Fipil, the Gaiarigonian region."

Dertujia let his sword rest. He took the cloth Xorna offered to clean the gunk the eye left behind on his sword. This was going excellently. The Gaiarigonian lands were a lot further towards Eropus areas. They had cut off a lot of miles with this shortcut. A fortuitous blessing.

"This curse," Leahnina asked. "What is it?"

"You are the seer," the eye answered.

Leahnina bit her lip. She narrowed her eyes. “May I touch you?”

It bounced again, but Leahnina took it as an affirmative response.

She reached out and touched … Dertujia looked away. He had put up with a lot of sights before, but Leahnina’s slender hand touching the bare white of a giant eye and squishing the slime between her fingers wasn’t something he needed to see.

“Oh!” she emitted. “You tried to save your lady. He was a knight.” This she put towards Dertujia. Xorna and he shared a look of understanding. Neither cared.

Leahnina didn’t seem to notice. “Eropus cursed him. He already lost his body from being crushed in the earth, so that’s why he can control the earth now.”

Dertujia loved the woman in front of him, which is why he bit his tongue.

“You did the second part. He needed his wings cut off by a fearless person. Pretty impossible, until you, Dertujia. The last thing he needs is for someone to give up the water they desperately need. If only we had filled our waterbags, we could have freed him completely.”

She, unbelievably, stared at the thing with compassion and sympathy.

“We need to go.” Dertujia turned on his foot, forcing Leahnina to follow. He left the disgusting thing bouncing and squishing over its cursed wings.

“It was sad,” Leahnina said, shifting her bag with the items inside.

“Yes, too bad his goddess couldn’t help him,” Dertujia said.

“She died,” Leahnina said. “Eropus drained her energy. Took it away from her so he could live. It must have been before he turned to the earth. Padonum was a victim.”

Dertujia felt the sides of the tunnel. They were getting smaller. The three started going single file. Good thing, it ended the conversation. Dertujia was starting to despise Eropus. He left victims behind. Dertujia couldn’t feel sorry for an eye that would have killed them all, but this goddess. She had given words to save them. Had provided water to quench their thirsts.

If it hadn’t been for the mysterious goddess, they wouldn’t be alive. And Eropus had drained her.

Dertujia had seen the man, but in his mind—unfair—he had thought maybe there had been two sides to the story, that maybe Neesh had been overexaggerating his evil.

But now he knew.

“What are you thinking?” Leahnina shot back to him.

Dertujia answered. “How much Eropus has just bought my disfavor. I look forward to repaying him for this lovely stay in the tunnel.”

He could hear Xorna chuckling. She always teased him when he, according to her, was overdramatic. But this time he meant it.

Eropus had earned Dertujia's personal anger today.

The tunnel wound deep under the earth. No sky. No light. It grew narrower and narrower. None of them were claustrophobic, thank the gods, but even Xorna was getting impatient for this journey to be over.

"Only a little longer," Leahnina promised. She was at the front and guiding them even as they had to crouch and then crawl.

"This crawling is rather aggravating."

"Keep your mind on something else," Xorna replied from behind him.

Dertujia nodded but all he could think about was Leahnina crawling ahead of him. *That* didn't help anything! "Hey, why not tell us about Padonum," Dertujia suggested.

"Dertujia more than me," Xorna said. She was trying to keep it light. This journey was getting to all of them, though.

"Padonum was the goddess of prophecy."

Dertujia put one hand in front of the other, thinking about that. How odd that the woman he loved had that ability as well. And she knew about Padonum, like they had a connection somehow.

Being deep in the darkness, no sight, no light, Dertujia felt increasingly paranoid. No shadows to talk to. No way of knowing when this horrible journey would end.

Leahnina had shut up about who Padonum was. In fact, she didn't speak at all. At this point, Dertujia was grateful for Xorna. She kept on muttering and making quick ejaculations. Lots of inventive swears.

He knew now six different languages that insulted someone's mother.

It helped him grin.

If it weren't for her, he'd be driving himself crazy. Suddenly … he knew. They were almost free.

He felt the shadows from the moon, whispering to him.

"We're there!" Leahnina said, and he reached forward and squeezed her foot. He could feel her warmth as she nudged him back. Finally, they exited the long endless tunnel.

They were deposited out of a hill … and right into a whole lot of swords, and one shadow underneath the moon lit sky.

"Hold it right there. We want the future teller. Refuse, you die, and she doesn't reach the king in one piece."

Dertujia stood up slowly, watching the blade at his neck. "This is not possible."

The grin of Captain Bartoe made bile move in Dertujia's stomach. The beast inside him stirred. It had started when he saw his first village that had been taken over by a war runner. The situations the peasants had found themselves in. All working for one. Anything that one wanted given without thought. No matter how much suffering it caused.

Dertujia had to make a choice long ago. To keep that beast down. If he let it go, Dertujia might become just as bad as the cruel people he fought.

It was easier fighting monsters than humans. Like with the centaur, he knew what to expect. But humans surprised him every time.

And, as he looked around at the army that wanted the love of his life, he felt the beast stir. He wanted to kill every single person there.

"We will kill you, make no mistake about that," Captain Bartoe said. "Eropus will see to it. He wants you to know that he helped us get here. He knew where you'd emerge."

Dertujia could barely see. Rage kept his eyes in almost slits. Xorna tugged on his elbow twice. Their old signal.

Of course.

"Okay, fine. take her. I grew bored of her anyway," Dertujia said. "But you will pay me for her."

He could hear Leahnina's gasp of indignation. Far from important now.

"Okay, now you're seeing reason. Though I don't have to, I will give you a bag of gold for the woman."

As Captain Bartoe turned to his bag, Xorna leapt into action. With a quick flip, she landed behind him on the horse and held a dagger to his throat.

"Hi," she cooed. "Now, either you call off your army, or I slit your ugly throat."

He visibly quailed under her blade. He swallowed and said, "But I heard you valued life."

"Not when the life wants to steal my friend and kill my partner. Sorry. Tell me your choice." She pressed the dagger tighter against his throat.

Captain Bartoe froze. He saw his options.

Never had Dertujia been more proud of Xorna. She was holding him back. The shadows of the soldiers were separating. He could have used his powers. The moon was bright. Their shadows military. Easy.

But Captain Bartoe valued his life. "Retreat," he said slowly.

His warriors gaped and gasped, but they listened to orders. Soon every soldier was gone, and only Bartoe was left behind.

"The king will not give up," he added. "And we will have more help from Eropus."

Dertujia clenched his hands into fists. Xorna glanced at them and then nodded decisively. "You come again, and we will kill you. There will be no negotiation. Make no mistake."

Then she jumped to the ground and slapped the horse on its rear, which sent it galloping into the night.

"You didn't see them?" Dertujia asked Leahnina.

She shook her head. "No. I didn't. Eropus blocked me."

Dertujia squared his shoulders, but a small fear crept up his spine. Eropus could block the future seeing …

The three decided to keep traveling. As tired as they were, they were on a mission. That desert had set them back, but at least they were on the other side. But as far as rest went, they needed four walls around them. A door that could be locked.

Maybe then they'd feel at peace.

But somehow Dertujia doubted it. At every turn, evil seemed to be growing. Using the name of Eropus.

Travelling signs started showing on the long and dusty road. They were the only life—or mark of—as they walked. The occasional tumbleweed struggled by, blown by little breeze. The desert was behind them, but it was still near, reminding of its presence.

Never before had Dertujia wanted a journey to end as much as this one. He had let his guard down. He expected Leahnina to know everything, to spot danger and warn him accordingly. Just like his shadows, though, hers had limits. And one was named Eropus.

Chapter Eight

"You okay?" Xorna asked. He had to laugh at his friend's face. She was filthy. They all needed a bath. After the sand from the desert and the tunnel's dark and dirty paths, a good night's sleep wasn't all they needed or wanted. Dertujia didn't answer. He couldn't. He didn't really know if he was okay or going to be.

"They say that Firebranch is close by," Xorna said.

Leahnina frowned. "I don't like the name of that village. I can't tell why."

Dertujia couldn't figure that out. But whether her dislike was just a hatred of a colorful moniker or if it was a premonition, it didn't matter. They were tired. And Firebranch was the only village on the horizon.

"Is it possible to get two rooms?" Leahnina asked, making Dertujia's heart skip a beat. But he couldn't assume.

"For you alone?"

Leahnina shook her head. "For us together, and Xorna alone. This place isn't dangerous. The army is gone for the time being. Eropus won't try anything."

Xorna stomped one step extra hard. "Can you be sure of that?" The path widened and started heading down into a great valley. To Dertujia's relief he saw trees. A great chasm was to the east of the village. The desert sands were disappearing. Far in the distance, a mountain range cut the sky like teeth, but it was too far off for any travel.

"You were lost when we were attacked by Eropus' magic." Xorna wouldn't let this go.

"I don't care! I can't see everything anyway!" Leahnina poured her words out like rain dropped from the sky—yes, it was raining. The blessed drops caressed their faces. "I need … You know, Xorna. You know what I need."

Xorna rolled her eyes. "This is so not the time or place for …"

"I almost got us killed." Leahnina stopped walking. "I should have seen the army or the will of the general at the very least. And I have wanted Dertujia for so long. The way this journey will go, we'll all die without any …"

Dertujia was absolutely clueless on what the two were talking about.

But Xorna was nothing if not bold. "So, a night in a bed rolling around with Dertujia will cure your ills? Trust me. It's nice. But you'll still feel like a failure in the morning."

Dertujia's jaw dropped, and suddenly he felt warm. Now he got it. Leahnina wanted to consummate their relationship in a bed, throw all her fears and worries away. Come to think of it, Dertujia needed that too.

Then he turned a heavy scowl on his friend. "And what do you speak of? You talk like you've had experience. I haven't."

Xorna giggled and shared a look with Leahnina. "You were always noble, Dertujia, but did you really think I spent all those nights in inns by myself in my room? There were always many who were grateful to me."

Now Dertujia was gaping. "And you just gave in?" The rain was increasing. All the times, he thought his friend was as chaste as he had been. He felt like a fool. "But what about consequences?"

Xorna cuffed his shoulder and finished up with a push. "Let's just get to Firebranch. One of these days, let me tell you a few things about how I can prevent consequences."

Dertujia didn't know what to feel. The looks Leahnina were giving him made his legs warm. So far, he had wanted to do many things with her, especially as her warm body moved next to him at night, but he had kept true to what he'd been taught. Xorna, however, didn't seem to think it was that big of deal.

It was clear, though, she was going to leave them alone. If only Eropus wouldn't send anything tonight, he could finally get a chance to stay a real night with Leahnina. To see her without her garb. To undress her and feel her fully.

The idea was intriguing to say the least.

Xorna wouldn't judge him either. With an extra bounce to his step, somehow it didn't matter anymore that Eropus was out there, or that their journey would end with pain and suffering.

He was getting a real night with Leahnina. Nothing else mattered.

The forest that brushed around continued until it built up all alongside the road. The sun started to set, casting its glow across the brilliant forest. It looked like it was being set on fire, all golden and orange. What he could see of the village was small with one mighty castle about a stone's throw away from the it.

Monarchy. Well, Dertujia had dealt with them before, though he hadn't seen such a small village with a ruling family. No matter. The village was big enough to warrant signs, which meant an inn was sure to be available.

He grinned at Leahnina and took her hand. She took his comfort, but she was shaking. She had relied too much on her visions. But still she was amazing.

"You told a story about the eye better than any bard," he assured. "You have items that … Will they help us?"

She shrugged, her face gray. "Maybe. Who knows? I can't be sure. I'm useless. Your shadows are the real power here. I just watch the future. Your shadows are omnipotent."

He smiled. He liked that she thought so, but he'd better tell her about his lack of control over shadows and how weak it made him—if there was any time for talking at all tonight.

Once again, he squeezed her hand. Eager for the village to finally be around them. Firebranch was certainly a beautiful city. The buildings had the Jascot architecture Dertujia had seen a few times. Jascot was a man in love with swirling metals and tall roofs to put that metal on. Elegantly designed and curling to the ground from the tower type houses made for a lasting impression on his eyes.

The sun glinted against the metal designs.

"It's pleasant," Dertujia said as they walked under a burnished metal sign with the Firebranian letters spelling out its name. Luckily, the village also had the language from Gaiarigona, so Dertujia was familiar with it.

"It's amazing," Xorna crowed. "It'd be like living in a work of art, a painting."

Dertujia grinned.

And finally, they were properly inside the village perimeter. The border was only a mark between wild grass and the city's stones. Dertujia heard a wild river, and they were soon crossing the small bridge over it. The thing was big enough to rush by fast underfoot. Soon enough it'd eat away more and more until it took over a big patch of the city.

"One day, this city will rise up and rule all," Leahnina said, surprising him.

"This small town? It's a hamlet at best."

Xorna slapped his shoulder. "This *hamlet* has a huge castle. Pay attention, my old friend. This place is a lightning caterpillar, stored inside its cocoon, waiting for its chance to burn."

Dertujia laughed. He didn't see it, but he trusted Leahnina and Xorna. He put away his doubts and paid attention to the people. As they had stepped onto the main road that led through Firebranch, a rocky path with flat boulders making a barrier wall that separated the houses from the path, the people were getting more prevalent. He guessed he and his friends were heading towards the main square. That was where the inns would be. And his night.

Again, all thoughts disappeared. All he could think about was how pretty Leahnina had looked in the moonlight. Maybe he could leave the window open and let its light cast all over her body. It would be a wonderful night. How glorious …

"Dertujia, watch out!" Xorna yelled and sliced a spear away from his head right before the point got uncomfortably imbedded in his temple.

Dertujia growled. Embarrassed. He had been taken off guard. Sure enough, they had hit the town square, and dozens … no, more were taking up arms. They wanted *them*.

But unfortunately for the crowd, each shadow was separate. Highly defined by the afternoon sun. He gave a grin as he flattened his palm, and then crunched into a fist. Everyone froze, held down by their own shadows.

"Did you have a problem with me?"

A man nodded. The rest were too afraid to speak.

"Then tell me. Are you working for Eropus?"

The man shook his head. He was a strange sort. Aquiline eyes with the darkest hair that Dertujia had ever seen. He was taller than his neighbors. He had the most piercing green eyes, but they weren't cruel. Just determined.

"Who are you? Speak up."

"Prince Tenpert."

Xorna snorted. "Aw, a prince. You can tell he is one with his princely robes."

Tenpert blushed and looked down at his simple tunic that covered thick rugged pants. But Dertujia knew he was telling the truth. His ears wore jewels. No normal peasant would be so well decorated.

"I am the prince. My father and mother rule this kingdom. They encourage us to mingle with the people. To show that we are all together. And you are not welcome here. You have until nightfall to get out of this village, or the royal army will cut you down where you stand."

Dertujia had trouble understanding this. Never before had he encountered someone who was good, but still biased against him for a reason he could not tell. "Like that man already tried?" Dertujia asked. He held the shadow tighter of the person who had thrown the spear. A blowhard with copper hair. Not nearly as blood red as Dertujia's own.

He glared at Dertujia but could do nothing.

"I do not condone my officer's attack. It was cowardly and without honor. But I do warn you. After that you will be violating Firebranian law. You are not welcome here."

Leahnina gripped Dertujia's hand. "Because they have a future teller here, too."

Dertujia cast a look at her empty eyes, wondering what she saw.

"Yes," Tenpert agreed. "Our oracles tell us a man with red hair will bring doom to Firebranch."

Dertujia took a step back. It was a little weirder when the fortune telling was done by someone other than Leahnina. With Eropus out there, could it be true?

Leahnina shook her head. "The oracles lie."

Tenpert stared at her, wondering what her game was. He didn't know. That meant this couldn't be an attack from Eropus, a cowardly attempt at stopping Dertujia before he went and visited that god. These people believed in what they said.

"How can you tell they're lying?" Dertujia asked Leahnina anyway.

Leahnina rolled her eyes. She was getting her faith in herself back. "I don't see that you will be anything bad for this town. That's ridiculous. You've never even heard about this place until now. And we'll leave."

"We will?" Dertujia asked.

Leahnina spun on her heels, scowling. "They won't take no for an answer. If we stay, we will be attacked."

Dertujia felt his soul failing him. Yes, he was indeed interested in Leahnina for a night of certain discoveries, but that wasn't the only reason. He, too, needed a night where he was normal. Did the normal things, not hid from gods and ran from armies. He didn't think about his shadows or what the future might bring.

Just Leahnina and him doing what lovers do.

Now they had to travel. Kicked out of a village that had seemed so welcoming. Dertujia had always loved exploring different palaces and castles, seeing how the higher-up lived. Every royal seemed to love gigantic paintings or sculptures of themselves and their families. He wanted to see if the theme remained the same.

Dertujia had seen them grow more and more ostentatious and a tad ridiculous, with certain body parts over-emphasized and embellishments of beauty, becoming godlike.

But instead, he and his friends were escorted out by the military and all the way down the south road. The trio was silent as they walked.

"I hate that place," Xorna finally broke the silence. "Even if what they said was true, they could have easily let us stay on the outskirts, give us some food and … I *really* hate that place."

Dertujia concurred. He didn't make it a habit to dislike any place or people, but in that one declaration, they had made him an enemy. He didn't want to continue on now. After that desert, that tunnel, the army … was it too much to demand to have a simple night?

It seemed so.

This journey became more and more cursed as he traveled it.

But it still continued. He couldn't go back. He had no idea how even if he wanted to. Besides he had gotten powers for this trip. Eropus had targeted him. Dertujia had no choice but to walk.

And walk.

And walk.

They hunted and found streams. Xorna did her best to ignore the meat and ate vegetables, but her strength weakened until she was forced to share in the meat just to keep her protein up. Each day brought more and more of a ragged appearance. Their clothes were wearing out. Their shoes and even their scabbards. Xorna and Dertujia were hard pressed to even keep their swords sharp as the hours continued. How much longer did they have to travel this misbegotten path?

The trio were the only ones who walked this road. The land around grew more and more desolate, and the mountain range grew bigger. Dertujia focused on Leahnina who tried to stay chipper. She pointed out the orange thump rabbits which populated this area and flew around them as sunset approached. Sweet faces watched in quiet awe as they fluffed their cheeks up to show their menace. They didn't bother the group but made for a surreal feeling as the sun went away.

Dertujia enjoyed Leahnina's voice, and her words wrapped around his brain, making him ignore the journey, but every step away from Firebranch brought his ire. One day, he'd have to repay that village for their kindness.

The only sign of life was from animals now. But soon enough Leahnina stopped, and her eyes widened. "We need shelter. Now!"

Dertujia didn't ask why. He just started scanning the world around. The road spread through brush that was spiky and thick and spread across the landscape for miles and miles. No structure was around that would be good enough for shelter.

But Leahnina's concerns were valid. Rain started up.

"One moment," Dertujia said. Though he was too tired for much, he bumped the shadow of an inn's overhang from very far away into existence. "Is this enough?"

Leahnina bit her lips and said nothing. Dertujia swallowed and watched the liquid fall.

Thirsty, he cupped his hands outside and let some fall into them. Pink? He rubbed it between his fingers. Then he carefully touched it with his tongue. "This is sweet," he noted.

"Really?" Xorna asked with a smile. She had quite the sweet tooth. She stuck her finger out and brought it to her mouth. "Mmm, like honey mixed with maple syrup. Hey, got any bottles? I'm going to use this on some pancakes when I get some kind of flour for them. Oh, and milk. Plus …"

Leahnina clapped loudly. "Quiet. Do you hear?"

Dertujia didn't like the look on her face. But soon he did hear.

BUZZZZ.

Dertujia cocked his head. “Do I want to know what that is?”

“No, you really don’t,” Leahnina admitted.

But he had no choice. As he looked out trying to see through the sheets of rain, there they were.

Gigantic orange heads with protruding mouths that slurped unceasingly along the ground. The sound was as unnerving as the BUZZZ. The things had two round circles of a body. One a head, and the other the place where two engorged wings kept them afloat even through the heavy rain.

“Bees,” Dertujia muttered.

“Big bees,” Leahnina defined.

“They like the nectar!” Xorna laughed and relaxed. “Creatures after my own heart. Is this what you were worried about, Leahnina, or was it the rain? Because I wouldn’t want to be drenched in that stuff.”

“Would you keep quiet?” Leahnina hissed.

Xorna had put a lot of faith in Leahnina’s prophecies before, but this time it looked like she was wrong. The bees were big but hardly a threat.

One hung like a heavy fruit and flapped over to them.

Its eyes were like beads, big and round, filled with some liquid that only sharpened their eyes. It saw them. Like a human, it cocked its head as if it were puzzled by the very sight of three such unusual creatures on its doorstep.

Dertujia usually attacked. But he saw Xorna’s shake of her head. She grabbed his arm.

"They are just eating the rain. Not dangerous by any means. I wonder if they understand language."

The bee got ever closer. It definitely had them in its sights. Dertujia reached out for any shadows, but the rain made them flicker if he could get a bead on them in the first place. The sun was covered. The light, gray and shy.

The other bees squirmed and buzzed, watching the first bee.

"They're kind of cute," Xorna said. "Come on, little guy. Come closer," she clicked her tongue.

Dertujia had to admit they were. Xorna reached out her fingertips into the rain. It spread across her hand, dripping down to the ground. The bee was close enough. It reached out its long tongue and slurped the rain off her fingers.

"Aw," she said with a smile. "It wants the stuff on my … Ow!" She yanked her hand away. Dertujia saw the blood mixing with the pink rain.

He snapped his vision back to the bee which opened its long mouth to reveal three-inch-long sharp teeth, glistening with blood. It angrily buzzed some more and shot its way into their enclosure. It bounced around, opening its mouth wide.

The trio jumped away from it, into the rain.

And got drenched. And sticky.

"Ugh!" Dertujia said. "Why do you always have to make friends with dangerous beasts, Xorna?"

He drew his sword and slapped it against the bee that was trying to take a piece out of his forearm.

But the rest of the bees had seen what happened. In unison, they opened their mouths to reveal the same sharp, finger-long teeth.

In a group, they dived at them, grabbing bites where they could, slicing like razors. Dertujia yanked the shadows of the bees but all it did was make them angrier.

"You insignificant insects!" Dertujia yelled.

He shot desperate eyes at Xorna who had fallen, her sword out and slicing with great skill. But the bees were everywhere. Drawn by the sound of the buzzing, a whole lot of other bees had joined the fray.

"Stay still!" a voice yelled. Dertujia didn't recognize it. A danger. But considering the bees were about to swarm him, he froze. Flames leapt around the area, turning the bees black, dropping them. The majority saw this death and turned to the new arrival, but flames leapt through the rain, burning it away before it could touch them.

The bees halted as one and decided to find a new target. They buzzed away.

Dertujia looked around to see that the new arrival still had his fire up, wrapping them in a warm bubble. He couldn't move though. The rain was drying into paste.

"Thank you," he said with a heavy breath.

The man pulled Xorna up. "You okay, milady?" he asked.

Xorna smiled. Her eyes weren't blinking, but that was because the rain was freezing her eyelashes to her face. "I'm good now. Who are you?"

Before he could answer, though, Leahnina started gasping for air. Her nose was completely covered, and her lips were frozen shut. Dertujia could do nothing. He couldn't even gesture.

He couldn't even call her name. The rain was cement, and it was forcing them into statues. They would still die.

"Oh! Hold on."

Fire leapt through the area again. The rain had blessedly stopped. But the man was trying to kill them. He was burning …

The rain off them. Roaring a fire to evaporate all the disgusting pink liquid. Fire was its cure.

Dertujia opened and shut his jaw and then ran over to Leahnina. She was able to breathe now. He held her tightly. "Are you okay?"

She hesitated but nodded. "That rain was … Oh, good it stopped."

The clouds were retreating, bringing the sun. But it would have taken way too long to do them any good. The new arrival had saved all of their lives. Something that Dertujia couldn't, wouldn't forget.

He took a look at their savior. The stranger certainly didn't look like he was anything that could control fire. Blonde hair that fell down to his shoulders. A scruffy short beard on his chin made him look older than he was, and above that were red eyes. He wore all black except for a red backpack on his shoulders. He was armed with a sword on his hip, a dagger on his arm, and a bow slung over his back.

A mercenary. That made sense. Who else would be out here?

"You have our eternal gratitude. My name is Dertujia. The woman whose hand you're holding is Xorna." She jumped and yanked her hand away, as if she had forgotten he was holding it. "And this is Leahnina."

The man grinned. His beard moved with its power. "Name's Cetphur. What in the name of the gods are you three doing out here in the Wild Areas?"

Dertujia tried to remain standing. He had lost a lot of blood. Almost as if Cetphur sensed that, he rushed over to him. "Okay, well, you're bleeding, my friend. Let me see."

"I know first aid," Dertujia complained.

"And even if he didn't, I do," Xorna said.

Cetphur gave her a grin, and she held a hand to her heart like that grin had seared her soul. "But none of you can do it quite like me. The good thing is that the rain has great healing attributes. You just need to close the wounds. Hold on. This *will* hurt."

Dertujia gasped and gritted his teeth as all over his body, wounds started being burned, cauterized. Closed up with fire. It took minutes for the ladies to be treated as well, but Cetphur held Xorna's arm longer than was necessary.

"Handy trick," Dertujia said. He moved his body around. No permanent damage. No muscle injuries, but he was exhausted. "Did you too go to Dragon Tower?"

Cetphur gave him a look of confusion. "Where?"

"The place where one gets powers. It is how Leahnina can tell the future. And how I got my power to do this," Dertujia said and pulled on the remnants of his energy to yank three shadow horses into being.

It was risky telling this stranger of obvious strength anything, but there was something about him. Dertujia cared for him upon meeting him. He was a man anyone could like. Xorna had already blushed a few times at his touch. Leahnina smiled at him. It was like coming together, they had found the fourth of their group. They were supposed to be together.

Cetphur laughed and ran over to pet the shadows of horses. "That's incredible!" he craned his head back to look at Dertujia. "To answer your question, no. Nothing gave me this power. I was born with it. My father was too. This power is why I became a mercenary."

Dertujia smiled. The danger was over. He felt better. Just tired—more than tired. He wanted to fall down and sleep. He needed some rest. Gods-awful Firebranch! He would never forgive them. They had almost gotten them killed. Had Firebranch just allowed them in for the night, they wouldn't have come across the bees at all.

He'd always have a thorn in his stomach, and it had come from that city.

Chapter Nine

Cetphur glanced at the horses again. "Is one of these beasts for me?"

Dertujia nodded.

"I'd rather not. If you would just send them away. I don't take advantage of animals if I can help it."

"They are shadows," Dertujia answered, baffled.

"They're alive. It doesn't matter. I'd rather walk." Dertujia gritted his teeth. He sent the horses away and instead brought back a horseless carriage. It should work the same.

"Will you travel with us, then?" Xorna asked.

"Makes sense. I don't turn down a free ride or forgo a chance to look at such a beautiful woman."

Xorna giggled and blushed more as he helped her board the carriage.

"What am I? An Octogob?" Leahnina asked.

Dertujia gave her a grin and slowly kissed her hand. "Far from it, and as soon as we can get somewhere to be alone, I'll prove it to you."

Leahnina laughed herself, but she put out a hand for him to board first. He chuckled and scooped her into his arms, depositing her in a seat.

"Refuse my hand, get my vengeance," he teased.

"Ooh, I'm terrified," she said with a flirtatious wink. Surviving the bees had put them all in a good mood. Dertujia was taking a risk to use the carriage—the shadow could give out in any minute depositing them on the ground. At high speeds that could be risky. But he needed to ride. Leahnina needed it. The bees could have killed them.

"So, you're a mercenary?" Xorna asked. "Where do you come from?"

"A small town called Firebranch."

Dertujia brought his fists to his sides. Cetphur noticed. "You hate my town?"

"They were far from hospitable," Dertujia agreed. "We're headed towards Gaiarigona now, just to get some food and shelter."

"I was going there too," Cetphur said. "It looks like we were meant to travel together."

Dertujia laughed. He wasn't quite sure he believed in the destiny that made people do things against their own will. "Then we should travel together. Even if your home isn't as nice as you are."

Cetphur leaned back. "They weren't always so bad. But not long ago, a town called Neonea was overtaken by the peasants. The royals there had treated them cruelly. Instead of fighting, all the nobility abandoned the town and looked for a new home. They found Firebranch. They built a castle, forced their rule on us, and now friendship and loyalty are a thing of the past."

His blood red eyes looked sad. "One day I want to return there, but it's so different."

Xorna stared at him. Dertujia had never seen her act like this. Smitten, that was the word. Her eyes made copies of Cetphur's face in her brain and played them over and over.

"Maybe you should go back and fight," Xorna said. "Take back the rule."

He stared at her and grinned. "Maybe. But that'd take forces I don't have. As it is the only way I can get money is fighting in wars or to help people."

"I'd like to see Firebranch then. When you save it from evil royals." Xorna blushed and turned away. Dertujia laughed but only internally. He wouldn't embarrass his old friend in front of her crush. Later, she was fair game.

"What's in Gaiarigona?" Dertujia asked. The carriage bumped over rocks. Stray ones would hit the shadow windows from time to time.

"A war runner."

Dertujia hissed. He had fought at least seven war runners in his years. Across Telda, people were different. They had different rulers, different governments. Kind or cruel. But war runners were all the same. They had one word in their vocabulary. Mine.

"His name is Dubruck. The letter I got asking for help says he's destroyed half of their people, murdered, raped, and pillaged. When I come along, he'll see the fires of hell taking him to justice."

Dertujia nodded. "I'd appreciate it if I could help. We are heroes of our own. Have you heard of us?"

Cetphur hung his head. "Every single day since I was old enough to hear stories, I've loved the ones about heroes. But yours were something else. It always gave me hope, hearing someone my age going out and making a difference. I didn't want to mention it. I especially loved your cause, Xorna."

He shined his eyes at her, and she fixed her armor, trying to look perfect.

"What are we going to find in Gaiarigona?" Dertujia asked, changing the subject. He liked someone worshipping him, but something felt off. Like he was being elevated. Dertujia was no god. He didn't want to feel like one. Something his mother always warned him about. "Never get high or someone will make sure you get low."

He knew she was right.

"They'll be a people at the end of their rope. We need to bring their hope back," Cetphur said.

Dertujia smiled. "So we shall."

"And if Dubruck gets in our way, he'll regret it," Xorna said.

Leahnina was quiet. Dertujia held her hand. "Is there a problem?" he whispered. "Is Cetphur …?"

"He's one of us. I just …"

Then Dertujia realized she wasn't tense, she was blushing. A bright red. What did she see in …

Oh.

Dertujia whistled as their journey continued. He had a feeling they'd find a warm greeting in Gaiarigona. The opposite of Firebranch.

He looked forward to it as the rocky mountain shoved its way forward in the landscape.

Cetphur was an amusing companion. He loved stories and myths. Cetphur let them in on who the goddess who sent them on this journey was. Bynneeshia was very much for the people. She even had made a great lake in a drought ridden town. She accidentally overdid it, and now the town was built on poles.

And also, he talked about the goddess who made the items they carried. Padonum was a goddess shrouded in mystery. She had told the gods future dealings and more, but her demise was many years after the other gods.

As the carriage bumped and sped across the land, and Dertujia kept his mind on the far-off sun that cast the shadow they rode, the conversation led to showing him the items.

Cetphur laughed as he held them. Gently, almost reverentially. "Amazing. They exist. They really do."

"What are they?" Xorna asked. Dertujia held a smile back. Xorna had never cared about gods or their artifacts before. But one word from Cetphur and she was absorbed. Of course.

"This is Padonum's Box," he said. "It has the most power here. It can transport people long distances, but it does have to have a connection with where it is going. Mainly one of these trinkets." He held up the necklace.

"It creates storms that lift things into the air."

Dertujia shook his head. He already knew most of this stuff.

Leahnina decided to voice her own thoughts. "We already know what they do."

Xorna gave her a hard look. "I don't. How much could they do?"

Cetphur turned his head to look at her face, so close to his, thanks to the closed in confines of this carriage. He was silent. Lost. Finally, he shook his head and looked at the necklace again. "This could lift a city."

Okay! Now that sounded helpful.

"And the mirror?"

Cetphur shuddered and handed the mirror back quickly. "It connects to a land none of us want to visit until we're old and gray. The Underworld, keeper of the King. Death, my friends."

"You're right, and you're wrong," Leahnina said, carefully putting the items away again. "It does communicate with the underworld, but it also can make things bigger."

Cetphur cocked his head, leaning forward. Xorna glared at Leahnina. Dertujia held a smile again. It wasn't Leahnina's body Cetphur was interested in (otherwise his own shadow might lay a few punches on him). It was her mind.

"How big? I never heard that before."

Leahnina gazed at him. "Very, very big. Reflections can be magnified depending on how close or far away they are to the mirror. It can utilize that. Padonum was amazing."

Cetphur clasped his hands together. "And you know all this?"

Dertujia decided he wanted to get in on this conversation. He and Xorna were getting ignored. Dertujia didn't like that, not at all. And if Xorna kept looking at the back of Cetphur's head, pretty soon she might cut Leahnina's eyes out.

"I told you, she has future visions, much like my shadows."

He shook his head vigorously, his red eyes alight like they were on fire. "That's not all. It can't be."

Dertujia scratched his brow. This journey was taking forever. "How so?"

"We are not only these bodies, my friends."

No one balked at his terminology. They had become close in only seconds, knowing each other somehow.

"We exist through space and time, using forms of flesh when we need but go onto the next when these expire."

"What are you saying?" Leahnina asked, narrowing her eyes.

"You may very well be the goddess Padonum reincarnated."

Xorna cleared her throat. "She is just a normal woman. Gained powers by the Dragon Tower."

For the good of everyone's health, Cetphur turned back to Xorna and gave her a rugged smile. "And what did you get, milady? The beauty of the gods?"

Xorna giggled. Dertujia breathed freely. He wasn't usually the jealous type. Then again, he never had to fight for the cause of a beautiful woman. He was attractive, he thought, but he didn't have that deep cleft or that handsome mustache that Cetphur had. Surely, Leahnina would be happier with the blonde hair that this guy had and not Dertujia's own deep red locks.

Either way, if Xorna had Cetphur, there would be no worries.

Leahnina laughed quietly next to him.

"What?" he asked in an undertone.

"I have watched you for years. You know this."

Dertujia did. He had felt her eyes on his leaving form every day he left the village for heroics, and hers were the first he saw on return. She had always been there. It was only now how gratified he was that was true. Which made him all the more worried he'd lose her. He hadn't shown her his appreciation always.

"You're jealous. And I like it."

Her lips were close to his ears, the whisper a tickle. But it made him feel better. For whatever reason, Leahnina still worshipped him. A heavy sense of happiness took him over.

But what Cetphur said bothered him. He wasn't only this body? Could he have lived before? It was strange that Leahnina had powers even before the tower, how Dertujia could hear whispers of things he'd never known. Maybe they had lived before. Maybe they'd all live again.

But if she was Padonum, who was he?

The city of Gaiarigona was finally close enough to drive into. It was a simple village, huddled into the mountain like a chick into a mother hen. And Dertujia could see the damage from the war runner.

Being so close to the mountains, the architecture was stone and rocks. But all had been smashed almost into rubble. The citizens were living outside, keeping together around fires for warmth. There were no structures to live in.

Eyes turned towards them as they entered. Dertujia collapsed the shadow carriage, just as the light left its owner. Funny, the eyes were tired, scared, and wary, but they weren't angry or mean.

They didn't ask them to leave.

Dertujia hailed a passing woman. There was something earthy about her, light green hair and a narrow face. Long appendages. "Hello, we need to speak to your leader. We need a place to sleep first. We are tired."

He expected resistance, unfriendliness. Instead, she gave him a broad grin.

"I can do you both, strangers. Though you'll have to sleep under a lean-to, and you'll have to speak to me in the morning. I'm Queen Tiabana, ruler of Gaiarigona, or what's left of it. You'll be safe in the night, but in the morning, you'll have to move on. The war runner Dubruck comes at dawn."

She seemed awfully happy for someone who had this fate coming. When Dertujia noted it, Tiabana kept her grin with difficulty. "That piece of unholy feces wants us all to be miserable. But happiness is a way of life not what happens to you. I love visitors. You all have such great stories. I bet you have one about that shadow carriage you arrived in. And if I'm not mistaken, you are Dertujia and Xorna, aren't you?"

Dertujia nodded.

Tiabana laughed again. "I knew it. I saw a tapestry of you once. I recognized you easily. I am so honored."

"While as, we're just chopped Octogob meat," Cetphur murmured.

Leahnina laughed.

Xorna and Dertujia preened though. "Good of you to follow our journeys," he said. "But I do have to remind you that Dubruck is coming. Joviality is a bit foolish. We may not be able to fight him."

Her grin, if anything got bigger. "You'll *fight* for us? That's incredible. But, no, Dertujia, great master, I will always smile. I can be happy until I die. Happiness is one thing I *won't* lose. Right now, I'm not in pain. Right now, I'm not being tortured. Now, I'm listening to the great Dertujia and waiting for the great Xorna to speak. Can't I be happy?"

Dertujia nodded. This was a better reception than in Firebranch.

"You can be happy," Xorna spoke up, giving Tiabana what she wanted. "Because we will free you of this curse. Then you can be happy and not tortured at all. Tell us about Dubruck."

Now Tiabana lost her smile. She gestured for them to follow her past many, many people who were homeless. It got worse as they traveled. Tiabana filled their ears with the crimes of Dubruck. He and a group of people were faster than anyone here. They roared forward every week or so and demanded people to give them what they wanted. The best food. The best drink. Any man or woman they wanted in bed. If the Gaiarigonians refused, they would murder every child they saw. The inhabitants thought it better to give in than to lose their future.

But it left the Gaiarigonians a bruised people. No real will to fight back anymore.

Dertujia's heart broke. Not because of the bruises he saw on the men and women, showing their dealings with Dubruck and his thugs were far from gentle. Not the starving people or the shade in a lot of eyes.

No, what hurt was that the people were forcing smiles. Trying to be brave for their children. Come morning, a lot would have to give their best to the war runner, or they'd suffer.

"My shadows will have an intimate conversation with his spleen, and the livers of his men. Their hearts," Dertujia said.

Leahnina froze. They had reached a bed that was obviously for the queen. Soft and cushioned under a lean-to. Tiabana gave it up easily for the group, and Dertujia sunk into it.

"The first thing we'll do is rebuild," Cetphur said. "After killing the rotten enemy. I saw that the inn isn't in bad shape, and neither are a lot of the houses. Just a little crumpled. Some look as if it's just the entrance that's destroyed. A little fire. A little shadow. Perfect."

Xorna nodded. Leahnina burrowed into Dertujia's shoulder. "I saw the future after we fix up the place. But …"

Ah, the visions he looked so forward to. There was death in her tone though. "What is it?"

"Now that I'm here, the visions are coming, Dertujia. They're coming at a rapid pace. You can easily kill Dubruck. Xorna will take down the first lieutenant. Even I will get a little action with my dagger. No worries about Cetphur."

Dertujia crossed his eyes. "Then what's wrong?"

"The children have been used as hostages before. Dubruck will do it again. They die, Dertujia. The people will rebuild, have children again, but for a lot of them, they will never recover. Dubruck is going to kill all the children."

Dertujia sat back. This … No. He was supposed to save them all.

"Can we go after Dubruck? Meet him earlier?"

Leahnina shook her head. "He can get past us. He is soooo fast."

Dertujia threw everything out of his head. Maybe a defensive wall. No, a fast person could just run right up a wall, and how long would it take to …

He thought of the mirror. Padonum's Mirror. Made things bigger. His thumb glanced against a small rocky shell discarded from a boulder-crab.

If it were bigger …

"Leahnina, give me the Mirror. I can use it?"

Leahnina relaxed. She gave a mighty grin. "Yes, yes, you can. You are wonderful! It's no wonder …" She blushed again, seeing the future that was coming.

Dertujia chucked her chin.

He got to work. He picked up the shell and ran as fast as he could out of the city. He took the border path towards the mountain behind the city, using his shadows to climb with huge, towering pillars formed under his feet. The sun was coming. Dawn was almost here.

Faster.

His back against the mountain, he had a good view of the city. He placed the shell down. When it grew, it'd encase the city. Protecting it like the shell had once protected its owner. He held the mirror up and reflected the shell. "Please, Padonum. Help me. Give this city shelter."

A loud noise echoed off the plains behind him. Like a hundred people were running very fast.

Dubruck was coming.

"Please, Padonum," he begged. "Help me. I want to protect these people."

The mirror glowed. The rocky shell burst upwards, roof first until the mountains overhead were blocked. It kept growing and growing. It spread across the tents, the groups who had stopped what they were doing and looked up. The shell got so big it took over the city.

Only seconds later, a large noise hit the front of the city. The entire place had been encased. No way in.

Oh, but Dubruck's unfortunate group had been running just a bit too fast. Splatted like an insect against a moving Koorsgald.

The shell was in place.

Dertujia grinned. Well, that was easy!

He moved the mirror. The shell overhead groaned. So, Gaiarigona was protected but only as long as this mirror stayed right here. He couldn't bring it with them, not if he wanted Gaiarigona safe from future attacks. He had lost one of Leahnina's items.

When he returned to her side, she shook her head. "Losing the mirror is inconsequential. You don't know the danger this city will face. It is for the best, and Padonum is happy to help."

He shot her a look. She just smiled. She didn't believe *she* was Padonum.

No one saw the sun come. It would be eternally dark until someone made a better light.

But, funny, none of the Gaiarigonians cared.

The children laughed as they played.

The inn was the first place Dertujia and Cetphur repaired, but they went on to help rebuild all the buildings and made a very large gateway in the shell. Cetphur showed his skill and artistry with fire as he formed out of the rock two gates with giant horses on them coming out of the walls as if crashing through the gates from the city.

Gaiarigona would be forever protected from any outside influences.

The building was done. Cetphur had taken beams of metal and molded them with his fire to stick to others to form structures from a molten stone he had also concocted. A very useful man to be around. Dertujia helped, once someone villagers lit many torches, by making a hundred-man shadow army to put in furniture and chimneys and the like.

Leahnina and Xorna organized the villagers and asked what kind of houses they wanted. Well, Xorna asked. Leahnina just foretold. By the end the whole group was adored.

As it came time to rest, Dertujia looked at Leahnina and nodded towards the inn. It was time for her visions to come true. Thanks to the daily activities, they had been too exhausted to spend much time together. Dertujia was used to being a hero, and helping people came first, a habit ingrained in him since childhood.

Leahnina didn't, to Dertujia's surprise, jump to standing when he offered her his hand as they sat in an outdoor garden in front of a newly made stone restaurant. The sun had gone down outside, not that it made much difference. If not for the torches glittering merrily every foot or so, the city would have been pitch black.

"We didn't get him," she said in a tone he was starting to recognize as her future telling.

"Didn't get who?" Dertujia asked.

"Dubruck."

The name chilled Dertujia. He had never exited the city to see whose bodies were out there. Let the Violet Crows have their nutrients. But to think that …

"What happened?"

Leahnina just shook her head. "He is outside now."

A voice slammed through the city.

"Gaiarigonians!" it yelled. A thick voice, full of menace. "You have stopped me. Congratulate yourselves. But you are not free of me. I want Dertujia."

It settled down across the city. Dubruck asking for Dertujia by name.

Heads poked out of the windows.

Dubruck's voice continued. "I have been blessed by the god Eropus. He has enhanced my speed. He has given me strength. I *want* Dertujia! Send him out alone or the city will suffer."

Seconds later, the whole shell shook.

"Dubruck is running into the city," Leahnina informed. But Dertujia could figure that out on his own. It wasn't hard to see his intent. If Dertujia didn't go out to face him, as per Eropus' request, Dubruck would slam into the city until the shell gave in. It would collapse. All inside would be crushed by the very thing that protected them.

"I am really growing a hatred for Eropus," Dertujia said. "If not for him, I'd be having a much more pleasant life."

He stood up to go.

Leahnina grabbed his arm.

"No, Dertujia. It's pitch black out there. No shadows."

Dertujia caressed her arm, spreading his fingers on her smooth skin. "Will I die here?"

Leahnina shook. "I can't tell. But …"

"Have faith in me, Leahnina. I can take a war runner."

Leahnina pulled herself up into his arms, pressing her cheek against his chest. "But Eropus has enhanced him. Eropus knows our mission. He wants you, above all else, dead. He knows you're the biggest threat to him."

Dertujia kissed the top of her head, inhaling her pleasant scent. It set his body on fire. He had a great incentive to come back alive. "You've foreseen our night, Leahnina. Don't doubt your visions."

Leahnina's eyes fluttered against him. He felt the small movement even through the shirt he wore. "They have changed. We can change them.

Eropus can change them. It's like … he knew I could foresee a good future, so he waited. Then he changed it. He's outside of time. He is a god."

Dertujia put two strong fingers under her chin and gently pulled her face up so he could look her in the eyes. "Leahnina, I have gone into battles that were hopeless before. Every single time I have won. I will never lose. Because I am right. Right wins. Not evil. Dubruck may be a powerful man, but he fights for the cause of the flesh. He wants only to send thrills to his body. But that isn't worth dying for.

"My cause is. So, I will win. He will die."

Leahnina gave a tremulous smile. "I can't see whether we share our night together."

Dertujia kissed her slowly, pressing his bottom lip to her top and sending his breath into her nose. "We will. I will not die without experiencing you fully. You are my hope. Leahnina, I don't have only good to fight for now. I have you. That is going to keep me alive."

Leahnina slammed both of her hands down on his muscular shoulders. "It better."

He hugged her fiercely. Inside, he was in turmoil. It would have been much more hopeful if Leahnina had told him he easily won.

Dertujia had faced death before on many different occasions. He had fear then, too, of course. But he went into battle for a cause bigger than himself. Death was just another thing to fight.

Chapter Ten

A few minutes later, in a house made for defense, he put his armor on. Xorna helped. "You by yourself?" she asked, buckling black armor in multiple places. "I can come too."

"Dubruck said alone," Dertujia said, hurriedly putting a black helmet on his head. The Gaiarigonians were kind enough to offer him a full suit of armor. There had been a few more announcements from the enemy. Dubruck was giving them time for Dertujia to get ready.

"Stupid," Xorna muttered. "We've been partners for so long."

"Not this time."

The tension was thick. Dertujia had always gone into battle with Xorna. This would be the first without her even meeting him after the battle began. This was one-on-one. Only one survivor.

"I'm afraid," Xorna admitted. "Dubruck didn't get squashed, though he couldn't possibly know you were going to put the shell up. He is here. Eropus has set his sights on you, and you alone. What about me?"

Dertujia chuckled. "Is this what it's all about? You were looked over?"

Xorna punched him in the stomach. His armor took the blow.

"Hey, this does protect me pretty well," Dertujia joked.

Xorna didn't even look like she hurt her hand. "I'm not offended. All this time, Dertujia, our many battles. Our mission. We fought together. Celebrated together. Made a name together. But with this god, he has singled you out. He blames you just for going after him."

Dertujia sighed and pulled on his leg greaves along with the boots that went under them. "Many have hated me."

Xorna shook her head, handing him his sword. "This isn't about hatred. Eropus is playing with you. Like a wasp-cat would a mouse. He doesn't hate you. Nor does he fear you. He is waving you on. Challenging you. He *knows* he can win."

Dertujia felt a weakness in his stomach at her words. She was right. It was a personal enmity he made when he stood by and watched the god attack that creation. Neesh chose him, and that was all Eropus needed.

"Well, I do *hate* him," Dertujia said, strengthening his stomach. "And righteous hatred is all I need. Oh, and he is wrong. He won't win."

Dertujia left through the front door, leaving Xorna alone.

"But Dertujia," she said to nobody. "I'm afraid he will. We can't be victorious."

Xorna hadn't wept since she was a child. But now somewhere inside, she knew this would end badly. Once, long ago, Xorna had a dream. It was a simple one. She and Dertujia were traveling on an endless road. The sun shined. The birds sang. For that part of the dream, it was perfect. Peaceful. But then a fork came in the road. Dertujia went left. Xorna went right. As soon as they separated a tornado roared up and smashed the sun away. The peaceful purple sky became gray. The birds died. Everything was chaos.

She had awakened with one thought. If she and Dertujia ever separated, something would go wrong. And here and now, she couldn't join him in battle. Dubruck would smash into the city. He'd destroy it. If he was truly so fast, how could either Dertujia or Xorna stop it?

Tears filled her eyes. They slowly swept her face. No one ever saw Xorna weep. But she did now like she was a child.

***

Dertujia walked out of the gates alone. They were closed up quickly as possible, as he had ordered. If Dubruck had other forces, they wouldn't find access to the city.

Behind Dertujia stood the mountains. Behind Dubruck were the long plains that went into the Wild Areas.

Dubruck looked different than Dertujia would expect. Oh, he was ugly, of course. War runners were never attractive. Their soul had been tainted by giving into evil. But he was muscular. Usually, war runners were fat, having given into indulgences all their lives.

Dubruck stood on the battlefield like a tree, tall and ready for battle. He wore one sword on his hip, and armor that included a face mask, but he was arrogant. Lots and lots of places for Dertujia to get a wound in. Under his arms, through his belly. Half piece of armor over massive chest. He strained against the armor like a horse pushing against a harness.

Long black hair flew down to his hips. Another arrogance. Hair got in the way, which was why under his helmet, Dertujia had pinned his hair tight against his head.

"So, *you* are Dertujia," Dubruck said with a sneer on his rugged face. "Eropus told me to fear you."

That was gratifying at the very least. Somehow, though, Dertujia didn't think Eropus feared him. "And you are the scum I will kill," Dertujia acknowledged.

Dubruck laughed. "So, you have a tongue on you. Let me cut it out."

Dertujia knew as long as Dubruck was talking, Dertujia was safe. But based on the Gaiarigonians' tales of how very fast Dubruck was, Dertujia might be in the underworld before he realized he was dead.

"Will you use your speed in this fight?" Dertujia asked.

Dubruck laughed again. A hollow sound. Nothing amused this dead piece of flesh anymore. He had given himself too much, destroyed his own life by indulging. "I can kill you without my speed. I can refrain. And though I don't keep my word much, to you I will keep it when I promise, I will slice the flesh from your bones slowly."

Dertujia held up his sword. "Then I will return the favor and not use the shadows." The moon had come out from behind the clouds so there was truth to Dertujia's promise. The moon cast some shadows.

Dubruck ran at him. He was still fast. Dertujia took the blow, remembering Xorna's and his own training at the foot of the teacher. Never be on the defensive.

Dubruck had taken Dertujia by surprise, and he got the first blood as he sliced through Dertujia's armor. A long line appeared on Dertujia's chest. Dertujia gritted his teeth, placed all pain to the back of his brain. Fight. That was what he had to do.

Like a dance, he used his moves.

Dubruck brought his sword down, Dertujia blocked it. Dodged a lower cut. Dubruck slammed his knee into Dertujia's armor.

Like he had been shoved against a mountain.

A sinister voice in his ear. "I never promised not to use my god-given strength."

Dertujia held his teeth together, bracing them for his uppercut into Dubruck's face. He was satisfied to feel bone crunching. He had gotten past his face armor.

"And I never promised to not use my own honed and tried strength. You are a fool." While Dertujia talked, he hit Dubruck again. Same area. Right in his teeth.

Dubruck groaned and recoiled. Now he was on the defense.

"Spare me!" he moaned. Ah, the battle had turned, so he showed a different side. Cowards. All of them.

"I will spare you," Dertujia said and slammed his gauntlet into Dubruck's helmet. "Like you spared the Gaiarigonians."

Dertujia spun around and slit the armor from the body, leaving Dubruck without defense. Then he sliced again. "I will show you the mercy of the children you threatened to kill all so you could ruin the parents."

Rage built more and more. He hated Dubruck for what Dertujia had heard about him. He hated him for the wound he'd gotten. It burned like fire, reminding of weakness. Mortality. He could have died by that one blow.

More, he hated that this lousy human being was used by the enemy Dertujia hunted to *toy* with him.

Finally, he hated him for his cowardice. Dubruck couldn't just give Dertujia the satisfaction of dying like he lived, instead making Dertujia feel almost sorry that he was ending his life. Because he was so damned pathetic.

"This is for the wound!" Dertujia finished and stabbed his sword right through the heart of his enemy. Like his soldiers, Dubruck would never hurt anyone again. And the loser cried out like Dertujia was murdering him not executing a monster. Like Dertujia was the one in the wrong.

In previous battles, Dertujia had killed in the heat of it. None of the others ever whined at his feet. Never had they been helpless in front of him as he slaughtered them.

"No," he muttered and let the corpse fall. "I will not feel sorrow for the enemy. Anyone who goes against me is against the side of justice. That's what I live for. That's who I am."

He cleaned his blade and left the body for the birds. Let them feast anew.

***

The people of Gaiarigona hadn't ignored the battle. They wouldn't wait for morning. All of them hung out windows, waiting for him to return. People had left their new homes and camped out near the entrance to the gates. As the gatekeeper watched the battle, he had thrown down words dictating the actions of the two combatants.

As the gates opened for Dertujia, cheers filled his ears. They made him forget his pain. He had been praised before but never like this. Being a hero brought with it admiration *and* hatred. It had tempered the praise. But nothing could compare to these screams and yells. Men gave him hugs. Women gave him kisses. The joy swelled his heart, and he told himself, "See, this is why I do what I do. Look at the gratitude."

The offers roared over him. Food. A house. Bed partners. But he only wanted one.

And she came running towards him along with Xorna.

"Where were you?" Dertujia asked.

"We scaled the wall up to a small hole that let us see the battle," Leahnina said, panting from the climb and run she'd done.

"We watched." Xorna gave a grin and patted the bow she carried. "I wasn't going to leave the battle to chance."

He pulled his old friend into a hug. Everyone cheered around him. But he was on fire from the battle, the killing, and the crowd around him. He only wanted one thing.

"People!" he yelled and jumped up to climb a low hanging roof on one of the stone buildings. "I appreciate what you offer. I did what I could to save you all. But, please, I want one thing. The rest of this night to be mine. I will be in the inn. I want no interruptions whether it be storm, beast, evil man, or demon. Got me?"

They all cheered him again. He pulled Leahnina into his arms and practically ran towards the inn.

She kissed his chin. "It could wait," she argued weakly.

"No, it can't. The battle stirred me up."

"But you're wounded," she said in an even weaker voice as he ran his lips down her neck.

"Leahnina, I will always be wounded. Or fighting. Or worrying. Let this night be ours."

Leahnina shut up and allowed him to carry her all the way to the inn and up the stairs into their room. He locked the door just in case. He didn't trust these people not to ask if he needed anything. This was all he needed.

"How …" Leahnina stood in the room like a lost woman, sliding one hand down her arm. "How will we do this?"

"Slowly." Dertujia grinned, his heart starting to beat more so than even in battle. "I have been waiting for this."

"Good." Leahnina gave him a mischievous grin. "Then you'll let me clean your wound, slowly."

He quickly started unlatching his armor as she brought over a damp piece of cloth. She slowly brought it down his wound. It stung, but it was made better by the trial of her soft warm fingers, touching him intimately.

"Leahnina," he groaned. "If you must clean me, do so in the nude, so I can watch you. Burn my appetite before the main course."

Leahnina blushed. "Surely you've seen a naked woman before," she argued, dipping the red cloth into the water, staining it.

"I've always averted my eyes. That is the gentlemanly thing to do. And even if I had, I've never seen you."

Leahnina laughed. She put the bowl down and her slim fingers went to work untying her laces. After what seemed to be an eternity and teasing pieces of flesh, she let it all fall. The flickering light in the room showed the most beautiful sight Dertujia had ever seen …

He felt his eyebrows come together. "You're beautiful. But … I may have averted my eyes in the past, but even I know that a woman is not see through."

Leahnina swallowed and looked down, fingering a path of skin right below her breasts. Or was it just not there? "Oh, Dertujia. I'll put my clothing back on."

He pulled her forward, gasping as her skin touched his directly on. What could feel like this? "Don't you dare," he begged. "I just wondered. What is wrong?"

"Nothing." But her voice was empty. It changed quickly into fire. Her passion was growing as his fingers trailed her bare back. "It's part of my future telling. I think I use too much up. I … Oh gods above, touch me again right there."

Dertujia did as she wished, and his mind got distracted with her touching him exactly where he wanted.

Their conversation was forgotten as the evening lasted well into the morning. Dertujia had never known such pleasure before, and he vowed he'd have it again and again.

It was only after they left Gaiarigona that the worry troubled him. Why was Leahnina disappearing? Her skin was there, sure, he could feel it well under his hands. But it was invisible.

He could see portions of body parts that only appeared when he cut someone through.

Leahnina was healthy enough.

But would she someday disappear forever?

Luckily for him, he had more worries on his mind.

Eropus had sent two evil people after Dertujia. He would do more. This adventure was just beginning.

The road turned hilly as it paralleled the nearby mountains that were the ridge of Gaiarigona. A city they left behind of love and worship. Dertujia could swear people were planning to build statues of them after they left, no matter how much he and his friends had begged them not to.

Dertujia had left two kinds of innocence there, if he was honest. One, which he gladly accepted, and that was the innocence of what it was like to be with a woman he loved. He knew her well now, and he could never return to what he was before. He knew what he'd miss if he didn't have it.

And he wouldn't for a while.

Traveling with Xorna had been bad enough, but now there was a new wheel. Too bad. Dertujia would have found any place or hidden patch of grass to do as he and Leahnina had done inside that inn. He shelved those thoughts, though he sent hidden looks to Leahnina whenever he could.

The second innocence was worse though. He had killed someone on their knees. If that had happened before, Dertujia would have stayed his hand and allowed the law to have its say.

This time, though, he hadn't dragged the miscreant to the Gaiarigonian justice. No, he had meted out that judgment. There was a question. What if he had been wrong? Maybe Dubruck wasn't really responsible for all the crimes. He could have even been a fake, trying to get attention by pretending to be someone who had caused so many crimes. It had happened before.

That innocence, Dertujia had thrown out. He didn't need it. If Dertujia had made a mistake, the gods would sort it out. He did what he had to do. It was really Dubruck's own fault.

Dertujia's group rolled along in style. The sun was high up, giving a positive shadow. Dertujia was getting better with them too. Though the shadow he dealt with went in and under trees, he kept it solid. Like his will alone made it live, not the sun.

The journey still continued, but Eropus' land was getting closer and closer. Not many traveled this way. The stain of Eropus was long across the land.

"No town for miles," Cetphur complained. "I'm sick of riding in this contraption."

Dertujia glared at him. "No offense taken."

Cetphur laughed and thudded his hands down on his knees. "It's just so boring. I want to walk. Can you stop so I can? It's better to move the body then sit in this godsforsaken pose for hours on end."

Dertujia slowed the shadow carriage by clenching his fist. “Very well. But I think you’ll like it again when your feet ache.”

Cetphur shook his head. “By the gods you do take offense easily. Was he always like this?” He shot that question to Xorna.

She had been reading a Gaiarigonian novel to pass the time, but as soon as Cetphur asked a question, her eyes shot upwards. “He’s different now,” she admitted. “Dubruck must have shaken him.”

“I am right here,” Dertujia said crossly. He brought his hand down. The shadow under Xorna and Cetphur just happened to drop while the one holding Leahnina and Dertujia stayed firm. “Walk.”

“I will too,” Leahnina said with a squeeze to his hand. “This riding thing does get old. We are meant for walking.”

Dertujia gave her a hidden look. “But with them out, we could …”

Leahnina gave him a smile he was starting to yearn for, permission. She wanted him too. But she shook her head. “Not with friends nearby. We can wait for the next village.”

Dertujia watched her climb down and walk over to Xorna and laugh with her about Dertujia’s unceremonious dropping.

“You can,” Dertujia muttered. He bit his lip as his eyes ate up Leahnina’s form. But there was nothing they could do. He had to remind himself this was no honeymoon. It was a mission.

He collapsed his shadow carriage, no matter how much he didn't really want to walk, and joined his friends.

Before they could continue, a being shrieked overhead, and Dertujia paused, watching the sky. Something was familiar about that shape. A man with wings, fury on his face. Red with anger.

"Wait, I know that creature."

Xorna rubbed her backside and gave Dertujia a glare. She hadn't let him have it for his stunt. "You've met a flying man?"

"It's a Flitelike. I named it." Then the being fell and thudded into the earth.

Dertujia started running to catch up. There were very few trees. One could see far off a long way in this place. Just as the landscape went up, the eyes could go towards the end. Far from something on the horizon, the bird man had fallen. He screamed and screamed.

Dertujia ran up to him and placed a gentle hand on his shoulder.

His wild eyes pierced him. Like a bird's. Slanted and black. Shiny eyes.

"Calm down. You are injured," Dertujia spoke. The rest of his group ran up behind him. Leahnina jumped in, trying to wrap the injuries. There were multiple ones. Thanks to Eropus.

"Do you remember me?" Dertujia asked.

The Flitelike nodded, huffing, but in too much pain to be able to rage. So, Eropus wasn't perfect. The Flitelike could calm down.

"You …" His voice was rusty, barely used. But he knew language. "You were there with mother goddess when I was created. You are my father god?"

Xorna laughed. "Oh, he's no god. Believe you me."

Dertujia shot her a look. "I am Dertujia. We will take care of you. Where were you headed?"

The sharp eyes shot towards the lump on the horizon. His wings flapped and hit the dirt. A little shrill cry of pain came out as Leahnina slammed his arm back in place.

"Dislocated," she muttered.

"Is there a village?" Dertujia asked.

The Flitelike nodded. "My home. Our home. One of war and pain."

Dertujia bit his lip. The goddess had created this being relatively recently. Could he have already gotten a village?

"How many of your kind are there?" Cetphur asked. "And what is your name?"

The Flitelike gave a tremulous smile. "My name is Fetgur. We have over two hundred Flitelikes. After the cursed god infected me, the goddess mother tried to make more. Every single time, we were born angry. She did her best, but she gave up after two hundred of us. We flew and flew, always mad. We took the abandoned city of Aieranolea. It was supposed to be in the air, but the mother goddess had urgent business somewhere else. And now? It isn't. We have to hate. We have to make war."

Dertujia helped him up, letting the small man lean into his shoulder. "You reason. You have a choice."

Fetgur shook his head. Already, Dertujia could feel his anger mounting. "We are beings of the sky, forced to the ground. I was trying to fly, but I already felt gravity fight against me."

Dertujia brought a shadow horse up, but Fetgur moaned and buried his head in Dertujia's shoulder. Lovely. He'd have to practically carry him the whole way.

"But you don't hate me. You don't rage against my friends."

Fetgur unburied his head and looked into Dertujia's eyes. "But you, Dakchin, are our leader. Your friends are our friends. It's everyone else who is our enemy."

Dertujia bristled at the wrong term. "Why do you call me Dakchin? It is not my name."

Fetgur looked at him like Dertujia was a god. It was … good. Even better than the Gaiarigonians' awe. "Because if you are not a god, you must be an emperor. That is the name of an emperor in the Flitelike tongue."

Dertujia shook his head. Now, Dakchin … nice name. But he was no emperor. Why keep correcting this guy though? "You have just come into being. How could so much have happened?"

"The goddess took us out of time. She hoped time away from Eropus' influence would save us. But we wiped out too many lives in that sphere. Now only two hundred remain. She set us free and gave us our village. If only it was in the sky …"

Dertujia kept walking. He started seeing signs of a city. Tall buildings reaching up and up.

It was made of a shiny material that blended into the horizon. As they got closer, they could see it clearly.

"Why would that make any difference?" Xorna asked. "You seem to rage so much you couldn't possibly enjoy it."

Fetgur gave her a smile. "Because we only feel at peace in the sky. If we're earthbound, we hate everything and all. Bynneeshia had hopes we would be able to make the city fly. But in truth she couldn't give us any more attention. She told us that if she did Eropus would notice and give us more problems. We weren't supposed to be like this at all."

Dertujia nodded in sympathy. He had seen this creature before Eropus' hand had changed him. He had seen the peace in Fetgur's eyes.

There was no road to the city. They had to make a path through spiky brush. Xorna used her sword. Dertujia, a shadow, and Leahnina? She was showing more skills. She'd just point at the plants in her way, and they'd wither. Turning into dust.

Leahnina noticed him watching her and said, "I control time. Not too much. So, don't get your hopes up."

Dertujia laughed. She was growing in power—and so was his attraction for her.

Once they finally made it into the village, Dertujia helped Fetgur into a hammock. There was no way to get inside to a bed. Dertujia didn't know why. The buildings were well made but had no doors. Only smooth shiny material that wouldn't allow entrance.

But if Dertujia had thought Gaiarigona was bad, he didn't know what it would be like to have a people who were practically born angry let loose in a city. Only the shiny buildings stayed up. Everything else was broken, destroyed. Smashed by hands. Old blood stained every inch of the city. And as Dertujia looked around more and more, he saw Flitelikes angrily watching them, eyes flattened to points.

"Why are they all so angry?" Cetphur asked. "I too have my own temper, but it's like a fire in front of a volcano."

Dertujia grimaced. He above anyone else here knew why. Eropus had cursed them. Just because his own creation had been made better. These Flitelikes would never know peace.

Leahnina pulled on the edge of Dertujia's sleeve.

"What is it, Leahnina? Will we be attacked?"

She shook her head. "The Pendant. It will make the city fly. Don't you remember what it does?"

Dertujia gaped. "But they're your items. You already lost one. If we use it to …"

Leahnina wrapped her arm around Dertujia. "I have everything I need in my hands right now. I didn't know at the time, but I wanted these items for this. For Gaiarigona. For Aieranolea. Let the city fly, and the Flitelikes will have peace. It's because Bynneeshia brought these beings into life that they're angry. Eropus' curse works only on her creations. But if left alone, if given peace, they will create their own offspring. Ones that might be free of the automatic anger that comes with their blood."

Dertujia felt a smile creep up on his cheeks. More, the beings Eropus cursed living happy lives would piss him off. His stupidity would be stopped. Just one, but a small victory was better than what had been happening recently. All the wins that Eropus had gotten. The taunting. This would fix one of his deeds.

"As long as you're okay with losing your toys," Dertujia teased.

Leahnina slapped his bicep, letting it land and trail down to his elbow. "I'm fine. Besides we could use a new bed to stay in. A night before we take down Eropus."

Dertujia couldn't agree more. Besides there was something else. Just like Eropus was targeting what Neesh did, he was also doing the same with Dertujia. It was only a matter of time before Aieranolea was threatened. No matter how much they were doing it to themselves first.

Leahnina handed him the pendant.

He shook his head. "You do it. You're the one giving this to them. I am pretty full of myself already."

Leahnina gave him a kiss and spun around, letting the pendant rise into the sky. It flickered in the sun and sped up to the top of one of the buildings. It settled down.

Then the whole city shook.

It moved and breathed, fluttered and flew like it had wings. The ground was left far behind. The Flitelikes squawked their indignation, but they caught on.

Like night and day's difference, suddenly peace came over their faces. They swooped down as the city took its place in the sky.

It was done.

Chapter Eleven

Almost immediately the Flitelikes grabbed ahold of the four and flew them off the island in the sky.

"What?" Cetphur burst out as he was picked up.

"We're no longer welcomed," Xorna said, looking like she had just sucked on a sour humfruit.

Leahnina laughed. The only one who knew what was going on. "No, we're being honored."

To Dertujia's surprise, they carried them over and under. Then he saw. The buildings had entrances from underneath. This city *had* been in the sky once. Flown to. Someone had downed it. And it wasn't hard to see who. Eropus had planned this to play with Dertujia again. The Flitelikes would have tried to rip the group apart, and they would have had to kill them. Dertujia would have killed Neesh's creation, and Eropus would have laughed at losing both problems.

But unfortunately for Eropus, Dertujia had Leahnina.

The inwards of the buildings all connected. Light shined right through making a city of light.

The Flitelikes put the four on some glass couches and settled down. Their wings reached towards each other as they hugged.

"We're flying!" one said. "We're home."

In the sky. Dertujia laughed.

For the rest of the day, the Flitelikes flew in and out bringing supplies to help their future and guests. Not one was younger than adulthood. Their celebrations included a whole lot of love, to make up for the hate they had always had. Which meant soon this city would be bringing in a whole lot of babies.

Once again, the group was pampered and spoiled. Dertujia was asked to stay on for a week so they could figure out who could rule this place now. Dertujia and Leahnina put their free time to good use. But they weren't the only ones.

Cetphur and Xorna were falling in love. Cetphur put into motion his courtship plans. He was an old-fashioned type of guy, believing in marriage first. Since the next stop was Eropus' place, and they had no real clue if they'd return, Cetphur made his intentions known to Xorna.

On the fifth night, after Dertujia and Leahnina had separated from them, Cetphur finished talking about the king Ingborn who had taken his throne in Firebranch and was worried about where his firstborn son had gotten off to, he stopped and looked into Xorna's eyes.

"Xorna, let's walk. The city is quiet. The birds are asleep."

Xorna chuckled. “They’d hate you calling them birds.” But her eyes were shiny.

“I say it with affection. They like it,” Cetphur excused himself. “Don’t worry I asked them. But I have another question.”

And they walked.

The city flying in the sky felt more underground than Gaiarigona. The buildings were dark now that the sun had stopped its shine. No night air touched them, and the sky had a roof.

There was no sound except the pitter patter of their feet, and the only scent was the sky roses, blooming even after the crash and subsequent revival of the city. A sweet perfume. Xorna enjoyed it more than ever, because Cetphur’s question had a loaded weight.

The fact that he was waiting to ask her just weighed it down more. Xorna was scanning her mind, trying to figure out her answer. Her journeys with Dertujia had been escapades. Enjoyable adventures, even the not so enjoyable ones. The arguments they shared had been almost legendary.

Dertujia and she were like two sides of a coin, opposites as similar as their desires were. Xorna knew Dertujia inside and out. But Cetphur? He was a mystery as like to her as he was. He valued life. He would have sided with her about the centaur. He even said as much when she told him the tale.

But his thoughts were not known automatically, not like Dertujia’s. Cetphur’s mind was intriguing, and she never knew what to expect. He was exciting and stimulating.

As they walked, they climbed a little higher so the glass grew thinner, and they could look out at the darkened landscape far below. A silver stream reflected from whatever light was in the sky matched by blocks of black shadows.

Xorna glanced at her companion's rugged face. He was certainly her type, the kind she would have searched for to spend an evening with. Yet, neither mentioned the inn. Neither talked about it. Their newfound relationship was too important, too precious to only focus on the matter of the body.

"What is your question?" Xorna asked, trying to sound like it wasn't important. She went to work braiding her silver hair. He took her hand, and her hair fell down, caressing her shoulders.

He stared at her for a few minutes. "Normally, I'd ask if it was allowed that I start courting you. I'd plant flowers that grew to mark our days together. Though I am far from Firebranch, I'd still want to do its customs and take you to the forest and ask the trees for their blessing."

Xorna kept her tongue. Asking the trees? Such a weird idea. But her heart was too big. Cetphur was falling into it.

"But you can't?" she asked.

Cetphur shook his head. "No. We don't have enough time. I've done a lot of research on Eropus. He's connected with this world. When all the other gods died, he lived because he is tied to the earth. I don't like the odds against us. We leave tomorrow. Leahnina tells me we should reach Eropus' land in only a week. On the way, well, I expect us to be waylaid. You told me of your journey. First, that army. Then Dubruck? This journey is fraught with struggle. One of us might not live. We might lose our friends we travel with.

"So, my question drives straight to the heart. Will you marry me here? In Aieranolea? Will you give me your hand in marriage and let us celebrate our love sooner rather than later? If we survive, I will court you … Wherever we will live."

Xorna knew this was coming. Still, nothing had prepared her for the joy that was coming into her. She had never considered marriage. Not once. It seemed a shackle to tie her down. How could she live her life if she had a husband and children at home?

But everything had changed. Surely, she'd earn enough of a reprieve if she helped end Eropus' threat. Xorna had saved so many. Maybe it was her turn.

"Cetphur, do you miss your home?"

She startled him. He expected a yes or a no. But Xorna wasn't going to give in that easily. She loved him. But not once before had she given in without some kind of fight.

"Yes. I do. It is so beautiful. The river. The chasm nearby. The forest. I miss my family. I even miss hating the nobility. Why do you ask?"

"I have no home. Long, long ago, my village was attacked and destroyed when I was but a child. A group of wanderers took me and my sister in. They taught me how to fight and protect her. When I met Dertujia, they had all come down with an affliction, so Dertujia and I became a family. Our home was where we went, and my sister and I settled in his village. But it was never truly home for me. I want a new one.

"Firebranch was flawed. I'd like to fix it. I'd like to live there with you, as my husband."

Cetphur's mouth slowly widened to a grin until he was positively laughing. "You said yes! I got a yes. That was a yes, right?"

Xorna nodded and leaned forward to kiss him. They held each other with passion but then let go.

"I want to be married before," Cetphur said. "I want our union to be as husband and wife."

She nodded. For the first time in her life, she agreed with waiting. It would be pure, not the sordid relationships that had left behind broken hearts and a few regrets.

The two separated after a few more kisses. The next day, Xorna asked Dertujia if he'd delay leaving until they could find someone to marry the two.

Dertujia snorted. "You don't need a legal union. It wouldn't be valid in Firebranch anyway, as the royalty there probably have to approve the marriage. And in our own Shymis, Xorna, anyone can marry a couple as long as they approve."

"Will you marry me?" Xorna asked.

Dertujia gave her a wink. "But I thought you wanted to marry Cetphur."

She gave him a warning glare. She was so serious about this!

"Okay, okay, I will. Leahnina, will you be a marriage watcher?"

Leahnina was sitting on a bench against the glass, letting the morning sun filter through to light up her hair. Dertujia watched her for a few seconds. Her hair was … blonder? The past few nights, he did notice that her skin was growing in invisibility. No. He had to ignore it. Surely, there was a stop. An end to her disappearing.

"Leahnina? Is there something wrong?"

Leahnina looked away from the glass and gave a big grin. "Nothing at all. Let's celebrate. We don't have time for a lot. But I'm sure the Flitelikes will bring flowers and songs."

Leahnina was proven right.

They even found a perfect place to hold the ceremony. At the top of the city there was an area that was through one of the glass buildings. Outside and looking down into the valley below. High cliffs and hills that scooped out showing grass and far off trees. The area was quickly decorated with gems, flowers, and more.

The sun shined on all, exploding the area with color.

A Flitelike made a dress for Xorna of simple gray, the bridal color of Shymis, and Cetphur got the red marriage robes of Firebranch.

Simple, really, not even near as elaborate as it would have been in his hometown. Of course, neither was Xorna's dress. This was the best they could rummage up, thanks to the quickness of the wedding.

Dertujia stood on a raised dais and placed his hands out. Inside, something stirred. He was happy for his friend. Xorna deserved happiness. But what could come of this? Separation, definitely. They already had told him of their plans to go back to Firebranch, the city that had thrown them out. Xorna wanted to fix it. Cetphur wanted to go home.

But as Dertujia tried his best to remember the wedding vows of his city, which he had witnessed only once, there was more. Leahnina hadn't jumped to approve. She had acted like she was happy, but she wasn't. Yes, something was very wrong.

"Will you entwine your lives together?" he asked. "Will your pain be his pain? His worries be yours? Will you think of the right way first? You first, because taking care of yourself will take care of him. Then him. Then others?"

Xorna peered into Cetphur's eyes. Her face was round with pleasure and happiness.

"Of course."

Dertujia repeated the question to Cetphur who instantly said yes, even over Dertujia's words. He finished up, feeling the loss. This was over. Xorna and he were no longer partners.

This had always been a possibility. Whether Dertujia had chosen to settle down or if Xorna had, a separation was in their future. Dertujia had even considered marrying Xorna on a few occasions just to prevent that future. But he knew they'd kill each other if they were husband and wife. Cetphur and Xorna fit together. If anyone could save Firebranch from the assault of royalty, it was them.

But all that happened after Eropus …

The ceremony ended, and Dertujia told them in his and Leahnina's eyes they were married. As Cetphur and Xorna kissed in a tight embrace, Dertujia leaned over to Leahnina. "What did you see?"

Leahnina smiled at him. "Oh, silly. I see love. A future. Lots of love and happiness."

Dertujia breathed a sigh of relief. He had been worried. It must have been something else on Leahnina's mind. He gave a look at Leahnina's hair as the lovebirds went to consummate their union. The group was leaving in the afternoon.

"Your hair is blonder," he said. She gestured him to the outside garden, and they watched the ground as the city floated. It wasn't moving, just pushed with the breeze but like it had an invisible anchor, it stayed in its position.

"Your love could strip the color right out of me," she teased and kissed his hand.

But Leahnina wasn't the same. She wasn't the boisterous girl that had followed him around. The fan that had loved him. She still loved him of course, but she had grown quiet, subdued.

"Leahnina, you'd tell me if something was wrong, wouldn't you?"

Leahnina nodded. She shook her hair to let it fall out and tickle Dertujia's arm. "As long as we can prevent it, you know everything."

That response wasn't at all what he wanted.

"Eropus is coming closer. We will be at his home. Do we go in swinging? I can age him, make him lose some defense—at least for a little while."

Dertujia sat back, holding Leahnina's hands and pondering that. This was what he should have been planning with Xorna. Things were changing. "Leahnina, I am a warrior. You are not. I have to admit, I don't know what that makes us. When Xorna and I went into battle, we'd agree or disagree, but she knew the consequences of what would happen."

Leahnina laughed and brought a piece of the cake to her mouth. The Flitelikes had made chocolate with yellow roses. It was decadent and wonderful. Leahnina quickly put a piece in his lips, and he was silenced.

"You forget, I know everything. I know the consequences. I can be your equal."

Dertujia swallowed and smiled. "Then maybe we should be married as well. Xorna has always had to one up me. But I can follow her example. Will you marry me?"

Leahnina nodded. "Yes, I will. I have wanted to answer for days."

It was sure hard to keep a secret from her. She knew his question. By Hetahaunder, she probably already saw them married way back in Shymis. He knelt down beside her and started making the same vows he had asked Cetphur and Xorna. Leahnina and he needed no watchers or legalities. They would always be married in their hearts.

Leahnina made the same vows.

As they joined Xorna and Cetphur much later, he realized that Leahnina hadn't really answered his question about Xorna's future.

But two wedded couples were flown down again, and this time Cetphur didn't complain about the carriage.

No one did much of anything. The ground turned black under them. Not the black of shadows. Nor the black of the machines in Tajfac. No, it was the black of death. Eropus' land was coming.

No people were on the road. There was no road. Trees that were black. Not from fire. There was no natural destruction. The trees were just sapped of strength.

Worse, there were no attacks. Not a one. But Eropus had sent an army after them. Then a war runner. Finally, he had downed the flying city. What, had he just given up?

Dertujia doubted it. The air was grim. They held each other's hands. Not only the couples. All of them. Even the sky turned black as they entered the peaks of Eropus'.

Dertujia had to force out words. He could barely breathe. "I can barely sense my shadows here. There's no natural life. I'm not sure I can use anything around."

"It's the same with my fire," Cetphur said. The two shared a look. If they couldn't use their abilities easily, something was very, very wrong.

The journey continued until everywhere they looked the world was black. The mountains crept ever higher. But they were lovely in their own way. The mountains weren't evil. The ground wasn't. It was Eropus' evil stain that marked it up. If not for him, this would be an ideal place.

Dertujia could see barren waterfalls, water stopped and halted just by the presence of the god. Six or seven would cascade down the mountains. In the center there was a dual peak, but only a tad separated, pressed into almost one line. At the base was a house. Of course, house was a generous term. It grew almost as big as the mountain it was near. The entrance was a courtyard.

Dertujia's carriage faltered, though the sun from far away wasn't gone.

The group tumbled to the ground and walked the rest of the way.

The courtyard had an open gate. Thick wood with lots of pointed metal. Dertujia and Xorna drew their swords, but Eropus was nowhere to be found. Six fountains all in a row guided any visitor inside. Another door stuck out of a wall of metal.

"Where is he?" Leahnina asked. "Shouldn't he be here?"

Dertujia didn't show his nerves. When a fortune teller asks what's going to happen, one didn't feel safe. Not at all.

"Cetphur," Xorna said and tossed him a short dagger.

He caught it and looked at it. "I have my own weapons, but I rely on my fire."

"You can't have too many arms here," she said.

Leahnina gave her a tight grin. "And me? I have none."

"Oh fine!" Xorna exclaimed and produced a dagger from her boot. Xorna was armed and ready.

Dertujia had never imagined that his own powers wouldn't be much use here. He had gotten the abilities for this very purpose.

"I thought going to Dragon Tower would help us," he muttered to Leahnina. "It will do us no good."

Leahnina squeezed the dagger in one hand, Dertujia's in the other. "The powers weren't for Eropus. He won't be hurt by powers."

Dertujia did his best to force all his fears down. Eropus was somewhere. If he wouldn't come out, the four would go in.

"Come," Dertujia said. "Obviously the coward hides from us."

When they opened the door, he had to take a breath. This house was as big as a city. Statues were everywhere. Of the same man. Eropus.

"Quite the arrogant one," Dertujia mentioned.

They walked forward, small in the enormous space. The ceiling went into the mountains. Millions of tiles held onto the cliffs and fought back the mountain. Pillars acted as supports, but they were bigger than trees, and even if Dertujia had six men with him he wouldn't have been able to reach around the base.

Staircases were everywhere. Dertujia could tell four of them went into towers. The steps were like poured rock, smooth but cold.

"This is nonsense," Xorna exploded. "We could spend a year exploring this place and still not find him. If he doesn't come out, we will …"

"I bid you welcome," a voice called.

Xorna gave a vicious grin. "Ah, how nice of him."

Like black and brown cream dripping from the ceiling, Eropus appeared. He was as thin as ever. He wore a one piece of cloth over his shoulder that fell down to his feet which were bare. His black hair, wild and untamed, whipped around his face. He had his fingers pressed together on top of his chin, and a glint was in his eyes.

"I am Eropus. I have met the red-haired shadow man. But I haven't met the other three."

Dertujia had spent a lot of time on this journey. He had expected to come after the villain every day, but he hadn't thought about what to do when he got there. In the past, lots of villains did the first move. Attacked. Ran. Begged for leniency.

But Eropus acted as if this was a party. That he had invited them there. But he knew that Dertujia was here to end his threat. He did, didn't he? That was why he had sent the bad after them.

"I am Xorna," she announced, noticing Dertujia's puzzlement. "This is my husband, Cetphur, and that's Leahnina."

Eropus walked slowly. The splat of his bare feet against the floor was sickening. Disgusting. Dertujia couldn't say why.

"Ah, you control fire, don't you?' he asked.

Cetphur looked unnerved. "Yeah. What do you control?"

Eropus didn't answer. He passed him by to walk closer to Xorna. "You control naught."

She nodded. All of them had been thrown out of their comfort zone. This wasn't going at all as they expected. It was almost humorous that Xorna and Dertujia still held their swords out and that Leahnina and Cetphur held daggers. It was like attacking a host.

But Dertujia gripped his sword tight. There were shadows in this place. And he heard them.

Urging caution. Speaking to him. Nobody else heard. "*Death, Master. He has killed our bearers. We remain. Death ...*"

Eropus interrupted the shadows only Dertujia could hear. "And the reborn goddess," he said looking at Leahnina. Now Dertujia was getting angry.

Eropus didn't look *nice* when he talked to her. He separated his hands and pulled her hand up to his mouth.

"Padonum, we were enemies once. Do you remember when I slit your throat? I bathed in your blood. I felt it in every crevice of my body."

Finally! Dertujia knew what to do. He knocked him away from Leahnina who was recoiling in disgust.

"God, we have come to either command you or kill you. It's your choice."

Eropus giggled and whipped his hair around. "You have come because I have allowed it. Because I like you being in my home. It's much better when you can rip people apart on your own turf."

Dertujia had heard enough. He ran towards him. Sword out. If it weren't for killing Dubruck mercilessly this might be a harder choice. Eropus hadn't done anything yet. He only threatened. Dertujia had heard a lot of villains threaten over the years. And they were the best ones, because they were true cowards using words to hide their fears.

Dertujia didn't care. He had to strike.

His sword never met its mark. Eropus caught the tip and gave him a tight smile.

"And I thought we could be friends."

"You tainted the Flitelikes, sided with war runners. Almost stole my beautiful bride away from me. I will not hesitate." He struggled and pushed his sword further down. Eropus looked intrigued. A crooked smile.

"I believe you could kill me."

Dertujia smiled grimly and yanked the sword down. It slit Eropus' arm, but he danced away.

"Blood. The most humbling liquid. We both have it."

Dertujia looked towards Xorna. "Easy."

She nodded but looked as if she couldn't believe this would end so well.

Leahnina fell. Dertujia ran over to her.

"What is it?"

"You …"

Eropus ran at Dertujia. He couldn't do much but deflect his hand. Yes, Eropus was using his hands, sharp as blades now.

Xorna rushed to help out.

Cetphur thought the battle was decided. He rushed to help Leahnina, looking for a wound of any kind on her. But she was in shock. She just kept saying, "No. No."

Dertujia gave Xorna a look. She got it. As Eropus came down the middle, they split and went behind, landing a wound on his back. He was quick.

"No!" Leahnina shrieked.

Dertujia risked a look back, but Eropus took advantage. A slice down the back of Dertujia's head. If Dertujia hadn't moved, Eropus would have gotten his ear. Dertujia fell to the floor.

"Distractions, so useful."

"Shut up!" Xorna yelled and they continued the fight.

Dertujia shook his head, a little dizzy.

"You opened the pit. You let them out," Leahnina said. "Don't, Xorna! Don't!"

Dertujia had no clue what was going on. Cetphur had joined Xorna's side and were trying to drive the giggling Eropus back.

Leahnina crawled over and cradled Dertujia and let his blood pour on her. "Dertujia, Eropus is *connected* to the earth."

Dertujia knew that.

"It's his strength and weakness," Leahnina said trying to stop his bleeding. "He is invincible. Any wound given him destroys the earth."

Dertujia felt like more than Eropus' blade had hit him. This was all pointless then?

"He knew that. That's why we weren't heavily deterred. He can't be defeated. He was just playing with us. Wearing us down until he could kill us."

Dertujia watched the battle. Eropus was just dodging and running. The wound had sealed up. Eropus wasn't wounded. But Dertujia saw blood on both Xorna and Cetphur.

"There has to be a way." Dertujia was *not* leaving here as the loser, not after all this time. He'd win. He had to!

"Yes. There is a way. My box. The Padonum's Box. It is the key."

Dertujia hated not beating this god himself, but he'd take anything. He couldn't allow the god to run rampant.

"Then give it here. I guess we can lose the last one." He gestured for her to give it to him.

"Xorna will die."

That stopped him. "What? I thought we …" A scream from Cetphur made him snap his head up. Too fast. His head hurt. Cetphur had gotten a wound on his leg. But Xorna had Eropus on the retreat again. He was dancing behind the large pillars.

"We prevented that."

"It is what it has to be. Xorna will be dead if Eropus is. I don't know why. I can't tell. But she dies with Eropus."

Dertujia closed his eyes. Despair hit. He couldn't kill Xorna.

"And it will do worse. The wounds are on the earth. Healed on Eropus still ache in the lands. It's not good. But to kill Eropus, you'll have to rip him apart. It will destroy the world too."

Dertujia stood up. It was over. He pretended it was for the world. He didn't want to rip it apart. He didn't know the consequences. But as soon as Leahnina had said Xorna would die, his mind was made up.

What had Eropus done to them? Nothing until Dertujia started hunting him. "If he isn't stopped …"

Leahnina shook her head. "Beings will be hurt. Bynneeshia will die. I can't see much. I'm looking."

Dertujia grabbed her arm. "No. Don't strain your abilities. You don't need to. We're going."

He stood up and looked at Xorna and Cetphur. "Cease!" he boomed out.

Xorna looked back but listened. She looked at him like he was insane.

"Come now, Xorna, peace at all costs, remember. Cetphur stay your blade."

Cetphur was bleeding profusely. Xorna had red all over her. Eropus walked back over to the group and cocked his head.

"Peace? Now that I didn't see coming."

"We will leave you if you leave us alone."

Eropus walked up to Dertujia. The two of them made a strange contrast in the big and empty city house. Black hair wild, red hair calm. Blood on Dertujia's temple. Nothing marring the god's skin.

"A deal?" he asked. His sharp eyes roved Dertujia's face, looking for something more.

"A compromise. You haven't hurt mortals. Keep it that way. The battles of the gods aren't meant for mortals. If you will let us leave, we will not bother you."

Eropus spilled his head back and forth, head hitting shoulder until he nodded. "Of course. I do have other things to do. But a coward doesn't impress me."

Dertujia held himself back. He wouldn't lose Xorna. Never. It was bad enough to lose her to marriage, but she would be out there. They could visit each other. He could see her children if she had them, and she could see his.

"Call me what you will. This is over."

Eropus walked backwards but kept his face forward. "Okay. So, it is. Leave."

Dertujia gestured to his group, beaten but victorious in their own way to turn their back on the god.

As they walked along the big area, Dertujia felt empty. Lost. He had let a bad guy live. What was he …

"Dertujia, look out!"

Eropus slammed him into the floor, bashing his fist into his head, back and legs. Over and over again, until Dertujia could barely move.

As he lost consciousness, he heard that voice. That slimy voice.

"Never turn your back on a god, puny mortal."

Then he went out.

Pain. A red haze of pain, and that was all.

Blessed darkness, his old friend claimed him.

Chapter Twelve

The light hurt. A white dagger slicing his eyes. "My poor champion," a voice soothed.

He didn't want to wake up. The pain was on the edge, but it was knifing through him, ripping him awake.

"Ow," he said, trying to sit up.

"No. Don't. You are broken. You need to let the wounds heal."

Dertujia groaned and blinked his eyes open. But it was tough going. They were against the light. Brightness hated him. He tried again and again, finally to see Neesh holding his hand.

He didn't know where he was. But it was bright. The wind told him he was somewhere far away from Eropus' place. There had been no wind there. "Leahnina," he whispered. Great, was his throat caved in too?

"Eropus smashed every part of your body," Neesh explained. "Your friends screamed out for me. I fought through Eropus' powers to find you. You're at my home now."

"Leahnina!" he said again, stronger. His throat felt better.

"You were wounded. Every step towards health will have to go through stages as my healing abilities help you." Her hand caressed his brow.

"Goddess," he said stiffly, "either tell me where Leahnina is, or I leave and find her myself."

"She is not far. She wouldn't leave you. I had to make her sleep. But your kiss will awaken her. All of them would have died watching over you. I have made it so they slept."

Dertujia felt a bit better. In all sorts of horrendous pain, but better. They were alive. "Did Eropus hurt them?"

"No. Just you."

Dertujia considered something. "Will I have to kiss all my friends?"

Neesh laughed, though she sounded sad. "No. A hug or a shoulder shake will suffice. I don't know what happened."

Dertujia went over the battle in his head. He couldn't recall the last part, where Eropus hit him from behind. But he could remember giving up.

"Neesh," he said, trying to sit up, but gave up that goal too. Minor wounds were healing at light speed, but complete fractures were much slower. Faster than it'd take normally, but they still hurt. "I am sorry. But your battle will have to remain. I apologize. I didn't know."

Neesh sat down on a golden branched chair. It was woven from a tree Dertujia had never seen before. Not that the beauty mattered. Everything on him hurt. If it wasn't for the pain, he'd notice that the room he was now in was round, going up into a tower, but it was made of a soft violet color. On the ceiling were pictures that his eyes could take in, if they weren't crunched.

"You didn't know what?"

Dertujia tried to move, but razors sliced his bones. He tried not to move. He looked at the pictures. Gods and goddess were painted up there. Golden and glowing. One brought his attention. Padonum. The one who saved them. The one who had been murdered by Eropus.

"I didn't know that Eropus' death would destroy the world around us."

Neesh snapped her fingers, and a bowl appeared in her hands, giving off steam and smelling of home. But his stomach wouldn't eat that. It was still raw and bruised. "Drink this broth. It is the last from the fruit of the gods, but I want you to have it. I wasn't aware myself, my young champion. Your friend told me. It is what it is. You should not feel guilty about leaving the whole world to its fate."

Dertujia kept his mouth closed, like an obstinate boy who didn't want his medicine. But Neesh kept the spoon hovering under his nose, and he couldn't help it. He opened his mouth and she fed him.

He drank it down and tried not to weep.

"Cry," she advised. "It isn't a weakness. It's a release. Do not bottle yourself up, or your future will pay."

Her comfort, her sympathy—the fact that she wasn't angry with him for failing her. It all came out in tears. Dertujia couldn't help but cry. He had never given up before. Never had he been hurt so badly.

Mortality. What an interesting concept that Dertujia didn't like at all. Yes, he had been wounded. But this went deep. He could die.

Without leaving anything but a heroic legacy behind. What was life worth when one left it so easily? It wasn't how many people he had saved. That would be lost and only remembered in books telling his story. But hadn't he read about heroes? They were fun reads but not important.

What was, was a legacy.

Somehow, Dertujia was all too glad that Neesh was okay with him giving up.

He dried his tears and finished the broth. By the time the last droplet hit his stomach, the wounds felt like just sprains not breaks. He was able to sit up.

Neesh took his hand and walked him to where his friends were.

The violet tower opened to a long hallway that connected to another tower. And that one to another hallway until it went around four times. Four towers around one gigantic courtyard holding what looked like an old court. He could see it through the clear, large windows. The area was overgrown with grass. But it held six thrones, and lots of stone tablets had made a floor.

"This is the home of the gods. Or it was. It is the pantheon. Before Eropus, we would sit there and decide what was best for mortals."

Dertujia stopped and leaned on a windowsill, a little dizzy. He was almost whole, but he was still half now. "What was best for mortals? Shouldn't they decide that?"

Neesh frowned at him. "Yes, the war runners do decide for mortals, don't they? And the kings. The emperors or the dakchins as the Flitelikes call them. Funny, I thought that's what you were fighting against your whole life."

Dertujia couldn't answer her. She was right.

"The ones with power are the only ones qualified to lead, Dertujia. As well you know. Because that's what made your life. You had extra strength. You had inimitable powers even before Dragon Tower. That gave you the right to make the decisions. Let me give you an example. I watched your threads, Dertujia."

Confusing. He looked at her, feeling better. His shadows slipped under him to support him. Without his command. With his healing came his abilities restored at a greater strength. "My threads?"

Neesh clasped his shoulder and tried to help him, but he shrugged her off. He was Dertujia. He needed no help. "There is a room in this pantheon where gods can look in on destinies. It's … difficult." She put a hand to her head as the sun from the sinking redness hit her hair and made it gold. "Only the three sisters ever could make heads or tails of it. But Eropus could read them. I think it's how he knew you'd go to Gaiarigona."

Dertujia glared at her. "And how you knew he did what he did there, correct?"

Neesh stared at him. She looked as innocent and sweet as a child. Dertujia lost his anger. "I only know a little. But you are destined for greatness, Dertujia. You are above. And you know it. My example is the centaur.

"I know it was you and Xorna who chased it far from another village. I know you had decided to stop it."

Dertujia wondered where she was going with this. It troubled him more than he liked to admit that she was telling him something he was starting to believe. The ones with power had a right to rule. But not Eropus. There was a problem with his belief. Eropus didn't have a right to rule.

And yet he did rule now. Dertujia had left him alive.

"You could have let it roam."

Dertujia turned to stare at her. Leaning hard against the window behind him, looking at the goddess. He had been in awe of her when he first saw her, and yet he had walked up and talked to her like equals. And that's the way he felt now.

"If it had roamed, it would have killed people, destroyed crops, which would have made children go hungry, and that centaur might have made more pain."

Neesh cocked her head, beatific in her judgment. "And so, you chose to kill the centaur over the people he would have killed. You chose."

Dertujia was silent. She was right. He had. He wasn't threatened by the centaur. It hadn't been defense. Even now, the centaur's corpse probably hung on the fence near Shymis. Xorna had argued with him. She had wanted it let go. Dertujia wouldn't have been able to live with himself had he spared the beast.

But he had let Eropus live, and why? To save Xorna. As an added benefit, the world was safe too. But in that very reality, Eropus had the most power, and so he still ruled.

A tricky puzzle.

"I'd like to go home," Dertujia said. He heard it in his voice. He was tired. He was also done. His mother would scold. His father would be disappointed. But Dertujia was finished fighting. Finished being a hero. Finished making the choices for everyone else.

He had almost died. Even now as he walked, aches echoed through his body. Not just Eropus' wounds. But also the cut he had gotten from the war runner. The injury he had to nurse thanks to the evil Octogobs.

Those wounds were a part of him now. He wanted to go home.

Neesh took his hand. "And so you shall. I appreciate you trying. No other mortal has done the same. I will move you home. And your friends where they want to go. It's a trial for me, but not so hard."

Dertujia was glad. He could have easily summoned shadows, but this way would be faster. He wouldn't have to go any length of distance, and who knew how far the pantheon was from Shymis.

"Thank you, goddess. What will happen to you? To the Flitelikes?"

Neesh didn't answer him. She turned away with a hidden frown. Dertujia couldn't bother himself to ask what was wrong. He had earned his rest.

Neesh brought him to another room, far down the hall from one of the towers. It was a room of beds, an infirmary, maybe, but what the gods needed with that kind of thing Dertujia didn't know. Only tiny windows were here, and right next to each other were his friends, each one on an elaborate bed made of silk with marbles on the ends of the blankets. Clear and shiny. White soft pillows were under their heads. He went towards Leahnina first.

He couldn't help but care about her foremost.

She was asleep, her black-blonde hair—a lot more blonde than ever before—splayed out across her ivory pillow. Her hands were clasped across her breast, and she wore a long purple gown that swept the bed. She looked innocent and lovely in her silence.

But he disliked her eyes being closed. It was too much like death this sleep. He had a strange thought. What if she was dead?

He leaned down and kissed his beloved, and her eyes shot open. She focused on him and leaped upwards, grabbing him around the chest. Her tears fell fast and unending.

"Dertujia, you were so …"

He took her hands to his breast and kissed her long and soft. "My wife, we can go home now. Shymis is waiting for us."

Her eyes filled with hope and happiness. But it wasn't enough for him to show that he was fine. Even Neesh's assurances didn't help. Leahnina had to poke him in all the places injured.

Pleasant as well as painful. Her touch could still make him gasp. "Now, Leahnina, we can do this later. The goddess has offered to take us home. It's over. Our journey is done. No more hurt feet."

Leahnina grinned as she remembered the beginning. How far she had come. From the woman who complained to the silent partner who spoke great import whenever she talked. Dertujia missed the chatterer but loved every part of the woman he married.

He, too, had become more silent.

Dertujia shook Cetphur awake and then Xorna. The hugs and reunion lasted for a while. Neesh brought them food and drink, and a going-away party was thrown for both couples. Xorna and Cetphur were going home to Firebranch. Leahnina and Dertujia to Shymis.

When it was time, Dertujia took his old friend in his arms and held her ferociously. "I will miss you. Our travels together. Our war."

"We have a new one," Xorna said, muffled, but he heard tears on her voice. "Cetphur and I do not go home to a willing place. The royalty has to pay for its crimes. We need to fight back against them."

Dertujia wished he could say he'd help. But he couldn't. He looked across the room at Leahnina. Her face was alight with happiness. She was happy to go home. He was too. He couldn't go with Xorna. Their fighting days were over.

"You'll be fine," he said stiffly. "Just remember to punch them hard if they disagree."

Xorna chuckled and pulled away, her shiny eyes looking up at him. "Dertujia, I don't go to Firebranch to fight them. I go to war with peace. Without weapons. We will talk them into giving back as much as they got."

Dertujia smiled. "Good luck with that. If you need me …" He couldn't finish. He wouldn't come. She knew it. They had been partners for too long. She knew he was finished. And, more, she understood.

"Dertujia, you are owed this break. You have been … hurt."

The most uncomfortable times were when either of the women in his life brought up how badly he was injured. The fear in their eyes, the what-if questions, would play out long in their lives. Eropus could have killed Dertujia. Xorna knew that. So, she forgave him his breakage of their partnership and awarded his rest with no resentment.

Dertujia didn't wish things were different. He was ready to lay down his sword. He only wished he felt guilty about this. He'd only see Xorna if there was peace, as he wouldn't come to Firebranch as its enemy.

Finally, the hugs had ended, the goodbyes were done, and the four were holding their traveling bags, their cloaks, and standing in front of Neesh.

"I send you home to Firebranch," she said to Xorna and Cetphur. "May you have luck with your endeavors, and know that you have my favor."

Then she kissed the tips of her fingers and blew a ball of light off towards Xorna and Cetphur. Dertujia had only a second for one more quick goodbye, but then she was gone. For the last ten years, he hadn't gone to bed without knowing where she was. Whether on the opposite side of the fire from him or in another room in an inn. She was always nearby. Like a sister.

Now it was time to grow up and be on his own again.

"I'm going to miss them," Leahnina said. "And I know you will too."

He squeezed her hand. "But time changes all things. This is the end of one life and the beginning of another."

He nodded to Neesh who once again kissed her fingers and brought that light. It enveloped them, and Neesh stood alone.

"Oh, Dertujia, if only you knew how much would come. Your destiny isn't finished. Not for a very long time."

Then she sat down and wept. She wept for Dertujia's future. She wept for hers. And she wept for the world's.

***

Shymis sat like a jewel in the night, shiny and welcoming. Dertujia couldn't believe he was back. He walked with Leahnina holding her hand as he headed towards his parents' home.

"We'll have to get a house," Dertujia said.

Leahnina laughed. "With what money?"

He frowned and wiggled her hand. "Okay, I'll have to get a job. Or maybe run a farm. What do you think?"

Leahnina turned her cute little nose up at him. "No, thank you. I think I'll tell fortunes. I can get a lot of coin that way."

Dertujia felt his brow tighten. "And what will I do? What is my future?"

Leahnina sighed. "I can only tell little stuff. I …"

Dertujia remembered her disappearing body. He got it. She was retiring in more than one way. She couldn't just keep telling the future. It robbed her of her very skin.

"If I just tell some villagers things about lost items, true loves, and so on and so forth, it will give us money."

"That's a risk I will never take. It's up to me to take care of us. Forget using that ability. Please."

Leahnina nodded. She looked sad. But she understood the cost of her own abilities.

Dertujia watched the road disappear. Finally, he was at the garden outside his parents' house. "What shall I do?" he asked, but he wasn't asking the future.

"You're strong," she said. "You could raise horses. They get money."

Dertujia quickly agreed, though it sounded dreadful.

"Oh, also, I've heard about some steeds far away. You could own a whole different kind. There are large birds called Koorsgalds. Maybe a Reathmop from—"

He held up his hand. Leahnina was trying. He would too. But he was damned if he'd talk any more about raising disgusting animals tonight.

"Then there are the shadow beasts," Leahnina quickly added, giving him an understanding smile.

Now, that did sound good. But first things first.

Dertujia knocked on his parents' door and waited.

His mother came out. Her lined eyes relaxed when she saw him.

"Dertujia, you're home! And Leahnina! You too. How did it go? Tell us all about it." She pushed him through the door, letting Leahnina follow. "Your father's asleep but he'll want to wake up for this."

Some things hadn't changed.

Another party broke out, and Dertujia reveled in it this time. Who knew when the next party in his honor would be? Leaving behind Eropus and that warrior life also meant leaving behind praise.

He was okay with that. As he told his parents about his marriage to Leahnina, they laughed. He felt better than ever.

This had never been his journey. It had been his parents'. Now he finally could make a life his way.

And he welcomed whatever future came with Leahnina.

But as he told his parents about his new life, they cried.

"Son!" Brani exclaimed. "There are a whole lot of people who need your help. You can't just give up on them."

Dertujia narrowed his eyes and again at his father shaking his head.

"Mother, there are forces in every land that work against bad people. Laws and order. I am not needed."

Kaytal crossed his arms and leaned far away from the table they sat at. Dertujia then noticed a lot of new things that weren't here before. Rich vases, silver water jugs, paintings of wonderful things. "You can't give up on your journey just because you're married now. You'll have to just leave Leahnina here and …"

"Father!" Dertujia said, standing up. He had expected this. Every single time he had wanted to quit before, his parents gave him the same lecture. "I almost *died.* I was broken in every bone of my body. Lacerations. If not for a goddess' help, I wouldn't be standing here."

Leahnina nodded. "He's right. I was so afraid."

Kaytal wasn't hearing it. "You don't give up riding if the horse bucks you."

Dertujia opened his mouth ready to scream. Maybe then his father would finally hear him.

To his surprise, Leahnina said something first.

"You have no choice in this. This is our life. I will not watch him die again. Never. If you will not give us your favor and blessing, you can wither and die …"

Dertujia's eyes widened, but he grinned. Leahnina was defending him. It was wonderful!

He wasn't surprised when his father looked at Leahnina, enraged that she'd dare speak to them like that. Kaytal had always been quick to temper. Dertujia took after him in a lot of ways.

Which was why the look in his father's eyes only made Dertujia refuse to let his own temper loose. It was, after all, an uncivilized way of living. Dertujia hadn't spent his life across from kings and queens without learning something. The more you stayed dignified, the more you were respected.

"I have made my decision, Father. Mother. Now, you may stay a part of my new life, or you can choose to get out. You will not ask me to fight anymore. You will not even bring up this course of action ever again. Understand?"

They were surprised. Dertujia was as well. He had never stood up for himself before. Not once. Though over the years he had many issues with this course his parents had set him on, he had plowed along like a good son.

Of course, never before had he had a cause to fight for. He looked across the table at Leahnina who had defended him. Who had mourned him. Who had stood by him through everything. He couldn't disappoint her. If he died, now, she'd be left behind. And what would he do if she died?

"What is your choice?" he asked. He had somehow risen to standing. Even though he was sure of himself, his heart beat a steady tune under his shirt. He wore no armor thanks to coming from the goddess' home. He'd never need it again.

His parents shared a glance. They sighed together and tapped the table. "Dertujia, you don't understand. We need you to … You see …" His mother was blushing. Dertujia forced himself to sit down again. He hadn't changed his determination. But he was curious about what his mother was not saying.

His father didn't look him in the eye. There was something wrong here.

"We made our livelihoods through you, son."

Dertujia had always taken for granted that his parents weren't well off. But he never asked about their jobs. As a child, they had been farmers. But the land had become overgrown, the animals lost.

"How do you receive money?" Dertujia asked.

But it was Leahnina who answered. "They share your stories." Her face was pale. She was angry. "I see it."

Dertujia tapped her elbow. She wasn't supposed to be using her gift. She quickly eased his worries. "No, this was from before. I never understood my own gifts. Now I know. They sell your tales. Like the bards do, but they have real fact and a heroic name to back them up."

The air became still. The shadows crept up around the house. Both his parents looked left and right to see faces of wolves in shadow form sniffing near their throats. Dertujia quickly controlled himself.

But he was angry. Now the shadows noticed. It was getting stranger, these powers of his. "You gained coin from my life and death situations?" he asked. Great, he sounded young. As if he had never stopped playing with toys.

"It was Darneah's idea," Brani quickly defended. "When I was pregnant with you, the farm failed. I couldn't work. It was such a hard pregnancy."

Now she was blaming Dertujia? The shadows darkened.

"She told me tales about her own child. A prodigy who had started making a name for herself in medicine. When you were born, you were so strong. You rode a horse at only two.

You learned to shoot a bow so quickly. It was only natural …"

Dertujia was standing, he had his bag over his shoulder in a heartbeat. "You sent me into battle to earn your way. You made me unbeatable to fill your pockets. I was your only son."

"Yes!" Kaytal said. "That's why you can't retire. We'll lose our way. Surely you wouldn't wish that fate on your parents."

Dertujia spun to get out of the house. The walls of his childhood home oppressed him. Tight and confined, filled with new items that weren't his, new rooms that were from his work but didn't benefit him.

"I make the choice," he said as he reached the front door. "You have no son. The only family I have is Leahnina."

He pushed the door open, slamming it against the outer wall. His parents were very lucky he didn't tear the house down with his shadows.

Chapter Thirteen

He stood under the sky. It darkened, making him lose his friends. Little pitiful spurts of yelps, and they were gone. Like they were living. Maybe they were. Hadn't he been warned by the remnants of people in Eropus' house?

"Are you okay?" the soft wonderful voice asked. It was strong. It'd be something to rely on. Something that would never leave. His partner. She had promised a while back that they'd be together for centuries. Remembering that, he felt whole. Complete.

He needed no mother or father.

"I am perfect." He reached out around her waist and brought her in for a kiss under the newly arriving stars.

"What shall we do first?" she asked after getting her breath back.

"We need a place to sleep."

He tugged on her hand, and they walked. Dertujia had the perfect place in mind. On every journey he undertook with Xorna, he had come back, entering the village on the east side. As he did, he always climbed down a simple slope full of grass and trees, and down at the base was an old, abandoned house.

The owners had died of some sickness or other, so the mayor allowed it as an up for grabs property. Anyone who wanted it could take ownership.

Problem was, nobody wanted it. The sickness had been so wretched, so horrible and contagious, just the idea of living where it once roamed was insane.

But Dertujia had always liked the area. The house was made of stone and rock, pushed together with a soft material that when it dried lasted for centuries. The grass was spotted with wildflowers. The house was big enough for a family. Dertujia knew that Leahnina loved putting patches of cloth together in order to make wearable items, and there was a room for it.

In addition, Dertujia could take the roof for practicing his shadows, as it cast some wonderful ones from the many curlicue designs on top. There was a kitchen, six other rooms, a large and amazing foyer, and long hallways. The fields around would be perfect for animals to roam.

More, it was empty and available. He'd take anything right now just to feel home. Living with his parents was out on so many levels. For one, they had revealed this night that they had never wanted him as anything but a moneymaker.

And two, he needed his own place for him and his wife. And their children.

The walk was wonderful. After having been in bed so long, he loved the feel of his legs stretching and bending to climb across the countryside. Leahnina also had slept, so she too enjoyed the walk.

"Where are we going?" she asked.

"To the Nacksun Ranch," he said.

Leahnina stopped, but he gave another tug on her hand, and she continued. "But Dertujia, the sickness …"

He gave her a grin, picked her up and spun her around. She looked lovely in the dark, her hair glinting against the many sky lights. "Come now, my love. Do you really think a sickness could take us down?"

She lost her worry in seconds. She laughed as he spun her around once more. Then he let her gently to the ground and gave a soft kiss to her forehead. "We aren't meant to die. Remember? When you were still telling the future? What you said? Centuries."

She tilted up to kiss him. But it was getting later. And their home awaited.

It took longer than he thought to get to the Nacksun … no the Dakchin Ranch. He chose the name of the Flitelikes' emperor. It sounded better. The dawn sky was pink and orange as they finally hit the shadow of the house.

"Dakchin Ranch," he said. Then he shot worried eyes at Leahnina. What if she didn't like it? He should have asked her opinion. This would be her house too. It came as a realization to Dertujia that should have been obvious. This life was no longer just him alone. Leahnina was his wife. That meant they were partners. Everything he thought now had to be duo. What Leahnina thought as well.

"That's an interesting name," she said. But she was quiet.

"Leahnina, please. Tell me if you hate it. It doesn't have to be. I thought it was nice. You know, the Flitelikes called me Dakchin. And I can't bear to call it the name of who was here before."

Leahnina silenced him with a smack to his butt. "You worry way too much. I like it. Sometimes I will be quiet, Dertujia. But it's just because I have seen so much, and I sometimes try to make sense of it all. I see … Or I *saw* one day that you would adhere to that name. I just don't know why."

Dertujia didn't mind. As long as she liked the name. "It's because our ranch will be known the world over."

Leahnina walked forward with a small smile on her face. "Maybe."

The walk tired them. Dertujia brought up a bed in the biggest room from a morning shadow far across the world. His powers were truly magnificent. They would have to get more furniture, stuff that wouldn't disappear or be at angles as the sun moved.

But for now, the two collapsed in the bed holding each other.

***

Time passed. They tried to make the farm work. Dertujia brought food forth with his shadows, again not caring where it came from. Maybe he'd be honest as money came in, but for the time being he had to steal. Dertujia and Leahnina's supplies were dwindling.

Dertujia hated to admit it, but it wasn't looking good for the two of them. The house was in need of repair. Dertujia couldn't keep his shadows working all day, and getting food, and everything else that seemed necessary. He tried to get an hour practicing with them every day to make himself stronger.

But just living brought the need for strength.

Leahnina watched from the ground as he brought up many shadows, but then yelled. "The roof!"

He quickly stopped to reach out blindly for any shadow that would hold it up.

"Dertujia, we need constructors. You're wearing yourself out."

Dertujia grunted, pulling a beam out of one wall to shore up another. It'd hold for the time being. Using a shadowy staircase, he walked down to Leahnina who held out some of the drinks he had stolen … Yes, stolen. Dertujia was a common thief. Had he been someone else, Dertujia would have gone after him and took him down.

"You look sad," Leahnina said, reaching out to massage his shoulder. Her wonderful fingers invigorated him. Gave him strength.

"It's taxing. I admit it. I thought I could do it all."

"Dertujia, maybe we're doing this wrong. Let us get money coming in, then fix the house. Then live. If we go into town …"

Dertujia sighed. Going into town wasn't something he wanted to do yet. He wanted to come as a profitable member of society not as he was. A thief who needed charity.

"And do what, Leahnina?" he asked. "We have no money."

"And we never will if we don't do something soon. Look … I didn't tell you this, because it was a sacred trust that I wasn't supposed to touch."

Dertujia's ears cocked up. "What? A scared trust?"

"My grandmother left money behind. It wasn't for me, but for my children. It is buried next to the river. Deep down in the bank."

Dertujia was constantly surprised by her. "Why haven't you told me this?"

Leahnina swished her skirt. It looked very worn. "I was told it wasn't mine. I only knew, because my children were supposed to dig it up. I tried to ignore it. But if we don't dig it up, there will be no children. It's not a lot of money, but it will buy us things we need to get started. We're not doing well, Dertujia."

He looked at his wife. She was looking thinner. So was he. Dertujia didn't like stealing regularly when he wasn't even on a journey. When he was helping the world, well, the food was just payment. But now he was just helping himself.

Dertujia rubbed his tired neck and brought up his shadow carriage. It wobbled a bit. Dertujia was exhausted.

"Let us go into town. What will we buy?"

Leahnina climbed aboard and put her head down on the back of the dark cushions. "There are lots of animals to buy. We'll just need two of each."

They were off. Dertujia sighed as he stared out around his home. It wasn't the worst place to end up. But he had once been a hero, wandering around, praised wherever he went. Living like a king, or like a Dakchin. Now they had to rob what Leahnina considered not even hers after already being thieves for weeks.

The town showed up, its cobblestone path making clattering noises as they entered between two buildings. Truth was, Dertujia rarely went into town when he came home. It had changed from when he was a boy. More construction. More homes.

Lots of children running on the streets.

When he saw a small boy run to get out of the way of his carriage, he grinned, at ease. They did what they'd have to. Dertujia needed his own children to run around. What would they be like?

The river was straight through town. Dertujia watched out the window as people stopped and stared at his shadow. He didn't see much amazement. More wariness and anger.

Was he showing off? He was just driving through town.

"Look at them. They are all envious of us." Leahnina giggled.

"Envious of the poor? How wonderful." Dertujia rolled his eyes. The river wasn't far now.

But a crowd had been gathering, matching the carriage until it was so blocked up, he couldn't even move.

"Disperse, please," he said, sticking his head out the window.

"What is this, huh?" a boy asked. He was one of the few who weren't looking hostile at it.

"My carriage. I drew it from the shadows of one far off. Would you like a ride?"

That seemed to be the thing to say. The crowd relaxed. Ah, so if he brought himself above, they hated him. If he acted like he was one of them, they accepted him. Even though not one of *them* could draw shadows out of thin air.

Dertujia calmed himself and wasted time letting people ride. He and Leahnina watched as everyone laughed and squealed at the sensation.

"They're having fun," Leahnina pointed out. "A wise strategy. If we are to be a part of this town, then we should be known not for being arrogant but for being giving."

Dertujia gave a tight smile. He wasn't better than these people. Just because he knew how to bathe. Just because he wouldn't push people out of the way just to get a chance to ride what he would anyway.

He lost his patience fast. “Okay, that’s enough. We have errands to do.” He dropped the villagers out of the carriage. They rubbed their butts and glared at him. “Hey! We weren’t done yet!”

Dertujia narrowed his eyes and snapped his fingers. The man’s shadow rose up to stare him in the face. The man quailed and shut up. Control. That’s what these whining people needed.

“Where is the animal dealer?” he asked.

The man pointed. “A few paces away from the river.”

Dertujia smiled. That was quite convenient.

The two walked the rest of the way. They ignored the people that were following them. In awe, not anger or hatred. Like Dertujia and Leahnina were being worshipped. They could stay: after all they were doing what they should.

Leahnina showed him where the money was buried. It was in a stone box, deep in the bank of the river. He burrowed down with his shadows and then dragged it up. He took a great sigh of relief when he saw the many round disks that represented value.

They walked to where the man said the animal dealer was. They smelled the place before they saw it. It was a small ranch, full of wooden fences and narrow stalls. The animals looked dreadful.

The dealer was inside fanning himself as he read a scroll. It was the popular thing to do now, read fantastic adventures. Somehow, Dertujia didn’t care to do the same. He rapped on the door to get his attention. The dealer saw him through the window, gave a smarmy smile, and ran to greet them.

There was a narrow path between the stalls. The dealer made his way towards them. Dertujia and Leahnina stayed where they were. The path looked muddy at best.

As he reached them and started shaking their hands, his mouth moved faster than a horse ran. "Hi oh, Gerdin's the name. I have little animals. I have big ones. Need a steed? I got it. Need an animal for the field. Got it. Need one to hunt. Got it!" He quieted suddenly as he looked at the people who were still following Dertujia and Leahnina. They had all caught up and settled behind them, resting on the nearby fences or stumps. Gerdin's face got less friendly. A bristly mustache wiggled as he frowned.

"What is this, then? A mob? Don't like my prices?"

Dertujia hurried to assure him. "Not at all. We are returning heroes, that's all."

Leahnina nudged him.

"Oh, yes, and I also control shadows, so that made them interested in me."

Gerdin gave an almost grin. "Shadows? Well, that is interesting. Who are you?"

"I am Dertujia. This is my wife, Leahnina."

Now Gerdin lost all suspicion and fear. But for some reason he turned on his foot and ran away, back to his house. Before Dertujia could even question what had happened, he returned with the scroll he had been reading from. "Oh, please sign this. I read all about your adventures. You are *the* hero, you know."

Dertujia and Leahnina shared a look and Dertujia read the scroll. It was a good thing that Xorna had known how to read when they had met, or Dertujia wouldn't have known what all these squiggly marks meant. His parents had kept him from the schools in the village. They were more concerned about how he swung a sword not whether he could read the scholars' works.

It didn't take long for him to realize this scroll was based on his battle with the Octogobs. He had come home exhausted. His mother and father had hung on every word. Little did he know they were committing it to memory so they could sell it.

Dertujia handed it back. "I don't know what you mean. I won't put this on a sign."

Gerdin laughed. He was starting to get on Dertujia's nerves. "No, no, no! Haven't you ever learned to put your name down?"

Dertujia glanced at Leahnina, but she was as baffled as he was.

"Your name," Gerdin repeated. "You know how to write, don'tcha?"

Dertujia wrinkled his nose. He did not. He barely knew how to read, and that was Xorna's doing. He was no bard. He didn't have to write.

Gerdin got the point. "Oh! Well, since your name is so well known, this will be easy. Just …" Gerdin ran off again. He returned as quickly. He held out a quill that looked like it had ink already in the end.

"New design," Gerdin said. "Rarely runs out of ink. Just copy me."

He put the letters down and handed the quill to Dertujia. He clumsily copied the marks, but his looked like splotches and drips.

"Wonderful!" Gerdin enthused. "I taught Dertujia how to write!"

Dertujia's bad mood was growing. Here this animal dealer, this Gerdin, was beyond happy to see him, and yet he took the attention he was giving Dertujia and quickly turned it back on himself. Dertujia liked the first attention but started to see that it was tightly wound up with Gerdin's sense of self pride.

"I am not here to 'sign' scrolls or anything else. I've come for animals. I want to start my own business."

Gerdin grew positively less friendly. "Hey, now, I'm the animal dealer in Shymis."

Dertujia leaned over Gerdin menacingly. "I want to buy two horses."

Gerdin turned his smile on. "Of course, of course. Anything else?"

Dertujia glanced around the pathetic animals who looked unhappy at best.

"I will buy everything." He ignored Leahnina's gasp. They didn't have the money for everything.

Dertujia didn't care. This wasn't how it was done. Countless times Dertujia had risked his life for this village, and Gerdin in tandem. Whenever Dertujia had saved someone before, the person would give Dertujia all sorts of supplies and help.

Whatever Dertujia wanted. If he wanted these animals, no one would stop him. Certainly not a fanatic who took Dertujia's hard work for his own.

"Leahnina, why don't you go to the strange shop."

Leahnina gave him a glance. "The Mysterious Mondger?"

Dertujia nodded. "He might have some special products."

Leahnina gave him a steady look, but then she smiled. "Of course. Do I need to leave you any money?"

Dertujia shook his head. "Not a coin."

Leahnina walked off. Half the audience followed her.

The remnants buzzed with excitement. They knew something was coming. Dertujia wouldn't disappoint. These people were the right kinds. Gerdin was the wrong. Dertujia had saved Shymis. All there should look up to him with awe, respect, and honor.

Gerdin would soon learn that.

"You will give me all these animals," Dertujia said. "Call it a charitable donation."

Gerdin sneered. "Yeah right. Thanks for coming. Have a nice day."

Dertujia clapped his hands together. The animal's shadows came together. They rolled across the yard rising up over Gerdin who shook like a leaf in the wind.

"What is that?"

"These?" Dertujia said kindly. "They are the shadows of the animals you have. The ones you starve, imprison, and sell to hunters. They don't seem happy, do they?"

Gerdin fell to his knees as the snarling shadows seeped around him.

Dertujia was doing the right thing. He knew it! There was a small bit of conscience complaining. That this wasn't right, that Dertujia didn't have the right to steal something. But when he got in touch with the animal's shadows, he felt their suffering. Gerdin paid no attention to their plights. He wasn't suited for this job.

Dertujia would take it.

"If you don't have the animals to the old Nacksun place—now known as the Dakchin Ranch—by nightfall, I will have the shadows rip you apart. Am I making myself clear?"

Gerdin was on the ground, holding his hands over his ears to stop the onslaught of shadowy growls. Dertujia took the nod to be acquiescence.

"He's incredible." Dertujia heard the words behind him. He turned with a half-smile. He wasn't sure if incredible was good or not. But beaming faces met his gaze.

"Gerdin's been abusing animals, overcharging us, and making a nuisance of himself for years," a tall woman said. "You will be a much better choice. Let's cheer Dertujia!"

Now, that was more like it.

Dertujia basked in the joy. The people crowded around and tried to touch him, some falling to his feet to praise him.

See, he told his conscience. *I did the right thing.* This was no different than the centaur. Morals were all well and good, but sometimes those with power had to choose a new way.

Sure, Gerdin owned all these animals. Dertujia had in all legalities just threatened and coerced the man into giving all to him. But Dertujia would take care of the animals. He would feed them. Care for them. *Wouldn't* sell them to hunters looking for easy prey.

No, all in all, Dertujia had made a good choice.

How could he think differently with everyone around practically carrying him on their shoulders?

Dertujia met up with Leahnina outside Mysterious Mondgers. She held a bag with four items inside. She gave him a smile.

"And what have you been up to?"

"Rectifying injustice. We'll have the animals and feed by nightfall. You?"

Leahnina held up the bag. "I got four eggs. They're so small. But supposedly they'll hatch into amazing beasts. Koorsgalds. Reathmops."

Dertujia tried to smile. He hadn't realized until then, but he'd have to take care of these animals. From morning to night. Worse, he'd have to sell them. That was how he was going to put food on the table now.

When before all he had to do was hunt outside or take the gifts given him for being a hero. Dertujia glanced at the still worshipping people who now hung on buildings and fences through the main square of the village.

Surely, he could just go about this another way. Sell the animals all at once to someone who'd take care of them. Get offerings from the villagers.

He forced a stop to that line of thinking. He was no god. And the difference between a god and a mortal getting gifts was vast. One was an offering. One was charity.

Dertujia wouldn't beg. If these people wanted to give gifts on their own …

"Can we help?" the tall woman from earlier said. "Food? Clothing?" Her eyes shot an unwilling look down at their torn and worn clothes.

Dertujia should have said no. In a few weeks, he could sell the animals and earn his own way.

But what he said was, "Yes. Anything you want to give Leahnina and me will be accepted. Come to Dakchin's Ranch and lay your offerings …" Ah, great. He went there. Well, maybe he wasn't a god. But he was close.

"Put them down on the flat rock near the entrance. In addition, we need constructors to remake our home. Bring them forth as well. And you have our gratitude."

Then he brought up his carriage, boarded it, and they were heading home again.

"Well, that went better than I thought it would," he said. A smile broke out on his face. He had started the day with nothing. Now he was relatively positive that the villagers would bring all sorts of stuff to make him rich.

"Yes," Leahnina answered. But she sounded quiet again.

"Are you embarrassed?" he asked. "Because we are not beggars. We are heroes."

Leahnina took his hand and held it. "I am not opposed to being given items. I … You'll find me silly."

Dertujia knew that was impossible. "What is it?"

"I don't want to live like this!" she exploded. "I once owned a shop. It was horrible. The greed. The bottom line. You were the only thing I looked forward to. With your gifts, soon I didn't have to work."

Dertujia remembered. He hadn't liked Leahnina at the time. Or so he thought. But he would always try to bring some pure gold or ruby gifts for her. She had sold those instead of the stupid wares.

"But now," Leahnina continued as if his thoughts were known. "There is no hero to come home and give us stuff. Only villagers who most can't afford to. I mean, what will Gerdin do without his animals? Live in poverty?"

Dertujia hadn't thought about that. Of course, the malcontent deserved it for how he treated the animals.

"It's just … life is like a loose thread. Pull on one end, and it could unravel the whole thing. I'm just beginning to understand that."

Dertujia hurried to comfort her. He took her to his side and rubbed her back. “Leahnina, don’t worry. We’ll only take the first offerings. My fame will bring customers, and there will be no need to worry about doing well. We won’t take any more from the people. We’ll only give back. We will be happy, you and I.”

“Will we?”

She was crying! Dertujia held her tighter, not knowing what to do. He could barely breathe. What had made her cry?

“Leahnina, what is it?”

“Someone tried to rob me.”

Dertujia startled. “What?”

“In town. The people saw me taking the money. They knew what it could buy. He grabbed my elbow and said he’d be my escort. He managed to lose the rest of the crowd as we walked. Then he pushed me down and pulled a dagger. He demanded all my money.”

Dertujia pulled her face up to look at him. “Who? I’ll kill him. Did he hurt you?”

“He’s dead. I aged him to death.” She said it coldly, but there was something more. No, she couldn’t have guilt. She didn’t like killing. It left a mark. Not guilt, because an evil person who went around shoving people to the ground to rob them didn’t deserve the killer’s guilt for having done it.

But she was marked just the same.

“It’s life and death,” Dertujia said quickly. “You have to make those choices sometimes.”

Leahnina pressed her face against Dertujia's shirt. He felt her tears soak through. "But what gave me the right? I should have talked with him. Maybe just made him lose his grip on the dagger."

Dertujia stroked her head, shushing her. "You did what you had to." He chose the words of the goddess. "Power gives you the right to make the decisions. You were above that robber."

Leahnina was listening. Dertujia was still amazed about how much power he held over his wife. Whatever he said, she'd listen to. Of course, if Leahnina had condemned Dertujia for taking the animals, he would have given everything back.

Oh, what strength the heart had over the body!

Chapter Fourteen

The day was busy. Every hour, something new was delivered, and workers showed up and got to work fixing up the house. They were all dedicated to helping their new celebrity.

Dertujia and Leahnina tried to aid all the workers, but they were scolded and told to stay out of the way. None of the villagers would have them work. Dertujia and Leahnina relaxed and watched the flurry of activity around them.

"I could get used to this," Leahnina admitted.

Dertujia didn't want to say he already was. This was way more like what he had lived. Soon enough, though, the villagers would disappear. Then Dertujia would have to do better at working.

For the time being, though, he just relaxed, drinking from the cups that some of the villagers brought and served them with. Eating fruits and nuts.

Dertujia was proven right, though. As the day darkened into night, one by one the people disappeared. The animals had been delivered on a huge wagon, and Dertujia was now called upon to start his life.

As the villagers left, he made sure to tell them if they needed a new steed or a special animal, come by. He felt like that stupid Gerdin. Worse, he sounded like a used wagon dealer.

"You're doing great," Leahnina said as they were in bed that evening. She felt his tension.

"I'm my father," he said feeling sour. "I have become about the money. My life is *normal*."

Leahnina giggled a bit as he frowned. "Welcome to my world. Every single day when you went off on your adventures, I stayed at home. I ran my shop. I lived this life. It's not so bad once you get used to it."

Dertujia didn't want to get used to it. He never wanted to become his father. Maybe this life wasn't bad if you were a normal villager, but Dertujia was used to dining with gods.

What choice did he have though? He had given up that life. This one wouldn't kill him.

"You're right," he conceded. "I just have to get used to it."

But getting used to it was harder than he expected. The animals were big, smelly, and strong. As he fed them and cared for them, they got stronger. They wouldn't go where he told them. They had their own minds, even being the dumb beasts they were.

He started to wonder if Xorna had been right. That animals had the souls of people.

If that was true, he was enslaving people. He tried very hard not to think like that. But some of those horses …

They did the exact opposite of what he wanted.

Dertujia had no energy to practice with his shadows at the end of the night. He worked from sunup to sundown. He barely even had energy to show Leahnina attention in bed, but he made that a priority. It was the one perfect spot in his life.

It took a few weeks for someone to visit who wasn't at all welcome.

Dertujia had no clue who he was, but he heard the clattering of a carriage's wheels from a long ways off. He wasn't too surprised. The people had been dropping by to visit every day. Just dropping off the stuff wasn't enough. They wanted to make sure Dertujia and Leahnina were doing okay, being as far removed from the village as they were. Leahnina had made good friends with a woman named Nutra, and she gave all sorts of advice about how to make food that lasted and how to start a garden. She also brought lots and lots of filled jars and bags.

Leahnina would have to make their food. How demeaning. Dertujia hadn't realized how soon the villagers would only bring help. Not serve them. A naïve and stupid mistake, but Dertujia hadn't thought he'd need to work.

Dertujia had just checked the eggs, which had doubled in size. He didn't know how it was possible for eggs to grow, but they had. He guessed which were the Reathmops. A swirling colorful rainbow of an egg.

As he pounded a fence post that had been pulled out of the ground by one of the horses—on purpose, Dertujia swore—the carriage showed.

It was not the normal, poor, wooden wagon that usually came. This one screamed money. Dripping cloth with a gold symbol of a silver bell on the side. The man who stepped out was dressed as well as his carriage. Long half cape that fell down this back, buttons up the front that were rubies. Nice and new pants that were impractical for traveling, fighting, or, really, living.

"Hello," the man called and stood next to his carriage, looking at all the dirt on the way from the street to Dertujia.

Dertujia humored him out of pure curiosity. Besides, he hadn't used his shadows in days.

He flipped out a path made from shadow stones, and the man didn't even look grateful. In very fact, he acted as if Dertujia had taken too long in the first place.

"You must be Dertujia."

Yes, I must be. Dertujia leaned against the fence and rubbed the tendrils of his red hair that escaped and had stuck to his brow. "I am the owner. No one else would be here."

The man gave a tight smile. "On the contrary, you looked like a servant, but I saw no one else. Far from the impressive Dertujia, the hero that I've read about."

Dertujia straightened his tunic. It was rough and rugged, not even close to as soft as the inside of the armor he had worn or the stuff the goddess had given him. That had disintegrated in a day. But never before had he been judged on his clothes.

It didn't feel good.

"Who are you?" he asked.

"I am Maplen, Grand Operator of Shymis."

Dertujia had never gotten to know the ruling class in his village. He was used to kings, gods, maybe mayors. But never had he heard such a self-important title. "I am Dertujia." Hm, that sounded lacking. "Uh, Master of Shadows."

Maplen gestured to the shadows. "I see that. Well, master, make a shadowy gazebo where I can get out of the sun, and we can talk in style. I refuse to enter that …" He wrinkled his nose as he looked at Dertujia's house. It looked better than ever. Leahnina had been busy painting it a wonderful color. Her touch could be seen through the windows where ruffled curtains waved in the breeze.

Dertujia's mind seemed to tighten inside his head. First his clothes, now his house.

He was about to refuse, but then he noticed that Maplen hadn't come alone. Two guards had flanked the carriage and were walking forward, hands tightening on spears. Maplen obviously wanted to be ready if Dertujia turned hostile.

As if two guards would help him if Dertujia did. Only Eropus might be enough.

But Dertujia wasn't the hero anymore. He felt out across the world for a gazebo that was in the right sun and spilled it into an opening on the field. He did it one better and made two thrones for them to sit on.

Would Maplen accept? Or would he say it was too high for him?

Maplen climbed the steps and sat down within an instant on the tall-backed throne with lots of shadowy gems.

Dertujia took a seat next to him. Funny, Dertujia had put them in equal seats, but Maplen was so far beneath him. One gesture from Dertujia, and he'd be on his backside.

"So, what do I owe the pleasure of a visit from the Grand Operator of Shymis?"

Maplen moved his lips around his teeth. "You are new to the village. Your parents have been here for a while, and they've paid their taxes on time and respectfully."

Dertujia had heard about taxes before. Always about them being too high, but he never had been affected by them. He thought only the normal people … Oh, right. He was normal now.

"I will pay my taxes." He sat back. "Um, what are they?"

Maplen looked at him as if he were the biggest dummy in the world. "Taxes are the way that people help out the greater glory of the city. They build homes, make roads, help with war."

Dertujia felt in over his head, but he still asked. “Why doesn’t the royalty do that? I mean … um, king?”

Maplen spoke slowly. “Our Headcrown isn’t a king. But he follows the rules of the king of Srashan. The Headcrown is the ultimate power.”

Okay, that didn’t answer his question. “Isn’t he already rich? Why wouldn’t he use his money to pay for those things?”

Maplen gave him an ingratiating smile and patted Dertujia’s knee like he was a child. He felt very much like one right now. “The Headcrown’s money comes from the people. It gives him a nice home, security. It pays for jobs like mine. That comes from everybody. One coin out of a pocket is better than a hundred, isn’t it?”

Dertujia saw a certain logic to that. Except he had seen the Headcrown’s homes. They far outweighed the simple one he lived in now. And to think that the people paid for it but didn’t live in it …

Dertujia had fought unfairness his whole life. But to come home and end it all, only to have it follow him?

But this is what he had chosen. The little bit of money he had to pay to help out his home was nothing. Better than dying. Better than feeling the slam of a god who had attacked him from behind.

“Okay, so I pay one coin?”

Maplen laughed again and looked around. “Couldn’t you supply food and drinks?”

Dertujia didn’t want to supply anything. Maplen was growing tedious. “I’ll give you my coin when I get it. I'm going to start selling animals. I already have one buyer coming next week."

Maplen shook his hands. "No. Not one coin. It all depends how much you make. Those who are better off should pay more, don't you agree?"

Dertujia gaped. How was that equal? How was that fair? "Um, and you? How much do you pay?"

Maplen's face tightened. "I am exempt, being a servant of the people."

Dertujia was beginning to realize something. As long as you were part of the receiving money, you lived quite well.

"Okay," he said. He was too tired to argue. "How much?"

"Twenty percent of what you bring in."

Dertujia hadn't wanted to do the numbers, but he forced himself to sit down with Leahnina and hear out what they needed to earn in order to survive. The offerings wouldn't last forever, and they were already beginning to dwindle. In order for them to have food, take care of the animals, and clothe themselves, they had to make a certain amount.

Now that was already knocked down twenty percent. And for what? This man to not pay taxes? The Headcrown to put another wing on his house?

Dertujia didn't like what he was seeing. Had he been in charge, the money would have come from the ruler's own hard work not the people while the rulers got fat like Maplen here.

Dertujia was already down two pant sizes. Maplen didn't look like he worried about that at all.

"I'll get you the twenty percent."

Maplen stood up. "Great to know. Oh, and make sure you keep records. We wouldn't want you giving us a thin purse, am I right?"

Dertujia had no clue what he was talking about. Then he understood. Maplen wanted records to prove Dertujia wasn't making more money than he claimed. He wanted to know every single cent.

Dertujia hated being normal. But he agreed and sent Maplen on his way.

He didn't feel like doing much for the rest of the day. If he didn't earn money, they couldn't take it. Like common thieves that were entirely legal.

By morning he had shaken it off and vowed that he wouldn't let normal problems beat him.

It worked out well for another two months. He did get used to it.

He was accustomed to being dirty and smelling like the beasts he spent all day with. The Koorsgalds hatched well, but the Reathmops? They were taking their sweet time. Every week, the eggs doubled in size.

The customers started coming, regularly buying from them. But Dertujia wondered if it was the animals they wanted or just the interaction with their hero. His tales lasted long after he'd done the deeds.

Sometimes he'd have to be reminded what exactly the peasant was praising him for. "I did what? When? Oh, yes, that was ten years ago."

Didn't matter. To the villagers it was yesterday thanks to the scrolls the seller brought into play.

But it irked Dertujia. Every single time he made a sale, he couldn't rejoice. He had to automatically take twenty percent off. When he decided to raise the prices twenty percent, Leahnina just pointed out that would probably lose the sales no matter how much they adored him, and, besides, the money coming in would still be taxed.

As time went on, though, Dertujia began to enjoy this simple life. The birth of new animals. The same cycle over and over again never got boring. The steady customers who came and asked just for one more story, paying for the animal and his time.

It was good.

After a few months, Dertujia was even used to taxes.

As he worked in the field one summer afternoon, wearing a straw hat to keep the sun off his head, he got a letter from an old friend.

He stopped everything and waved it around, jumping with joy. Xorna had written him!

He had sent many letters her way, dictating them to a helpful scribe, asking for advice, sending greetings, and more than often wondering how the whole thing in Firebranch went. It was impossible for him to get away to visit her. A sickness had spread across the animals almost immediately. It didn't hurt him or Leahnina or the Reathmops still in their eggs and protected. It did however kill a few horses, still weak from the maltreatment from Gerdin.

Dertujia had taken it personally, but the lucky thing was some of the deaths were after the pregnant foal had given birth, so they left behind a legacy. Still, those last breaths took Dertujia away from this for a while. Death was never so obvious as it was here. Not even on the battlefield. He had always imagined that anyone fighting chose to. Any death could have been avoided by not going to the battlefield. It had been a choice, maybe a bad one, but the person in battle had accepted the possibility of death.

An animal made no claims to that. None of them had chosen to be taken by Dertujia and brought to a place where sickness ravaged their bodies.

That was all on him.

"Leahnina!" he yelled. She stuck her head out the window of the inside room of the place where they released their bodily waste. She looked pale.

"What is it?" she asked, but she sounded like she didn't much care.

Dertujia held back his worries. He couldn't face this right now. It looked as if Leahnina was getting the sickness. No. He couldn't manage without her. So, he put it away.

He wouldn't deal with it.

"I got a letter from Xorna!"

She gave a simple smile, and then frowned. She escaped from the window, and Dertujia heard her retching.

He let the letter fall.

He would read it later. Yes, that was it. He had work to do. He couldn't think of Leahnina …

What if he lost her? He'd be alone.

Once again, he ignored life, and focused on work. Once all the animals were fed, hooves clipped, eggs shined—they looked ready to burst—talons trimmed, and beasts let out to roam, along with fences repaired, he headed inside, cleaned himself up, and sat down to dinner.

Leahnina wasn't doing well. He tried his best to ignore it. But she wasn't eating. Her face looked green when he offered to share his spoon of food with her. She loved doing that before, an intimate romantic gesture.

"Please get that smell away from me," she said grouchily. "Are you finished yet?"

He cocked his head at her. She really looked terrible. No … He couldn't …

"Yes, I am." Though he could have eaten another three servings. Working all day took his energy.

"Good. Shall we read Xorna's letter? Unless, of course, you've already read it?"

Leahnina's eyes narrowed. If he had, she wouldn't let him hear the end of it.

"No! It's on the post outside. I …" He didn't say more. Leahnina was in a very bad mood tonight. He rushed outside to get the letter, came back as quickly as he could, and patted the big chair with black cushions and a sculpted wood back for Leahnina to curl up next to him.

He was grateful she did so without complaining. She hadn't been as in love with his touch as of late. But now she sighed with ease and put her head to his shoulder. He wrapped his hand around her forehead. A loving gesture—at least according to Leahnina. But he wanted to see if she had a fever. That was the first sight of the sickness.

She felt cool.

He closed his eyes and let Xorna's letter fall open. It was long, rolling all the way to the floor. She knew how to write and well.

Greetings, my old and dear friend,

I will start this letter by saying how much I miss you. Don't hate me. I received all your letters, but I didn't have the time to answer them.

We started a peaceful war, Cetphur and I, as soon as we got back. By constantly dialoguing with the misbegotten royals, we made them see, finally, finally, finally! That the people of Firebranch were not their enemies and that the people had a right to have a say in what the royals did with everyone's lives.

There's been progress, my friend, even though sometimes I want to use your approach and execute the lot of them. Privilege has not brought compassion to these people. Still, to defend my approach, they are like children who never got the chance to grow up. They need discipline and patience to let them see what's past their own noses.

It's going slow. Glacially slow. But it's going, so don't even say ha ha, I told you so. This will bring peace. It will just take a while.

I live now in a tiny house just north of the White Lady River. I got into a lot of trouble when I laughed at the term for such a small piece of water. I had seen rivers that would choke the life out of this one.

I have to change a lot of my abrasive behavior here. I learned quickly royals don't appreciate sarcasm. Yeah, that's right, Dertujia, I'm becoming a diplomat! Scary, huh?

How are you? I really expected more than what you've told me. Okay, so you're running a ranch. But that doesn't tell me how much you're having problems. Hello! You are Dertujia, a warrior. Controller of what the sun brings. Yet, you tell me that you live happily messing with animal dung?

Hm, doesn't add up. More, give me more. How are you feeling? The last time I saw you, you were so ... Well, I worried, old friend. A lot. Your eyes lost their shine. That's why I let our partnership go. Maybe it was past time to retire. I should have known that.

Way to miss the mark, Xorna! But, seriously, how are you? I hope when you look in the mirror you can see the shine in your eyes return. I miss it.

Okay, maudlin tones aside. I've got good news. I am pregnant. That's right, me. The one who swore she'd never let herself have a baby has decided to let one grow. It's a long story, Dertujia. But something about moving furniture into our house, something about how Cetphur's eyes lit up when he watched the village children at play, something about the babies in the village cooing at me ...

I can't wait to have my baby!

It's not all pleasant. For a while there, I thought I was coming down with a serious illness. But I'm doing great.

Speaking of parents and children, I know you told me you and yours have had a falling out, but I'd reconsider if I were you. Forgiveness brings light. Your eyes are turning dark. Bring the light back. Maybe I'm just biased about the whole thing thanks to missing my own parents.

They'll never see my baby.

Great, now I'm crying. My tears are going to stain this scroll. I hate this emotional wreck I've become. The Firebranian doctor tells me it's a part of my hormones acting up. But I control them, not the other way around.

Tell me how Leahnina is doing. I didn't think I'd miss her as much as I miss you. We became friends so fast, and I miss some of our deep philosophical conversations.

Well, I feel like an Octogob is eating me, so I have to finish this letter now.

I love you, my friend. I miss you and our travels. But I know we're where we need to be.

Be safe and healthy, and if you need anything ... Well, just wait six months to need anything, got it?

Your friend, partner, and mentor,

Xorna of the house of Pyre.

PS Yeah, I've got a last name now. They shorten it to Pyre, so I'm Xorna Pyre. I didn't know that Cetphur's last name was Pyre or that the tradition in Firebranch was to take the father's last name or I would have called the whole thing off. Kidding! I had no house, so I'm proud to belong, besides it makes sense. I could have had this baby with any man in this village. This name tells everyone it's Cetphur's. Okay, bye again.

PPS Cetphur's doing great too. He's so excited about the baby. He's gotten a job with the castle as main liaison between the Firebranian poor and the king. Pays well. I'm working in the same field, but the king respects my warrior background and has made me enforcer of the peace. Of course, it's his *peace he wants enforced. I just make sure the peace is fair for everyone. Okay,* now *bye.*

PPPS Sorry. Wow, that's a lot of P. But I just wanted to say that I'd like you to be nearby when my baby is born. I am scared. I've had wounds before but never like the one the village midwives say is going to happen to me. You've been a comfort to me when I've been wounded before. Please. Promise me you'll be here. My letter is really done now.

Chapter Fifteen

Dertujia sat back, thinking about what he had just read. He felt tears fall to his chin. He had missed so much. Maybe he should have asked Leahnina if it would be alright for the two of them to settle down in Firebranch instead of coming home. Shymis wasn't as good as it once was. Or maybe it was as good. Dertujia didn't even know why he thought he had to come back.

"Amazing that Firebranch is welcoming them in, the way they treated us," Leahnina pointed out. She was on her side down, an arm across her eyes.

Right. That was why he didn't join his friend. He still hated Firebranch. He would always remember it as the village who didn't give him respite. But why did he come all the way back here?

"Leahnina … do you think we made the …"

Leahnina jumped up and ran out of the room holding her mouth. Again? Dertujia let the letter fall and bent to his knees. She had thrown up so much recently. She was getting sick. He would lose her.

He had made so many mistakes. Why did he choose this place where he knew sickness had raged? Why had he been so arrogant to think they wouldn't succumb to it?

Everything was … Dertujia cocked his head. Something occurred to him. Maybe because he couldn't face the truth. Or maybe it was because he had hope. What had Xorna told him in her letter? She had thought she had come down with a sickness. But she was pregnant. Dertujia had been untouched before Leahnina, but even he knew that the things they did together sometimes brought a child when the circumstances were proper. Could it be? Not a sickness but a baby?

He leaped to his feet and rushed towards the bathroom where Leahnina was just standing up. She looked paler than normal, but when he touched her forehead, she was cool.

"I am getting very sick of seeing the meals I've eaten again," she said tiredly.

"Leahnina, is it possible? What Xorna said about thinking she had come down with an illness."

Leahnina gave him a tired smile. "So, you've figured it out. Yes, my husband, I am pregnant."

Dertujia hugged her fiercely, relief washing away the despair he felt. "Why didn't you tell me? I was so afraid."

Leahnina leaned back and clutched his face between her hands. "I apologize. Sometimes my future telling confuses me. I thought you knew. My visions …"

She trailed off as she realized what she was saying. Dertujia looked at her with darkness creeping up around the bathroom. "You swore you'd stop using your visions. Is this why your gaping holes got bigger?"

Anger overtook him, and he spun around, leaving the room. He didn't get far before Leahnina touched him from behind. She still moved slowly and quietly.

"I needed to know. I wasn't sure I wasn't sick myself. I had to know if I was going to leave you. Besides, if I only do a little at a time, only a centimeter happens a week."

Dertujia spun around on his feet to grip her arms. "How much have you been doing? What was so dire you needed to risk your body? What if it disappears for good? What if you do?"

Leahnina brought his head to her breast and held him, letting him hear her heartbeat. "I won't. That was the first thing I checked. I'll just lose visible skin, nothing else. No organs. I'm healthy. Except for whatever this little thing inside me is doing to me."

Dertujia couldn't breathe. But the sound of her heart soothed him. "But I can't stand seeing it. I like the sight of you without clothes, but I don't need to see you without skin. Please. For me. For our child. You know … he? She?"

Leahnina spread her fingers through his hair, and he closed his eyes. "He."

Dertujia's heart leaped. He could visualize it. He would have liked a daughter in equal amounts. But, hey, they weren't done. Maybe the next one. A son and a daughter. "Then you know he's fine. Is there anything else to know?"

Her heart sped up. "There is so much to know. We can't just leave it to a mystery. I can know. I can figure …"

Dertujia heard a whine in his throat. No matter what she promised, with every patch of skin that went away, he knew that it was stripping her from him. It was bad enough to wonder if she would stay with him for as long as he needed her—centuries were what she said. But when she willingly lost herself, maybe she was changing that.

"Leahnina, you are the most important thing in my life. As long as you are with me, nothing else matters. Not this ranch I have to take care of. Not this house that isn't exactly a castle. Nothing. I can't lose you. The baby will need his mother. You make me more frightened than even Eropus. Please. I am begging you, and I never beg. Don't ask the future any more questions."

Leahnina held him tight. Her heart was still fast as she responded. "I promise. I adore you. I'd do anything for you."

He moved down to see if he could hear inside her stomach. But all he heard was gurgles. No sign that their son was in there. But Leahnina had seen him.

"Describe him," he begged again.

"He will be called Juyolax," she stated. "His hair will be fair, his eyes blue. He will have my hair and your chin. He will be passionate and sweet."

Dertujia could almost picture him. "How long?"

"I'd say about eight more months."

Dertujia groaned and stood up kissing Leahnina on the mouth and then again for good measure. "How long really?"

Leahnina grinned. "Okay, okay. It will happen when the winter comes in. I will lose a lot of blood. My pregnancy will be a difficult one. Lots of pain. But I will live through it. Just remember that. It will be tough."

Dertujia stared at her. She welcomed the pain so easily. Maybe because their son would be worth it. "We will get the help of the midwives."

Leahnina took his hand and led him to the couch again. "Dertujia, they are too expensive. Besides I've been asking Nutra a few things. She will be helpful at the birth, taking my pain down by at least seventy-five percent."

Dertujia didn't like the idea of Leahnina being in any kind of pain. No matter what comfort Dertujia had brought Xorna, he had been a mess inside when he saw her wounds. When he sopped up the blood and stitched the parts back together. Outside he was calm, but sometimes he still had nightmares about some of Xorna's wounds.

"I will be next to you the whole time."

Leahnina looked troubled.

"Oh, great, now what aren't you telling me?"

Leahnina held his hand. "There will be a lot of stuff to do when he arrives. You won't make it home."

Dertujia glowered. Oh, wouldn't he? "I won't ask you to check the future to see if this changes anything, Leahnina, but now that I know, I will not do a thing that requires me elsewhere. I'll hire hands. They will do as I ask."

Leahnina shook her head. "With what money? We're barely making it as it is."

Dertujia narrowed his eyes. He'd figure something out. He would *not* miss the birth of his son.

He sat back, thinking about what Xorna had written. The fact that her parents wouldn't be there for her child.

"Can you go travel tomorrow?" Dertujia asked. With Leahnina's nod, he looked out the window at the dark night. "There are two people I have to give a second chance to. If only for Juyolax to have grandparents."

Leahnina smiled. She too understood the concept of family. It was too important to throw out.

They traveled with his shadow carriage, but it was different. Dertujia hadn't been practicing with his shadows nearly as much as he had been on the journey. The carriage flickered in and out, feeling … petulant. As if the shadow was mad that he hadn't talked with it in so long.

Dertujia was quiet as the thing rumbled and flickered. He hadn't had the time. That was all. It wasn't like he was ignoring the shadows he could control. Still, his mood soured into misery. He had once considered the ability the most important thing, and yet he had forgotten it. Hadn't he even announced himself as Master of Shadows?

Yeah, real great Master. The shadow was barely under his control. He furrowed his brow and put his anger into drawing it to full form. He was the master. No one else could control the darkness around.

"What's happening?" Leahnina asked gently.

"I have gotten rusty. It's been months since I practiced. The shadow is complaining."

Leahnina giggled and was bumped around, making Dertujia reach his hand out instinctively to shield her. After he found out she was pregnant, he saw her as weak as glass. One move wrong, and she'd break.

Leahnina was not amused by that. She kept snapping at him, "I'm pregnant, not dying."

He blushed a bit as she glared at him again. Just to change the subject, he asked, "Why were you laughing?" Maybe she'd remember and stop glaring at him.

"Oh, you make it sound like they're alive. Childish and immature. But it's a carriage. Not even a living animal."

Dertujia rubbed his jaw. He really had to start shaving again. The shadow on his face had already become a scruffy beard. He kept it combed, but he constantly caught glimpses of it out of the corner of his eyes. He preferred nothing marring his sight. In addition, he had never really liked the color of his hair. Like blood, his mother had once said.

"Leahnina, what if I told you I think all the shadows I control are alive. I don't know how either!" He threw up his hands as if to defend himself. He knew he sounded crazy. "How could darkness live or breathe? But I hear it. The carriage … Or maybe the shadow it casts doesn't like me forgetting about it. I need to practice more. Spend time with my, uh, children."

He looked out the window, seeing the rough road turning even rougher as it headed out onto the back roads behind his parents' farm. He could feel Leahnina's eyes boring into him.

"I am not insane," he said, his deep voice darkening.

Again, that laugh he enjoyed so much. Good, she was no longer cross with him. "I didn't say you were." She shifted to get comfortable. "I'm just wondering. When we were in the Endless Tunnel …"

"Yes, false moniker that."

Leahnina rolled her eyes. He smiled. "Would you stop? Names don't have to always tell the whole, complete truth about someone. Your name is Dertujia. What does that mean again?"

Dertujia grimaced. "In ancient Derigotan, it means hero. Or was it light? No, light hero."

"Exactly." Leahnina crossed her arms as if she had just won the argument.

Dertujia licked the corner of his mouth before responding. “Okay. Tell me how that’s not true.”

Leahnina scooted in closer to pull his hand onto her stomach. She enjoyed the feeling, and Dertujia was not complaining. “You aren’t light at all,” she pointed out. “You are shadows.”

Dertujia rolled his eyes. His mother had called him Dertujia because of what she wanted from him. And for many, many years, people would have called him a hero. It was true. Names should be true.

But he didn’t want to bring up an argument, not when Leahnina’s stomach felt so nice under his fingers, and she was melting under his touch.

She wriggled again. “Well, let’s not get off topic. When we were in the not so endless tunnel, I could feel so many lives before me. The goddess that supposedly shares a soul with me. Her life. The memories she had when she made the place as a way to escape Eropus.”

Dertujia’s stomach tightened inside. He hated hearing that name. It was the same word as failure. But he pushed it away again.

“Yes?” He had learned not to push her too fast. If he did, she’d forget what she was saying and let him have it for weeks.

“The elements around us. They aren’t just brought forth at our behest. They have a life of their own. Even Cetphur would agree. We had long discussions about it. He feels like his fire is a best friend, always having his back. He said his father felt like his fire was a lover, which was probably why Cetphur was an only child."

Dertujia stared at her and then saw the small raise to her pink lips. "Oh, ha ha."

"But the point is, he talks to it. Asks it to do things for him. So do you. Even Neesh told me she and Eropus have nothing to do with the elements. They became without the gods' help. They are their own entity. Your shadows are too. Yes, I do think you need to spend time with them like they are your children."

She tapped the shadow carriage.

"Do you hear that? I'll make sure he practices."

Dertujia noticed the carriage strengthen. It even stopped moving into an angle as the sun far away hitting it moved. It was a full carriage. Satisfied.

"Unbelievable," Dertujia muttered.

"They aren't your loves," Leahnina said. "Good thing for them. And they aren't your friends. They are your children. They need your hands to guide them."

Dertujia reached out himself and touched the shadow. Firm. Dark. And listening to him. He only said one more thing. "I'm sorry."

That was all he needed to say.

For the rest of the journey, the carriage stayed in one form. Dertujia didn't have to worry about his shadows. He could focus on the thing he came for.

Which made him angrier. "I will not apologize to my parents," he said. "I will tell them you're pregnant. Then they will get on their knees and ask me for forgiveness."

Leahnina stared up into his eyes. "I wouldn't have it any other way. They owe you. If they want to be in your life, they have to make sacrifices. You already have."

Dertujia stepped out of the carriage and cradled Leahnina as he sent the carriage away with a thank you. He let her down to the ground like a queen descending. Her regality still took his breath away.

His parents' house was looking a little rundown. It must have been hard when they stopped selling his new stories.

But the roses still lined the path, though grass overgrew it. Dertujia walked up to the door and rapped on it.

When the door opened, he saw his mother's face. What would he do? If she demanded an apology? Would he give it? Though he owed her nothing?

It turned out he didn't have to worry. Brani immediately fell on her knees and grabbed him around the waist. "Dertujia, my baby! You've come home. Please, please forgive me. I've missed you so much."

Dertujia felt his heart turning squishy inside his chest, but he wouldn't give in that easily. "Not just the money you received for my adventures?"

"I don't care about that! I thought I did. It was nice. But Dertujia, you're more important. I made so many mistakes. My little light hero. Can you shine on me again?"

Dertujia pulled her to standing and took her into a hug. "Of course. We have things to discuss. Where is Father?"

"Here." Kaytal watched the reunion from the doorway, and Dertujia let his hands drop. So, would his father give in? Kaytal was never much for emotional displays. He said that at least one person had to be the strength of the house, and he took that role, as Brani couldn't. She had never really matured, staying childlike the whole of Dertujia's life.

"You just left. You never told us where to find you. I was in town when I heard that you had taken over the Nacksun Farm. I was afraid …"

Dertujia heard it. The deep worry in his father's voice. Though the two of them had taken advantage of their son's work, they truly cared about him. They would want to know …

"There is no sickness there," he said. "At least not anymore. It ran itself out in my animals. Life is there now. Leahnina is pregnant. She will have a son. You will have a grandson."

Kaytal blinked. Then right in front of Dertujia, he fell to his knees. Both his parents had done as Dertujia had wanted. They had shown him worship. Then they were forgiven.

He took his father's hand and pulled him up. "Father, what shall we do? You know the farm is far away from this one."

"We're okay to travel," Kaytal insisted. But they weren't. They looked … old. Wrinkled.

Tired out from the harsh life they led by living on the outside of town. The money Dertujia had earned them hadn't lasted long. Their bodies were worn down.

"Move in with us," Dertujia said. "I'll bring more constructors to build on more rooms. You can be there for the birth. I will be there myself." Like a mantra, he had started saying that whenever he could, ignoring Leahnina's doubtful face.

"You'd forgive us? Just like that?" Kaytal was trying to pull the tears back into his eyes by sheer force of will.

"You are my parents. I want Juyolax to know his grandparents, unlike me. I didn't know mine. Juyolax won't know his maternal ones. I want to fill his life with family. Not the secluded lives you've led, Father and Mother. I don't want him feeling like he needs to be anything but a child. My tribulations will never reach his ears.

"Do you understand? Juyolax will *not* be a hero. You will not require him to be."

Brani squeezed his arms. "We were young and stupid and weak, Dertujia. Never again. You becoming a rancher even through our meddling is a miracle. We won't risk that again. Truly, Dertujia, we never meant to hurt you."

Kaytal also came in close. This was ridiculous. The whole reunion was happening outside on the front step. Dertujia pushed them and then had to push again. They held on like he was trying to pull them close.

"Let us finish discussing this inside," he said.

They listened, and many tears were shed that night. Dertujia realized he hadn't gotten the whole story before he had condemned his parents. The farm had been suffering. His parents had been desperate. And at first, they didn't sell his stories nor were they aiming for that. The heroic values they drove into his head were only a result of their beliefs.

Kaytal and Brani belonged to the old religion. One that demanded self-sacrifice and honor. Loyalty. They taught him to hold a sword in order to defend himself if a bully hurt him or if he needed to defend someone else. They still believed in that utterly.

And so did Dertujia. He had made his life with those morals, and he needed to instill the same kind of values in Juyolax. But he would do it differently. Juyolax would not be called upon to go and fight in wars or make his name as a hero. But he'd know what was right and what was wrong just the same.

Dertujia would have his parents to help. Their bad example would help his son be the hero he needed to be without all the pain and suffering. Juyolax would learn to use a sword. That he agreed with his father on, as Kaytal packed his stuff up to come out to Dakchin Ranch that night.

Kaytal shared with him all the pain and suffering he had to go through as a boy, being the littlest in school. He had hated it so much. Juyolax would not feel that pain. Dertujia couldn't be with him all the time. And what kind of child would be raised if his father fought all his battles?

On the way back, Kaytal and Brani snug in the back of his shadow carriage, and Leahnina and Dertujia in the front, he told Leahnina his plans, and to his surprise, she agreed.

"Yes. He'll need to fight. And fight well."

She gave Dertujia no more info. He wasn't even sure she had it. But the way she said that …

Dertujia knew. Juyolax's life would be about as complicated as Dertujia's was.

Hopefully, he'd have enough love to back him up. But their mission had been successful. Juyolax had grandparents.

That was whenever he showed up in this world in the first place.

***

Dertujia heaved his traveling bag onto his bed. It had been a while since he last used it, but he needed it. Xorna had sent word that any day now she would have her baby.

He had his misgivings about leaving Leahnina. She had predicated, as usual, correctly about the difficulty in her pregnancy. She had been exhausted, sick for two months straight, and had cravings that had Dertujia's shadows running to the far end of their world.

He had not neglected his shadows since. Even if he had wanted to, Leahnina made sure he didn't. He tried, at first, to practice with his shadows at the same time as watching over Leahnina, but she wouldn't have it.

Dertujia had to admit she had a lot of help. Her best friend Nutra and, to his great surprise, his parents. They spent time with Leahnina and made sure to get Dertujia if she needed him. In the meantime, they told her stories. Amazingly enough, they hadn't only been good at telling Dertujia's adventures. They knew lots about their world.

Far into the evening and to the next morning, they'd tell Leahnina all the things she wanted to know about the old gods. They told the tales skillfully and with entertainment, so no one got bored. Many times, Dertujia sat under the sun practicing with his shadows and heard the words soar up to him, and he felt at peace.

It was like he was a little boy listening to his parents tell him tales. But this time they weren't aimed at him, asking him to be a hero.

Dertujia shook his head and brought himself back to the present. Leahnina was staring at him, daring to say one more word.

He didn't disappoint. "Surely I am not needed." It broke his heart to think about betraying his promise to Xorna. But it broke *him* with the idea that Leahnina's prophecy came true that he wouldn't be here to see their son for the first time.

"Promises are important to be kept, Dertujia. It's honorable. Lying and manipulation are for the lesser, the war runners. The evil. We are good. Don't let her down. I told you I will be fine."

Chapter Sixteen

Dertujia stared at Leahnina. She had a shiny glow to her face and skin. She looked more beautiful every day. The lessening, what Dertujia called her skin being lost, had stopped. Her stomach rounded into a pleasant shape hanging low. She had grown in beauty so much that Dertujia didn't just catch his breath when he looked at her, his knees actually got weak.

Now this vision wanted him far from her.

"But, what if …?"

Leahnina sighed. "I know. Just … we've changed a few things. Your parents weren't in my vision before. The future may be different. I don't dare threaten Juyolax's health at this point to check and make sure."

Dertujia sat down next to her. She was in a huge chair, made by Dertujia's father, which had a high place with a pillow for resting her head, and it rocked, waiting for Juyolax to be in her arms. He took a little stool next to her. "And we discussed this. You promised me you wouldn't try to see the future anymore."

Leahnina pursed her lips. "I thought you'd change your mind if you wanted to know something."

Dertujia rolled his eyes. "Never. I wouldn't put my wishes over your health. You must know that about me by now."

Leahnina held his hand on her stomach. Juyolax was in there, kicking. "Go, Dertujia. You owe it to your old partner. There are weeks until my due date."

Dertujia tried to soothe himself. She was right. There was a lot of time. He had been getting very good at the size and strength of shadows, but not only that. The speed had increased too. Shymis to Firebranch was a good month's travel, but his speedy shadows worked like shadows did when the day moved. He could pass landscapes in minutes. He would arrive in Firebranch in only two days. Stay there for as long as it took and be back in plenty of time. Kaytal had taken over the fieldwork, overseeing the workers they had hired. The ranch was making a steady income.

Just the other day, the Reathmops finally made their debut. It had been a wonderful exhibit, honestly. The eggs had grown past the size of boulders. Then, throbbing in the middle of the field, large cracks started appearing. Beaked mouths broke off the shell while lots of legs kicked out the rest.

The Reathmops were truly ugly. Long and squirmy worm-like things with lots of fur and more legs.

Still, as Dertujia was an expectant father, he saw the beauty of the younglings and gave them a cleaning and a rubdown. The Koorsgalds hated them on sight, so he had to keep them away. As well as from the horses.

But Reathmops were in heavy demand. Only a day after their birth, people showed up asking for dibs on the eggs the new couple would have. The couple wasn't from the same parents, so they could breed. And the creatures had two eggs a day.

Money had started to pour into the ranch. Dertujia could afford to hire more hands.

All in all, it was a perfect time for him to go. Weeks before his special event, and he hadn't worked a lot anyway. Dertujia couldn't help thinking this was the way it was supposed to be. Not working so hard. Having many people to do the job quicker and more efficiently.

He loved it when he just headed towards the field, gave his father his list of what he wanted to do that day, and let him take care of the workers. He knew Leahnina also enjoyed the housework getting done by the other servants they had hired so she could focus on getting through this pregnancy.

Dertujia brought his mind back to the conversation he was having with Leahnina.

"Okay, I'll go to Xorna," he said simply.

He was surprised when her face paled. She had wanted him to go!

"But I won't go. If you don't want."

Leahnina quickly controlled her face. "I do want you to go. I just … had a pain. I love Xorna too. She must need you. I know I will."

He gave her a squeeze, stood up, and went back to packing. He couldn't argue anymore. Xorna did need him. Her recent letter had been masked desperation. She was terrified of what might happen at the birth.

Dertujia made his carriage appear, and minutes later he was zipping across the land like a shadow travels. He watched the scenery, remembering the last time he traveled this way. But it was different. He couldn't put his finger on it.

Then he realized. The land looked … tired. Like in winter, but it was early autumn. The trees were bare and even dead in some places. Dertujia felt a deep furrow ruin his brow. Neesh had told him that Eropus was connected to the earth.

Dertujia saw more and more as he traveled. The trees weren't turning. They were losing their leaves before they even changed color.

He didn't know why or how, but out of deep desperation he called her. "Neesh! Please, goddess, if you can hear me. Come."

The carriage shuddered as a power took it over, and the next thing he knew Neesh was next to him. "Hello. It's been a while."

Dertujia gaped. He had just summoned her. A goddess had come at his call! "I didn't think that would work."

"I am always near. You were my champion. Never would I not come if I am able. Tell me.

What's on your mind? I know you will have a child soon."

He grinned despite his worries. "Juyolax. I look forward to his coming in heavy breaths. I would like to have a daughter as well. I want a son and a daughter so they can play with each other and never be lonely. Like Xorna was to me. I'd like a sister for Juyolax."

Neesh smiled. She glowed but not like Leahnina did. It was a star's glow. A sunrise. Her long thick hair could have flown freely, but she kept it down at her waist in control. "I am glad you found the happiness that makes mortals and gods equals. It was all I could have wished for someone so true to me."

A glimmer of guilt rubbed his back, and he stiffened to prevent it from breaking him. On his last encounter with the thing he walked away from, his back had been broken. It could bear a little bit of guilt now.

"I wanted to ask," Dertujia said. He gestured to the landscape flying by. "Do you know what's going on with this?"

Her face grew shadows. Not the ones he could control. But they were black and angry. "Eropus takes what he needs for energy. He's still draining the world."

Everything inside crunched up into a ball. "This is the result? Can the earth take it?"

Neesh smoothed the shadows away. "No worries, my friend. I do my best to ruin his creations. When they turn their devotion to me, he has to give the power back to the earth. This will be a harsh winter, but spring will make a recovery. The world will endure."

Dertujia rubbed the tension out of his neck. That was a good thing. "And how long will this happen? Is there any end to Eropus' bond with the earth?"

Neesh didn't answer. She didn't have to. No. Eropus would use the energy forever.

Don't go there, he ordered himself, but he asked anyway. "Isn't there any way to stop him?"

Neesh looked at him with her face widening. "You'd ask that?"

He nodded. "Only for information. Maybe someone else can take my place in stopping him."

Neesh's face pacified. "The trick is to use a weapon against him at the same time restraining him with elemental control. Nobody can get close enough to use the Box otherwise."

Dertujia blinked. "The Box?" The one souvenir left of his adventure. Leahnina still had it on a shelf. He had forgotten about what had happened in the heat of the battle and why he had given up. After that had been so much pain.

"Right, Xorna has to die. The Box can destroy Eropus by ripping the world apart."

Neesh shrugged. She knew he already was aware of what had to happen. "But that point is moot. Xorna is giving birth soon. You have given up. I will just continue my work. Dertujia, please. There is really no need for you to wonder about this. You will be fine. This world has the most life in villages. The people fight back against

Eropus' power by just existing and helping each other. Kindness, compassion. He can't drain that. It's only the outer edges of the world that are suffering. And I will prevent that. I am the goddess of the spring. It's only natural you'd see the god of destruction win around wintertime when everything is dying and the hopes and faith of people lessen."

Dertujia told himself to drop it. It wasn't his fight anymore; he had done enough. "Thank you, Neesh. Goddess. I will always be grateful for what you have given me."

Neesh giggled. "And now you are dismissing me, a goddess. You have grown an ego, haven't you?"

Dertujia blanched. "That wasn't my intent, Neesh. I was just … The journey is almost over. I will see Xorna soon. I need my attention on that. I don't like Firebranch. I am going to try and see something different now. Xorna lives there. It's her home. Cetphur also originated from that village. It will be a struggle to forget that when we needed help, they turned us out. In addition, I'm pretty sure they still think I'm going to destroy them. A prophecy, you know."

But when his dialogue ended, the goddess was gone. Neesh had slipped away.

Dertujia narrowed his eyes. Surely, she should have said goodbye. Then he remembered. What did she owe him? He had failed her.

The carriage arrived at the forest of Firebranch. Now it looked like a normal forest as it was just hitting dawn.

Dertujia snapped his carriage away and landed on the ground, staring at the city.

He was back. His bias roiled in his stomach, and he told it to shut up.

Xorna was important. Her house was nearby.

He walked the rest of the way.

It wasn't long before people noticed him. He walked along the main road, alongside businesses. He could see the roads branched every now and again, probably heading towards the farms in the distance. The city had grown a lot since he had seen it. He knew Xorna and Cetphur lived in the city proper. He guessed that the tall buildings nearer the castle were what they meant when they told him the number. One Bird House Set. A group of homes squashed together. Not what he expected his old friend to settle down in.

But Firebranch was huge now. He had lost his shadow carriage, but he didn't dare bring it up. Not in a city that hated him and his shadows.

As he walked, people were putting out wares or washing the street. Shoppers mingled together while people on errands rushed in and out of the crowd.

It was a busy day in Firebranch. Soon enough he reached the square. His feet ached. He hadn't been walking for a very long time.

Dertujia sighed and snagged the elbow of a running person. "Is there a vehicle that will carry me around the city?" he asked politely.

The person's eyes narrowed. "You're not from here? You have red hair."

Dertujia tried not to grimace. "Very observant of you. Now as I asked …"

"There's nothing for you. Get out before I call the town defense squad." He pulled away and ran.

Dertujia glowered. After all this time, and yet the whole of Firebranch saw him as a demon.

He walked the rest of the way, remembering long ago Leahnina's complaints about her feet hurting. Now in his mind he made the same ones. How soft had he gotten? Never again. He'd walk long journeys whenever he could, not pull up his carriage as it suited him.

It took until midday to reach the tall buildings. They were pretty enough, golden to match the castle glimmering in the nearby view. But hardly good enough. As one got closer to the castle, the buildings weren't pushed together. Single family homes, huge and impressive. That's where the nobles lived.

He scanned the building and laughed out loud. A passerby, heading towards the castle from the look of the noble cape he wore, gave a curious look at him.

"Sorry to interrupt, but what is so funny?"

Dertujia favored him with a look. Since the question was genuine curiosity and not rude, he answered. "I just find it funny that there are numbers on each door." He gestured to the shared raised walkway and the lower levels. Each one had a branch with a swirled leaf design. Under each was a number. It was clear that Xorna's was the one with 1 on it. But it seemed a tad ridiculous that they needed numbers to identify themselves. He also snickered at the sketching of a bird that spread its wings over the entire building.

The noble wrinkled his brow. He himself had a coppery head of hair, not nearly as blood red as Dertujia's but it flowed down his back, resting on his shoulders. "How else would you find out who lived there?"

Dertujia covered a laugh. "Ask?"

The man chuckled himself. "Sir, there are over two hundred buildings like this in Firebranch. And more singular homes. You're going to ask every single person?"

Dertujia got his point. But it wrinkled his nerves. He didn't like feeling stupid. "Thank you."

The man nodded, a glimmer in his eyes. "So, you're not from here, are you?"

Dertujia shook his head. "And please don't talk about that stupid prophecy. I am sick of hearing it."

The man laughed. "I don't really believe in the ability to tell the future. It comes from our choices."

Dertujia wanted to tell him about Leahnina, but he decided not to. Why press his luck? This was the first person from Firebranch that he didn't want to slap.

"Well, have a good day." The man turned to leave and then sighed and looked back. "I do have to report you to the king and queen. Otherwise, I'll be breaking the law."

Dertujia lost his favor of the guy. All Firebranians were the same. "I'm sure the royalty already knows I'm here. My friend Xorna lives in that home right there."

The man nodded and left. He wasn't the bad type, but somehow … Dertujia got the feeling that there was something more to him. A feeling of destiny washed over him. That man with the copper hair … he was connected to someone.

Dertujia laughed at himself. He was seeing ghosts when there were none. Leahnina would tell him he was being silly.

He was surprised by the wave of emotion that hit him. Leahnina was about to give birth to their child, and she was so far away. He closed his eyes. It was like his arm was gone. He was sick. Stomachache. Chest pain. And she was the cure. Holding her in his arms.

He breathed in and remembered his promise. Xorna needed him too.

He walked forward and rapped on the door.

Cetphur opened it, saw who it was, and laughed out loud, grabbing him into a hug.

Dertujia laughed as well. "Cetphur! It's good to see you. Is your hair a little longer? Your beard more scruffy?"

Cetphur pulled him inside the house. "Hey, I'll have you know I've trimmed my beard and hair just recently. But I could swear there are more lines around your eyes, old man."

Dertujia shook with laughter. He had no idea how much he missed him.

"How's Xorna?" he asked.

Cetphur sobered. “Maybe you can convince her that someone in her condition shouldn’t be practicing flips and swordplay.”

Dertujia groaned. “Where is she?”

“Out back. Come on.”

Cetphur led him through the house, telling him about his job. Sounded dull. But Cetphur seemed happy enough. He wasn’t wandering, and he was well settled down.

Out the back through another door, this one with clear material that Dertujia almost bumped into, he could see Xorna. His heart melted a little. She was beautiful. Fully glowing and stomach bigger than big.

“Ah,” he said.

Cetphur grinned. “What?”

“I’ve missed her.”

Cetphur laughed and pushed him out the door. “Great. Go to her. Then we’ll have some lunch. I have made a masterpiece that will even please Xorna.”

Dertujia stopped in surprise as Xorna jumped into the air kicking wildly and coming back down. Then she groaned. Both men ran over to her.

“Are you okay?” Cetphur asked.

Xorna rolled her eyes. “I’m *fine*. I just didn’t land that move as well as I could. Dertujia!”

She tackled him, moving so well he could forget she was almost due.

“Xorna! Is this safe?” he asked.

Xorna pulled away. Her eyes shimmered with tears. “Hugging you? Probably.”

"No! The swordplay. The …" He gestured to the empty air she had just filled quite magnificently.

Her eyes turned sharp. No tears. "You're as bad as Cetphur. I have been fighting all my life. My baby is strong. I am strong. It's safe. I wouldn't do it otherwise. It's important to keep fit when you're pregnant."

Dertujia decided to ease the sharpness in his friend's eyes. "Okay, I'll remember that when I'm pregnant."

Xorna hugged him again. "Yeah sure. Speaking of which, how is Leahnina?"

Cetphur smacked his head as they walked in again. "I completely forgot to ask about her. What kind of friend am I? How is she?"

Dertujia tried to smile. He didn't want to talk about her. How she was when he left, he knew. He didn't know how she was now. "About the same as Xorna. Neither of you want to let us pamper you."

Xorna rolled her eyes. "I didn't like being pampered when I was not pregnant. Now it really gets on my nerves. Come on. I'm starving." She mopped her head with a silver cloth that hung on the wall. Dertujia now had a chance to look around.

It was certainly nice. Smooth floors with some kind of musical instrument leaning against the wall. Paintings had been done of the two, and they hung on the walls. Potted plants were everywhere. They fit the forest. Red on the top, green on the bottom. It was a Firebranian home.

Dertujia just couldn't like it. He didn't like Firebranch. That wouldn't change. Worse, he felt it was stealing his friend. Where were the swords? She swore she'd have a sword collection one day. He didn't see even a clue of Xorna's personality.

"Where is your sword collection?" he asked, sitting down at the table in the dining room. All around were pillars with flowers on them, a low hanging light source that held seventeen candles. The window pointed out, but because this house shared a wall with another, he knew there'd be no window on the opposite side of the house. Worse, he could hear slight steps from upstairs. They weren't living alone.

It was unsettling.

"I know you had a few. Shouldn't they be hanging on the wall?"

Xorna laughed. "When the baby is old enough not to cut herself, yes. We put them away. Didn't you see the small building outside? It holds my armor, my swords. My daggers. Oh, I got this great whip …!"

Cetphur interrupted. "That will be also not used until the baby is out, right?"

Xorna waved her hand at him. "I wounded my belly when I whipped it too hard. Right here!" She yanked up a portion of her shirt and showed an angry welt.

Dertujia stared at her. "Were you hurt?"

Xorna blushed. "No. Just my pride. But I see Cetphur's point. I'm a lot bigger than last I used a whip."

Dertujia settled back as Cetphur served them food. “Xorna, old friend, are you happy?”

She snorted. “Can’t you tell?”

He shook his head. “No.” Cetphur put a plate in front of him. It smelled wonderful, but he ignored it. “This isn’t what I wanted for you. You should be queen. Ruling. Not in this place.”

Cetphur gave her a look. But Xorna rallied back. “This place looks kind of bad. But when you consider I traveled for so many years, no family except you. No real home base. So much sand under my feet. I like a foundation. And we’re moving up in Firebranch. I don’t mind living here. And my sister has a house here too. She is getting married in the spring. I’ve got what I most want.” She held her stomach and Cetphur’s hand.

“But … you’re living like a peasant. You’ve saved so many lives. It’s wrong.”

Cetphur shared a gaze with Xorna. “Tell him.”

Dertujia tapped the table, waiting. “Tell me what?”

Xorna sighed. “Truth is, we’re not sure about staying in Firebranch. But we live here. My sister has a house. How can we just give up on that?”

“Just one more straw,” Cetphur muttered.

Xorna glared at him, but Cetphur changed the subject. “This is standard housing for people in my line of work. One day I could try my hand at being a knight. That’s the road to royalty. Then Xorna will get what she deserves. All in good time. Besides, we’re working with the government. You think this is bad? You should see the hovels. All farmers have to live in them."

Dertujia dropped his fork. "Did you say what I think you said? Farmers have to live in hovels? That makes no sense. They provide the food for the city, do they not?"

Cetphur sighed and sat down. For a few minutes, all that was heard was the sounds of clinking plates and glasses. Cetphur stared at Dertujia. "Firebranch works on a certain system. It's tradition. If someone has lived in Firebranch for a long time, they can petition to join certain other areas. As they move up, they can become nobles. No one else can do that. Like Xorna told me of other villages. Ruled by kings. Born a certain way, you stay that way. In Firebranch it's not the same. What you do elevates you."

Dertujia slammed the table. "I'm a farmer. I should live in a hovel?"

Cetphur shook his head. "I don't agree with it. Like I said, we're working on the king and queen. Trying to change the government. Every week I bring petitions from the farmers."

Dertujia narrowed his eyes. Maybe he should have a few words with the royalty. Negotiating with shadows. A hero shouldn't live where Xorna and Cetphur were living. Farmers who bring the food shouldn't live in hovels. He knew that some of the ones he met had to have multiple children. Not because they wanted big families, but as needed to have extra hands on the farm to make it work. But here? They'd all live in hovels.

He was starting to loathe Firebranch.

"Ow!" Xorna exclaimed.

Dertujia forced a smile. "Did you bite your tongue?" he asked.

Xorna looked at him. Her eyes were wide. "No. The baby is coming. And it really hurts!"

Cetphur jumped up so fast he knocked the table over and spilled food everywhere. By reflex Dertujia brought up his shadows quickly to spare his outfit and was over by Xorna's side in a minute.

"Where are we going?" he said, lowering her to a shadow bed he snapped into existence.

"There's a hospital not far away." Cetphur rushed from room to room, grabbing bags and sliding them over his arms until he looked too big to get through the door.

Xorna gripped Dertujia's hand.

"Something is very wrong," she whispered.

Chapter Seventeen

Dertujia didn't want to hear about anything going wrong with Xorna. He gently pulled her through the house until he reached the street. In front of a crowd, he brought up his shadow carriage, longer to fit her bed, and they were off.

The crowd followed.

Dertujia didn't notice. He was holding Xorna's hand, whispering softly. "Everything will be okay."

Cetphur was on the opposite side, holding her other hand, staring into her eyes and mopping her forehead which seemed to have exploded with sweat.

"Everything will be okay." Dertujia wished he could believe that. Xorna looked bad. Going from bad to worse in seconds.

No. Everything would be okay. He'd make sure of it.

Xorna was, as always, a silent sufferer. He could see it in her eyes, though. The deep-set pain. The barely contained tears. She gripped

Cetphur's arm so tight, she was drawing blood. He didn't notice. He clutched back.

The couple of them were both good at hiding. But Dertujia saw. He himself was an expert.

The hospital Firebranch had was more modern than what he was used to.

Secluded rooms for the mother to be. A window that pointed out onto the Firebranian forest. Had so much time already passed?

The forest was on fire. Sunset. And still she hadn't given birth.

The doctors didn't know what to do. Six had been sent into her room, each more useless than the last. They scratched their heads and pointed at scrolls, wondering what the best procedure was.

The procedure? They should have been able to help her give birth. Babies came into the world the same way all the time. How could one be so wrong?

But it was. Xorna got weaker.

Cetphur's eyebrows didn't unknot.

Xorna looked up at him even as the sunset made her silver hair glow.

"It's not going well," she whispered. No strength to speak.

Dertujia hissed. "No. But you won't give up. Above all things it won't be childbirth that destroys the legendary warrior."

She gave him a small smile. "No. But it might kill my baby. I knew this was wrong. All of it. I had too much sickness. Too many sleepless nights. Dertujia … She's dying!"

Dertujia felt like she had punched him. The baby was dying. And back where he left, Leahnina could be going into labor. She could be dying. That's who he took the she to mean.

Dertujia closed his eyes. He had to do something. There was nothing, though …

"Cetphur," Dertujia suddenly yelled. "Shine a light between her legs."

Cetphur gave him a look Dertujia chose to ignore. Did he think that Dertujia was trying to get a cheap peep of his wife in labor? Silly fool.

"The baby needs a shadow. She needs to tell me what's wrong." He gestured and expected Cetphur to do as he said.

But he just stood there. Hope was leaving his face. He was too used to giving up. Not this time.

Still holding Xorna's hand he pulled the shadow up from his and made it grow. Larger. Then he used it to slap Cetphur across the face.

"I told you. Give me a light. Now."

Cetphur looked shocked, his haggard face registering some emotion.

But he ran around Xorna's legs, shoving the pondering doctors out of his way. "Leave!" he screamed.

The doctors didn't care. They were only waiting for an excuse to leave. They couldn't help. Dertujia watched them go, glowering.

Xorna finally screamed out, the pain too much.

"Hurry!" Dertujia prodded.

Cetphur lit up the entire area, keeping the fire at a safe distance, but the light spread through the room.

Dertujia listened, he closed his eyes and felt.

There! A little shadow. There was so little light. But it was enough.

He listened, heard the plea. It couldn't breathe. There was …

The cord that attached mother and child, it had tangled around the baby and somehow wrapped around the throat.

So little light.

So strange of shadow.

"More," he whispered to Cetphur who increased the flame. Xorna opened her legs wide in order to help.

"Don't push," Dertujia said. "Not yet."

The light was finally enough.

Using the baby's tiny shadowy hands, he twisted the cord off the neck. Untangled the most horrible knot in the world. The baby could breathe.

"Now! Push, Xorna," he said. She shuddered and gave the most impressive push she could manage, and out came a ball of goop. So much prettier in shadow form.

"That is disgusting," Dertujia noted, but he was breathing again. His chest wasn't so tight. His life much better.

Cetphur gave him a dirty look but wrapped the baby in fire, burning off the goop. It nestled her in warmth, destroying only the blood.

Xorna flopped back, breathing but exhausted.

Cetphur put his fire away and wrapped the baby in a blanket and helped Xorna support the head as he pushed himself onto the bed next to her.

"A girl," he said. "A little girl."

Dertujia could almost float away, the relief and happiness were so bubbly. Like one of those drinks the merchants sold at the fairs in Shymis.

So, Xorna had been right. She needed him there. The doctors were useless. Again, if it had been up to Firebranch, Xorna would be dead. She and her child.

"She was trapped. Wrapped up in something that didn't allow her to move," Dertujia said.

Xorna gave a pathetic nod of her head. "I knew it. I just did. That's why I did the flips. I thought I could untangle her. I failed."

Dertujia shuddered. "It wasn't natural. Was it?"

Xorna shook her head. "Another curse from the evil god. Right before we left with your broken body, he had said something like, 'Enjoy childbirth.' I knew this was what he meant. Well, now I do."

Dertujia gritted his teeth. "Will his shadow ever leave me? The shadows of an angry god …"

"He's done now, Dertujia. He failed," she said. Her eyes were bloodshot, but she was already healing. She was strong. Her girl was too.

"Isn't she pretty?"

Dertujia smiled. "Now that the yuck is off her tiny form, yes."

Xorna chuckled. But she looked as if she could sleep for days.

"I'll fetch the doctors," Dertujia said. "They can finish this up. They'll know better how to take care of a new mother."

Xorna nodded, expecting Dertujia to turn and walk out. But he didn't waste time with things like that. The doctors had been useless. It was time for them to earn the Gilar they charged.

He waved his hand. The doctor's shadow yanked him into the room. He gaped at Dertujia.

"What in Hetahaunder do you think you're doing?" he demanded.

"Care for your patient. Better than before."

Then he turned back to Xorna, holding her hand.

"I have to get back. You understand right? Leahnina is due soon. If she goes through what you did …"

Xorna heaved a big breath of air. She gave him a weak smile. "You did more for me than anyone could ever, my friend. Go. We can take it from here."

Dertujia kissed her forehead and turned to go, ignoring the doctor's glare, who started checking over Xorna and the baby.

Xorna stopped him with a word. "Dertujia, you saved my life. You saved hers. We will always be together, right? Friends forever."

Dertujia smiled, feeling tears in his eyes. "Yes. Forever."

"And we'll live in the same area. Cetphur and I'll go to Shymis."

Cetphur nodded even as Dertujia looked at the both of them with surprise. "Seriously?" he asked.

Xorna grinned. "This was the last straw. My daughter almost died! When we're all ready to travel. Firebranch is not what we expected. And think … our children can grow together. Maybe they'll fall in love. Get married."

Dertujia felt his heart swell, imagining that. His best friend next door. His family growing with Xorna's. The little Juyolax on the floor with …

"What's her name?"

"Tomphane."

Dertujia didn't know what that meant.

Cetphur filled him in. "It's my great great grandmother's name. She died long ago. But she could control ice. And while Cet is our word for fire, Tom is the word for ice. Not that ice is here anymore. There hasn't been one in my family for many generations. And there probably won't be one for many more."

Dertujia walked forward, dodging the doctor to clasp hands with Cetphur. "I hope this is what you want as well. I hate to take you from your home."

Cetphur glared at the doctor and gave him a push. He was finished checking over the patients, and now he was just standing there staring at the three of them. He obviously was disgusted with their lack of patriotism.

He walked out glaring. He rubbed the place where the shadow dragged him in. With one more glare at Dertujia, he disappeared.

Cetphur heaved an angry sigh. "Firebranch isn't my home. I'm not sure it ever was. And the changes I would love to make won't happen in my lifetime. It's taking too long."

Dertujia agreed. He turned back to Xorna and gave her a hug, holding the baby between them and smelling her new scent. Somewhere across Telda, his wife would soon produce a similar baby.

"I have to go. But I look forward to the day when you show up in Shymis. That is where we'll all be happy."

Xorna held up her baby. "You hear that, Tomphane? You're going to see Shymis. You beautiful baby, you."

"She really is. Hey, would you look at that? She has your eyes, Xorna. It's incredible. What a miracle."

Xorna bit her lip to stop from laughing. "Not really. That's how it works, Dertujia."

They all chuckled together. "I'll look for a home near mine. Oh, wait! I'll build one for you. On my homestead. Like a miniature castle. You'll never live in a wretched building like the one you are in now." He quieted. He felt an overwhelming urge to get back to Shymis. To get back to Leahnina. But he had time. He quickly closed his eyes, sending a message through his shadows. Asking questions.

It worked. The shadows near his home whispered back.

"*She is fine. She sleeps now. Fitfully, but she waits for you.*"

He pulled up a chair. A little longer wouldn't hurt.

"What made you change your mind?" he asked. "You seemed pretty intent on staying here. Dare I say that you were even proud of that pathetic hovel?"

Xorna's eyes closed. She was falling asleep. Cetphur pulled the baby into his arms and held her even as Tomphane followed her mother.

"I think it was the doctors," Cetphur admitted. "We were thinking about it already. We missed the two of you so much. No one can have conversations about old tales like Leahnina can. And Xorna loves you."

Dertujia felt his face get hot.

"You know that," Cetphur scolded.

"And I love her." He wasn't used to admitting things like this. But Cetphur wasn't judging him. He was a good man. "I have missed her like I would if I lost my leg. But you were intent on staying in Firebranch. Fixing it."

Cetphur placed the baby in a tiny bassinet nearby, staring at her in awe as he touched her tiny toes in reverence. "It won't fix for my daughter. It won't even be fixed for hers. I'm not sure we are doing any good. And in Shymis we'll have friends. But we were holding out. I didn't want to abandon my home again. I didn't want the royalty to win.

"But these doctors almost killed Xorna, Tomphane. I can't stay here. Let someone else save this world. I want to be happy. I want my daughter to have a friend like you. Your son. My daughter. Friends from birth. Wouldn't that be amazing!"

Dertujia nodded. He threw out his shadows again. He realized something. He could leave them as sentries, watching Leahnina. Sending a message if even for a second she went into labor.

He set that up but looked at Cetphur.

"I know. You have to go. Such a short visit."

Dertujia clasped his arm and then drew him into a hug. "But soon there will be no need for goodbyes at all. I am overjoyed you will stay in my home."

Cetphur sat back, yawned and leaned his head against the wall. "It's been hard."

He said no more, as he let out a light snore.

An exhausted family.

Dertujia tiptoed out.

He left the hospital and was ready to pull up his carriage when he noticed torches. More importantly, people behind the torches, staring at him.

So many shadows.

But they were one.

"Can I help you?" he asked.

"Yeah," a big burly man with thinning hair and an oversized belly sneered. "You can die."

Dertujia's instinct told him to duck. An arrow whizzed past his head.

He felt the sword's shadows around him. The anger and wrath coming together.

And across the world, he heard.

Leahnina screamed.

She was going into labor.

A fist came towards him. Too many shadows.

Dertujia started fighting. All the while, his wife moaned.

A heavy metal thing came down upon his head.

There was no more light.

***

Cetphur awoke to a much brighter day. He quickly glanced over to where Xorna was, still asleep, her hand holding the baby's in her bassinet. He grinned and stood up, stretching. He looked over Xorna, but he felt like someone punched him. She looked so bad. Her skin wasn't glowing. Her hair was bland, not shiny. That pregnancy had taken it out of her. That was why she had spent so much time on the fighting moves she had learned in her youth. It was the only thing that made her feel better. Without it, he wondered how fast the baby would have died. Surely, she had helped the strange knot that the cord inside had been making.

He sighed. Eropus hadn't been lying. He had cursed Xorna. That strange pregnancy was just a part of it.

Her eyes flashed open. "Cetphur," she said with a groggy smile.

"You look beautiful," he said.

"What a liar," she responded. "Is Tomphane okay?"

Cetphur touched the baby's forehead, not letting go of Xorna's hand. "Doing better than you. Her color is so pink and healthy. How long was that cord trying to strangle her?"

Xorna shrugged, heaving a huge sigh from the effort. "I'm not sure. But I felt it keep trying. Or maybe it was my fault. Maybe I tied her up."

Cetphur gripped her hand tightly. "No. Don't do that. It had to be Eropus. It was wrong from the very beginning. Remember, Eropus broke Dertujia. He wouldn't let you walk out unscathed."

Xorna rubbed her eyes. "What about you?"

He felt the vice clench his heart, but it was finally releasing after all these months. "If I had lost you and the baby, that would have been the worst curse. He knew that. He knew everything. But it's all over now. Dertujia saved her."

"Dertujia!" She tried to sit up, but she couldn't. This would be a long road to recovery. "Has he left?"

As soon as she said that, Cetphur recalled his dreams. He had been surrounded by people yelling at him. Were those screams real? "He must have. He wanted to get back to Leahnina. As soon as you can travel, oh, and the baby, we'll move there."

Xorna looked around the room. "Were there people in here? I thought I heard yells. A fight. Someone got punched."

Trust her warrior nature! Maybe those screams he heard hadn't been a dream. "I heard them too."

They shared a look. They both knew what Firebranch said Dertujia would do. "Has Dertujia gone home?"

"I'll find out," Cetphur said. But there was a knot of worry in his belly. "You get rest. Popung?" There was a nurse for the baby that was very pleasant. Better than the doctors and not at all jaded by her years in this business.

"Yes?" she asked as she walked in. "Is it time for the baby to feed?"

"I can give you twenty Gilars if you take care of her while I'm checking on something. Will you?"

Popung just smiled. "No need. I love helping people. You go. We'll all be here when you get back." Cetphur trusted that.

He walked out, trying not to yawn. It was hard to believe now after all the stress and worry that Tomphane had been born. Dertujia had saved them both. He couldn't have asked for a better friend.

But something was wrong. He could feel it in his gut.

An hour later, Cetphur should have been relieved. The castle guards told him that Dertujia had been escorted out of town. A few people said they saw him leaving the city.

It was all over. Now the only thing needed was to have Xorna rest, recover, and then they'd all travel to Shymis.

He couldn't put his finger on it, but there was something still wrong. He tried to ignore it and headed back towards the hospital. When he entered the room, he was gratified to see Xorna sitting up. She still looked as if a Koorsgald had run over her. But she was smiling, holding the baby.

"Did he leave?" she asked immediately.

"No," Cetphur responded, surprising even himself. "I mean, of course he did. The guards told me they saw him. A few people."

Xorna's eyes narrowed. "A few?"

"Is that bad?" Cetphur asked.

"Yes. Cetphur, Dertujia is a legendary hero. You know the name we've made for ourselves. In addition, this stupid town is sure he'll destroy them. And only a few saw him leave? A mob should have escorted him. Whether friendly or hateful. This doesn't make sense. And one thing I've learned is that if something doesn't make sense, it's a lie."

Cetphur spread his hands out, scooting up next to her. "Xorna, what can we do? All we can do is wait for Dertujia to send us a message or go ourselves. Once you're well."

Xorna shook her head. "No. You go. Now. You can get to Shymis fast with your fire feet."

Cetphur sighed. "No way. I'm not leaving you."

She held up one hand. "Cetphur, without Dertujia we'd all be dead. Me and the baby. You because you wouldn't live without me."

Cetphur couldn't argue with that.

"So, do this for me. Go to Shymis and find him. If he's at home give him help with his baby. Then return. I'll be sleeping most of the time anyway."

Cetphur opened his mouth, intent on arguing.

"I am begging you. I need to know that my friend is well. I can't recover if I am worrying. Do as I say."

Cetphur wanted to say no. He felt like either choice he made would rip half his heart apart. What if Dertujia wasn't well? What if he needed help for his child? What if Leahnina needed him like Xorna needed Dertujia?

But he couldn't leave his family.

"I am begging," she said again.

He made the choice. The hardest one. He pulled on traveling boots made of steel to withstand his fire, wrapped himself in fireproof material and was out the gates of Firebranch heading towards the dusty roads so he didn't burn up too much stuff.

His feet threw fire down as he ran. Making him move beyond the speed of any vehicle or animal in Firebranch.

He made his way to Shymis, a ball of bright fire.

Chapter Eighteen

Dertujia never liked the dark. But now he was waking up practically blind. No, there was no darkness. It was his eyes, sealed shut to withstand the pain in his head. He blinked and could see a little. Red smeared his vision.

He shook his head a few times, calling out to shadows.

But there were none.

"Don't bother," a voice told him.

Dertujia took three steady breaths and tried to open his eyes again. Thankfully vision came back. He was in a small room. Only a few feet and there were stone walls. A small toilet. No floor coverings. Maybe what he woke up on could be called a bed, if you could only sleep on the ground.

Maybe Dertujia would have preferred the ground.

Across the way where the voice came from was a solid door with a window of bars. A face appeared. He recognized the prince of Firebranch all too well. Tenpert's green eyes looked down on him. Faking sympathy.

"You will let me go," Dertujia said. But inside he felt like a boy. Where were his shadows? What was happening with Leahnina?

"We can't." Tenpert sighed. "You can't escape either. I have the ability of light."

Dertujia gasped. Light? How could that be possible?

"I studied your journey, Dertujia. You gained access to the Dragon Tower. You never had shadows before. It was simple for me to follow in your footsteps. It's not much. But I block your darkness."

Dertujia looked around again, now that he could. It was unbearably bright in here. No darkness around the edges. None of his old friends. "So, what?" he asked glaring at Tenpert. The seed of hatred this city had pushed into his heart when he first came was slowly growing into a tree. "You will execute me?"

Tenpert nodded. "Yes."

Dertujia bared his teeth, standing up. If the door didn't separate them, he would have ripped this prince apart. "You'd dare? Let me go. I mean you no harm. But that will change if I can't get home. My wife … she's in labor!"

Tenpert pursed his lips. "Not likely anymore."

Dertujia felt sick. Like his insides had stopped existing. No stomach, no heart. Just ash. "What do you mean?" Had Tenpert decided to wipe his whole family out?

"You've been unconscious for a long while. Without your shadows, you don't heal fast, do you?"

Dertujia clenched his fists. Fury overtook him. He slammed forward and grabbed the bars. Tenpert jumped away. "What did you do to my wife?"

Tenpert looked confused. "Nothing. You're our enemy. I only said that because you've been out for a week. No woman would be able to sustain a week labor. So, she probably already gave birth."

A new sickness took over. He had missed it. Leahnina had been proven accurate again. His son had come into the world, and he hadn't greeted him. He had greeted Xorna's, held her baby, but his own remained without the comfort of his arms.

He shook the bars. "You have no right to keep me here. I've violated no law. I have only helped people."

Tenpert bit his lip, but his eyes remained steel. "You have been prophesied to destroy us. That's all we need. Just relax. You'll be fed a last meal. A scribe will come and take your final thoughts, a letter to your wife and child, perhaps. After six more hours, you will die."

Dertujia shook. "Why are you doing this?"

Tenpert stood up tall with his righteousness. "It's the best for all. You *will* ruin Firebranch. What is the worth of one man's life over many? You'd do the same thing if you were in my position. I know of your heroics. You should be sacrificing yourself for the best for all."

Dertujia wished he could get his hands around that prince's scrawny throat. "I am an innocent man. I do not believe in killing innocents to maybe help the best for all. If you were a real ruler, you'd wait. You'd see my threat. I have done nothing but visit your city."

Tenpert glared at him. "Yes, and one day you will visit with the worst intentions. I will not allow that. And I know I am doing what any good person would do. What a hero would do."

He spun around on his heels, letting his cape flutter as he stomped to the stairway at the end. Dertujia could see the long bright corridor. Not exactly what he was used to in dungeons. It had been created with him in mind.

For a few minutes, he wondered. Was he really that great of a threat to Firebranch? Or was this whole thing ludicrous?

He settled down to the floor as he let the thoughts wash over him. He'd die. His son would grow up without him. His wife without her husband. A farm without its master. All because of a what-if scenario. When he had done no crime and had saved so many.

No, this whole situation *was* ludicrous.

But he could do nothing. The door was strong, locked with ten locks. The light obliterated his shadows. He hadn't realized how much he relied on them.

Even before Dragon Tower they were his allies, giving a second sight that helped him in battle. Now, they were just gone.

Soon, he would be too.

There was no way of telling what time it was. No windows. No time keeping devices. Just a hole in the ground. He couldn't even tell if there were other prisoners, though he called out, desperate for the sound of a voice, unfriendly or not.

And the smell! How many prisoners had been in here? Leaving their refuse before they too had been executed? It was moldy and smelled of the ammonia of urine. The acrid scent which left a taste in his mouth.

Finally, he heard steps on the stone floor outside.

He jumped up, hope still alive. He would not just give up. All the way to the end. He'd even spit in the face of his executioner.

It was not, however, the executioner that was coming.

Rather a guard escorting a clumsy scribe who kept dropping his quills. He wore a long blue robe that fell down to his feet. At the base of the neck was a huge collar that scraped his ears. He was balding with long silver hair on the edges of his scalp. His face was weathered from years in the sun. A farmer. He bore the marks of a farmer, not a scribe. Strange.

The guard next to him rolled his eyes and sniffed with a sour face. The man stunk. Dertujia grinned. Anything that made the Firebranian guards uncomfortable was wonderful to him. Dertujia didn't much care for its citizens either, but its government had a special place of hatred inside.

"Open it up," the scribe said, noticing the expression. But to Dertujia's surprise, he just stretched and spun a bit, letting the air carry to the guard's nose.

The guard gave an expression of disgust, covered his nose, and opened the door quickly. As the scribe entered, Dertujia smiled. The scribe didn't smell bad at all. Earth and a little bit of manure, sure, but it was smells of the farm. Nothing horrible. The stuff that made plants grow. In fact, it reminded Dertujia of home.

The guard slammed the door shut behind him, muttering as he walked off of smelly farmers.

"So, you're the destroyer?" the scribe asked.

"So, you're the one who will hear my last words? How was your Beato crop this year?"

The scribe's eyes widened. "How'd you know?"

Dertujia sniffed. "The smell of Bortmire manure. It is supposed to help Beato. Trouble to cook though. I gave up on farming it myself."

The scribe relaxed. Dertujia had a feeling he had just earned a friend for life. "It is difficult! But I know its secret. One day I'll pass it down to my …" He trailed off. Sadness overtook his face.

Dertujia knew the man was here to give last rites. But he couldn't help it. His heart went out to him. "What?"

He swallowed. "I won't have children. I won't pass my secrets on to anyone. I always wanted a family. But my wife …"

Dertujia's heart clenched. Leahnina was never far from his mind, entwined as she was with his heart. But every statement anybody made brought him back to her. Was she well? Did she have troubles like Xorna did? She would have foreseen her own death. She would have told him … wouldn't she?

More than his own sentence of death, more than anything else, this was what he worried most about now. The unknown.

Dertujia struggled with himself and asked, "What happened?"

The two shared a look. Both understood each other. Both loved someone more than themselves, with the passion the poets talked about.

"She wasn't far from town when a storm hit. She died when one of the trees of Firebranch fell on her. She was out gathering wood. We're farmers."

Dertujia tried to smile. What he wanted to do was scream. "Yes, I could tell. So, what are you doing in scribe's clothes?"

He sat down next to Dertujia. "Well … Hey, we should introduce ourselves. Name's Nockhun."

"Dertujia, the condemned," he reminded.

Nockhun hadn't forgotten. "Yes, I know. But you asked me a question. I'm attempting to become something more than a farmer. I owe it to Bethiope. She hated being poor. Never wanted to be a farmer. When she married me, she married down."

Dertujia harrumphed. What a stupid world the Firebranians lived in. Marrying down just because the man was a farmer.

"But we're allowed to seek other jobs. Work for a long while, and you can change your circumstances. I have always loved history."

"So, there you go," Dertujia finished for him. "You'll work your tail off in two jobs just for the chance of being more." He didn't bother to hide his disdain.

Nockhun deflated. "Yeah, but it's all I can do now. All I can see whenever I close my eyes is her face as the tree hit her. I was there for her last moments. I can't forget."

Dertujia stood up, letting out the rageful scream he was holding back.

Nockhun didn't condemn him. He just said gently, "Who is she?"

"My wife. Leahnina. She's given birth by now. Or maybe she's dead. And I wasn't there. The worst thing is I don't even know. I'm stuck here with this travesty of justice. I haven't done anything wrong, and yet they condemn me."

Nockhun stared at him. In such a short time, somehow the two had become friends. They had similar wounds, similar fears.

Nockhun cleared his throat. "Okay, so I guess we should get on with it. What are your last words?" He scrambled to get a quill and scroll ready for writing.

Dertujia could say nothing. Think nothing. "Only to my wife. I'm sorry."

Nockhun's mouth crumbled, revealing the light hairs on his face. "That's all?" He paused. "Why are they destroying you again?"

"I am to bring destruction to Firebranch. Their oracle told them tales, so I will be executed."

The silence settled in the tiny prison cell. Nockhun glanced at Dertujia and then back at the scroll in his hands with the two words. Suddenly, he rolled it up and stuck it back in the bag he carried on his back.

"You know …" Nockhun said slowly. "There's only one guard down here. The rest were told to go home and get some sleep for the main event. Prince Tenpert expects resistance on your part."

Dertujia gave a bitter smile. He was right about that!

"When the door opens, I could distract the guard. You could run. They say you can command the very shadows under us. Well, once you got out of the hallway there'd be a lot at your disposal. Prince Tenpert's power only goes so far."

Dertujia couldn't believe what he was hearing. This scribe also farmer was coming up with an escape plan!

“In addition, if you took the castle turret to the south, it comes down over the chasm. If you used your shadows, a bird’s wing perhaps to fly down over that, they wouldn’t be able to follow.”

Dertujia wished he could double check this scribe’s honesty. But he couldn’t. He trusted him as if he were his brother. “Why?” was all he asked.

“Because you’re good. I can see it in your eyes. What’s happening to you is wrong. And … if someone could have helped me save my Bethiope I would have appreciated it. I can’t just write down your last words, knowing this is wrong.”

Dertujia stood up, feeling hope burn. It was people like Nockhun that made Dertujia not give up on Firebranch completely. “But if they find out you helped me?”

Nockhun looked out the small window to the hallway and then glanced back at Dertujia. “I have nothing left to live for. I was just living. This is a good way to go out, helping someone who’s innocent.”

Dertujia couldn’t think that. No, he wasn’t going to just …

“Get ready!”

Dertujia clenched his fists.

“Guard, I’m done, open up,” Nockhun yelled.

The guard took his sweet time coming to the cell. Dertujia felt his tension rising with every step.

"Okay, make sure the prisoner is against the wall!" the guard snapped.

"Oh, he is," Nockhun said, knowing full well the guard couldn't see past his body to notice that Dertujia was right behind Nockhun.

The lock opened unbearably slow. The door squeaked open.

"Hey, your face," Nockhun said looking at the guard and keeping Dertujia behind him. "I've read some old scrolls that say the face can tell your future. I think that line right there …" Nockhun conveniently blocked his eyes. "Says you're bound to have a passionate love affair with royalty.

Nockhun gestured behind him for Dertujia to scoot past. There was only a narrow passage between them.

He moved past. The guard didn't notice.

"Yeah? The queen? Or the princess?" he asked eagerly.

Dertujia snorted. How ignoble did a man have to be to betray his kingdom by coveting an affair with the queen or princess?

He shouldn't have made a noise.

The guard jumped and looked down the hall.

"Hey!" he yelled. "He's escaping."

Dertujia turned to run. He heard behind him the guard being tackled. Had Nockhun really …?

The next thing a punch was heard. He hoped it was Nockhun doing the hitting but was made obvious it wasn't as the guard yelled. "You helped him escape! You are dead!"

Dertujia stopped. No. The scribe wouldn't be killed because of him.

He ran back. Slamming his feet into the floor, he came down on the guard who was still punching Nockhun.

Dertujia wrapped his hands around the guard's throat. He hissed, "I am the one you should have gone after. But you're a bully who saw an advantage to attack the less fearsome of the two."

Dertujia pulled him up and slammed the guard's head hard against the floor. He stood up and gave a hand to Nockhun. "You won't be able to live in Firebranch. Not unless I kill the guard. And I loathe to do it while he's unconscious. But you freed me. If you ask me to …"

Nockhun rubbed his face, wiping away a smear of blood. "No. You need to get out of here. The guards will return any minute."

He was ready to listen to him. But there was little way this could be covered up. Someone had records that the scribe Nockhun was going to come down here. If he was here, the guard injured, there'd be little doubt that Nockhun had played a part in it. And as much as this city looked down on farmers, Dertujia was sure they'd condemn him.

"You have nothing left to live for." Dertujia held out his hand. "Then come with me. I'll show you a home in Shymis. Where a farmer is honored not condemned."

Nockhun hesitated only for a second but took his hand. With a shake, they ran down the narrow corridor and out to blessed shadows.

The devastatingly bright light was gone.

"That way!" Nockhun yelled, and Dertujia heard them, the soldiers.

With narrowed eyes, he tightened shadows.

Nockhun yanked on his arm. "What's more important?" he asked. "Revenge or your wife and child?"

Dertujia felt very tired all of the sudden.

"You know that answer."

"Then move. The soldiers of Firebranch are trained well. With all due respect to your legendary abilities, I don't think you can take the entire castle."

Dertujia let a grim smile play on his mouth. "Maybe one day I'll find out. For now, though, I see your point."

Running took over Dertujia's mind. There was a large area between him and the staircase. A mezzanine that peered down onto the large throne room. Two humongous thrones where the king and queen would sit. They weren't there, but a whole lot of guards yelled when they saw him.

Panting, he tried to keep his breath steady as he smashed into the staircase, climbing upwards.

Arrows whizzed past his head. His shadows rose up behind him, catching the arrows. But if this onslaught kept up, he'd falter. He could see what Nockhun meant. These Firebranians were very, very good.

"Higher," Nockhun urged.

A tower appeared and rose upwards. One of six. Golden and with intricate brickwork. A small window peered out, as Nockhun predicted, onto the chasm. A black hole. But there were still a lot of shadows around. But sunset was coming. Lack of light. Lack of shadows.

He closed his eyes and asked for a large bird's shadow. It came back flighty and light, but it'd bear them.

"Get on!" Dertujia yelled as the sounds of a half dozen soldiers echoed up the spiral staircase.

Nockhun looked dubious. Dertujia didn't waste time. The shadow bird reached out a talon and grabbed him, holding him tight.

Then Dertujia got on and they were airborne, flying through the sun. While the light got ever closer to the horizon.

"You won't get away!" A voice screamed. Tenpert was standing on the tallest tower, aiming a crossbow. "The light is lessening. So are you!"

Dertujia gritted his teeth. The bird dodged an arrow.

"Remember, Dertujia," Nockhun yelled from his place in the talons. "There are shadows everywhere. This world isn't the only one. All you have to do is find them."

Dertujia was confused. He didn't understand. But the sun slipped beneath the horizon. The bird was obscured in darkness wherever it was.

They fell.

Chapter Nineteen

Falling wasn't a pleasant experience. It was actually the worst experience Dertujia could imagine. Not because it was terrible. No, it was freeing. Beautiful. Like all your cares and troubles could fly away.

But there was reality. At the end, you'd die. And that took away anything pleasant you should be feeling.

Dertujia scanned his brain frantically. Taking less than a second, he thought about what Nockhun had said. Different worlds. Was there light in different worlds? Shadows. Could Dertujia actually reach out to them?

Well, why not? He had set a sentry on Shymis to tell him about Leahnina, even though the shadow was gone now without the master to sustain it.

Desperately, with only one hope, he reached out for anything. Any shadow that'd talk to him. Not one by a flickering fire. No. One that was fully lit by the heat of the sun.

He was too weak. They were too far away.

This was how it'd end.

Leahnina … was she alive? Was she waiting for him?

The thought bolstered him. He had to know.

Reaching out further than he could even imagine, he begged. "Shadows, I am your master. Come forth. Save me!"

And feathers slammed into him. Catching the other falling man, it flew high again. No more falling. No thud.

Dertujia just breathed heavily closing his eyes in cooling relief.

He was alive. Nockhun was alive. "Towards Shymis," he ordered the beast, whatever it was.

He hadn't had the time to look. He sent out his shadows to ask about Leahnina's condition. Nothing. Like they were smothered. How …?

He couldn't think. But as the journey commenced, and more immediate concerns appeared, he had to continue on. No focusing on the near death he had just experienced, both of them.

He shot a look at Nockhun to see how he was faring. Like Dertujia, he was freezing. All Dertujia could see was his frame shuddering.

It was cold up here. The air was thin.

Nockhun surprised him. "Mind if we sit closer together?"

Dertujia cocked his head.

"Body heat. Staying together keeps more heat in. It's freezing up here!"

Dertujia scooted over to the man and pushed his body against his. Strangers, but they both needed each other's heat.

"That's a bit better," Nockhun said. "This is incredible, Dertujia. Flying. Falling. I felt so incredibly alive back there."

Dertujia managed a wry smile. "Yes, and if you had hit the ground, you'd feel amazingly dead."

Nockhun shuddered but laughed. "Yes, I suppose so. I never realized though what it was like to actually have an adventure. I always had my nose buried in books or my hands in the soil."

Funny, did Dertujia hear a longing in his voice? "What is it?"

"You'll think me mad, but I just want to go home. I miss my farm."

Dertujia didn't think him mad. He understood. But thanks to Nockhun's sacrifice, Dertujia was alive. While Dertujia was going home, Nockhun wouldn't.

"You'll always have a place with me. I'm sure I could use a person on my farm. If you want, I can build you a house, not a hovel, and you can farm again. Or you can study. Do both. Whatever you want. I owe you my life."

Nockhun nodded. The night got colder, and they both shut up.

As they winged through the frigid air, Dertujia turned his attention away from his shivering and towards the beast he had called.

Funny, but it didn't follow the wind currents. It didn't flap and then glide. It just soared.

What had he called forth?

As dawn approached and Shymis' border showed, he knew too that it was fast. It had taken half the time a normal shadow bird would.

The light appeared on the horizon illuminating the mystery under him.

Both men gasped at the same time.

"What is it?" Nockhun asked.

Dertujia didn't know.

Now Dertujia could see what it really looked like. A black and red dragon with a long body, four feet with sharp claws, and a long serpentine neck. Patches of skin were there. Others were, well, he didn't know what. But he had summoned forth an otherworldly dragon. It wasn't a shadow at all.

It was big enough for three more people to sit on. None of them would be dislodged by its wing movements. The back was as soft as silk, and the feathers …

Dertujia swallowed. "Are those bones? I thought them to be feathers."

Nockhun, more scholar than scared, tapped them. "They are soft," he marveled. "But yes, they are bones. There's nothing covering them. No muscle. No skin."

Dertujia didn't know what else to do. He was more than a little unnerved. This being wasn't his. He only controlled it. He didn't create it. He had so little time with his shadows so far, but as far as he could tell, all he did was get in touch with the being or object that cast the shadow and brought it to life.

This dragon had already been … alive. Maybe. But where did it come from?

"Dragon, tell me your secrets."

Nockhun laughed. Dertujia felt more than a bit ridiculous. It was a dragon and he expected it to answer?

"*I was birthed in Hetahaunder. I breathed through the dead. I bring souls to their afterlife.*"

Dertujia nodded. "I'm really sorry I asked."

But the dragon wasn't finished. "*You connected with me. Freed me from my servitude. I am grateful. But know this, the Hetahaunder King doesn't take lightly to theft from his kingdom.*"

Dertujia gaped. His head swirled with everything, and suddenly it was all too much. Almost being executed for a crime he didn't commit yet, the falling and almost death, summoning a dragon from where he didn't know, and then having it speak and tell him it came from the underworld?

"Crying doesn't make you weak," Nockhun mentioned casually as if he wasn't doing anything but stating a fact.

Dertujia couldn't help it. He started weeping. He put his head on Nockhun's shoulder and cried. There was so much more that he needed to cry about. Leahnina had already given birth. The people of Firebranch—not all of them—hated him when before he had been loved by all people.

He had come within feet of his own demise, and what had he accomplished? Sure, saving people. But what was that worth when the very people he attempted to save turned against him? His baby could be dead. His wife. Then what would his life matter?

Nockhun became almost like a father in that instant, patting his back and murmuring, "It'll be okay. I know it."

As his misery subsided, embarrassment replaced it. He barely knew this man. Yet he cried on his shoulder like a child would.

"I apologize," Dertujia said, shifting on the strange beast below him and rubbing his eyes. "I am not usually so showy of emotion."

Nockhun settled down. Now that the sun was out, it grew warmer, and he basked in the heat. "No problem. It's always best to allow your emotions. Not bury them. I know how it feels though. I cried for a week solid after my wife died. So many either walked away from me or snickered. Like I was less of a person because I freely grieved. Only a few were sympathetic, but they disappeared when I cried for more than they'd allow. Me? I say let the person cry as long as they want."

Dertujia had to disagree. "No. As a good friend, you should allow a proper time, but then they'd have to be slapped out of their grief. It can destroy people if they let it."

Nockhun sat up on his elbows. His face lined in the sun. His white hair damp with the dew of morning. "And who decides what is the proper time? I'd think that was up to the person grieving, am I right?"

Dertujia pondered that. It was a strange question, but enough to make him think of that and not what awaited him in Shymis. Could another person look at someone and judge them to be ready to heal? If they saw the person sliding into ruin, wouldn't it be better to take matters into their own hands?

It grew in his head. It wasn't just grief. It was everything. For example, Firebranch. That was a city imploding on itself. It had strange rules and designs that made a good portion of its citizens unhappy. Xorna and Cetphur swore it'd be free one day by constant diplomacy. But Dertujia saw a damaged city, overcome by its own rule.

Like a person grieving, did Dertujia have the power to get Firebranch out of it? Would it be best to allow the city to figure out its own problems?

As he recalled the cell he was put in, the elite guard who took to abusing an elderly man instead of taking on a worthy opponent, the execution that waited him just because he might cause problems later on …

No. If a person was too consumed with grief, it was up to their friends to get them out of it whatever way possible. If a city was destroying itself, it was up to the person who had more power to stop it.

The roads underneath turned green, the rocks shoved together with moss, pounded down by feet and wheels. Dertujia felt his heart swell. "I'm home."

"There's nothing like it, is there?" Nockhun asked. "The smells. The sights. The familiar places. It's like slipping into a warm bath at the end of a hard day."

Dertujia nodded. He was home. Firebranch wasn't his. He was a farmer now, not a hero. Both he and Xorna gave up those lives in order to settle down. Besides, governments weren't exactly monsters or centaurs. They weren't evil war runners. They were the people in charge. Surely the people could save themselves. If not, what did it matter?

Dertujia had other responsibilities.

Funny how the mind could have two different paths that warred with each other. One mind, so torn apart by conflict. He used to be a hero who saved people. But he had turned his back on Eropus, and now he was turning his back on the world. On the other side of his conflicted mind, he yearned to see Leahnina, to cuddle her in their bed, to hold their child. To awaken and play with the soil and animals to encourage a profitable future.

The second path was more important. He never knew how much he'd fight for that. Family. Home. Let the rest of the world suffer. It wasn't his responsibility to save it. He had done enough.

Like turning his back on Eropus, he made his choice. No matter how much he wanted to go back and make Tenpert pay for daring to attempt an execution. No matter how thrilling and pleasurable it'd be to choke him with his own shadow.

Those thoughts hurt. The ones with Leahnina didn't. He focused on the ones that made him who he was.

He was Dertujia, a farmer. Once a hero. Now he would live simply with his best friend and wife and a new friend of Nockhun. His life was going to be perfect. Leahnina was fine. His son was fine. She never said anything about seeing his or her death. As Dertujia turned to his new path, there was no way it could be stolen from him.

Yes, everything would be …

"No!" Dertujia yelled almost jostling the dragon with his scream. His homecoming was far from perfect.

Shymis was frozen over. Everything was ice and snow everywhere he looked.

The road that was covered in moss ended in a line of frost. There was no proof any town existed, and as he flew on, he could only know where his farm was by memory of location. There were no landmarks.

"What happened here?" Dertujia asked. His dragon dropped, an unnatural landing. No gravity, no impact. Just a drop. Gently landing against the cold stuff.

Dertujia slid off and gaped.

His farm was unrecognizable.

Snow, blank spaces. Desolation. Mounds of white even as a flurry hit his face.

A cold underworld where no life existed.

***

A week earlier …

Leahnina had never experienced such pain. Brani filled her head with what to expect, but nothing could have prepared her for this. The ache split her stomach, traveled down her legs. Even her head was affected, screaming in pain.

Brani had set her up as best she could in a wonderful bed, but Leahnina didn't stay in it. She spent the time walking, bending over to hold her stomach and moan, and then walked again. It was just better for her to be moving.

Hopefully, it'd keep her mind off the fact that she was going to do this alone. In the last few months, she hadn't dared to take a peek at her baby or the future. But Dertujia not being here was coming true.

"Any sign of him?" she asked as Kaytal stomped in, shoving the wooden door closed. He gave her a look of sympathy. She hated it. Both of them had been horrible. She would be fine!

"There's no sign of him."

Leahnina clutched her heart and almost fell while holding her stomach as another pain wreaked havoc on her.

Kaytal rushed over to her side, trying to guide her to lie down. As if it'd help.

"I want Dertujia!" she moaned.

She couldn't be strong anymore. It was time. Their baby was coming. And it hurt. Worse than ever before. She had always tried to be strong ever since the first look of pity and irritation hit Dertujia's face on their first journey together.

This was too much pain. It was almost like she was dying.

She screamed again.

To her surprise, a knock thundered on the front door.

“Dertujia!” she cried.

Kaytal, failing at getting her to move back to bed, shook his head. “Why would he knock?”

Leahnina clenched her fists, trying to hold back the scream she wanted to utter.

Kaytal opened the door to see …

“Cetphur!” Leahnina said. Her pains were gone. Only an icy chill. If he was here, then where was Dertujia?

“Is Dertujia home?” he asked.

Leahnina fell but was caught by Cetphur. He sure moved fast. “He’s not, is he?”

Leahnina shook her head, biting her lips. “What happened … Oh!” She squeezed her eyes tight as another spasm shook her body. Like her stomach wanted to come out with the baby, yanking on all her organs while it did.

“It’s okay. We just got separated. He’s fine. Just using another route.”

There was forced joviality to his voice. Leahnina didn’t believe him. But it was too late for her to do anything. She couldn’t stand anymore. Could barely breathe from the pain.

“Here, sit here,” Cetphur urged. There was a wooden chair nearby, next to the table but facing away so she could sit on its warm cushions.

“Your baby is coming. It’ll hurt, but I’m sure you’ll be fine. Dertujia told me about the son you’ll have.”

For the moment, Leahnina smiled. It was true. She had seen him living, breathing. That meant she'd be alive to see him. Why else could she see the baby in the future?

"Okay."

"We need to get her to bed. This walking around can't be good for her."

Cetphur smiled at the man. "At least she's not flipping."

The door slammed open and shut again. Brani came in, followed by Nutra, with a whole lot of supplies from the village.

"No one is coming," she announced. "No doctor. Only us."

Kaytal slammed his fist into the top of the table, making it rattle. "It figures. They sure make promises to come but when …"

Brani cut him off. "It's not their fault, Kay. There's a storm coming."

Leahnina stretched her neck up, holding back her pain. Cetphur tried to bring heat to her muscles. It sure felt good but couldn't stop the wretched pain that attacked her.

"What kind of storm?" he asked and upped his intensity.

The warmth was incredible. It almost made her feel like she wasn't having this baby.

"Ice. Snow. Dark clouds." She shuddered a bit and rushed to get a fire started. Kaytal got in her way and put the wood inside the fireplace.

"But it's so early in the season," Kaytal complained. "Too early for the storms."

Brani shuddered again. “This one doesn’t seem natural. It’s already destroyed all the crops in the village. I fear for the animals.”

Leahnina gaped. No! She wouldn’t have Dertujia come home to an abandoned farm, empty of crops and animals.

She closed her eyes, feeling Cetphur’s fire warming her, easing the ache inside.

The future …

What would …

Her hands fell to her side. She was glad she was sitting.

“Cetphur, leave me, and get the villagers. They need to come here.”

Cetphur gave her a wry smile. She saw the bags under his eyes. He was worried about a lot of things. “This farm isn’t big enough for the villagers.”

“Cetphur, please. How long can you heat up an area and how big of one?”

Cetphur shook his head. His heat on her belly faltered. But she ignored the returning pain.

“This whole farm, I guess. But why?”

“This storm is evil. It will kill everyone within its borders. Everyone in Shymis. But you can save us. Your fire.”

Cetphur didn’t know how to answer her. But he saw her desperation. This wasn’t good. She had to focus on the baby inside her. Nothing else.

“If it will make you happy. Brani, you just came back. Take care of Leahnina. Kaytal, I’ll need your help.”

He nodded. Though the two had just been introduced, they jumped into action as allies.

Cetphur used his fire feet to first make a fiery perimeter with one large opening. He made it like a fire building, overtaking the entire space where the animals and buildings were, including Dertujia and Leahnina's house.

Once that was done and the fires were burning eerily under a black sky, Cetphur and Kaytal jumped into a wagon that Leahnina used when Dertujia's shadows weren't available and the two rushed into town.

Thanks to the devil cloud hanging overhead, they didn't need to do much convincing to get the villagers to line up.

Snow was already falling, slicing cheeks. As a huge group, the ones who listened followed Cetphur. The ones who were too stubborn stayed in their houses. Cetphur didn't begrudge them that, though the look on Leahnina's face was unnerving. The future was death.

When they arrived at the farm, one vehicle after another, they all found spaces to rest. A lot were taking it as a big sleeping party.

Quite a few glanced at Cetphur's flames with suspicion and fear, but when they saw the snow over their heads whirling like a demon, and the icy tornado stripping the plants right outside, they settled down. The looks turned to hope and care.

Families stayed together. None were allowed into the house. Cetphur wouldn't have Leahnina's birth be interrupted.

But they were happy enough outside. His flames made for a bonfire type setting, hanging all around them. People started roasting pieces of food, and someone made a sticky concoction that became black in the flames, and they ate it with relish.

Cetphur reinforced his fire barrier but looked up with a grim face.

"What is it?" Kaytal asked. "I don't know you, but I know that look. You're worried."

"Look," he responded. "My fire's not melting that ice."

Kaytal looked too and his jaw dropped. "It's unnatural."

"This is of the gods. It's making a shell. An icy shell around the fire. Is everyone in?"

Kaytal nodded. "Anyone who was coming. But there could be a few stragglers. Should we …"

A wild tornado of ice and fire burst into the opening in the fire. Cetphur threw his hands up.

Like fighting a monster, he dug his feet into the ground and shoved it back.

There was little ground given, but he screamed and pushed it back.

Inch by inch, centimeter by centimeter, he shoved it out the gap and closed it up. It quickly tried to get in again, like a wild monster tearing at the door.

"It'll hold," Cetphur said. But he felt exhausted. "It's trying to kill all of us."

"No. It's trying to kill me," Leahnina said, suddenly at their elbows. Looking exhausted, frail and very much in labor.

"I tried to stop her!" Brani yelled running up behind her. "Come on, we need to focus on the baby not …" She shot a horrified look at the snow outside. It was encasing them already. Piling up like on a house, the fire against white, not making a bit of difference.

"It's after me," Leahnina said. "It's Eropus' handiwork. He's trying to kill me."

Brani convinced her to go back inside. But everyone was quiet now. There were no burnt confections. No laughing faces. All of them huddled together, watching the snow continue to bury them.

Would they ever get out of this?

Leahnina was escorted inside by all three.

It was more peaceful in the house. No worried faces. No swirling storm, though they could still hear the whine of it all around, like the very peaks of the mountain were trying to come down on them in snow and ice.

Cetphur ignored it. He had one task. Since Dertujia wasn't here, he had to make sure Leahnina's baby was born like Dertujia had helped his.

He did wonder how much of a village would exist when Xorna and he moved here.

Finally, Leahnina was exhausted. Cetphur had to carry her to her bed. As the snow demon outside roared, she moaned and pushed. Cetphur did his best to ease the ache with his fire, warming her, but she was in labor and what could he do about the internal machine?

It was finally time.

Leahnina grabbed onto Cetphur's arm and screamed. "I want Dertujia! I want my husband!"

And all Cetphur could do was feel helpless. He wanted Dertujia here too. He wanted Xorna. His fire was strong. But he already felt taxed.

"Just give the baby your attention. Dertujia will want to see him." *If he's still alive*, Cetphur thought. He wouldn't show it. But if Dertujia wasn't here, then he probably hadn't left Firebranch.

Something had gone terribly wrong.

"Just breathe. And give a push," he soothed. He hoped desperately the baby wasn't like Xorna's. Everything was nightmarish. Leahnina screamed more than Xorna had. Her eyes were bloodshot from pain. Her hands tight on his arm, digging in with her sharp nails.

And outside the demon fought the fire, trying to find a way in. The people huddled together wondering if this would be their last night on earth.

The ones who foolishly stayed in town were buried by the first pass of the snow demon. Their tombs were of snow and ice.

But a baby's wail echoed out under the fiery roar and the windy wail.

Juyolax was here.

Cetphur cleaned the baby, and Leahnina fell backwards exhausted. She immediately went to sleep as they tended to her wounds with the doctor's help. Halfway through, the doctor had volunteered, and she took care of her while Brani, Kaytal and Cetphur cooed over the newborn.

He looked like Dertujia but had a head of sandy blonde hair. Bright blue eyes. And a chubby set of cheeks.

"He is so cute!" Kaytal exuded.

Brani chucked the baby's chin and looked back over the sleeping Leahnina.

"Where is Dertujia?" she whispered.

Cetphur couldn't answer that. He had no idea. There was no way he'd make it in here even if he had left Firebranch.

There was a good chance Cetphur would never get out himself.

All the while the fire fought the snow. But the fire weakened. Day by day. As the people huddled together, getting more and more cold as the fire flickered, the only thing to do was wait for the storm to abate.

But it might never.

Outside the fire, the demon screamed, wanting a way in. Trying to kill the fire.

Chapter Twenty

There was a moment when Dertujia gave up. When he saw the frozen wasteland underneath, when no sign of life showed, he wanted to crash the dragon and let his pieces scatter where they may.

How many times could he have hope? He had expected to come back and find out if Leahnina was alive, if their son was. But now it looked as if no one was.

The snow swirled around his face, the howls of a demon attacking coming over the eerie silence of the snow.

"It's an ice Dart," Nockhun muttered in terrified but reverential tones.

"A what?" Not that he cared. Nothing mattered. How could anyone withstand this?

"An ice Dart. A demon from Hetahaunder."

Dertujia felt as cold inside as his skin did out. Nothing mattered anymore. "Like the dragon?"

"Yes, summoned by someone, a god perhaps."

Dertujia's mouth wrinkled. He could guess which one. "Nockhun, I want to drop you off somewhere else. Afterwards I'm going to come home and lie down in the snow. Let it bury me forever."

Nockhun gave a snort of disbelief. But then he took another look at the beaten man in front of him.

"No, Dertujia! Don't despair. Don't you hear the angry howls? The frustration in the demon's voice?"

Dertujia hardly thought that mattered. "So?"

"It hasn't succeeded in its master's will."

The world slowly started moving again, his heart joining with it. "Are you saying that there are survivors?"

Nockhun threw his shaky fingers towards an area more covered in snow. A hill? No there weren't any hills that large there. "It's attacking there. And it grows ever more frustrated. If it was done, why spit snow? Why continue to fight?"

Dertujia nodded. Not only because Nockhun made sense, but because the only way he could live anymore was the fact that Leahnina was alive.

He urged his beast towards the mound. There was nothing to distinguish it from anything else except the sheer size of it. But there were patches that seemed to be caving in.

"There's the source of the ice and snow!" Nockhun crowed. "It's beautiful, isn't it?"

Dertujia snorted. Nockhun had a strange sense of beauty.

The demon was like a giant leech, swirling a snowstorm around its head, an open mouth belching only ice and snow. It was attached to one part of the mound, its mouth open wide. From time to time, it stretched its rubbery skin and bellowed.

It had the same sheen to it as Dertujia's dragon, showing their connection.

But while someone could almost mistake the dragon for a living animal, there was no way anyone could mistake the Dart for anything but a monster. Its coat was slimy black with red patches like open wounds. At times, gaps showed bone and muscle working together.

The snow around darkened it almost to the point of shadows. At the end was a split tail, oozing orange goop that froze on its end and became an almost mace.

"Something is stopping its force," Nockhun surmised. "But it's weakening."

Dertujia understood. Somehow, they had made a defense. The villagers. His wife. But it was faltering. They needed help from outside.

"Demon!" he screamed, and the Dart moved its eyes towards him. Yellowish orbs with black flakes inside, matching the snow but like a black mirror image. Its mouth curved upwards.

"*So, the little victim has showed his face. Eropus will be pleased. I came to kill you as well as her along with everyone else.*"

Dertujia glared at the thing. So, it could talk. That made things nicer. It wasn't just a mindless animal that had no control of what it did. No, this thing was sentient. It was evil.

"I'll send you back to Hetahaunder," he declared. Then he urged his mount on.

Flying through the sky, he clenched his hand around no weapon. But before he even asked a blade appeared. A shadow sword. Was there no limit to his abilities?

He sped through the air, the snow and ice becoming blades that slit his cheeks. He felt nothing. He was already numbed from the cold. Good. He could feel the pain later. His main goal was his enemy.

Just inches from the creature, though, it spread its body and leaped into the air, using its own air currents. Then it spun around making a tornado appear.

"*Die*," it mentioned.

The tornado sliced the air, hitting Dertujia's dragon. But lucky for him, it wasn't one of his shadows.

The dragon spoke, surprising Dertujia. "*So, the Dart wants to play in the air. I was born there.*"

Then his steed rolled, dodging the tornado and shot towards the Dart.

Dertujia didn't know what to do exactly. He didn't need to command his ride. It was his ally. And it sure hated the Dart.

Dertujia got ready too and twirled his sword through the air, catching on the Dart.

It squealed even more as that orange goop spread through the frozen air, becoming solid rocks, but the demon spiraled towards the big mound of snow.

The Dart impacted and spread the snow in orange.

Dertujia could see now … fire? Was the fire stopping the snow? But … that made no sense. The only person that controlled fire was Cetphur. Was he here?

No time!

The Dart flew again, undulating in the air, slamming into the dragon and Dertujia. The contact was horrible. As if all the pain and suffering of Dertujia's life was combined and reminded in a single touch. He writhed out from under it.

Nockhun tried to help. He grabbed at Dertujia's sword.

Silly fool! The blade wouldn't work for anyone else!

But it was the distraction he needed. The Dart didn't know that Nockhun couldn't fight back, he writhed in the air to fly towards Nockhun. Dertujia brought the sword down on its neck and again on its back. Who knew where the weak point was.

It sprayed them with orange gunk but suddenly vanished.

All the orange did as well.

"I love it!" Nockhun laughed. "No messy clean up."

Dertujia agreed. If only all monsters could be so accommodating.

The snow around stopped. Almost like a summer day, it just evaporated. The clouds vanished. The temperature warmed. And Dertujia could see.

An intricate frame of fire covered his farm! His farm! He was home. There were lots of people under the …

The fire fell apart as he looked at it. Dertujia had killed the Dart right before mass disaster would have come.

"Wow," Nockhun said. "That was amazing. If we had come only a little later …"

Dertujia shuddered and forced his dragon to land. When it touched the ground among all the people, it nodded to Dertujia and disappeared, back to where it came. Funny, like a soldier on the battlefield, Dertujia was sorry to see it go though he had no idea who or what it really was.

He scanned the huddled people. They were so scared they hadn't realized it was all over. They had closed their eyes and fallen asleep, waiting for the death.

"Up you go!" Dertujia announced, clapping his hands and using shadows to run through the area, their clatter awakening even the most dead of sleeper.

"Where is Leahnina? What has happened here?"

Dertujia recognized the elderly baker. A man of huge girth and stature. "She's inside. She was in labor," he noted. "Good that you're back. I take it you are the one who saved us?"

Dertujia just gave a nod but headed inside. Around him cheers broke out, the people gratified for his presence. Right now, he didn't care. Maybe he had become jaded. But their praise wasn't what he needed.

At one time he would have basked in the glory. But he had matured. If Leahnina was alive, maybe he'd feel that way. But for now, the worry still ate at him. The battle and the prison weighed on his shoulders.

He slammed his door open to find …

"Cetphur, so you are here!" Dertujia said. clasping his friend into a hug.

"And you are too! Why were you so late?" he asked, holding him at arm's length to take a look at him. "And who is your friend?"

"My name is Nockhun. I saved him from prison," he interjected. Dertujia hid a smile. Though this was true, Nockhun was trying to look impressive in Cetphur's eyes.

"You were in prison?" Cetphur didn't look all that surprised. "I should have known."

"Where is Leahnina?" Dertujia demanded. "How is she?"

Cetphur washed away his worries by grinning.

"She's wonderful, old friend. She sure likes complaining, but she delivered normally. No complications. And your son is the cutest thing I've ever seen, oh, minus my sweet little daughter. What happened anyway?"

Dertujia didn't answer. He rushed into the backroom where he saw Leahnina sitting up and holding Juyolax. She had all her color returned, looking more beautiful than ever.

He fell on the bed losing all strength. He held her tight, almost crushing Juyolax in between. "Aw, my sweet. My life. My reason. I have missed you."

Leahnina pursed her lips, trying to fight her smile. She was angry with him. Little did she know he hadn't chosen to be late. "Glad you could grace us with your presence," she said.

Dertujia picked up the baby, said one thing, "I'll look at you later, little one," and drove the baby into Brani's hands who was sitting in a chair making a blanket. Then he caressed Leahnina's face, marveled at her form. Her perfect face. She held him so tight, with only a little more pressure, bones would crack, but he held her too.

"You knew," he whispered. "You knew it all."

Leahnina nodded and kissed the side of his face. It wasn't enough so she wrapped her arms tighter around his chest and kissed his neck. He showered her with the same, stopping before his mother got embarrassed. "I would have been here if I had been able. You know that too."

Leahnina finally let out the laugh she was fighting. "I know. I just wanted to scare you a little. Come, meet our son."

Brani walked over with the baby and side-clutched her son. "You're back. Did you see that storm? It was a nightmare."

Dertujia didn't answer. It was a nightmare. He'd have it for a while. That sickening thing from Hetahaunder wrapped around him.

"Juyolax," he said, taking the baby into the crook of his elbow and staring. Everything fell apart inside. He felt tears roll down his cheeks. It was a good thing that none here thought tears were a weakness, because he collapsed in on himself. This was the epitome of perfection. Holding a creation he and his wife had bonded to make. The little toes! The eyes so blue like a flower in the field. He had strong legs which jerked as his eyes stared at Dertujia, not sure if he was friend or foe.

"Come, let us hold him together. I haven't had enough," Leahnina said.

Dertujia sidled up to Leahnina on the bed and looked back and forth between them.

Let Eropus do what he must. His best plans weren't enough to stop them. They would always succeed. As long as Dertujia had Leahnina, his son, and his friends, Eropus would never truly win.

He was a useless god who could only make faces at him. He hadn't even taken him on one on one. It was always an army, or a monster, or attacking from behind, or using a city.

Dertujia still really hated Firebranch.

But Eropus would always lose.

After an hour of just marveling at his son and Leahnina, finally it was time to send all the people to their homes.

The snow had evaporated, not even floods to show its presence. So, all they had to contend with was the damage to the houses and the burial of the people who hadn't listened.

It took a month for Xorna to heal enough to travel, but when she did there was a home for her.

Xorna had left a lot to be with them. Her sister had remained in Firebranch with her husband. But Xorna hoped one day Gampralle would join her. But everyone here was happy enough. They spent a lot of time in the house talking and reminiscing while the babies played on the floor.

Both had taken an immediate liking to the other. Good thing, because now their sets of parents were inseparable. Cetphur and Xorna, when she was strong enough, became farmers.

At one point, Dertujia stood on his porch enjoying the sunset. The giant sun so big and warm it cast a glow across the mountains. The cold friend.

Xorna walked out and leaned on the big wooden column next to him.

"Peace. This is what it's like. I feel as if I've been in war my whole life."

Dertujia nodded. He was still feeling the effects from Juyolax's first "ba ba". He would one day call him dad. "Tell me about it."

Xorna frowned though. Maybe she couldn't let things go so easily. "I don't like it. You do know that Eropus most likely planned all of this. The delay at Firebranch, the ice Dart just happening to attack while you were gone."

Dertujia shook his head. “One more time I have to disagree with you.”

Xorna snickered. “What else is new?”

“He couldn’t have had hands in that many things just to torment us. No, his last effort was to send the Dart. Firebranch has their own set of problems, and they just coincided with ours. But it’s over now. Leahnina doesn’t do too much foretelling these days. The pregnancy took a lot out of her. I’m sure one day she’ll return to full strength. But she had one vison.” Dertujia let a smile break out on his face. He didn’t even bother to hide it. “She said we’ll be happy for years to come. Our children will grow. We’ll have no diseases. No war runners. Shymis will glow for the foreseeable future. I am content in that.”

Xorna opened her mouth to protest.

He held up his hand. “No more war, Xorna. It’s peacetime. Give your daughter the gift that was never given you. Relax and see peace.”

Xorna closed her mouth and did as he asked. The two warriors watched the sun set.

Chapter Twenty-One

Eropus was a stain on Dertujia's existence. As much as Dertujia attempted to forget him, explain all the troubles away—Xorna's childbirth, Firebranch's enmity—it was made quite clear that Eropus was far from done with them.

Staying put made for sitting targets. Two different occasions came to test Dertujia's faith that there would be peace in his life.

The first was when Leahnina came home looking terrible. It had been a month since the birth. Juyolax was doubling in size. She had reluctantly left her child to go into town to have clothing fit for her body. Being between birth and pregnancy her form was recovering. She desired new clothes that covered it up.

Dertujia didn't see anything ugly about the body that she held now, but she hated every piece of clothing she owned.

When she returned, she barely got out of the carriage before she fainted to the ground. Dertujia had been sitting on the fence, rocking Juyolax and showing him the people in the fields, when he turned back, alarmed.

"Leahnina!" he roared and managed to keep a hold on Juyolax as he helped his wife up with a shadow arm.

"I'm okay. I am." She gasped and moaned. "I just used my powers."

Coldness seeped in. "A bad future?" he asked. She had refrained from future telling, as her skin was slipping away again. But she must have had a need …

"No. Dertujia, I killed again."

He held her arm, as she pulled Juyolax into hers. But she barely had the strength to hold him up before losing it.

"Xorna!" Dertujia yelled.

She came running. She wasn't the warrior anymore. She wore coarse pants and a long tunic with no armor, no weapons, but she was still ready for battle.

"What is it?"

"Take Juyolax. Please. Leahnina is weak."

Xorna did as he asked. "What is it? A war runner? A thief? A king?"

Leahnina's face crumpled. "Vengeance." Her eyes fluttered closed, and they pulled her inside the house. It took another hour to get the story out of her.

She had been walking, enjoying the fabric of the new clothes she had bought when she saw something that hurt her.

"They were there. The two bandits." She covered her eyes.

Dertujia couldn't breathe. If they had hurt her …

"They were selling Cornbers!"

Dertujia blinked. "Cornbers are disgusting. Did the bandits attack you? Throw them at you?"

She shook her head. "They were a part of the town. I pointed at them, screamed at them. These monsters had killed my grandmother."

Dertujia understood. The ones she met up with were from her tale of woe. They were a part of Shymis now.

"They didn't take that well," Xorna noted.

Leahnina struggled to sit up against the cushion on her bed. The gray and red curtains around the bed got caught on her arms. She flung them off. "No. They apologized. They turned over a new leaf, they claimed. Wanted to be a part of a town. Not constantly running from the law.

"'Why didn't you go back to Srashan city then?' I demanded."

"And their answer?" Dertujia stroked her hair, trying to get her to lie down again. This had been stressful on her. Meeting up with the monsters who had killed her grandmother.

"They didn't want the law finding them. They wanted a fresh start. Real fresh start for the woman they murdered. She'll never be able to hold Juyolax in her arms."

Xorna rocked Juyolax. "So, you turned them in? And they didn't want to go."

Leahnina's lip jutted out. Her eyes filled with messy tears. "No! They agreed that if I was willing to call the guard and have them taken back to Srashan, then they'd go. They were older now. More wrinkles. Tired."

Dertujia was more than confused. What would have made her use her powers then? It had taken a lot out of her.

"I don't understand," he admitted.

"They had no right!" she wailed. "One of the monsters actually said he might be happy to go back even if in jail, because he had a sweetheart back in the town. Maybe he could look her up, he said."

Dertujia took her hand, pressing against her knuckles. "And?"

"I made sure they got their justice. Both of them. No returning to *sweethearts*. No future. No children. They stole my grandmother. I stole their lives. I aged them to death. I watched as their brown and black hair grew strands of gray and then got taken over. Their wrinkles became a million. Then … dust. All over the ground."

Dertujia took a step back, Leahnina's hand falling from his. She sounded … mean. Cruel. There was no guilt like there had been with the thief. She was cold. The only reason she had been crying was because she was exhausted.

"What happened to you?" Dertujia asked. He couldn't recognize his own voice.

"Motherhood. A child is connected with the parents, just as I was to mine, just as theirs were to them. And those monsters had no right to live if they took it away."

Xorna cleared her throat. She didn't like Dertujia's face in that moment. "I agree."

He deflated. He never thought he'd hear Xorna say that. "What?"

"She got her family taken away. Leahnina had every right to choose their judgment."

Dertujia had another of the same question. "What happened to you?"

Xorna gave a tight smile. "Motherhood. I remembered long ago. The fight we had about the centaur. That poor child it killed. If that had been Tomphane … Family. You protect it. Even if you have to kill."

Dertujia's mind was reeling. So, their philosophical discussion had ended with this. Somehow, that fact made everything worse. She had always been his conscience. Maybe he never agreed with her. But she was someone to listen to. Now?

Leahnina had done no wrong by murdering two men?

"The law." Dertujia crept closer to Leahnina, hearing Juyolax cry for her. She could take him now. He couldn't feel anything but love as he held them together. "Will they arrest you?"

"Should I check?" she asked, pointing at her head.

"No. Did anyone see you?" He knelt next to the bed. His legs were weak. "Will you be judged?"

She shook her head. "No. They knew who kept them all safe. They know what I could do to them. I am their goddess. They'd never dream about putting me under their pathetic excuse for law."

Her eyes drifted closed. Dertujia walked out with Juyolax, straight from the house and back to his vantagepoint of before.

"See the people?" he asked Juyolax. "They are good. Never raise your hand to them. They rely on you."

"Dertujia," Xorna said behind him.

"Go away," he said. "I need to raise Juyolax right. I'm afraid …"

"That you are becoming the villain?"

He turned on her. "Leahnina sounded … did you hear her?"

"Do *not* judge her," Xorna lectured. "You have no idea what it's like to have people stolen from you. Leahnina told me how those monsters killed her grandmother. Now, nice and sweet? Having redeemed themselves? For some things, there is no redemption. You once told me that those with power have an obligation to make choices. Like with the centaur. Like with Dubruck when you executed him.

"Leahnina just claimed her right."

Dertujia couldn't breathe, but his mind started tying itself up with words.

What, it asked, *you can kill but she can't? You can get vengeance, but she is too soft? Never judge for you can be judged the same.*

He lost his anger. Lost his fear. "Still. Juyolax should know what it means to be a hero. I will teach him."

Xorna shook her head and left him.

It wasn't over. Leahnina thought of herself as an elevated person in the town (Dertujia believed so too. He wouldn't allow any of those traitorous thoughts to condemn her again.) But the people were mad. Some who hadn't cared she had helped them all live or even worse thanked gods for saving them from the snow and didn't give her credit at all.

They sent word to Srashan City.

It wasn't long until someone showed up.

A week after Leahnina's vengeance, Dertujia heard his shadows warning him.

"*Warriors, Master. Thousands of them. They surround our farm.*"

Dertujia gave a slap to the rump of a feisty Reathmop and turned around. He hadn't even looked for anyone.

But then …

They came.

Like a living tornado, they tore down the side of the soft hills around the farm. The army headed straight for him, led by …

"Captain Bartoe?" Dertujia queried. "I had hoped you'd given up." He reached for his shadows, ready. He felt a glare almost breaking his brow.

He pulled back on the Koorsgald's reins, and the rest of the army did as well. Some screeched and turned around, showing the armor they wore "Srashan City has asked for help against a powerful seer. We are here to deliver. Give over the woman. We will leave. If not, we will kill everyone here, including the animals."

Xorna and Cetphur came out behind him. They had spotted the army too. Cetphur's fire was hesitant, but it was there.

"You have some nerve," Dertujia said. "I own shadows. My companion orders fire. My wife can age you. What do you have?"

Captain Bartoe gave a sinister smile. "Eropus' protection. One more chance."

Dertujia wasn't going to listen to this. Bartoe had been warned.

"Pull the interlopers from the mounts," he ordered his shadows.

They moved as one, a black mass across the ground. But they halted and fell.

Bartoe shook his head. "So, you choose to die."

He whistled. His steed roared forward. Cetphur's fire came down, but it was a wall, blocking movement.

Bartoe rode right through it. He drew his wicked looking blade and sliced it through the air.

Right towards Dertujia's temple.

"Stop!" Leahnina moved so quickly he hadn't heard her approach. The blade rusted and fell apart in swipe. Leaving a shower of rust on his forehead.

How could he have judged her? She *was* like a goddess.

"You are a simple fool," he told Bartoe. Dertujia knew the only way to end this for good. He turned to his wife with an apologetic smile. "Leahnina, they come to kill. My shadows don't work. Cetphur's fire. Eropus has given him protection."

Leahnina's eyes widened. She asked for permission without saying a word.

"Never. I will never judge you again," he whispered.

"Nor I you. We have the right to protect ourselves."

She turned to Bartoe. "So, you want the seer, do you? Let me tell you about your future. When you're old and gray, you and your warriors will all *die*."

She gestured. A sight to behold. A silver line of dust shot out of her fingers. It settled on the whole army.

Bartoe rolled his eyes, confident in his god's protection. But those same eyes grew bloodshot, old, faded. He fell to the ground with white hair. All the people behind him fell as well.

"Now, they are dust," she said. And the army disappeared. Dertujia didn't have to have Leahnina's powers to tell that King Veriton wouldn't send people after the seer again.

"Well done." Dertujia narrowed his eyes. "Now, it's my turn."

He sent out a summons. All the people in Srashan or Shymis heard the same warnings.

"People who know who I am. I am Dertujia. Master of Shadows. I aim to live a peaceful life. My wife, my friends. Anyone I claim as mine. If you turn one hand against them, you will match the army that came today."

Then he asked for the dust's shadow to rise up all across the land, replaying the death of the army.

"A warning." He finished up and looked at Leahnina. "I'm sorry for judging you."

She gave a small grin. "No more apologies. We have nothing to feel sorry for.

They turned back to their duties.

No one ever talked about Leahnina's murders again. The two families lived peacefully for a while.

Chapter Twenty-Two

The baby awoke Dertujia in the middle of the night again. He bumped into Leahnina on the way to his room. She yawned and laughed. “It’s my turn.”

Dertujia tried to get his bearings. His dreams were messy, but he was at his peace. “I believe it was mine. Didn’t you comfort him last night?”

By the light of the sickle moon that trickled into their home, he could see Leahnina’s brow furrow. She was being extremely selfish about the baby. She seemed to think Juyolax was her responsibility and hers alone.

Dertujia pointed back to the room.

Leahnina harrumphed. “He could be hungry.”

Dertujia felt way too tired to be having this conversation. Who knew a new baby would cause so much contention? “You fed him on schedule. He isn’t hungry. He’s lonely. He is the loneliest baby I’ve ever met.”

Leahnina held her hand against his shoulder. "You've only met two. Tomphane and Juyolax."

Dertujia hid a grin. Maybe it was the late hour, but he found it funny Leahnina insisted on calling the two by their full names. Not once had Xorna, Dertujia, or Cetphur used them. It was always Phaney, or Laxy, or Juo or the like. And that was if they used the names and not sweetie, lovely, baby, moo moo, la la, wah, wah wah.

The baby talk coming from the former heroes was almost embarrassing. But Juyo was so cute!

"Go back to bed. You'll need your energy for the next feeding. Let me help our son, Leahnina. Please."

Leahnina yawned and agreed, shuffling back to bed. Meanwhile, Dertujia headed towards the baby's nursery.

Juyolax could already stand. And he was standing against his shadow crib. His tiny hands were shaking the bars like the little one was a prisoner.

Dertujia smiled, overcome with the emotion he felt. This was a part of him. A connection. Someone to teach things to. There was so much he wanted him to learn. As he picked up the squalling boy and placed his head against his neck, patting his back, he started thinking.

Cooing to the boy, his mind wandered. Did he want him to learn what Dertujia had? That parents could be cruel? That the world was filled with unfairness and strife?

No. Dertujia didn't want his son to be anything but a boy and then a man. He wanted him to be heroic. He wanted Juyolax to know right from wrong. It was strange as he looked at this little face, so full of wide-eyed wonder and new life, Dertujia felt bad about all the thoughts he had. Like this baby would judge him. As if all his deeds he had done should be carefully weighed in front of those innocent eyes.

Dertujia took a look at his life. There was a lot to be proud of. But would he want Juyolax to judge a village on the crimes of a few? Would he want his father to turn into a farmer and not help people anymore? Would he be proud that without lifting a finger or even battling, a whole army was murdered in front of him?

Juyolax babbled, playing with Dertujia's sleeves.

"Don't worry, little Juyo. You will not be a hero. I will be one enough for the both of us."

He held him to his chest, feeling resolve come over him again. He was a farmer, true, but he also could help a whole lot of people. When Dertujia was young, he had been called upon to train to be a hero.

It was wrong in so many ways. But he wouldn't have traded what he had gained from it either.

He wanted Juyolax to have the same thing.

Dertujia let his head fall in the affirmative. Dertujia had retired from being a hero, but it had never felt right. The more he didn't help, the meaner he felt. Blaming Firebranch for everything, hating them as a whole.

These thoughts were mixing with what Nockhun had said earlier that day. He had been going on and on about Firebranian seed planting and how it was best. Dertujia had snapped angrily that Firebranch was wrong about everything.

Nockhun had given him a wounded expression and said quietly, “It was my home. I wish you’d respect that we were taken over. We didn’t choose the leaders.”

Dertujia had wanted to say, “Yes, but you didn’t stop them either.” But in the middle of the night with Juyo in his arms, he felt the offense his words had caused.

And the guilt of the army falling to dust in front of him. He told himself time and again, that they were going to kill him. It was him or them. But even with that, as he held his son, he felt lost. Anxious. He needed to get back to battle. He needed to help again.

It all seemed so clear to him. All his hate and despair melted away. Juyolax was Dertujia’s future. The past was needed to guide the boy. Dertujia disagreed with his parents on how they raised him, but sometimes he understood why they did what they did.

The question hit him severely at this hour, when the starless sky outside sunk into the distance, obliterating any light. Did he want Juyolax to feel that darkness? Or did he want him to see the light, the hope. Already, there had been rumors of war runners taking over cities not far from here. A few people had already traveled to Dertujia's farm.

He had turned them away, saying how he was more of a farmer than a warrior.

Xorna's face when she found out!

Xorna was still the hero these days. Though she had a baby to take care of, he could already see that she still desired to continue her role.

Dertujia hugged Juyolax to him. "I want you to be a hero. Not a coward. Not a farmer who ignores his world around him. I don't want you to be me."

"You are great, though!"

Dertujia spun around. He almost expected Leahnina, but there was no one behind him.

Dertujia tensed, holding Juyolax. Where had that voice come from? There was no one in the room with him. Out the open window, he only saw his fields or at least the shape of them in the vast darkness.

"Sorry. I'm out here."

Dertujia finally relaxed. It wasn't an enemy. Far from it. "Hello, Fetgur."

The Flitclike leader was in the sky. Dertujia had been looking at the ground.

"Hello, Dakchin."

Their name for emperor. He chuckled and placed Juyolax in the crib and stuck his head out the open window. He heard a lot of flapping noises. "It's Dertujia. And I hear that you've brought friends."

Fetgur landed. There were deep lines in his face, a result of the daily battle he fought with his anger. Eropus had really ruined these people.

"How goes it with your anger control?" Dertujia asked. They had sent many letters telling Dertujia, Dakchin, that they were doing better these days. As a whole, they didn't fight. That helped keep the rage at bay. All of them were pacifists.

Fetgur grimaced. "Not too bad. The new babes are dealing better with it than the ones who were born fully formed. They might be able to be free one day of our rages. One day."

Dertujia leaned on the sill, letting the night air tickle the hairs on his forearms. "So, what brings you here?"

Fetgur whistled, and the rest of the ones with him landed. Dertujia hadn't met a lot of them when he was there, but the ones he had were all here.

"We've come to pay tribute to your child. We heard that you have been gifted with a son."

Dertujia slid onto the windowsill to laugh. "Yes, I really have." He moved through the window and gestured to continue the conversation away from the house.

Fetgur walked forward but used his wings to keep his balance. He was barely visible in the low light. "Then we want to pay him homage. Give gifts. Make him the honored son of our Dakchin."

Dertujia tried very hard not to roll his eyes. This had happened only a few times with the ones he saved. Acting as if he was a member of their tribe or worse their leader. Usually, he managed to lessen it, but the Flitelikes knew he was there with their goddess when Fetgur was born. In a strange way, he was the father. Which meant he was the Flitelikes' father, and Juyolax was their brother.

He couldn't deny that.

"I just got the baby back to sleep. Surely this can wait 'til morning."

Fetgur nodded vigorously. "Of course. I just wondered if you'd give us safety. Eropus was following us."

That made Dertujia tense. It also reminded him how long it had been since he had practiced fighting with his shadows or even his sword.

"Into the barn." He scanned the night sky. The Flitelikes, five in total, scurried across the darkened field and slipped into the barn where Dertujia heard the Koorsgalds squawking at their new neighbors. The Reathmops, luckily, were all in another barn, as they wouldn't appreciate their sleep being interrupted. Dertujia held his fists, wondering if he could possibly know if Eropus was here.

"Boo," a voice whispered in his ear.

Dertujia growled in his anger, trying to find the voice.

Suddenly, the night was lit up. There was the man Dertujia sometimes had nightmares about, the one who had left him broken. Was that what he was here for now?

"Nice farm," Eropus said snidely. He stretched his narrow limbs and moved his shoulders. The robes he wore now showed him to be royalty. He even wore a solid silver crown on his black hair.

"What do you want here?" Dertujia asked. He was proud that his voice neither faltered nor wavered. If Eropus came here for a show of fear, he'd be disappointed.

But Eropus just smiled, cocking his head. "I hear the baby's gurgles. What a soft sweet sound."

Dertujia was confused. This sounded an awful lot like Eropus was here for the same purpose as the Flitelikes. He tensed his throat but relaxed as much as possible. It'd be better to be friends with a god who could break every bone in his body not an enemy.

"He's a sweet babe. I hope you're not here after the Flitelikes."

Eropus gave a smile. Thick lips twisted, almost purple. "Not at all. My sister and her toys mean as much to me as a single grain of sand in a desert."

Dertujia moved towards the open window where just across it slept Juyolax. "You cared before."

He placed a hand against his chest in offense. "I cared because Bynneeshia ruined my creations. It's a brother sister thing. Do you have siblings?"

Dertujia had to admit he didn't. Maybe it was foolish, but Dertujia was beginning to listen to him. What did he truly know about Eropus? The bards said he was evil. His sister, a goddess who was just as interested in ruining lives as he was, had confirmed it.

But Dertujia knew next to nothing about him. "You almost killed me," Dertujia pointed out to his own mind and Eropus.

"You were attacking me. Coming to stop me from so-called draining the world."

Yes, that was true. Dertujia conveniently forgot the fact that he had been leaving when Eropus tried to take his life. Dertujia leaned against a fence post. Perhaps the Flitelikes were just overly paranoid about a god who ruined them.

"Question," Dertujia said, quickly. Old habits died hard. He wanted to protect them. "Can you reverse what you did to the Flitelikes? Restore their good nature? It would mean a lot to …"

Dertujia felt like a fool, but surprising him, Eropus just waved his hand.

"Of course. I want no enmity from you. You are something else. A hero that has renown. If I had only known who you were, I wouldn't have hurt you."

Dertujia felt the rest of him relax. This was not an evil god. He was just put in the wrong light. War runners didn't speak so sweet. Evil gods didn't apologize. Not that Eropus had, exactly.

"But I have to admit, I am a little disappointed. You were a hero. Now you're a farmer."

There again with the same snide tone. It shamed Dertujia. Like nothing had before.

"I …"

Eropus waved his hand and gave a grin. "No offense. I just wanted you to know that many people looked up to you. And Xorna too. To think you've let them all down."

Now that hurt. An ache attacked him. Hadn't he just been upset by that very thing? Now Eropus was here telling him how wrong he was. Almost as if Eropus was the real hero, and Dertujia was the bad guy.

He wrinkled his brow. "I regret it."

It was simple enough. Eropus was not mortal. If it had been anyone else, this conversation would not be taking place under the dark sky right near dawn but still in the throes of deep night. But he brought a worm into Dertujia's heart. He should never have given up being a hero.

"Great thing about regrets," Eropus said with a smile. "You can fix them. Return to who you are. Don't make that baby grow up to think his father is a coward."

Dertujia felt it deep inside. Eropus was right. Dertujia had given up being a hero. Because he had been afraid.

"Tomorrow I'll check on the war runners I've heard about recently. I'll return to what I am. But my son …"

Eropus chuckled. "Your son will be better knowing his father is out there fighting. Do you know what happened when the old gods died?

My father? I resented him for giving up. I hated him. You don't want your son to hate you."

No. Dertujia couldn't stand that. All this time, he resented his parents for making him a hero. He had tried to give it up, but he had never thought about what it'd be like for his son to know what happened. What would Dertujia tell him? Would he say that after a bad injury he had been too scared to fight again? That he had given up training and even tried to prevent his best friend from helping people? That the only battle he had taken place in was one-sided, and he had done nothing? How would that go over? What would Juyolax think?

"Thank you, Eropus. I never thought about that before."

Eropus gave a grin that made Dertujia uncomfortable. But there was no reason for that. Eropus was a good god. Neesh had just been telling her side. But he had to ask. "Are you draining the world? Neesh told me …"

Eropus slapped his knee and walked towards the barn of Flitelikes. "She has always used that one. No. This world has seasons. Like winter or fall, but it's just going into a winter for a while. That's why the scenery is drained. But it will be reborn like a spring breeze. Don't worry about it. That concern is for us gods. Not mortals."

Dertujia breathed a huge sigh of relief. Eropus was telling him what he wanted to hear. He couldn't take it if anyone, god or other, was draining the world around. Yes, Neesh had been lying, and Dertujia had believed her. How foolish! Just because she was lovely and seemed kind meant nothing. There had been a lot of queens who appeared sweet that were more sadistic than an average war runner.

"I thank you for your visit. Now if you'll just release the Flitelikes."

Eropus' chin fell down in the affirmative, and his eyes looked out under his eyebrows at him. "Bring them out then."

Dertujia gave a yell. To his surprise, the Koorsgalds didn't squawk. They usually loved the sound of his voice, breaking into a cacophony of noise when he called out. Now there were little murmurs of coos, but they remained silent. They must have been terrified at the Flitelikes in their midst.

But the Flitelikes came out, looking angry.

"It appears I did you a wrong," Eropus said. "Let me rectify it."

He snapped his fingers, and suddenly all the tension left Fetgur's body. The same happened with the other Flitelikes.

It was done. What had started this whole journey was over. Dertujia smiled. "Come in, surely you can drink with me," he offered.

Eropus shook his head and walked off, disappearing into the darkness around. Dertujia looked at Fetgur who wiggled his fingers in front of his face. "Odd. He fixed it. I didn't think …"

"We all gave into fear," Dertujia said. "Go home. You're free now. No longer pawns of either god."

Fetgur laughed. But he didn't go home. Not until morning. After the group had adored Juyolax for a while. But they didn't leave alone. Dertujia packed a bag along with Xorna and they left their farm to go towards the war runners. Both trained on the way in the grasp of the Flitelikes who gave them a ride halfway.

Meanwhile, Eropus watched the bubble he had brought up as he lounged on his throne. How gullible mortals were. Say a few pretty words, do a little bit of a show, and they do everything you tell them.

"What are you doing?" Neesh said, appearing next to him, looking so innocent. Her expression drove him nuts. Had he the power, he'd rub her own blood all over her face as he smashed it into one of the stone pillars around his throne room.

"Dertujia was living with his family. You …"

Eropus snapped a whip of living black energy at her. The life in her just spat it away. "I missed him being a hero. You should rejoice, sister. Your Flitelikes are back to normal."

"You never do anything without an ulterior motive. And you still drain the world to one day destroy me. So, am I to believe you've turned over a new leaf?" The innocence in her ocean blue eyes wiggled his nerves. How could she be so good? Even after all the pain they had suffered?

"Believe what you want, sister. I just know that I really liked breaking that hero. It's not fun to make an omelet with already broken eggs."

Neesh hissed at him. "He was healing after all the pain. He needed that relaxation. His son needs his father."

Eropus cocked his head and laughed. "Yes, it sucks doesn't it. But it got you here."

He wiggled his finger, and the earth opened under her. She flew as it pulled her down, fighting against it.

"This is where I drain, sister," Eropus said, shoving off the throne and watching her kick uselessly against the air. She'd lose against the maelstrom. She was weak. And he had the energy of the earth.

"What are you going to do?" she yelped, slowly sinking. He snapped his fingers and beneath her chains reached up, wrapping around her arms, throat, and legs. Yanking her to her prison. She would not bother him anymore. "Will you kill Dertujia?"

Eropus yawned even as his prisoner disappeared. He lounged on his throne. "No. Not yet. I like waiting. Let Dertujia think he's a hero again. Let him regain his confidence. Then I will smash it like his bones. A few years ought to do it."

He thought back to when he watched Dertujia holding his son. He couldn't wait to watch his own game play. Let the hero return. Then Eropus would play the villain again.

He laughed and sent out another wave of energy.

Far across the world, the Flitelikes in the middle of a game of ball, turned on each other. Screaming and fighting. Ripping each other's wings off.

Games were a little war, and Eropus had restored their anger.

"Be a hero, Dertujia," he whispered. "But you will fail. Always. And when you do, then I will take your life. It will be … sweet."

He heard the screams of Bynneeshia down below. Trapped. Their game was over. The god surroundings were his.

He was the last god standing.

Now he wanted to have fun.

Chapter Twenty-Three

Leahnina finished putting the Koorsgald in the enclosure and latched the gate to make sure she wouldn't find them roaming come morning. It was coming time for supper, and her boy would be hungry.

She waved to Nockhun, always feeling the same way. Happy to have a friend there but upset at the same time. He wasn't her husband, and yet he was more familiar to her than Dertujia these days. He had been gone far too long this time. Two years now, after two years of traveling. Her son was turning five soon. And he barely saw Dertujia.

Leahnina made the way across the long field, walking in to see Brani stirring some fragrant food, while Kaytal looked over the oven with some bread in it. Leahnina was more than grateful for Dertujia's parents.

They filled his gap. Though, nothing could.

"It's almost time for dinner," Leahnina said, taking her hood down. She wore one to prevent the sun from burning her face. It seemed so sensitive these days. Of course, her whole upper half felt sensitive. She had been trying so hard to keep an eye on Dertujia and make sure he was okay. But his future was getting harder and harder to see. The more he tried to prove himself, he flitted from village to village, from cause to cause.

Leahnina had to be careful not to tax herself. She needed to see when real danger would hit. Not his life away from her. She didn't admit it to anyone how many times she watched her husband. Was he safe? Eating enough? Finding his diversions elsewhere?

"Where is Juyolax?"

Brani smiled. "He's playing with the building blocks I gave him."

Leahnina nodded and walked towards the playroom.

As Brani said, he was in front of his blocks. The little tyke had built up a whole city with roads and houses. Even a castle.

Leahnina just watched him, laughing internally as he measured and made sure it all fit together.

Then to her shock and surprise, he stood up and started kicking the whole thing over!

"Juyolax!" Leahnina scolded. He looked up with surprise and gave her a sheepish grin. "What are you doing?"

He shrugged. "I'm a bad guy."

Leahnina clucked her tongue and pointed at the pieces for Juyolax to start cleaning up. "You're the son of a hero. You are a good boy. Not the bad guy."

Juyolax frowned. "Nope! Bad guy. Maybe then Daddy would love me. Maybe then he'd see me."

Leahnina's heart clutched. He was so innocent, but his pain was so raw. Dertujia hadn't been home for more than a couple months a year ever since Juyolax was born. And the last two birthdays had been missed, and maybe this one too.

"He's doing great things for the world," Leahnina said, kneeling down next to him and rubbing his knee.

Juyolax shook his head. "No. He's with the bad guys. I wanna see him. I want him to like me as much as he does them."

Leahnina pulled him to her, crying. What had gone wrong? In the name of saving people, he was turning his back on his own son.

When Dertujia returned home, she pointed him into the living room and paced in front of him. "Dertujia, you're staying home now."

Dertujia rubbed the dirt off his face. He was ready for a long bath, not a lecture. He pulled off his boots, worn and getting a hole. He should have used his carriage more often, but even he couldn't climb up mountains with it. And he didn't think using the shadow dragon necessary just for traveling.

"Leahnina, I am not in the mood for this. I am making a better world. Becoming the hero Juyolax needs."

She pointed an accusing finger at him. "He needs a father. A role model. Just earlier he was playing with his toys and becoming the villain just to have you spend some time with him."

Dertujia leaned back, comforted by the scent of the chair he sat on. The rug under his feet. The house around him. He wanted to stay home more than anything. But what kind of man would he be then? A farmer? How could Juyolax look up to him then?

"Dertujia! I can see him hating you."

He let his hand fall from his face. "I thought you had given up seeing the future. Is your body still whole?"

The same concern and love he had always had for her surrounded her. It washed away the aggravation she held in her heart. She slipped over to him and fell into his lap, the smell of the road and his body enveloping her. "I'm fine. I just wanted to check. Dertujia, I barely see you. Juyolax barely sees you. Don't be a hero. Be a father."

Dertujia put his hands around her waist and held her, kissing her shoulder. "I'll take him with me," he said slowly. "If that's okay."

Leahnina tensed and pulled away. "What?"

"I need to show him what I'm doing. But he also needs to be with me."

Leahnina stared at him. "Take him with you? As you fight evil war runners and the cruel kings?"

He touched her face gently, missing her. It seemed that's all he ever did was miss her and Juyo. "If he wants to be a villain, then he has to see what they are."

Leahnina saw his point. But somehow, she didn't want that. She wanted him to come home. This was supposed to be their new life, away from all that pain.

"We'll get ready tomorrow." Leahnina wasn't going to argue on this.

He made a face, but she put two fingers on his lips. "It's all of us or none of us. We have been without you for far too long."

He finally gave in, holding her tight. He wouldn't have it any other way. He just thought that his family should have a choice. He breathed in and made a face. "I need to bathe first," he claimed and sent a kiss to her head.

"Do you want company?" she asked, showing the hidden yearning. The months without him. Once again, he questioned the wisdom of leaving her.

What was he doing?

But he tabled those thoughts.

***

The next morning, he asked his parents to take care of the farm as he and Leahnina along with a grinning and excited Juyolax boarded his shadow coach.

"Room for two more?" Xorna called. She plopped down beside him shoving her own traveling bag onto the top of the carriage.

Dertujia gaped at her. "I thought you were staying with your husband and child this time."

She shook her head. "Hey, we stay together. I wouldn't risk my child, but we can keep her safe. And Cetphur is coming too."

Dertujia jumped as Cetphur swung in, laughing. "An adventure."

"What is this?"

"You are going with your family," Xorna said stiffly. "I want to make sure you come back. Cetphur does too. There's been too much time apart recently."

Dertujia had to admit she was right. He sent the shadows on, relishing the feeling of the past. This time, however, he held Juyolax on his lap and pointed out all the things he could see for the first time.

Leahnina held his hand, and the journey continued.

There were rumors of some horrible thugs attacking a village in the north. As they traveled, Dertujia started lecturing. It was time for Juyolax to see what villains were.

"They take without cause, smash and trash anyone who gets in their way. It isn't noble, son. It's damaging and selfish. Never be that."

Juyolax nodded.

The journey continued. They slept in a copse of trees as night fell. Dertujia played with Juyolax and a wooden sword while the little one jumped and stabbed imaginary creatures. Tomphane watched with a wide expression. She would be a peacemaker not a warrior.

Dertujia was all too happy that Leahnina had suggested this. Although Xorna and Cetphur worried about what could come, they had fun.

It became much more like a two-family vacation not a warrior trip, and Dertujia wondered if that's why Xorna had come with her family as well. Maybe this wasn't even a training lesson. Maybe it was just trying to keep Dertujia from being that warrior.

He was lost. He admitted it. All the people around him saw that he was making a mistake. But what Eropus had said! He couldn't imagine being a farmer in Juyolax's eyes.

"Hey look, Daddy!" Juyolax said. "I know that picture. It's your shadow." He crowed this as they passed a sign for a village they were heading to. "Shadow Land."

Dertujia smiled and tussled his hair. "That is Shadoria, my boy. Shadow Orian. In the old tongue."

"What's there?" Xorna asked. "I've never seen it."

"Spider warriors," Leahnina pointed out. "I've seen them. They exist in the deep darkness, spinning webs for their city. We must be cautious. If they can't handle a threat, then what could?"

Dertujia closed his eyes. His vacation was turning into work. As they traveled, the road grew darker. Not from shadows but from stone.

Dark and deep, stuck together tight with some kind of black muck that became so hard it would be impossible to tear apart. The journey was smooth under his shadows.

But then … the sound he had been dreading. Why was he bringing Juyolax into this? Screams echoed around them.

Dertujia halted his shadows.

"Stay here."

"No!" Leahnina argued. "You want him to see what you do? Show him. All of it."

He stared at her. "But he is just a child."

"So are some of the people being hurt today."

She stared him down, and he let the carriage continue. He wondered about the wisdom of letting children so young see what was happening. But if Leahnina was worried, maybe she had seen Juyolax grow to become a villain. He wouldn't allow that. And if Xorna agreed then little Tomphane would learn a lesson today too.

The road headed downwards. In the distance, he saw it sink into a huge chasm. That same black stone was all over the place, covered in colorful cobwebs. No matter how pretty, they were still webs, things to stick you tight. So, the spiders could eat?

Dertujia clutched his sword.

The spiders were half people, half spider with big hairy legs. Long, wide, thin, and fat.

The human forms on top were as varied. All of them were gathered in the main square and they looked up into …

"Flitelikes!" Dertujia yelled.

Winged. Armored. Angry. Spilling blood as they swooped down.

"Daddy," Juyolax yelled. "I'm scared."

"They were supposed to be peaceful!" Dertujia said, jumping out.

"Eropus lied." Xorna was spitting fire. She rushed into battle holding her sword up and lopping off the wing of one who came at her ready to cut her head off. Dertujia also got into position. Cetphur and Leahnina held their children, soothing them.

The war was serious. Dertujia didn't know what to do here. The Flitelikes were innocent. Twisted into this horrible place. Dertujia should never have trusted Eropus. All of this was ridiculous!

The battle was ugly. Webs shot across the sky. Feathers fell. Blood drenched the streets. Dertujia had only one recourse. The only thing he could do.

"Flitelikes, I am your Dakchin." He flew up to the top of the shadowy buildings. He stood there and put his hand out. "Listen to me."

One was familiar. Fetgur flew over to Dertujia and looked at him. "Dakchin, what …?"

"End this now. You are terrifying children. You don't want this. Listen to your Dakchin. Please."

Fetgur's eyes cleared, and he nodded, looking around in horror. He pulled up and screamed a whistling retreat sound. They were gone. The spiders down below screamed their pain.

Then a voice added to it. "Dertujia! It's Juyolax!"

He swooped down, terrified. To his distress, he saw a red web covering his son. Juyolax was shuddering and choking, trapped by the web. Dertujia made a shadow knife and slit all of it off.

"How dare you?" he demanded.

One Arachnialon walked forward and raised his hand, daring to slap Dertujia across the face. "You led them here. You deserve much, much more. Get out. Now."

Dertujia shuddered with anger, wanting to throw his fist into the guy's nose. But Juyolax was watching. Dertujia stood tall and pointed. "You are very lucky. We saved you. But I will say goodbye now."

The group left, leaving a city who was crying, watching, and blaming.

No one could quite figure out what had happened. "Dertujia, Eropus …"

Dertujia didn't need Leahnina telling him. Eropus had manipulated him. He was still a villain. And he was playing with Dertujia.

Dertujia had trusted him! Had listened to him. He hadn't bothered to go and see what was going on. On his trips around the world, he saw more and more draining, and he had dismissed it as a winter season.

It was a somber group that boarded Dertujia's shadow carriage. Juyolax sat in stunned silence. "I don't want to be bad," he finally said.

Tomphane nodded her tiny head. "Yes. We should be good. That was scary."

They stayed true to their parents and didn't cry. A lesson was learned, but Dertujia didn't know which one he had learned.

As Shymis showed up … Dertujia stood up, removing the top of the shadow carriage. There was something very wrong in the air. Silence, the same as when the ice Dart was raging. Three pillars of black smoke rose in the distance.

"Flames!" Cetphur said. "I can feel them."

Dertujia urged the shadow carriage on. As he entered the village proper, burning heat met his eyes. The village was on fire. Everything.

Again, they rushed into battle, but this time it was Cetphur doing most of the work, taming the flames. But there was nothing he could do. A fire Dart roared through the streets escaping as Dertujia threw shadows.

They had arrived too late. Most of the people were burned alive.

In stunned silence, Dertujia returned home to see his farm was in fire ruined ashes. There was no sign of anything left alive.

He stepped out. He didn't feel a thing. His home, his life was in tatters. He moved through the wreckage like he wasn't there. Far away. The bodies of his parents, of Leahnina's friend were ash. Nothing was left …

Suddenly he heard movement. He ignored the barn. Nothing was left alive in there. But in the silo, under a wooden beam …

"Nockhun," he said and pulled him out, feeling the wall breaking. No. He had to stay far away. Not up close and personal. "What happened?"

He gave a bloody grimace. Xorna started wrapping bandages around him as Cetphur assessed the burns. "Eropus. He said he had a message for you."

Dertujia's teeth felt like they'd break through his skull. "What was it?"

"Only that he wishes you were here."

Dertujia clenched his fist, keeping his emotions closed.

"What are you going to …?" Leahnina asked but then gasped. She saw. This future was too powerful.

"I'm going after him again. This time I will kill him."

He stood up, ready to leave. The numb cloud wrapped around his heart. To his surprise, Leahnina put her hand on his arm, along with Xorna and Cetphur. "We're going together. We will finish what we started."

He shook his head. "No, the children need to be protected."

"I will take them to Firebranch," Nockhun said. "They will be safe there. You know that."

Dertujia did.

"In Firebranch, find my sister, Gampralle, and her husband. She can help," Xorna said to Nockhun.

The numbness stayed around his heart as they prepared two shadow carriages, one for Nockhun.

Nockhun took the children with great solemnity. None talked. None cried. There was no time to cry or think. The deaths hovered like a locust cloud on the horizon. They knew it was coming, but it wasn't the time to mourn. So many had died. Leahnina's friends, Xorna's and Cetphur's, but nothing was as bad as what Dertujia had lost. Not one there felt right to feel anything deep. Not until Dertujia did.

But Dertujia was frozen.

Nockhun clutched Dertujia's hand into a hug and then pulled back. "I will watch these children with my life."

"You'd better." Dertujia gestured for Xorna and Cetphur to board, and the two carriages crunched over broken and burnt debris as they shoved off.

Cetphur spoke in a monotone. "Should we fly? Nockhun told me about what you did to leave the prison. This carriage will be slow. We need swift revenge."

Dertujia nodded. He hadn't thought of it. He could only move onward, one foot in front of the other. No feelings. He slowed the carriage and called it forth.

The being bled out of the ground, shaking its head at Dertujia. "*Master, you called. So many have met the underworld king. I expected you to follow.*"

Dertujia inclined his head. "Yes. But I will not go down so easily. I will rip off Eropus' head and you will see only the body come to your realm."

The dragon shook its head. "*That isn't how it works, but I respect your promise.*"

They all boarded, and the wind was their companion as the dragon creature shot towards Eropus' place.

He held Leahnina in front of him in his arms. She craned her head to look up at him. "Dertujia, this beast is from death itself."

He nodded, holding tighter.

"Then could it give a message. To all the ones …"

Dertujia finished her sentence. "All the ones I failed. Yes, tell them how pathetic I am. How I could have stopped this god and saved their lives, but instead I listened to cowardice."

Leahnina rubbed the back of her head against his armor, her hair brushing the exposed neck. "You know that's not true. You were listening to me. I told you what I saw."

"But I am a hero. It's what my parents pushed me into. And my lack of heroics just got them killed. Gone, Leahnina." His voice was broken. He worked his hardest to strengthen it. "I won't let any more die. Tell me what you see."

She looked up at his chin. He wouldn't look back. "I thought you didn't want me using my skills."

"Things change, Leahnina. We need to know. Does Xorna still die?"

She closed her eyes. It had been a while since she had tried to see such a big future. As usual, it spilled through her head. "Yes. The world is split apart. Millions die."

He gasped. He rocked her, opening his mouth in a silent cry. When he recovered, Xorna poked him on the shoulder. "Dertujia, don't forget our rules. If one is in danger, the other saves the people. Sacrifice the one for the greater whole."

"But this is lots of ones," Dertujia cried. "I can't call for the death of so many people. He is only draining the world now. It will take years for it to die out. And I am supposed to kill many to save more?"

Cetphur grunted. "You don't have a choice. We don't have a choice."

Dertujia turned on him, twisting his body in half to stare. "You're talking about your wife."

Cetphur leveled a glare at Dertujia. "No, I'm talking about both of us. Leahnina, tell him what you saw. I knew this was coming. I had hoped by returning to Firebranch, it'd stop it. But she always saw Tomphane an orphan. We are supposed to die. Tell him!"

Dertujia couldn't breathe. He looked at Leahnina. She nodded.

"The box has to tear him apart. It's connected with the world. But to do so, Xorna has to take him on physically, match his might with hers. Cetphur has to throw the elements at him. I have to use my powers to the max to hold him, and you have to …"

"Take the box and ask it to split him in two. Since Xorna is fighting him and Cetphur is using fire, they will be at ground zero." Dertujia nodded. "We all have to die then."

Leahnina sobbed into her hands. "No. We survive. We are immune to the split. So is Juyolax and Tomphane."

He gulped. His tongue felt too thick. His chest too tight. What were they doing here?

"Then let's go home. Bring us to Nockhun. We will all make Firebranch home and keep it safe while *he* destroys the world. "

Xorna inched forward to hold him from behind, while Cetphur took his shoulder. Leahnina finished up the hug by yanking him closer. "That's what we thought before," Xorna said quietly. "While we were gone, Leahnina had too many visions. Always watching over you and Juyo's future. But Eropus won't leave you alone. He won't leave anyone alone.

"He has captured Neesh."

Dertujia gasped. "What?"

"Yes," Leahnina was the one who answered. "He pushed her into the earth. I saw everything. I kept it secret. I denied it so we could be happy. You wanted to be a hero, but I was afraid you'd go after him …"

"But now," Cetphur continued. "He has hunted you. Tricked you. Dertujia, you are a personal project now. First an ice demon and then a fire? He will bring all the elements down on anywhere you live."

Dertujia felt their love pouring over him. He wanted to be angry that they would have talked about this, saw these things and not told him. But his heart couldn't move. It was trapped under the ice and fire that Eropus had used to destroy.

"I can't," he said. "To destroy so many lives based on my own happiness? No, unthinkable. To lose Xorna. To lose Cetphur. I will travel constantly. Never settling down. Take a different name. Hide."

Leahnina screeched into the night. Her pain was showing. Dertujia's was blessedly hidden. "We can't. What kind of life is that for Juyolax? It's over, Dertujia. We thought he'd let us be. But he is an unageing god who has the gift of time on his hands. Even if we get bored, he won't. Even if we die, he won't. He will always be after our blood. We will see from Hetahaunder his wounds. And it will be our fault. You can't put that on our conscience. The end of the world. This way it will spare the survivors. His way will end everything."

Dertujia couldn't respond. He was tired of all of this. He just wanted to sleep. "I can't. I am holding on by a thin tether. It's straining. If it snaps … My parents are dead, Leahnina. And you're asking me to lose my best friends."

"It's for Tomphane and her children," Cetphur argued. "It's for Juyolax and his. We will leave so they can live. If Eropus had just given up … I don't know. But this is right. I feel it in my bones. We leave this battle, more will succumb to ice and fire demons. Or worse. He controls the world's elements.

"I never told you, but I am … of Eropus' blood."

Dertujia's neck tensed even further. "What?"

"It's why I can control fire. You told me how your trip to Dragon Tower gave you skills. I never had to go there. I have a piece of the world in my blood. Eropus has control over all. Kill him, and the control will return to the netherworld. But think! He can torture so many."

Leahnina spoke up again. "Neesh held him off, using her own powers of creation to offset his evil. But when he started draining the world, she could do nothing. Now she's trapped. I saw it all. Dertujia, I tried to keep it hidden. I tried to live. But it's not possible. Not now. When he's killed, Juyolax will be safe. We can take care of Tomphane. Their futures will still exist. The rest of the world's futures will still exist. That's not guaranteed with Eropus in power."

Dertujia couldn't answer her.

"Dertujia! Juyolax won't just die! He will be Eropus' next target. He will find him. He will torture him but never let him die. His personal vendetta against you will keep Juyolax in pain for his whole life."

He clenched his fists over her head. "Why did no one tell me this?"

"Denial," Cetphur answered. "After all we've gone through, we thought maybe we could change Leahnina's visions by separating. But evil follows you. Do you really think it was Firebranch's idea to hunt you? To imprison you? Eropus' reach is everywhere."

Dertujia let it all sink in. His heart grew to stone. It was as it had to be. Juyolax would live. The rest of the world would suffer. But he had no choice. He just hoped the future generations could forgive him.

"Where is the box?" he asked.

Leahnina handed it over. "Your shadows need to touch it. Dertujia?"

He looked down at her. She too was stiff, unemotional. There had been too much. They had to fight the god. That was it.

"What?" he asked.

"I will always love you. We will always be together. Remember my promise."

That somehow inched into his stony heart and smashed it into pieces. He wailed and held her, and one by one all of them broke into tears.

But as the ground skimmed faster, turning into Eropus' area, their eyes were dry. Dertujia had been talking to the box, the same way he talked to his shadows. This box belonged to the goddess of old. She was blessing them.

On the way to battle, it was the only shield.

Dertujia and Leahnina clasped hands, while Xorna and Cetphur behind them said their goodbyes. Xorna scooted to the front of the dragon to whisper in Dertujia's ear.

"It ends tonight, my friend. Our partnership. Our friendship. You knew this was the end. No hero can exist without one day sacrificing themselves not without losing the moniker of hero."

Dertujia clutched her hand and took strength from his old friend's words.

She was right. This was just one more battle. It was the right thing to do. No one could hold them responsible. Eropus was asking for death. He wouldn't leave Dertujia or the world alone. After all, the world had spited him. He would treat it the same way he treated Dertujia.

Yes, Dertujia was doing the right thing.

The dragon landed. They jumped off. Xorna checked over Cetphur's armor for missing pieces. He returned the favor, and then held her. Dertujia and Leahnina held hands, as Dertujia swung the box, wondering when he'd get a chance to use it.

"Here we are at the end," Xorna said. "I want to say something powerful to make sure the bards can repeat it. A witty line of poem. All I can think to say is I can't wait to punch that god's face in."

Cetphur gazed at her in fascination, edged with abject despair. "Couldn't have said it better myself. But I plan to burn his skin off his bones. You, Dertujia?"

"I will glory in tearing him apart. Revenge is sweet. But against a god? It is a decadent dessert indeed." He paused and nodded. They looked up at Eropus' castle. Dertujia could see him watching them. He was hanging over one of the many balconies, waiting and grinning.

"How foolish. It is time to end him. Shall we?"

And the four walked inside to the final battleground.

Chapter Twenty-Four

The door was open. All they had to do was walk in. Eropus was waiting for them. They took strength in each other's nearness. Battle made them lose all thoughts of anything but the god.

Dertujia watched everything, everywhere. The main room was like a throne room with two stairs leading up to another level. Eropus lounged on the banister watching them.

"Oh, so you did come, Dertujia, hero. I thought you might want to bury the bodies. They burned nicely, don't you think?"

"Watch yourself, Dertujia," Xorna warned. But Dertujia didn't need her warning. This was what he had trained his life to do.

The decision he made had encased his heart with a thick stone. It beat. But it beat strong with no emotion. This was war. No time for weakness. No time for second guessing.

"Are you going to come down to fight? Or do we have to chase your tail like the coward you are?" Dertujia asked.

Eropus grinned and with a whirlwind flew down, landing in the middle of the four. With one swing of his arm, he flattened Xorna and Cetphur. Cetphur didn't get up before fire attacked the god. He giggled and took the fire whip Cetphur sent and clutched it in his hand, sniffing it.

"My blood. Trying to hurt me. Amazing. Which one are you? One of my millions of spawns or what?"

Cetphur shot a wild look at Dertujia.

Dertujia understood. This shouldn't be happening. Eropus shouldn't be able to resist his fire.

Dertujia leaped up and brought his sword down across Eropus' wrist. But it clanged like there was metal in there. Eropus laughed and shoved him backward. Dertujia flew, slamming hard into the stone pillar in the room.

He heard Leahnina running, getting out of Eropus' way. Seeing his target and avoiding it. Eropus roared in anticipation and chased her out of the throne room. Dertujia ran to help Xorna up.

"What is happening? Is this a lost cause?"

"There has to be a reason," Cetphur said. He sounded desperate. Ready to scream.

Was this indeed a lost cause?

"Help …" A tiny voice called.

Dertujia didn't care. He heard Leahnina's footsteps, knocking things over. Evading the unbeatable god. She needed him. Who cared about …

"It's Neesh," Xorna said. "Where is the sound of her voice coming from?"

Dertujia scowled and turned to run.

"Dertujia, stop right there!" Xorna yelled, holding her ribs. The fall must have broken something. "You do not run from the helpless. You go towards them. No matter who is in danger."

Dertujia spun around, his armor making a thudding noise with his armband. "Leahnina is in danger. That piece of excrement is chasing her. If he catches her …" Dertujia's mind went to many bad places. "I won't let her face him alone."

Xorna slowly stood up, leaning on her sword. Cetphur helped her as best he could, his face a mask of pain matching hers. "She can evade him. But Neesh is calling for help. Be the hero, Dertujia. Your wife can wait. She is far from helpless."

Dertujia knew she was right. As he searched for the voice, he couldn't put away the thoughts about Eropus. He knew what he'd find if Leahnina wasn't fast. Very fast. And it killed him. If that happened, he'd never forgive Xorna for forcing him away from the god.

He looked down at the middle of the room. And he heard it again.

"Please, help me."

So weak. Under … something. Where was she?

He churned his shadows, ripping up the floor. A hole appeared. Underneath the castle room was a deep pit. And at the bottom chained was Neesh.

"Neesh!" he called.

Her eyes looked up, and she fell apart in front of him. "Dertujia, you came. You came."

His heart broke, and shame covered him. Had he really been about to abandon her? He swooped down on the wings of shadows, landing next to her. It was a wretched place. Nothing was around. "What is this?"

"It's where Eropus penetrated the earth, taking its strength into his body. It's where he took my strength." She sighed. "Now you can end it. Kill me."

Dertujia stepped back. "Now do not talk foolishness. I need to help you and then find the god."

"Eropus is invincible. He has my strength. He has the earth's."

Dertujia nodded, wishing he knew how Leahnina was. His heart seemed to beat too hard, breaking its rocky shell. He never expected this. "I will end his life by breaking apart the world. I have the box. I know its secrets." He held it up.

Neesh fluttered her almost transparent eyes. He finally took a look at her. She was indeed almost gone. Drained by Eropus. She had lost the war.

"The box will end him. But not if my shell exists. He knew what he was doing. He made sure no one could beat him. Even he knows the extent of the box's power. He was playing with you, but he knew when he pushed you far enough, you'd come with the box.

"Then he planned to laugh at you, invulnerable. You see, Dertujia, he doesn't like to lose. So, he doesn't do a thing without knowing how all angles could turn out."

"But killing you?" Dertujia asked. "How would …"

"Your shadows. Let them surround me. They will take me to Hetahaunder. I will die. And Eropus will have nothing left. It will be the end. Please, Dertujia."

If Leahnina wasn't being chased right now, if Xorna hadn't been holding her ribs as if she were trying to hold her body together, and if Eropus hadn't been immune to every attack they had tried, Dertujia would have hesitated. Begged for another way. But all of the above had occurred.

He flicked his fingers and called forth the shadows from Hetahaunder. They came, a dark cloud descending. They surrounded the weak goddess, and she was obscured.

Out of nowhere, a roar shook the castle to its foundation.

When the shadows lifted, Neesh was gone.

The roar echoed again.

Dertujia flew up and checked Cetphur and Xorna, but they weren't making the agonized noise.

He shot his eyes up to the top where Leahnina had been running. She returned. She was okay. Grim, angry, tired, but okay.

"What was that?" he asked.

"Eropus didn't expect my dagger in his eye." She held up her dagger, covered in blood. Funny, considering even Cetphur's fire hadn't done a thing.

Leahnina ran down the stairs and joined him even as Eropus flew into the air above them.

"You stole my sister!" he screamed. "She was mine. My protection."

Dertujia slowly drew his blade. "Now, Cetphur."

Cetphur threw his hand up and dragged the god down to the ground, burning every part of him. Xorna forgot her wounds and ran forward to strike, coming down on Eropus' sword. He was fighting back. His skin was blistered and red, but he wasn't going down easily.

He blocked a blow with his wrist, but stupid fool. He didn't realize the blade would slice his hand clean off.

"No!" he screamed and swung his stump into Xorna, sending her flying. He held his wrist up and suddenly it reappeared. Hand and all.

"I can regrow," he spit. "Can she?" He raised his sword to chop off Xorna's head, but Leahnina reached forward muttering.

"Wither and die, you useless creation," she said, hands reaching out like she was strangling him. His burned and blistered skin withered as she asked, wrinkles exploded on him. White hair fell to his feet.

She was aging him.

"Leahnina?" Dertujia asked, feeling lost. How had she gotten so much power?

"Dertujia, please, end this," she said. Her face … vanished. Her skin at any rate. Her brain was working clearly, the synapses firing in front of him. Everything was gone.

"Leahnina?" he asked.

"Do it!" she shrieked. "Now!"

"I love you," he said. "We'll always be together."

He watched as Eropus writhed. He fought back the fire. He fought back the age. He struggled against Xorna's sword.

Dertujia said one more thing. "Goodbye."

Then he sent his shadows into the box. "Box, I am your master. Tear the world apart. Tear *him* apart! Break him. Make the worthless god suffer."

The box lit up, making a swirl against his shadows.

Eropus's eyes widened. "You are using the box. Dertujia! Please, we can have an understanding. I can make you a king. A god. Don't do this."

"Do it, Box!" Dertujia screamed. "Now! End this!"

The dark and light swirl sped across the room. Eropus struggled, pushing Leahnina down. She lost her hold. Cetphur stopped spewing fire. Xorna stumbled.

But Eropus could do nothing. The light-shadow bolt from the Box hit him on the chest. He screamed in agony as it slowly but surely stripped him of his skin, diving between his chest and ripping.

Dertujia heard Eropus' ribcage break. He split right in front of them.

The world shook.

Eropus shrieked and screamed.

"That's for all you took from me," Dertujia said with clenched teeth.

Eropus' eyes had changed from hateful to terrified as he fell, two sides shooting blood across the room.

But it wasn't done. The world wouldn't stop shaking.

Dertujia could hear screams coming from everywhere all at once.

But he rushed over to Xorna and Cetphur. Leahnina was okay. She was next to him as always.

They held Xorna and Cetphur. Both sides of them. They were already dead. Split into the same two that Eropus was.

His old friend. His companion. His new friend. He couldn't even hold them as they took their last breaths. They were gone. He brought up shadows and covered them, buried them in his enemy's home.

Dertujia and Leahnina sat in silence, listening to the world groaning around them.

He held Leahnina and ignored that he could see the room through her. The world shook for hours as they sat there, crying their mourning song.

As everything quieted, they could only hear their sobs. The silence was too overbearing. The sound of burgbugs erupted. Dertujia had never heard them this loud. Waterfalls splashed down, showing Eropus' power was no longer holding them back.

The end of their enemy. His body gone.

Dertujia snapped his fingers, and the dragon appeared next to him. "Tell Xorna I love her," he said. "Tell Cetphur."

"*Oh, master, you don't understand. They aren't there. They have been returned to life.*"

Dertujia's heart leaped. "Truly? Where are they? I want to find them!" Everything would be okay. It wasn't over.

"*No telling where or when. They could return in a minute or a thousand years. They aren't your responsibility anymore. And I can't be with you either. The Hetahaunder King knows. He is watching.*"

Dertujia gaped again, the deaths fresh. "I thought …"

Nothing in life is easy, the dragon spoke and vanished.

Leahnina dried her tears and stood up, slowly walking over to a hanging drape. She pulled Xorna's sword out and sliced a crude hood. "Come, Dertujia. Let's go home. I won't feel good until I hold my child in my arms."

Dertujia took her hand, and they walked out of the blood-soaked halls.

The world had changed. Valleys had disappeared. Mountains. Villages were gone. As they rode in Dertujia's shadow carriage, he sighed. They had won. Now was the time to see how badly the world had suffered.

But he had Leahnina. Xorna had done what she always warned might happen. She had stayed true to her herself and died at her husband's side.

Juyolax would be safe, and so would Tomphane. And wasn't that more important? Not the few? The many.

"They will honor you," Leahnina said. Her voice was rusty, but she held him with love. Dertujia couldn't feel happy. That wasn't right. But he felt relieved.

He hadn't expected Neesh to be there. To have to kill her. But the battle would have ended so very differently if Eropus had been allowed to …

"How'd you come to stab him?" he asked, holding her.

"He had caught me. He was about to tear me apart. Then suddenly he shuddered, and I stabbed him with my dagger. Took out his eyeball. It was very satisfying."

Dertujia nodded. His heart was stone. But his logic was also rock hard. Eropus had been invincible. He would have hurt so many. But he was stopped now. And maybe the gods had decided to punish the evil. Maybe the ones torn in half along with Eropus were evil war runners. Then it'd be justice.

It was over.

It was time to go home and make a new one. Maybe Firebranch could be their new Shymis.

New friends and family. People still lived. They would live for a long time.

And that's what Dertujia had been fighting for.

He needed to hold his son and tell him he didn't have to fear anymore.

The way to Firebranch was blocked many times. Entire mountains had been sliced clean through and fallen into the way. Roads were buried. Forests ripped from their roots. All the duo could do was travel and look. Nothing was familiar.

"Where did the ten rock turrets go?" Leahnina asked. "They were amazing. They were right there, next to the …"

She couldn't finish. She saw their rubble in the next few minutes.

The world was breathing hard, heavy in its wounded state.

"Gaiarigona did okay," Leahnina mentioned. She sounded numb. They passed its rocky shell and its solid mountain range. "We protected it. I'm guessing the same is true with Aieranolea. The goddess' items took care of them."

Dertujia didn't feel as if he had protected anyone, ever. He remained silent. It was coming in slowly. Everything. Nothing.

"The Dragon Tower!" Dertujia exclaimed. They passed right where it used to be. It was in pieces. Rubble. Gone. Even the lava fields were nothing more than smoking ash. "Nobody can get powers now. Do you think the dragon …"

Leahnina didn't answer. They both knew that if the tower was gone, the guardian was too.

As they traveled, trying to make it to Firebranch in the entirely changed world, Leahnina pointed. "Snow," she said. "It's snow."

But it wasn't. There were little pieces in the air of something, but it wasn't ice. Dertujia put his hand out to let a few settle on his hand only to yank it back inside. "Fire. It burned me."

Leahnina took a closer look. "No. It's not fire. It's everything. Lightning. Earth. Fire. Water. Everything that makes up this world. Where will they settle?"

Dertujia had no answers. His stony heart was melting off. It ached with pain. He'd never see Xorna again. She was dead. Cetphur was gone too. No journeys together. No … nothing. He wouldn't see Xorna have another child if she wanted one.

He had saved her life in childbirth only to let her die. He gave a low groan. But it kept coming. Like a slice repeatedly on one part of his soul. "How many have died?"

That answer was not clear, but it was somewhat obvious that a lot had met their end. Bodies were spread across the villages like trash. Some split in half. Some just divided from their heads.

The slices kept coming. "Mother and Father …" He was nearly delirious. He had forgotten they had already died. It had happened so fast. "Are they split in two?"

Leahnina grasped his hand, pulling his head onto her chest to murmur in his ear. "We did what we had to do. Juyolax is fine. Tomphane. Nockhun. The rest of the world. The survivors. You can feel it in the air. Eropus' death let go of all the elements he was taking. Restoring the world. If we hadn't …"

Dertujia put one hand up to press his fingers to her lips. "You mean if *I* hadn't … It was my doing. My vendetta. Me as a target. I who got involved between the gods in the first place. My arrogance."

Leahnina cuddled him as he fell to pieces. She kept saying the same thing. "You did what you had to. You were in the right."

Slowly but surely, he started believing her. The world was a better place without that god. Hadn't the beast told him that Xorna and Cetphur would be reborn? What was death? That god had been a threat to everything living or reborn.

His eyes dried as he pulled his sense of conviction to his chest. He still had his son and Leahnina. They would all live together.

"Do you hear that?" Leahnina asked.

Dertujia sat up and listened. Shrieks. Mighty, loud. Angry. Something he'd never heard before. "What is it?"

Leahnina shook her head. "Can we move faster? I don't even know how long it is until Firebranch."

Dertujia begged the shadows to go faster, but the sounds continued. Like monsters who were dug up from the underworld itself. What else had the split done?

By the time the carriage finally went around enough to actually head back to Firebranch, Dertujia had reenacted the shield around his heart. It was done. No reason to feel bad. Everything Xorna had taught him echoed in his head. He couldn't expect to be immune to the laws of the hero.

She had told him more than once that if it came down to it, the hero had to die to save others. She had done that. He couldn't whine and moan about it just because it hurt so deeply. This was indeed a huge sacrifice, coming from people who didn't even agree to it.

They all needed this. Eropus had drained the world. Almost killed Neesh after tormenting her creatures. Surely, the Shadorians wouldn't be upset about losing the god who had created their enemy, the ones who had come to kill them.

Yes, peace would come back. Babies would be born. Heroes would be reborn. Dertujia had accomplished this. The people had huddled in their houses talking about Eropus and his rule. Mercenaries themselves had been terrified of dealing with him.

The thorn in the world had been removed. Now it could grow again.

That's what Dertujia would tell his son when he held him in his arms.

"We were right," he said, hating the weakness in his voice. "I was right."

Leahnina under her hood nodded. "We have to be. It cost too much to be a bad purchase."

He glanced at her, another part of him coming aware. "You will never look the same."

"I am still me."

He heard the pain in her voice. "Is it permanent? Will it spread?"

She shuddered, clutching her hands. "That is one thing I don't know. I apologize. If you wish to find another woman to share your life with, I understand."

Dertujia's heart ached in a whole new way. The option wasn't real. He couldn't imagine trying to leave her. No other woman had faced a god with him. No other had lost as much as he did. No other could be as beautiful with no skin.

"That is a stupid statement. I would never leave you."

She yanked her hood down, revealing her see-through head. Her lips were still pink. Her eyes had their pupils. Heavy eyebrows hung on a clear canvas. "You should! I am half a woman. I have nothing to offer you."

Dertujia put his fingers out slowly, as if he could go right through. But she still existed. He caressed her jawbone, down to her lips and bent down to claim them in his. Gasping and struggling to breathe, they poured out their pain.

When they pulled away, Dertujia put his hand against nothing, but he felt her skin. "You are not half a woman. You are the woman who owns me body and soul."

"I see it!" she shrieked, pulling away. "The horror. The revulsion. You can't love my face anymore."

Dertujia pulled her close. He vowed right then and there to never show that again. To never make her think of herself as less. "I was surprised. That's all. Your face was a beauty. I will miss it. But you have other parts I am obsessed with," he teased, trying for a jovial note in all this darkness. All around the moving carriage was death of land and body. Monsters were appearing he'd never seen before.

The very landscape had been torn up to form chasms and valleys, pushed mountains out of deserts. Castles had crumbled.

He couldn't feel the pain right now. Years and years would be his to remember. For now, he was with his wife. He still had her. She still had him.

"You are always beautiful, from the annoying person who followed me around to the invisible woman of which I wonder how far it goes down." He gave her another kiss to show he was teasing. "I have always loved you, Leahnina. I was scared. But we're still together. Like you said, always."

She shook and rubbed her face against his chin, kissing his neck. "I lost the faith in my own visions. So many are hitting me. I worry about Juyolax."

Dertujia froze, pulling her to look into her eyes. He kept it in how terrifying it was he could see through her. “Is he dead? He can’t be. No, I won’t believe it.”

Leahnina shuddered again. “He isn’t dead. He’s alive. I see his tiny face, looking around in horror at what has happened. Firebranch wasn’t affected at all. But outside it’s a mess.”

Dertujia felt a sliver of meanness slice his soul. So, that village didn’t get hurt at all. How unfair. He shook himself. No. That wouldn’t do. If it had been affected by the split, then Juyolax and Tomphane would have been hurt. It was better this way.

“Then what is the problem?” he asked.

“Futures are pouring in. So many choices will be presented. I can’t see as well. I took a lot away from me aging that god. I can’t pin down anything.”

He stroked her back as she sobbed. But he remained strong. As long as Juyolax was alive, nothing else mattered. Their little family would survive.

The road was long, so much longer. Everything got in their way. Dertujia and Leahnina settled back, thinking. With every minute that went by, reality set in. Every single thing had changed. His world was half of itself.

“Where did it all go?” he asked out loud, curiosity helping the pain ebb away.

Leahnina swallowed. He could see her delicate throat. It was still there. “Where did what go?”

“The other parts of the world. I see villagers and their bodies. Animals. Vegetation. But some stuff is just gone, nothing left. If it had been split, then where'd the other side go?"

Leahnina nodded and closed her eyes. He was about to tell her he was just asking, not to waste her energy, but she spoke too quickly. "Dertujia, the world did split. There are two now. There are little holes, and our world was sucked right through. It exists over there."

Dertujia pondered that. "So, who lives there? Did our people go?"

Leahnina shook her head. "No. Most people died or stayed here. I think monsters went over. They rule it now. I see …"

Dertujia took her hand. "What?"

"That world is moving along at a different pace. But it speeds to catch up. Someday it will run along the same time as this one. It's separate from us. It has its own life now. We lost everything, even our world. We are …" She started crying again. Dertujia held her, thinking about this other world.

What was it like over there? Better or worse than here? And could a new life be held in that place? But how to even know? It was intriguing, the idea of starting over. Not living in Firebranch where everyone hated him because …

He froze, gasping for air. They had been right. He had brought damage to their world. They would not be happy to see him.

"Hurry," he said to his shadows. They sped up even faster in response to his fear.

And as the castle of Firebranch appeared in the distance, surrounded by rubble and destruction, he saw the army waiting for him.

"They have come out to play," he said, anger burning in him.

As they got closer, he saw the prince and the king and queen at the lead of the army. To their right was Nockhun looking defeated, holding Tomphane, but a soldier had a sword to his heart. As if they had just dragged him out of his house.

The prince held Juyolax.

This was indeed bad.

Dertujia hoped they were ready to defend themselves if they got in the way of his son.

He stood up next to Leahnina. He let the shadows fall, as they walked forward, walking near bodies and piles of dirt.

The sun shone. What would be the end of the battle this day?

Dertujia narrowed his eyes.

"So, what do you have to say?" he asked as he got close enough.

Chapter Twenty-Five

The air was tense with anger and emotion. The destruction and death a fitting backdrop.

Dertujia was tired of it all. He had no mood appropriate for this. He needed to go home. But his home was gone. And the prince of Firebranch had his son, the only home he could find.

"Put down your weapons and allow us to place shackles on you. Do not fight back. You and your wife will be put to death for the ending of our world," the king announced.

This was it then. His good deed was going to be punished. But they had his son right now. It was too important to treat this poorly. "I had to do what I did. The god Eropus was draining the world. In years, he would have killed all of you. But you live. Give me my son. We will leave your village, but we won't turn ourselves over to your version of justice. Furthermore, Nockhun has nothing to do with this. Allow him to leave."

The king and queen glared, but to Dertujia's surprise, Prince Tenpert spoke up. "Yes, Father.

Mother. Nockhun is a simple farmer and scholar. I don't see how he is guilty simply because he was taking care of the monster's child."

The soldier lowered the sword and Nockhun walked over to Tomphane. Dertujia nodded towards him. Nockhun put his finger up, ready to argue. A sharp nod from Dertujia, and he gave him a torturous gaze and then took Tomphane by the hand. Turning their backs on the army, they disappeared inside Firebranch. Safe.

"We promised to protect her," Leahnina murmured.

Dertujia looked at her. How could he know how this was going to end better than she did? Her future telling was indeed ruined. But as he stared, she blinked and moaned low. Now she got it.

"Excellent. Now, Prince Tenpert, tell your parents to allow us to leave. They know what will happen."

He shook his head. "You are under arrest. You murderer."

Dertujia narrowed his eyes. "Give me my son!" he said, holding his shadows up, duplicating them until they were a mass.

The army stayed together. He couldn't use their shadows. They were too united. And the sun had begun to set.

Tenpert put his hand up in the air, threatening. Then he brought it down.

Across Juyolax's face. He wailed and struggled, trying to get free. Dertujia's shadows dropped.

"Leave him alone!" he said. Horror stole his breath and mind. Leahnina was screaming.

"It will be worse," Tenpert threatened, reaching his large hands around the child's throat.

Dertujia threw out his hand without thinking. A shadow spear impaled the prince. Juyolax was dropped, but the army went mad, converging on them. He couldn't see his son. Juyolax was screaming somewhere, calling for Dertujia. Calling for Leahnina. The young voice was swallowed as Dertujia and Leahnina started fighting.

Shadows were useless. His heart was on the ground with Juyolax. He searched for him even as blades came his way. Leahnina was screaming Juyolax's name, throwing power she didn't have.

"Mommy!" Juyolax's voice yelled.

"No!" Leahnina screeched as a blade reached her leg. Dertujia tried to get over to her, but someone grabbed his hair and yanked him down.

"It's over," he said. It was done. His last deed would be to save the world.

"It is never over!" Leahnina screamed, throwing powers out over the enemy. "We'll be free. You won't touch him!"

Somehow the world turned backwards, inside out. The people were there. Then they were gone.

Empty. Dertujia held his head, feeling it aching. There was nothing. Just the sound of quiet sobbing.

"Leahnina," he said, recognizing his heart.

"Are you okay?" she asked, sounding empty.

"I am wounded, but I'll live. What did you do to them? Did you kill them?"

He was beyond caring. He hoped they were all dead. All of Firebranch. "No … Do you see Juyolax? Did he come?"

Come where? Dertujia yanked his leaden body off the grass, seeing … everything was healed. The world was better. It was like the blow didn't happen. A dream? No, he remembered Eropus. Couldn't have dreamed him up.

"Juyolax," Leahnina urged.

He snapped out of his reverie to see that he was now nude. Nothing around him. The Box was gone. His pack. His food. Everything. He scanned everywhere he could see. "No. Juyolax is not here."

Leahnina screamed and pounded the earth. "I brought him. I brought him."

He looked towards her voice only to gasp. She was gone. From the knees up he could see nothing. Like she was ceasing to exist. He stumbled forward, bleeding. He grasped wildly. To his relief, her body was there. He could feel that she was clutching her stomach. By feel, he tried to surmise her wound, but there was nothing. This went deeper.

"Our baby. Our boy." She couldn't stop crying. He wrapped himself around her, feeling the skin comfort. She may have been invisible, but she was very much there. "What do you mean, Leahnina? Where are we? Can we get back to Firebranch? I don't think the rest of them would be as bad as Tenpert or his parents. Besides Juyolax would be a good bargaining chip for us. We just need to get our strength back and …"

"There's Firebranch!" she yelled. "Right there."

Dertujia had trouble understanding any of this. His mind was a rock. Not allowing anything but the smallest of details to come in. He looked up and saw the castle of Firebranch. No army. No angry mob. There were travelers on the distant road, but they were in a field, far away from a chasm and near the forest.

"What did you do to them?" he asked again, desperate.

"Not to them," she moaned, shuddering. "To us. We are in the future."

Dertujia's body seized up. The future … That's why Leahnina's body had been lost. "Then …" He desperately grabbed for anything. "The wound of Eropus is gone. They might have forgiven us. Let us find the ten-year-old Juyolax."

Leahnina stopped crying. He thought he was getting through to her, but when she spoke there was no emotion. "Further, my love."

Dertujia's jaw tensed. He bit his tongue to stop from crying. "An adult then. He will still need us."

"Further and further. I had no control. This is not ours. The wound left by the splitting of the world took a thousand years to heal."

It would have been better if she had slapped him across the face.

"Juyolax."

"… is dead. If he wasn't already before. That mob wanted blood. Ours, his. Nockhun was the lucky one. Only Xorna's line was safe. We are in the future."

Dertujia stood up. He wanted to cry, to scream, to rage. But it wouldn't do a bit of good. Everything was gone. Friends, family. One after another. This way there was no getting them back.

"Hey, are you okay?" a voice asked. A merchant by the looks of him was running towards them. Intent on helping. He saw Leahnina's legs and assumed the worst.

"By the gods above. Are you injured? Did the king's men get you?"

Dertujia only heard one thing. The king's men. "The king of Firebranch?" he asked sounding dark. The man jumped away.

"Um, yes. If not one of the king's men, then maybe an Element Manipulator? What could have caused such damage?"

Dertujia was in a foreign land, not his own. Everything was wrong. He had no clue how to step forward here. If he made the same mistake again, he and Leahnina could lose their lives. It was the last two things on earth they had, and he was going to keep it.

The man kept speaking. "Do you need help? I can take you to Firebranch. I live there."

Dertujia put out his fist and squeezed. The light from the overhead sun—how had he missed it was noon day again—choked him until he fell, dead.

"No. Firebranch will never help me again." He felt for Leahnina's hand and pulled her to standing. He flicked his fingers, and the shadow dragon appeared.

"*It has been a while, master. What has happened? You do know that the Hetahaunder King …*"

"I bow to no king," Dertujia said. "I am above all." He boarded, pulling Leahnina to be behind him. She still wasn't crying. Like him, they were both dead, though living in body.

"Dertujia, what are we going to do?"

"We're going home to Shymis. From there I will launch my war. First, though I'll need help."

"Revenge?" she asked, a fire burning in her soul. "Then take them now."

"No." Dertujia shot a look at the sleeping city. It hadn't changed. The army still was there, and who knew what had changed. A good tactician didn't rush into battle. He planned to savor his revenge and make sure nothing like what happened before happened again.

He had gone back to Firebranch without worrying. It was stupid. Hadn't his shadows warned him that there was someone following their progress, reporting back to Firebranch?

This time he would eke out every little piece of revenge until Firebranch was a shell. Then he'd kill them.

"Dertujia," Leahnina said.

"Do not call me by that moniker. Dertujia is dead. I am emperor now. I am Dakchin."

Leahnina nodded. He could feel it but not see it. "We are on the same page, my husband. I do not wish to be known as Leahnina. Just call me Oracle, because I foresee the future. I foresee death."

And the dragon flew on.

Shymis was in ruins. Dakchin had to rebuild.

Then he'd destroy.

Epilogue

Across the worlds, in a different time, a tiny child cried while surrounded by a mob. Power swelled around him. As he called for his mother, his father, two hands picked him up.

"Well, little one. You've been abandoned. Sh, sh, what's your name? Where are your parents?"

The boy cried. "Juyo. My daddy and mommy are getting killed."

The man looked around. Juyolax felt warm as fire spilled forth. Like Uncle Cetphur's flames. He relaxed and clung to him. "Save me," he whispered.

The man chuckled, but it sounded dry. "Don't worry. I too have lost my family. We'll be together. I have a castle. Wanna live in a castle?"

Juyolax nodded. He understood nothing except that the bad people had won. They had killed his father and mother. It was all over. He'd never go home again.

"My name is Cetbal Pyre. You will be known as my son. No one will ever come after you. You can trust me on that."

To bc continued.

Author Bio

Marianna Palmer is the author of many stories ranging from children's to young adult. She has been dreaming up stories since she was old enough to think. After a dare from her sister, she took on the scary writing thing. It was all she had to hold her together through years of seclusion, returning to college, and being afraid of every single thing that she encounters. After graduating with her BA, she disappeared from the world. If you look closely, you might find her walking with her sister, before vanishing again. Living in Tacoma, WA, she does everything in her power to avoid scary things and still live her life.

Made in United States
Troutdale, OR
06/14/2023

10604369R00232